SKIING

INTO

MURDER

*Book Three of the Laura Morland
Mystery Series*

JOAN DAHR LAMBERT
©2013

JOAN DAHR LAMBERT

JODAR BOOKS 2013

ISBN:13-978 1492202912

ISBN:10 1492202916

$12.50

BOOKS BY JOAN DAHR LAMBERT

WALKING INTO MURDER

Book One of the Laura Morland Mystery Series

WADING INTO MURDER

Book Two of the Laura Morland Mystery Series

CIRCLES OF STONE

Book One of the Mother People Series

CIRCLES IN THE SKY

Book Two of the Mother People Series

ICE BURIAL

Book Three of the Mother People Series

SEA HORSE MEMOIRS

A Novella

THE WOLVES OF PEAT MOSS FOREST

A Children's Novel

JOAN DAHR LAMBERT

Praise for the Laura Morland Mysteries

Laura Morland is an appealing heroine, perhaps too curious and impulsive, but delightful to follow around as she battles criminals with little but her wits, courage and a talent for getting people to talk to her. Her second mystery tackles a wrenching issue - the exploitation of children - but still manages to maintain a light touch. No easy task but well done! I'll eagerly await the next book in the series.
4.0 out of 5 stars **Charming!**, April 27, 2011

Absolutely charming. I'm hooked on Laura Morland and eagerly look forward to her further adventures. Lambert is a deft hand at pulling you into American college professor Laura's escapades as she finds herself repeatedly and unwillingly pulled into mischief and mayhem as she traverses England on a walking tour. A great addition to any cozy reader's library. Thanks, Ms. Lambert. And, ahem, when is the next one coming?

Once again, Professor Morland proves to be a very appealing, if flawed heroine. She's likable, admirable, intelligent, determined, and often reckless in the pursuit of her investigations. I'm anxiously awaiting more Laura Morland stories in the future.
5.0 out of 5 stars **Ms. Lambert Does It Again!**,

Ms. Lambert creates so many potential characters who could be the "bad guy" that it confuses the heck out of me until I give up trying to figure it out, and just hang on and enjoy the read. I highly recommend this author and Professor Morland...I am hoping that there are many, many more books to come!

CHAPTER ONE

Laura sank onto the nearest seat, breathless from racing to catch her train. As usual, she had been too busy people-watching to pay attention to details like signs and clocks. Only three minutes to go before departure.

The windows were clouded with frost, and she rubbed them clear with her scarf. This was the Golden Pass Train of Switzerland, famous across the world for its magnificent panoramas of lakes and valleys and mountains and glaciers, and she wanted to see it all.

A woman standing on the icy platform suddenly darted closer and stared through Laura's window into the train. She looked terrified. Her panic-stricken eyes were only inches from Laura's, but she was looking past her at someone in the aisle. Her face was twisted in an expression of desperate appeal.

Startled, Laura looked over her shoulder. The only person in the aisle was a tall blond man. The woman must have been appealing to him, but he passed through the door at the end of the carriage without looking back.

The train gave a subdued cough and moved slowly forward. When Laura looked out the window again the woman's face was sliding away, its image distorted by the increasing speed of the train.

She saw the woman dart into a parking lot and dash across it, watched her turn once to glance back in terror; then she disappeared from view.

The incident seemed out of keeping with this peaceful tourist-oriented country, Laura thought, disconcerted. But then, so was the job she had come to Switzerland to do. Violet, her improbably named six-foot-tall detective friend whose specialty was protecting children, had recruited her to help prevent a kidnapping during an international conference.

Pay attention to any unusual occurrence you see or hear from the moment you land, Violet had instructed. *Do what you always do. Watch people, chat with them, ask questions and poke around.*

Not a difficult assignment for her, Laura thought wryly. Curiosity had always been her dominant trait. And the panic-stricken woman certainly qualified as *unusual.* But how could she find out more about her?

The blond man – that was a good place to start. Slinging her pack on her back, Laura set off to find him. He had struck her as the type who would want a cup of coffee as soon as he got on a train. She would see if she was right.

The train lurched to a halt, its brakes screeching. Thrown off balance, Laura grabbed the back of a seat. A conductor punching tickets ahead of her glanced suspiciously at the emergency cord hanging nearby, and went hastily back the way he had come. Had someone pulled it to stop the train?

Laura scrambled after him to ask what had happened, but as she passed the lavatory a hand shot out, grabbed her arm and hauled her into the dark, stinking space. The door closed behind her with a thud.

Terrified, she opened her mouth to scream, but a pair of lips descended on hers before a sound could escape. The kiss lasted a long time, long enough for Laura to form an excellent idea of her captor's identity.

Unresisting now, she returned the passion in the other pair of lips. Then exasperation took over.

"How could you scare me like that?" she hissed. "It stinks in here!" she added, trying not to breathe. "And what are you doing here?"

"Sorry about the smell," the familiar voice said. "Closed for repairs, but this is the only spot where privacy is available. And we need privacy."

"Surely you don't mean…"

He laughed. "No, I don't. A soft bed in that nice hotel you've booked is more my style, though I doubt I shall get to it for a few more days." He sighed theatrically. "We need privacy so I can explain. Sadly, our rapturous plans have once again been side-lined by unexpected developments."

"Explanations are certainly in order," Laura agreed. "For starters, what *are* you doing here? When I talked to you yesterday you were in France tracking down long-lost paintings. And what about the weekend in Paris we're supposed to have when…"

Her words were cut off by another kiss. "Aren't you at all glad to see me?" Thomas asked mournfully when it was over.

Laura smiled. "Yes, I am," she said softly. "It's just that you have a habit of turning up in the most preposterous places. There have already been two unexpected occurrences on this train, so a third seemed a bit much."

Thomas was suddenly all attention. "Tell me," he said, "but we have to keep our voices down. That conductor is prowling."

"Trains like this don't normally stop so suddenly," Laura replied. "They're smooth, predictable and on time. That's one of the unexpected things.

"My guess is that you pulled the emergency cord," she added.

"That's a third odd incident," Thomas said thoughtfully. "I had planned to pull it if the need arose but someone else did it instead."

Laura frowned. "I wonder who – and why?"

"No idea – yet," Thomas replied. "What was the second occurrence?"

Laura described the woman's strange behavior. Thomas professed to be as puzzled as she was – which might or might not be the case, knowing Thomas as she did. "Maybe she wanted the conductor to stop the train," he suggested innocently. "Too bad I didn't give the cord a pull."

"Now you," Laura ordered. "I want to know what you're doing here. And no more prevarications." She sighed. That was exactly the line she had used the first time she'd encountered Thomas on a walking trip two summers ago, but the prevarications had just kept coming. It was no wonder she had pegged him as the murderer on that trip. After all, she had caught him red-handed with a body that he refused to explain.

Since that first memorable meeting, they'd had some equally scintillating but fortunately more romantic get-togethers. On those occasions, too, Thomas had turned up in unpredictable places just when she least expected him.

A beefy hand pushed past the door and fumbled for the light switch. Laura froze. Was this the men's room or the ladies? Somehow, being caught in a passionate embrace in the men's room seemed worse.

The switch clicked, but the light failed to come on. Thomas again? For all she knew, he'd pulled all the fuses and none of the lights on the train were working.

The door closed again and they heard footsteps recede down the corridor. Laura felt Thomas's lips brush her cheek. "We're almost out of time. I'm a conductor, so I need to get back to my post. All I can say for now is please look after Catherine if anything goes wrong for me, and this time, don't drag the poor girl into a confrontation with the murderer. It makes me nervous."

Laura bristled. "I didn't! If it hadn't been for you getting yourself captured by that sadist, we wouldn't have had to rescue you!"

Catherine was Thomas's daughter, and on their last adventure together she and Laura had embarked on a "rescue Thomas" campaign on horseback that had involved a near-lethal tussle with a murderer. Catherine had acquitted herself nobly. So had the horse.

A brisk knock sounded on the door. "Essayez la lumiere, s'il vous plait. Je pense que nous avons…" A jumble of words followed. *Try that switch, will you? I think we have the current going again,* Laura translated.

"Bien," Thomas called out. He pushed the switch, flooding the small space with fluorescent light that made Laura's eyes water. The men's room, she saw. What was she going to do now? Emerge in confusion?

Thomas solved that problem by flushing the toilet. Laura eyed it nervously lest it overflow. It didn't. Over its noisy gurgling, Thomas said: "I'll go out first and draw whoever is out there away. Then you can come out."

He really *was* a conductor, she noted, or at least he wore a conductor's uniform. His cap was askew, and she straightened it automatically.

"What are you doing here, please!" she hissed. "I can't be much help with Catherine unless I know. When is she coming to France?"

"She comes tomorrow so I need to get back." He grinned. "As to why I am here, did you know that Switzerland has a concrete bomb shelter under almost every house? There are thousands of them." Laura glared at him.

"I love to tease you. You're so tempting when you get all feisty," he said. "But seriously, find out anything you can about the shelters. They play a role, or I think they do, but my computer's been stolen so I can't find out."

His eyes were suddenly sober. "Laura, my darling Laura, and I really think you are that by now, for goodness sake be careful. You're heading right into the thick of things without knowing it. The case I'm on is all mixed up with what you and Violet are here to do…"

"Vite!" a voice commanded. *Quick*! Loud raps on the door followed.

"Un moment," Thomas replied. His lips touched hers again. "Catherine and I will be in Murren soon," he said. "I'll find a way to get messages to you."

He turned off the light and slid into the corridor. Laura heard him talking to someone. She hoped it wasn't another conductor. Thomas wouldn't fool a real one for very long. His French was adequate but hardly fluent, and she didn't think he spoke German. He was bound to be exposed soon, and that would probably land him in jail.

The two men moved away and she opened the door gingerly. The corridor was empty. Her brain felt empty too, but at the same time it was a whirlwind of conflicting thoughts. What was she supposed to do now?

Exactly what Violet and Thomas had asked: find out everything she could. Laura straightened her shoulders. Her penchant for investigating puzzles had already helped to solve two mysteries, one on that supposedly peaceful walking trip in the Cotswold Hills of England, another on a tour of that country's most atmospheric sites. There was no reason it wouldn't work again.

The thought steadied Laura. Start again where you left off, she instructed herself, and go from there.

****

Another conductor passed her, moving fast. He stopped on the platform between the cars and peered over the low barrier. Laura did the same, and wished she hadn't. This car of the stalled train hung precariously over the icy surface of a lake far below. She shivered and drew back. Not for her the dubious pleasures of Alpine water. Even in summer it was frigid.

She went through two more carriages and then came unexpectedly to the café. The setting was lovely. Huge windows gave superb views of untracked snowy wilderness on all sides. It was a deserted spot, with no villages or roads, but at least the café car wasn't perched over the lake.

More to the point, the blond man was sipping coffee at a table for four, empty but for him. So she had been right.

The elderly man behind the café bar looked at her enquiringly. "Thé avec du lait," Laura ventured, trying to resurrect her French through her sleepless, over-stimulated and jet-lagged brain. Her plane from New York had landed in Zurich at 6AM, and she never could sleep on those flights. Her train trip thus far hadn't encouraged relaxation, either.

The waiter seemed to understand her anyway and nodded. Encouraged, Laura continued her query. "Pourquoi nous avons arête?" *Why have we stopped?* The man shrugged in true Gallic fashion but made an unintelligible response in German. Laura gave up. Communication was going to be harder now that they were in a German-speaking area. She had better haul out her German dictionary.

"Merci beaucoup," she said, and carried her tea to the blond man's table. She studied him covertly as she sipped. He was strikingly handsome, with a broad, athletic frame and pale hair cut so short it looked almost white against his well-shaped skull. Laura got the impression that he knew exactly how attractive he was and used his looks to his best advantage.

He glanced at her with cool blue eyes that lingered only a nanosecond; then he made conversation impossible by pulling out a cell phone and punching in numbers. Irritated by his rudeness, Laura decided to play annoying tourist. Holding her camera in front of her, she focused it on the peaks beyond him and clicked ostentatiously, managing to get some excellent shots of his face.

The blond man frowned, but she wasn't sure if the frown was directed at her for waving the camera in his face or at the person he was calling, who wasn't answering the phone. Laura was struggling to think of a more productive way to communicate with him when the door banged open and two chattering girls burst into the café car. They reminded Laura of colts - all legs and arms and jerky movement. Both had long blond hair and bright blue eyes, and they were exactly the same size. Their clothes were extraordinary: thick leggings in brilliant turquoise and scarlet respectively, baggy sweaters in clashing tones of orange and purple and lime green, and huge clumping army boots that made their feet look elephantine in relation to their skinny frames.

After a moment's hesitation they perched nonchalantly beside Laura and the blond man, and began to speak rapidly in another unfamiliar language to a woman at the opposite table, who Laura gathered must be their mother. She had a good-humored face, and she parried their questions and demands with what sounded like consummate tact. The two girls slumped in dejection for a split second at the refusal of something that sounded like chocolate, and then sprang up again, excitement renewed, when their mother spoke a few more words. They bolted off, chattering volubly again.

"Energetique," Laura commented with a smile, hoping there was such a word and that the woman spoke French.

"Very energetic," the woman answered in lightly accented English. "Please forgive me for replying to you in English but I thought from your accent that you are American and I am anxious to practice that language."

"You sound as if you speak it very well," Laura replied.

"I must still practice, however. I am attending a conference for a child welfare organization which will be conducted in English, and I fear I still understand too slowly to keep up with the other people."

Laura's antennae quivered. That sounded like the conference Violet had been hired to protect. "What is the conference about?" she asked.

"It is on girls' education in the developing world," the woman replied, confirming Laura's guess. She was pleased to have met someone from the conference so soon. And, she thought, with trepidation, two of the children who might be victims of the threatened kidnapping. They were easy targets for criminals in a country where people felt safe.

"I believe there will be a representative from your country," her companion went on. "You are from the United States, are you not?" She clapped a rueful hand over her mouth. "Perhaps *you* are the American representative?"

Laura laughed. "No, I'm just a tourist but I am American. I'm a professor there and I'm meeting an old friend for a holiday," she answered. Violet didn't want anyone to know the real reason for their trip or that she was a detective, so that was the story they had agreed on. "We will be in Zermatt first; then in a town called Murren," she continued.

"That is where the conference will be held," the woman exclaimed. "And we too will go first to Zermatt. So perhaps we will meet again."

14

"I would like that," Laura replied. "I am a professor of gender studies and do research on the status of girls' education across the world, so I will be most interested in the results of your conference. In my classes, young women from developing countries often speak of how difficult it was to get an education."

"That is so true," her companion agreed enthusiastically. "The purpose of this conference is to find ways to ensure that the girls as well as boys get the education they need and the opportunity to use it."

"Exactly what I like to hear – and what I teach," Laura said with a smile. "We seem to have similar goals."

"We do indeed," her companion replied. "Perhaps you will be able to attend a few of our seminars, but even if that proves difficult, I shall enjoy speaking more about these issues with you."

Gathering up her papers, she rose to her feet. "I must follow my daughters now. I am Sigrid Olsen," she added, holding out a hand with a smile. "I am the Danish representative for the conference."

"I am Laura Morland," Laura replied, shaking the hand. "I am very glad to meet you, Sigrid. I too look forward to speaking again."

The café car had filled up while they were chatting and Sigrid' seat was quickly taken by a man with swarthy skin and hooked nose. His features were unusual in this part of the world, and Laura wondered if he was also a delegate to the conference, perhaps from one of the middle-eastern countries.

She was trying to think how to ask him politely when a movement at the end of the stalled train distracted her. A dark-haired man stepped down from the last car and dusted off his hands as if he had been... been what? Fixing the train or maybe the tracks? He had no tools, though, and he wasn't dressed like a repairman. He looked like a businessman, with his solid dark overcoat.

A pile of boxes were stacked on the ground beside him, and she wondered if he had been unloading them. But that made no sense. Why would the train stop in this desolate spot to unload boxes?

It had, though, she realized when the man boarded the train again and reappeared with another box. As soon as he stepped down, the train gave a jerk and inched ahead around a long curve. Laura frowned. That made even less sense. Why were they stranding the man him in this deserted place? There were no roads out there, not even any tracks in the snow.

Another question popped into her mind: was he the person who had pulled the emergency cord, so he could unload the boxes from the train?

She saw the man shove a hand into his overcoat pocket and retrieve an object that glittered. It looked like a gun, Laura though in horror. Why had he pulled out a gun? But surely she was wrong; people in Switzerland didn't go around shooting guns...

The blond man opposite her moved sharply, and she heard a sudden intake of breath. Laura twisted around to follow his gaze. A different man was visible at the other end of the train, leaning out of the platform between two cars as the train inched ahead. He looked like Thomas, except he wasn't a conductor now. He was wearing a ski jacket.

She looked again and was sure. Yes, it was Thomas. There was no mistaking that tousled hair. Why did his hair look wonderful when it was wind-blown or soaking wet, while hers looked like a badly built bird's nest?

A loud report boomed from the back end of the train. Thomas slumped down and disappeared. All she could see now was one arm hanging over the low barrier. It looked entirely limp.

CHAPTER TWO

Laura's chest contracted in panic. Had Thomas been shot? Was he dead? She was about to sprint to the front of the train when she saw the hand rise slowly into the air and perform a jaunty wave. Thomas's head reappeared too.

Laura collapsed into her seat and waited for her pounding heart to calm down. Being involved with Thomas was like being involved with a time bomb. On the other hand, even if he was hard on the nerves, he was never dull, unlike her ex-husband Donald, who had personified dull. Besides, Thomas undoubtedly thought she and Catherine were hard on *his* nerves.

Time to re-focus on the blond man. Determined to break the silence, Laura uttered the first sentence that came to her mind. "J'ai vue un homme la bas," she began in uncertain French, pointing to the back end of the train. "He was unloading boxes from the train, and I wondered why he was doing that," she finished, relapsing into English.

The man turned his cool blue gaze onto her face. "A repairman I believe," he told her in precise but accented English. "Perhaps that is why we stopped."

"But if he is a repairman, why was he left behind?" Laura persisted. "And why leave boxes in such an uninhabited place?"

"That I do not know," he answered shortly. He seemed to regret the curt response, and tried a friendlier tone. "I am a ski instructor in Murren," he told her politely. "I believe I will teach some of the young ones from the conference of which the lady spoke. So perhaps we will meet again."

Ski instructor fit him perfectly, Laura decided. He must cut quite a swath through the women in his classes. "I may need some lessons myself, since I do not ski very well," she answered with a wry smile.

"I shall be happy to help you," he said without noticeable enthusiasm. Laura caught a glimpse of herself in the window when the train went through a tunnel and wasn't surprised. Normally, she thought she looked reasonably attractive, but now her over-exuberant hair was wildly out of control, and the overnight flight had done nothing flattering for her admittedly middle-aged face. Maybe a few days of skiing would provide some glamour.

Thomas hadn't seemed to mind, though, despite the ghastly fluorescent light in that stinking lavatory. In fact, he professed to prefer her in a rumpled state of disarray, like covered in mud and straw or with her face smudged from a fast deteriorating disguise, as she had been during their last trip. She hadn't believed him until Catherine had explained that her mother, now Thomas's ex, never engaged in *any* activity without perfectly coiffed hair and an exquisitely made-up face. Laura wondered if that included activities normally confined to the privacy of the bedroom, but didn't ask.

Thomas even seemed delighted by her out of control curls, Laura mused. Titian, he called the color, after the painter whose women all had a mane of wavy dark red tresses. Sometimes he ran his fingers through hers...

Laura jerked her mind back to the ski instructor. "I believe a woman in Interlaken was trying to signal you

19

as the train pulled out," she said. "She looked very upset."

Irritation crossed the ski instructor's face. "I know no one at the station in Interlaken. Perhaps she wished to signal another person."

Laura sighed. Probably he had women chasing him all the time and didn't want to hear about another distraught admirer. She would have to think of another approach.

The ski instructor made that impossible. Rising quickly, he strode out of the café car. He looked arrogant from the back, Laura thought crossly, or maybe she was just prejudiced against unusually handsome men.

She stared out the window again, unable now to drag her eyes away from views so stupendously beautiful that at times her breath caught in her throat. Everything else went out of her mind, and she simply absorbed the wonder of the scenery. Truly, this country was a visual paradise.

As the train pulled into Montreux, the Castle of Chillon came into view. Laura hesitated, wondering whether to stop for a visit before going on to Zermatt, as she had planned. Maybe she should stay put and keep an eye on Thomas and the ski instructor instead.

Then, to her surprise, she saw both of them at separate exits, waiting to disembark. Grabbing her pack – thankfully the only piece of luggage she had with her since the rest had been checked through to Zermatt, Laura ran to the nearest door and stepped carefully onto the snow-slicked platform.

Thomas crossed to the platform on the other side of the tracks. He must be going to Geneva to catch a train for France so he could meet Catherine. Good; for the moment, she had only one person to follow.

The ski instructor headed for the castle. How unexpected! Or was it? Even ski instructors probably enjoyed the Castle of Chillon. One of Switzerland's most famous monuments, it had brooded over Lake Leman for centuries, and was as much a part of the landscape as the mountains.

Whatever the reason, she was pleased. She had never been able to resist a castle, and ever since she had read Lord Byron's *The Prisoner of Chillon* as a child, she had wanted to see this one. The poem told the true story of a young man who was shackled to a stone pillar for six years for daring to speak out in favor of peasant reform. At eight, Laura had shivered in horror and hoped the guard had a beautiful daughter who would rescue him. The forty plus Laura smiled ruefully as she remembered that innocence.

The castle seemed to rise out of the water as she approached, as solid and impregnable as the stones from which it had been built. On the south side it was an elegant chateau, with wide windows and balconies overlooking the lake and the beautiful scenery beyond; on the north it was an impenetrable fortress that guarded a narrow gap between the precipitous mountains and the lake. Even worse for those uncertain of a welcoming reception, the only way to pass the chateau was along a single ancient stone walkway under the gatehouse with its ever watchful guards. Imprisonment in the dungeons had once awaited anyone judged to be an enemy, rightly or wrongly. That poor young man in the poem hadn't stood a chance!

The ski instructor didn't buy a ticket, and Laura lost sight of him as she stood in line. She decided to go to the dungeons first, hoping that he, too, was unable to resist the lure of Byron's ghoulish tale. Ignoring the cold clamminess of lumpy stone walls literally dug out of the rocks, she kept an eye out for her quarry as she examined the pillar to which the unfortunate victim had been chained. Byron's name, scratched into it by the poet's own hand, was covered with a glass panel so contemporary graffiti lovers couldn't deface it.

Continuing her search, she explored tunnel-like passages where rats and mold and forgotten boxes had long been the only inhabitants; then she went upstairs and was stunned at the contrast. Here, large windows illuminated the rooms, many filled with a collection of beautiful old chests and well-furnished bedrooms. Compared to the horrors perpetrated below, the castle's legitimate occupants had enjoyed remarkably civilized surroundings. There were even rudimentary toilets and huge hip baths.

Eager to see the vista from the lookout tower where guards had watched for enemies, Laura labored wearily up five sets of steep stairs and emerged breathless and dizzy at the top. Grabbing the grey stone wall for support, she peered through a viewing slit at the black water lapping restlessly against the shoreline where the lake still hadn't frozen.

Immediately, she saw the ski instructor. To her astonishment, he was in a small boat that was plying its way through the choppy water to the castle dock. What was he doing there? She soon got an answer. When the boat reached the dock, he and two other men began unloading large boxes and carrying them into the castle cellars. Perhaps this was an extra job, Laura speculated, not a cultural visit. Ski instructors probably didn't make a lot of money.

Not a very significant discovery, she thought, discouraged. Shivering, she turned to leave. The damp chill of ancient stones seemed to have penetrated deep into her bones. Perhaps castles were best visited in the summer months.

Trying vainly to get warm, she jogged to the station, but it wasn't until she was settled in the café car of the next train with a mug of hot chocolate that her internal temperature returned to normal.

Glancing finally at her watch, she saw that they would soon arrive in Visp, where she would change to a smaller train to climb the heights into Zermatt. Excitement seized Laura. Another adventure was about to begin. What it would bring she had no idea but she did know she felt ready for any challenge. Even the ever present but always vague possibility of danger seemed exciting, at least for the moment.

Better remember that feeling. It might not last, the more cautious side of her warned, but Laura paid no attention.

****

The train that would take her to Zermatt was waiting across the track. It reminded Laura of old-fashioned trains in story books – simple and sturdy, and painted bright red. Many windows were wide open despite the frigid air, and cheerful faces hung out, watching other passengers haul gear inside. Laura climbed aboard and joined them, as excited as the rest of the crowd.

Her pleasure increased as the little train began its steep ascent. They were so close now to the scenery that each time they passed through a tunnel she was threatened with decapitation unless she pulled her head in. As soon as she poked it out again, more panoramas unfolded. Half-frozen waterfalls cascaded down steep cliffs; wild streams that had broken away from their blankets of ice and snow crashed through deep crevasses whose rocky sides showed black and ominous against the whitened landscape. Above them all, looking close enough to touch, were the mountains, like sentinels clothed in brilliant white standing guard over the towns huddled against their slopes.

Eager to see it all, the passengers roamed ceaselessly, noisily, between the windows on one side of the train and the other, snapping pictures, exchanging places without animosity, exclaiming in wonder at the beauty all around them in a variety of languages.

The light had dimmed and snow was falling lazily as they entered Zermatt. The town was just as Laura had imagined: a twinkling mecca of restaurants and hotels and shops against a backdrop of cloud shrouded mountains. Her stomach fluttered with anticipation. So many unaccustomed pleasures were about to come her way – luxurious hotels in glamorous places that were otherwise beyond her reach financially, the actual fact of skiing, however clumsily, in the magnificent Alps, the fantastic scenery all around her. Adding to the joy, she would see Violet again, Violet of the throaty guffaw and boundless energy.

The train came to a stop and practical considerations pushed aside all else. There were no cars in Zermatt, only carts that took visitors to their hotels.

The one she and Violet were staying in was halfway up the hill, Laura remembered, just past the graveyard where the many people who had been killed on the Matterhorn were buried. It was a sobering thought.

No carts came into view and she wasn't sure how to summon one, so she collected her luggage from the station and trudged slowly up the hill, pack on her back, skis on one shoulder, camera slung around her neck, suitcase rolling clumsily behind. She must look like an overloaded porter. On the other hand, most tourists probably arrived looking like this, unless they were staying at a fancy hotel where they would presumably be met and their luggage spirited away by one of the porters she resembled.

Pausing to catch her breath, Laura marveled at how crowded with buildings Zermatt was, but at the same time how harmonious they all looked. Dozens of restaurants and hotels with typical Swiss names like Alpine and Edelweiss lined the twisting streets. Most were traditional, with balconies and steeply pitched roofs, but a few modern ones were jumbled among them. And squeezed into every bit of empty territory were shops, some selling furs and luxury goods, others necessities like toothpaste. Most sold tourist items too – cuckoo clocks and Swiss army knives and decorated spoons. Had there ever been a tourist who had left without one of those trinkets to remind them of Switzerland and the mountains?

When she came to the old church Laura lingered by the graves of climbers, and then looked up at the mountain where they had died. There like a gift was the Matterhorn, bathed in an unexpected shaft of sunlight. The narrow peak sliced knife-like into its glow, its dark rock backlit into shining ebony. The sight was spectacular, unforgettable.

A tall redhead came loping out the door of the hotel beyond her. Violet! What a joy to see that lanky frame again.

Violet hugged her speechlessly for a long moment; then she stood back and grinned. "Tea or wine? You look ready for one of them, but then, you always are. Now, hand me those skis and the suitcase and we'll get them to the room. I'll give you five minutes before I drag you out to my favorite café in Zermatt. It's a good place for private conversations and we have a good deal to discuss."

Her Scots accent was more pronounced than usual, and Laura looked at her carefully. Underneath the cheerful banter, Violet was worried. Her face had a strained look Laura knew well.

"Has anything happened?" she asked anxiously.

"Another kidnapping threat came," Violet told her. "Just like the others – a scrawled note on a scratch pad without any identifying marks that is very hard to trace. But something else worries me almost as much, maybe even more."

"Is it connected to the conference?"

Violet grimaced. "That's exactly it," she answered cryptically. "I don't know but every instinct in me tells me it is." Without elaborating, she charged up the hotel stairs, suitcase and skis in hand. Laura followed, trying to contain her curiosity, trying even harder to keep up with those long legs.

Violet took care of the registration process; then they went up to their room. Laura exclaimed in delight when she saw the large glass doors leading to a balcony

26

facing the Matterhorn. She would see it every morning - if the clouds permitted. At any time of year they were likely to obscure the highest peaks, and the predictions of snow over the next few days weren't helpful. Still, she vowed to look each time she came into the room.

A quick glance at the now obscured view, a visit to the bathroom and a brush through her snow-dampened, uproariously tangled hair were all Violet permitted her before urging her out the door again.

"What's happened?" Laura asked again, worried by Violet's tension.

Violet shook her head. "At the café," she answered. "We'll go inside if that's all right with you. More private - and warmer. It gets cold quickly up here once the sun goes down."

Despite their urgent need to talk, Laura and Violet walked slowly through the now-crowded streets, enjoying the ambience. And that was precisely the right word, Laura decided. Zermatt had that indefinable *je ne sais quoi* called ambience. One knew immediately that beautiful people flocked here. Money seemed to be in the air, and power, or at least illusions of it.

The townspeople she saw, however, seemed remarkably unaffected by the influx of wealth that had poured into their town. Maybe catering to tourists willing to pay large fees to climb or ski the local mountains wasn't all that different from tending – and milking – cows, except the profits were larger.

The cafe was dimly lit, a bit smoky. Places where private conversations were held always made Laura think of old Humphrey Bogart movies, where wisps of smoke seemed to curl endlessly around the heads of the protagonists as they bent their heads together over the table.

The man behind the bar recognized Violet and offered them a table in a far corner. "Perfect," Violet told him gratefully. "This is my friend Laura," she said, "and Laura, this is Gustav."

Laura shook his hand. A strong face, she reflected. Good-looking but without that air of knowing it. She liked him immediately.

"Wine, I think," she said to his question about a drink.

Violet nodded. "That Sauvignon Blanc I had last night was good," she told him with a smile. "Could you bring water too? Laura just got off a plane so no doubt she's dry as a bone. I don't want the wine to go to her head. We've got a lot of catching up to do and I want to hit the slopes tomorrow."

"Sounds as if I'll need both," Laura commented when Gustav had left. "The wine to pick me up and the water for keeping my dehydrated wits about me.

"Now, tell me what's happening," she said firmly. "I refuse to wait any longer."

"Someone's been killed," Violet said bluntly. "A woman I knew, at least I've met her a few times. The last time I saw her was two days ago, just after I heard that someone is altering the orders for children's emergency aid supplies at the relief agency where she works. More boxes are ordered than are paid for, and then the extra boxes go missing from the warehouse where they're stored. Since Rosa, the woman who was killed, worked for the relief agency, I asked her if she knew or had heard about the orders or the thefts. She said she hadn't but would let me know if she learned anything."

"Did you believe her?" Laura asked.

"I'm not sure," Violet answered slowly. "I didn't see her as a criminal; she's all wrong for that. At the same time, I had the feeling that she was hiding something, or wasn't quite telling the truth. Or that she did know something but was reluctant to talk about it, or maybe afraid…"

Violet's voice dwindled away and Laura inserted another question. "When was she killed, and where?"

"This afternoon,' Violet answered absently. "Near the train station in Interlaken, where you changed for the Golden Pass route."

A terrible premonition shot through Laura. Impossible. Surely, it was impossible. She asked the question anyway.

"What did she look like?" Her voice had a strangled sound and Violet regarded her curiously.

"Nice-looking but not beautiful certainly. Dark hair and eyes. Here, the authorities faxed me a picture of her if you want to see it."

Laura took the picture, looked at it briefly, and closed her eyes. "I saw her," she whispered. "I saw her out the train window. She was afraid."

CHAPTER THREE

Violet stared at her incredulously. "You *saw* her?" Laura nodded mutely. For a long moment there was stunned silence.

Finally Violet shook her head, as if to clear it. "Laura, your ability to land precisely at the scene of a crime is uncanny. I'm beginning to think that all I have to do is follow you around. You'll find me the victim, probably the villain as well, every time. It's as if you have a magnet inside you."

"I don't mean to do it," Laura protested. "I don't even want to. This time all I did was look out the window. Everyone looks out windows on trains."

"It seems quite horrible now," she added with a shiver. "I guess she must have been killed soon after that."

"Sorry," Violet apologized. "It must feel dreadful. You must admit, though, that it's an unusual aptitude, if that's the right word." Her eyebrows went up at another thought. "As well as making you valuable to us, it puts you in danger. For goodness sake, don't tell anyone else you saw her."

"I won't," Laura promised.

"Good. Now, tell me exactly what you saw," Violet instructed.

Laura described the scene, how the terrified woman had been looking at someone just behind her. "She was appealing to him, I'm sure. And then she ran into a parking lot, looking panic-stricken."

"Appealing to *him*?"

"The only person I saw behind me was a blond man. He went through into another carriage without looking back."

"Can you describe him?" Violet's voice was sharp.

Laura felt abashed. "I can do better than that," she replied meekly. "I think I have one or two photos of him."

Violet's eyes widened in surprise, and she laughed. "I suppose you can also provide his name and his vital statistics?"

Laura grinned. "I don't have his name but I do know his occupation. He's a ski instructor in Murren. We should see him in a few days. As for statistics, I'd say he's about six foot two, short blond hair, athletic build. Blue eyes. In his middle twenties I'd guess. Very good-looking and knows it. Highly attractive to his female students, I should think.

"He might also have a job at Chateau Chillon, carrying boxes of supplies into their cellars. I saw him there when I visited the castle, helping to unload a boatful of boxes. It's a fascinating place, though a bit depressing in winter."

"I'd ask how you managed to get so much information out of him and take those photos, all between Interlaken and Montreux," Violet observed tartly, "but I'm not sure I dare. Quite a few half-truths were probably involved."

"Not at all," Laura replied primly. "All I did was take my tea to his table, snap a few pictures of peaks that happened to include his head, ask why the train stopped unexpectedly, and why a man who climbed down from the last car to unload boxes from the train and stack them in the snow was left behind in a place with no buildings or roads or even tracks, when the train went on."

Violet's gaze sharpened. "That does seem odd. So does the unscheduled stop. Those trains don't usually do that sort of thing. Did anyone know why it stopped - or why the man was left behind? Was he a repairman?"

"He wasn't dressed like one and he had no tools. I also think he was the person who pulled the emergency cord so he could unload the boxes but I can't prove it. When he finished with the boxes he pulled what looked like a gun out of his pocket and shot at Thomas, who was hanging out the other end of the train. He's all right, though. I saw him later."

Violet gaped. "Slow down and let me get this straight! First, what was Thomas doing there and what made you think he was shot?"

Laura provided details on her brief meeting with Thomas but omitted the interlude in the lavatory. With Violet's probing eyes on her face, she would certainly blush – an embarrassing weakness she abhorred.

"Quite an eventful train ride on the whole, I'd say," Violet commented with a straight face that Laura didn't quite believe. Violet had an uncanny way of intuiting what was going on in people's heads.

"A beautiful one too," Laura noted. "It's curious that there are so many boxes involved," she added, by way of changing a potentially blush-inducing subject. "Your missing ones, the ones being unloaded from the train and left in the snow, and the ones going into the castle."

"Did you happen to get a good look at any of the boxes?" Violet asked.

Laura reflected. "I'd guess they were about three feet long, half as high. "Do you think they could be the missing supplies?"

Violet looked doubtful. "That's about the right size, but I can't think why they would be taken to Chateau Chillon."

"Because no one would think to look there," Laura answered. "The boxes I saw in those old storerooms looked ancient, but that could be a cover."

"I'll send someone to check them out," Violet said. "The fact that the number of extra boxes ordered matches the number that disappear from the warehouse is intriguing, as is the fact that sometimes all of them are taken at once, at other times only a few are taken."

"Maybe that's because the number stolen sometimes has to fit into a smallish boat, or because taking only a few is less likely to be noticed," Laura inserted. "Do you know how long this has been going on?"

"For all we know, it's been going on for years, but apparently no one has noticed until now. It's not an easy deception to spot."

"I suppose not. I wish I'd paid more attention to the boxes I saw," Laura lamented. "I can't seem to remember if the ones in the boat and the ones being unloaded from the train were the same general size and shape."

"You had more important things to attend to at the time, like the errant Thomas turning up and being shot at," Violet said.

"Thomas said our case and his were connected," Laura told her. "He also wanted me to find out about bomb shelters in Switzerland. His computer had been stolen, so he couldn't."

"Paintings could be hidden in bomb shelters," Violet suggested.

"Paintings in boxes hidden in bomb shelters," Laura added.

"We'll keep it in mind," Violet said. "In the meantime, let's get back to the ski instructor. Did you get any impression of what he may have been in the victim's life, if anything? Or whether he even saw her?"

"Either he didn't see her or he didn't want to, which for some reason was the impression I got," Laura answered. "That's why I think any relationship that existed was one-sided. Maybe he wanted information from her or some other kind of help. If she thought he cared for her or needed her, she might have been willing to do what he wanted. Was she that type of woman?"

"I didn't know Rosa that well," Violet answered slowly, "but I think she may have been impressionable. Wanted to help people and might believe a man if he told her she was indispensable to him. Or want to believe."

"Could her death be connected to the thefts of supplies?

Violet nodded. "Since Rosa worked for the company that provides the relief supplies, it is certainly possible."

"What actually happened to her?" Laura asked suddenly, and then wished she hadn't. She shivered. "It really is horrible to see someone who is frightened and then find out they got killed. Nightmarish in fact."

"Yes,' Violet agreed soberly. "I wish now I hadn't got you into this in the first place. I genuinely thought all you would have to do was be watchful and have a good time otherwise. And ski."

She smiled grimly. "It doesn't seem to have worked out that way. But to answer your question - Rosa may have been followed from the station, and your description of her panic seems to confirm that. She was found lying on the ground and brought to the hospital. At first they thought that she had slipped on the ice and hit her head. Further examination showed that she had been hit from behind by an unknown assailant with the proverbial blunt instrument.

"If it makes you feel any better," Violet added gently, "she never saw what was coming or had any awareness of what happened to her."

"I suppose it does, a little," Laura conceded. "It also makes it essential to know why she was frightened and who she was frightened of."

"It does," Violet replied tersely. "And why someone wanted her dead. Unfortunately, the reason that comes to mind is that she was seen talking to me, which implies that someone involved in the thefts, possibly the killer, knows I am a detective. If that person is involved with the conference, I'm in trouble. I can be far more effective incognito. And that brings me to my biggest worry."

She took a deep breath. "Laura, I think you should just get out of the case and consider this a ski vacation. Things could get a good deal nastier than I'd thought when I asked you to help."

Laura sat up straighter. She didn't want to get out of the case. Watching from the sidelines sounded very dull. Anyway, danger wasn't her foremost worry. She grinned. "I was worried about keeping up on skis, not about the case," she confessed impulsively, and Violet laughed.

"Then you have an excellent excuse for just taking ski lessons and forgetting about the case. Think of it as a week to improve your skiing."

"I doubt it would work," Laura answered dubiously. "I already know too much, and I'm too inclined to snoop. I was looking forward to matching wits with a few more despicable villains, too. I fear I've developed a taste for it."

Violet raised her eyebrows in exasperation. "Enlisting you under these circumstances seems rather like leading a lamb to slaughter."

Laura bridled. "I'm no lamb," she protested hotly. "I've even learned karate and some self-defense. I'm told I'm pretty good at it, too."

Violet looked astonished, and then she roared with laughter. "I love it! That's my Laura. Always ready to take on the world."

"Besides," Laura added craftily, "since I'm rooming with you, anyone who knows who you are will assume I am a detective too, or at least helping you. I'd be much safer if I knew what was going on, so I could protect myself."

Violet sighed. "I suppose you're right," she admitted.

"Absolutely," Laura agreed. "There's also the fact that they may already suspect that I'm involved. The ski instructor could be one of the villains and he is fully aware that I'm both nosy and observant."

Violet sent her another exasperated look. "I don't suppose trying to keep you out of the action would have worked anyway," she muttered glumly. "You don't have to go looking for danger. It comes looking for you."

"That does seem to be my major talent in this business," Laura agreed, "which means if there's anything nasty going on, it's bound to find me, so you might as well make use of me."

Violet threw up her hands in defeat. "All right! But you *do* have to promise not to take chances. I can't watch you or have you watched all the time. I've got a few helpers at my disposal, but not many."

"I'll be very careful," Laura promised, wondering if that was possible. Last year she'd tried to be careful but got kidnapped twice anyway.

"I will also work hard on my skiing," she added mischievously. "I know an excellent ski instructor in Murren." Violet rolled her eyes and didn't respond.

"Now let's discuss the people in here," Laura went on in a business-like tone, watching the café fill up with glamorous people eager for after-ski drinks, any of whom could be part of the plot. "I want to know more about Zermatt, too. I can see that there are lots of beautiful people in temporary residence, but I want to know what it's like under the surface. There's a good deal of money here, that's obvious, maybe in those secret Swiss bank accounts I read so much about. And where there's money there are usually schemers, people who haven't got it and want it badly."

"There are plenty of greedy schemers here," Violet agreed. "Beautiful people have to be greedy to get where they are. Look at the older man wearing the new black designer ski outfit, for instance. He has a tall blonde with him – blondness seems a prerequisite for women in certain circles – who is at least twenty years younger. He once worked for the United Nations and is reputed to be involved in some shady, if not downright illegal, deals."

"Drugs maybe?" Laura asked. "I read recently that the faucets and door handles in U.N. bathrooms in Copenhagen are coated with cocaine."

"Not a very stellar report for the U.N.," Violet commented dryly. "And one that leaves the door wide open for all sorts of corruption, including blackmail."

The man in black raised a hand and snapped his fingers at Gustav. Laura saw irritation crease the waiter's face; he erased it quickly but he didn't hurry over. His steps were leisurely and he stopped once or twice to exchange a greeting or a quick word before reaching the table.

"May I take your order, Monsieur Guillard?" he asked politely. Laura saw the older man place a proprietary arm around his youthful companion. Gustav was young and attractive and she supposed that meant he was a threat. She examined Monsieur Guillard's face surreptitiously. Unless she was very much mistaken, he'd had a lift or two – and not the type that had to do with skiing.

"Do you think the blond is his wife?" she whispered to Violet.

"I doubt it, though she could be. Often there's an older wife who was left at home so the husband could have a little fun, but occasionally the men marry the younger one. The women are a varied lot, some professional companions, others students looking for help with tuition. If they're young and lovely and agreeably ready to dispense their favors, the men fork over quite a bit, enough to get them through a medical or law degree in some cases."

Laura studied the young woman's face. Intelligence was there, and perhaps ambition. Did that include wanting to marry a rich older man? She didn't think so. This woman was more likely to get what she wanted from him, probably funds for an education, and go her own way. So who was using who? What if the rich gentleman weighed three hundred pounds and had violent or quirky tastes in sex? However glamorously presented, prostitution was still prostitution, and the woman's job was to do what the man wanted.

She shuddered and Violet looked at her questioningly. "That's not for the woman and how she chooses to earn money," Laura explained. "It's just that the situation could get unpleasant for her, even dangerous, depending on what he expects for his patronage."

"Yes," Violet agreed. "I fear he's ahead in the balance of power. Her best weapon I would think is intelligence - out-guessing him."

"A bit risky," Laura noted. "The question is whether she can pull out of the relationship without repercussions if she wants to. Is she really her own boss?"

Violet shook her head. "Hard to tell. I hope so," she added fervently. "I don't like the look of him. And someone could be managing her. There are some nasty people in that business as we learned last year."

Laura examined Monsieur Guillard again. A cold man, she decided, and possibly a cruel one. Not much compassion in that face.

Her attention was diverted by a flurry of activity at the door. Three people had arrived, two men and a woman. Their faces were flushed with cold, and they were laughing and chattering as they stamped the snow off their boots. The woman was about fifty; slim and lovely, with wonderfully styled dark hair that looked as if it had never felt a breath of wind or a drop of snow. At the same time, Laura had the impression she had just come off the slopes.

"How do you suppose she manages to keep her hair so perfect while she skis?" she whispered to Violet.

"There's a new kind of hat out, a transparent bubble with a breathing hole that goes over the head to protect the hair," Violet whispered back with a straight face. "Quite expensive I hear but worth every penny."

Laura looked at her friend suspiciously and then burst out laughing. "I almost believed you. I was going to go out and get one myself!"

Violet grinned. "Actually, the woman in question is a bit of a legend. She won a number of downhill races when she was younger and she's still a fine skier. She also owns and manages one of the glitziest hotels in Zermatt and another in Vail, Colorado. She's an excellent businesswoman and is reputed to be remarkably nice, too. And no one has any idea how she keeps her hair that way even when she skis, except perhaps a discreet hairdresser waiting in the ladies room at the bottom of the slopes."

"She looks nice despite the perfect hair and all those enviable talents," Laura agreed, examining the woman's laughing face. It didn't look lifted, only healthy. "Do you know her name?"

Violet nodded. "Helga Braun. Her husband is behind her. He is well-liked too, and a sharp businessman – a venture capitalist, I believe. People know enough not to cross him – or her for that matter.

Laura examined Herr Braun. He wasn't tall or conventionally handsome, but he had an intensely alert and interesting face, large featured and deeply tanned, with sharp eyes that missed nothing – not even the fact that she was staring at him. He nodded politely in her direction, and Laura detected a slight smile on his wide lips. Embarrassed, she acknowledged the nod with a smile and looked quickly away.

"People around here would kill to get an invitation to one of their parties," Violet was telling her. "There's one tomorrow I think. I wish I had an invitation myself. We might pick up some useful information."

"Hans," Laura said immediately. "Surely he could wangle us one." Hans was a Swiss companion from last summer's adventures. He headed another child welfare organization and had hoped to join them at the conference, but at the last minute he'd had to back out.

Violet brightened. "Excellent thought. I'll give him a call. He's the source of most of my information about the Brauns so I'm sure he knows them.

"That's their son Nicolas with them," she added. "Hans says they used to call him the *Golden Boy*." Laura allowed her eyes to wander briefly toward the young man. The nick-name suited him, she thought. He was beautiful, like a young Greek God. A shock of light hair the color of golden wheat crowned his boyish face, and his large blue eyes were guileless.

He was also very sensitive. His gaze met hers immediately, as if he had sensed even her swift examination. Laura looked down at her lap, disconcerted again.

More people drifted in; some had just come from the slopes and repeated the boot-stamping process, other less athletic ones looked as if they had just been dressed by a wardrobe mistress for the après ski role. Laura watched with fascination until the food Violet had ordered arrived. It was a local specialty of melted cheese and potatoes called Rosti, and she tucked into it ravenously. Unfortunately, sleepiness moved in as soon as she had finished, threatening to have her head on the table.

Violet saw her yawns and beckoned discreetly for the bill. "There will be more time to people-watch tomorrow if we can get into that party, but at the moment you need sleep," she said crisply.

Laura nodded, unresisting. Violet led the way back to the hotel, this time through rutted, twisting lanes lined with wooden huts on high stilts. A few tilted at crazy angles, looking ready to collapse, and no light came from any of them. In the old days, whole families had lived in them while the farm animals sheltered underneath, Laura remembered reading. The heat of their bodies had helped to keep their owners warm.

Rustling sounds from the hut they were passing distracted her. Rats perhaps? Or dogs nosing around?

Violet stopped to listen. "Probably just a young couple courting," she whispered. "A nice love-nest - unused and private, if cold."

She didn't move on, though, but stood still, listening intently. Laura waited tensely beside her.

More sounds emerged, subdued gasps and hissed whispers. Laura didn't think they had much to do with love-making. They sounded too young, she thought, and too giggly. But that might not mean much these days.

"I'll have a quick look, just in case," Violet whispered. "Pulling out her flashlight, she crept silently toward the hut. Laura pulled out her own light.

A crash and a wild scream propelled both of them into a run. Violet hurtled into the dark hut, leaving the door swinging drunkenly. Heart thudding, Laura plunged in after her, flashlight held in front of her.

She gasped in horror. Lying on her back at the foot of a steep wooden ladder was a young woman. Her blond hair streamed out around her, and blood dribbled from her forehead. A young man holding a large chunk of wood stood over her, ready to strike again.

CHAPTER FOUR

An anguished howl emerged from the dark loft above the ladder. An accusing voice in accented English followed.

"What did you do to her? What did you do! Oh, Kjersti…"

"I did nothing. The idiot tripped and fell by herself," the young man replied dismissively. His voice was quintessentially upper-class British, the clipped sound marred only by his disdain. He made no move to help the young woman at his feet. "She always was clumsy," he added sarcastically.

"Brute! You are horrible. I think you have tripped her with that board! I saw you pick it up and hold it in front of her."

Another young woman with long blond hair crept carefully down the ladder into the pool of light shed by Violet's flashlight and bent over her fallen friend. She tried to pick up the bloodied head to cradle it in her arms, but Violet's voice stopped her. "Don't move her head until we know if she has concussion," she instructed sharply.

The blond woman whirled. "Concussion," she wailed, struggling to pronounce the unfamiliar word. "But what is that?"

"A severe blow to the head," Violet answered briefly. "Here, hold the torch." Obediently, the young woman took the flashlight and watched while Violet examined the woman on the floor with deft fingers. Only she wasn't a woman, Laura saw, only a girl. So was the second one at her feet. They looked exactly alike.

She went closer to make sure and then sat down heavily on the lowest step of the ladder, feeling dizzy with relief, or perhaps exhaustion. That chilling scream hadn't signaled murder, only a squabble between youthful late night explorers and, she suspected, an accident less serious than the frenzied howls and the blood indicated – an assessment that was confirmed when the girl on the floor eyed her curiously for a split second.

"The twins. It's the Danish twins," Laura muttered. They were dressed all in black now, like cat burglars, so she hadn't recognized them at first.

Violet looked up warily. "You're not going to tell me you know them too, are you?" She sighed. "On the other hand, I don't doubt that you do."

"They were on the same train," Laura explained defensively. "I talked to their mother. She's the Danish delegate to the conference.

"There she is, I think. Probably she's looking for the twins," she added, as a voice outside called out names in a language that sounded like the Danish she had heard on the train.

"It is Maman!" the flashlight holder exclaimed. Handing the torch to Laura, she ran to the door and yelled excitedly into the darkness.

"Did you trip her?" Violet said suddenly to the youth.

He shrugged his narrow shoulders. He was hardly older than the twins, Laura realized, when Violet's torch showed him more clearly. "She tripped herself," he replied nonchalantly. He looked bored by the proceedings, but Violet's next words brought a glimmer of fear into his eyes.

"We shall soon know," she said without further explanation.

Sigrid Olsen came through the door, holding a torch of her own. She shone her beam around the room, taking everything and everyone in with remarkably calm eyes while her standing daughter continued a volley of explanations in frantic Danish that eventually dwindled into silence.

Sigrid's beam caught Laura full in the face. "Why it is Laura from the train!" she exclaimed in English as she moved toward her fallen daughter.

"Now, child, what have you done to yourself?" she went on, still in English. Kjersti opened her eyes again, gave her mother a brief glance, and then closed them again with a dramatic moan.

"I don't think there's a concussion and the cut isn't deep," Violet said, looking up at Sigrid. "Still, it might be a good idea to have a doctor examine her." Kjersti shot Violet an alarmed look but her lids dropped hurriedly when she saw Laura watching.

Laura turned away, concealing a grin. "This is Violet McLarty," she said to Sigrid. "The friend I came to join. She knows first aid," she added, since it was obvious that Violet was more trained than most casual bystanders.

"And Violet, this is Sigrid Olsen, the Danish representative to a conference to be held in Murren. She told me about it on the train."

"I know a little about the conference, too," Violet told Sigrid as they shook hands. "My sister, a travel agent in England, organized the accommodations and meals at the hotel, the meeting rooms, all those details, and she has set me the task of making sure her plans are carried out well."

Laura was startled but tried not to show it. Violet hadn't told her that. Had she dreamed it up on the spur of the moment? If so, it was another excellent cover. Violet could get acquainted with all the delegates, ask questions and even pry into people's activities without arousing suspicion – unless, as she feared, someone already knew who she was.

"Ah! Now I know who to tell if I should have questions or complaints," Sigrid replied. "I cannot think of any so far, except perhaps how to control my too adventurous daughters.

"Thank you for caring for Kjersti and Kristin," she went on sincerely. "I have been looking for them for some time but I could not find them.

"I see you have come too, Reginald," she added levelly, watching the young man's face. "Did you see what happened?"

The young man's diffidence deserted him under her steady gaze, and he looked down at the ground. "She tripped," he muttered defensively. "Just tripped and fell on those steep stairs."

"I can see that much," Sigrid answered. "The question is, from where did she fall. How high was she? That will make a difference."

Reginald tried for another nonchalant shrug, but his shoulders were too tense to allow it to work. "I cannot be certain," he said finally in a formal lawyer-like voice. "It was very dark in the hut."

"I see." Sigrid continued to examine his face, her eyes quizzical.

Reginald edged toward the door. "I think I shall return to the hotel if you don't mind, Mrs. Olsen," he said stiffly. "Unless I can be of further assistance."

"That will be fine," she told him. "Please give my greetings to your mother. Are you also staying at the Hotel Couronne?"

"Yes we are," he mumbled, obviously aching to escape her scrutiny. When Sigrid nodded at him, he bolted out the door.

"He tripped her. I know he did," the second twin said accusingly to his retreating back.

"Did Reginald trip you?" Sigrid asked Kjersti.

Kjersti looked uncomfortable. "I cannot be sure," she mumbled.

Sigrid nodded. "Then we must give him the benefit of the doubt, as they say in the courtroom. It is possible that he did, but I also think it was very easy for Kjersti to trip in this dark place without his help."

She turned to Laura and Violet. "Reginald's mother, Ann Lawrence, is the English delegate to the conference," she explained. "He is her only son."

There was a wealth of understatement in the observation. Laura instantly formed an image of doting mother and spoiled, inconsiderate son.

Sigrid knelt beside Kjersti and spoke a few words to her in Danish while she wiped away the blood with a handkerchief. Kjersti responded with an exclamation that showed surprising strength.

"I have asked Kjersti if she feels well enough to stand, and that we must ask the doctor if she will be able to ski in the morning," she explained, and Laura saw the hint of a twinkle in her serene blue eyes. Sigrid was as aware of her daughters' dramatic flair as she was of Reginald's sneaky one.

"Kjersti thinks she will be all right, I am glad to say."

"I am glad, too, Kjersti," Laura told the girl sympathetically. "It would be terrible to be in Zermatt and not be able to ski."

"Now, my child, let us return to the hotel," Sigrid instructed. "Kristin, help your sister on the other side and we will get her on her feet."

Kjersti leaned heavily on her mother and sister but got down the outer steps with surprising agility, Laura noted. She might not have been unconscious at all, only eager to get Reginald in trouble. He seemed to be the twin's arch-enemy. She suspected he deserved it. He seemed unbearably superior.

Some of the other delegates were in the hotel bar when they returned, but Laura didn't stop. She could barely remember her own name after thirty six or more hours without sleep, never mind the names of a half dozen delegates. She would sort them out tomorrow. For the moment, reaching her room before she fell down was about all she could manage. Readying herself hastily for bed, Laura tumbled under the duvet and closed her eyes.

****

She didn't wake again until Violet appeared in the door with a tray holding a pot of tea and all the necessary accoutrements.

"Rise and shine," Violet said cheerily, flinging the curtains open to reveal bright sun. "I ran down for this to get you going. It's a gorgeous day."

"Thanks. You're an angel!" Laura stumbled to the bathroom, ignoring her tousled image, and careened back toward the tea tray. Not as good as English tea, she decided, but it still helped clear her jet-lagged brain. After a hot shower she would no doubt feel fantastic.

Remembering the Matterhorn, she hurried to the window as soon as she emerged from the shower. "Still clouds over the top," Violet told her, "but they're supposed to lift later. I reached Hans, by the way, and he is finagling an invitation for us. I gather he knows Helga quite well."

"Marvelous," Laura mumbled indistinctly as she pulled on a turtleneck.

"Now, while you get dressed for skiing," Violet announced, "I need to give you additional information about the conference. Some of the delegates may be at breakfast and I want to catch you up before you meet them.

"Briefly, the meeting was arranged because a group of anonymous donors has pledged a great deal of money for girl's education in four specific towns – two in the Middle East, two in Africa. In these areas, few girls now attend school, and maternal mortality and birth rates, especially among teenagers, are very high. The donors also plan to spend time and money convincing ordinary people that educating girls is the best way to help their families and their villages out of poverty."

"They're right. Educating girls really does work better than anything else," Laura commented, "but the idea must also alarm someone badly. Otherwise, why threaten to take the delegates' children hostage?"

"One possibility is that educating girls could threaten the power of local autocrats by empowering the female half of the population," Violet suggested.

"That's true," Laura agreed, "but dozens of conferences on empowering girls and women have been held in the last few years, and as far as I know, none of them have received threats."

Violet nodded. "Exactly - why this conference? That is the question we need to answer. For the moment, however, let's concentrate on skiing. It's a glorious morning and all we have to think about is turning properly, and then going to a glamorous party. There, we really can troll for information."

A number of delegates were already in the light-filled breakfast room. Sigrid and the twins were there, the latter clad in an outlandish array of cast-off clothes that bore little resemblance to ski wear. So were Reginald and his mother, a small, rather stocky woman with brown hair and an indeterminate face. Laura thought she probably wouldn't have firm opinions.

She was wrong. "I do not agree," the small woman said emphatically as Laura and Violet entered the room. "We must force these men to adhere to the rules. They are tyrants, and tyrants cannot be permitted to get away with their transgressions. To cater to them is not right."

"Perhaps we should try to make our views more palatable to them," Sigrid suggested. "Otherwise we may not accomplish anything at -"

"I should like another croissant," Reginald interrupted, pointing at the sideboard loaded with breakfast items. Sigrid looked startled, but Reginald's mother jumped up immediately. Picking out a choice croissant from the sideboard, she handed it to her son with an ingratiating smile.

"Growing boys are always hungry," she said. "But again, I do not agree. We have compromised long enough as it is," she continued firmly.

"These habits begin early in life, I fear," an elegant woman with shining ebony skin remarked. Her dark eyes twinkled but were innocent of malice. "In Africa, we women are taught to wait on men and in that way we teach them bad habits early in life. That is why so many men in Africa are tyrants." She had a beautiful, lilting accent and a rich, resonant voice.

Kjersti and Kristin giggled but the English delegate only looked confused, seeming not to grasp the connection. "I suppose that is true, but we must change those habits now," she insisted.

"One must start early for that, I fear." The dark-skinned woman, whom Laura assumed was the African delegate, sighed gustily.

"As you have done with me," a younger and equally elegant woman said softly in the same lilting accent. "In Africa we are taught to serve our elders." Rising gracefully, she took a croissant from the basket on the sideboard and handed it to her mother, or at least Laura assumed the African delegate was her mother. A delightful pair, she decided. No judgment, just a little lesson.

Still giggling, Kjersti rose, selected still another croissant and gave it to her mother. Not to be outdone, Kristin did the same. Now everyone except the English delegate was laughing. Finally she too gave a short laugh, but Laura was certain she hadn't grasped the joke.

Reginald paid no attention to any of them. He lathered his croissant with butter and jam and ate it with quick neat bites. Not a crumb landed on his hands or clothes. In fact, Laura noted, Reginald was neat in every way. His nails were clean, his hair perfectly brushed, and in contrast to the twins, he was sleekly attired in a dark blue ski suit that looked extremely expensive.

Sigrid thanked her daughters and then decided the teasing had gone far enough. "Let us say hello to the new arrivals," she said, indicating Violet and Laura. "This is Violet McLarty. She is the sister of the woman who organized our conference, so she will be making sure our needs are met. You can go to her if you have questions. And this is her friend, Laura Morland, whom I met on the train. She is a professor at an American University.

"I believe you met Reginald last night," Sigrid went on, introducing Laura and Violet to the people around the table. "This is his mother, Ann Lawrence, who is our English delegate. Next to her is our Iranian delegate, Doctor Ebrahim Nezam." Laura recognized the swarthy man with the hooked nose who had taken Sigrid's table in the café car.

He nodded to her, his face impassive. It remained that way all during the breakfast conversation regardless of what was said, she noticed.

"I should also like you to meet our African delegate and her daughter," Sigrid continued, "but I fear I still do not know how to say their names properly, so I must ask them to introduce themselves."

The African delegate complied, uttering a series of names for each of them that rolled off her tongue like music. Laura had trouble interpreting the sounds and if their puzzled faces were any indication, so did the others. The dark-skinned woman laughed. "I shall say them more slowly this time. My name is Makedu Nicato-Zalika, and my daughter is named Amina Abayoni-Kagiso. We are both named after former African queens. The names mean *a woman as capable as a man; born to bring joy, peace* and *fine warrior.*"

She smiled. "I think it will be easiest if you use only our first names, Amina and Makedu. We have many African queens in our history," she went on in her wonderfully lilting English, "though most people have heard only of those from Egypt, like Hapsheput and Cleopatra. Many more of them came from southern areas of Africa. These queens were all very strong women."

"Thank you," Laura said with spontaneous pleasure. "One of my first tasks when I get home will be to learn more about your queens. I am also eager to know more about the difficulties many young women in Africa face in gaining equal education. I am a professor of gender studies, so it concerns me."

"Excellent! How fortunate that you have come here," Makedu replied. "If your schedule permits, you must attend some of our meetings.

"As for your question: In sub-Saharan Africa, the literacy rate for girls is under thirty percent, while that for boys is double. Parents cannot afford to send girls to school as well as boys and they do not think it is a good thing to educate daughters anyway, so the girls are forced into early marriage, which means they bear a child when they are a child themselves, and so the cycle of poverty and abuse of girls and women continues...

"But I do not mean to monopolize the conversation with these problems," she apologized. "We will discuss them when the conference officially begins in Murren. Until then I shall hold my tongue!"

Her daughter, Amina, seemed not to have heard the last remark. Her large dark eyes were sad and far away. "Even education cannot help if there is civil unrest; we were there, you see, during the genocide in Rwanda..."

She stopped, compressing her lips tightly to hold back tears. Blinking, she looked down at her beautiful long-fingered hands. Her mother put a comforting arm around her shoulder. "It is difficult to keep up one's hopes after such sights," she said gently.

Then, to the others: "Rwanda was hell. I cannot understand such savagery. The men become worse than animals."

Laura shuddered, remembering the horror of those days. She had seen scenes of bloodshed and slaughter and rape and unspeakable brutality, as if formerly compliant schoolboys had suddenly been turned into monsters. The only good that had come from the genocide was that women had taken over as leaders, and now Rwanda was thriving.

No one spoke for a few moments; then Ann Lawrence's strident voice cut into the silence. "Religion is the cause of negative attitudes toward women," she said, her voice hard and unforgiving. She stared at Amina and Makedu, as if challenging them to disagree with her. Laura wondered if she had even heard their emotionally laden description of Rwanda. It wasn't going to be easy to tolerate the English delegate, much less like her.

The others looked as uncomfortable as she felt. Amina sent Ann a hostile glance. "Religion did not cause the genocide in Rwanda," she protested.

Again, Ann didn't seem to hear. "We must convince women that equality is not possible in religious societies," she declared. "Catholicism is bad, but Islam is the worst. We must get rid of it completely."

"A difficult undertaking," Violet commented dryly. "I suspect quite a few highly educated Muslim women would not agree."

"Then they are fooling themselves," Ann replied tartly.

A tall square-jawed man in a sleek grey ski suit entered the room as she spoke. "Now Ann," he told her, his tone placating, "I know how strongly you feel, but one point of view must not be permitted to dominate. One step at a time toward agreement, is that not right, ladies?" There was more than a hint of paternalism in his tone and Laura cringed.

"Good morning, Karl," Sigrid said in a bland tone that Laura suspected hid a similar reaction. "I believe you have not met Violet and Laura, have you? Or our African delegates this year?"

"This is Karl Hoffman, the representative from Germany who will chair our meeting," she said, providing him with all their names. Laura was impressed. Sigrid was worried about her English, but it certainly seemed excellent. So was her memory for names – and her poise. There was strength in Sigrid underneath that serene manner. She would make a good ally.

Karl Hoffman greeting them all charmingly. Laura sensed that charm was his strong point and when he sat down beside Ann Lawrence she was sure she was right. He bent over the English delegate solicitously, giving her his full attention and behaving alternately like a prospective lover and fond father. Ann Lawrence absorbed his attentions like a stone-dry sponge, seeming not to notice his patronizing attitude. She must have a very inattentive husband at home, or very little confidence underneath all that bluster. Laura wondered if Karl Hoffman was a womanizer or just good at handling people – or both.

Reginald lips twisted with distaste. Laura saw the small movement only because she was looking at him, curious to know what the boy thought of the rapport between Karl Hoffman and his mother. Was it her imagination or was Reginald angry? With his mother or with Karl Hoffman?

The expression left his face as suddenly as if a slate had been wiped clean. Without speaking, he rose and left the dining room. His mother looked after him in concern but Karl Hoffman quickly pulled her attention back to him with a remark Laura couldn't quite catch.

For the first time, she was aware of undercurrents in the room that went well beyond Ann Lawrence's dogmatic pronouncements. Tension and discord were inevitable in a roomful of strong-minded people with divergent views on an already incendiary subject, but she sensed a deeper, unknown cause that was entangled with the personalities and ambitions of the delegates.

Violet interrupted her thoughts. "Time for the slopes," she said, rising. The strained mood in the room broke as the others followed suit.

Makedu and Amina also rose. Both were enveloped in gorgeous robes of scarlet and indigo that swayed luxuriously as they moved. To Laura, they looked as much like queens as their namesakes, tall and statuesque and magnificent.

Makedu eyed Ann and Karl with interest as she swept out of the room. "The English delegate is an enigma, is she not?" she observed in a low voice. "Unless I am very much mistaken, she will soon find herself between his sheets with her mouth firmly shut by his. I think perhaps he likes women best in that position. She will protest all the way and be thrilled all the time, and he will enjoy the challenge." She grinned infectiously.

Laura laughed. This elegant lady didn't mince words! "Ann is indeed an enigma," she agreed. "I never cease to be amazed at how a person can hold such a strong view and behave in exactly the opposite way without even being aware of the discrepancy."

"Our British representative appears to have perfected that balancing act," Violet contributed dryly. Makedu and Amina laughed heartily and on that note they parted. Another pair of friends, Laura thought with pleasure.

Half an hour later, they were on the slopes. To Laura's relief, Violet was a competent but not expert skier, so they stuck to the easier slopes except for one memorable run when they found themselves on an expert trail by mistake. The terrain was well beyond Laura's capabilities and she spent more time on her face than on her skis. As she lay awkwardly spread-eagled across a huge mogul after one fall, Karl Hoffman, Ann Lawrence and Reginald sped past, waving cheerfully.

Laura watched with envy as they swept effortlessly away. Reginald and Karl were good skiers but to Laura's amazement, Ann Lawrence was the best of them all, transformed on skis from stocky middle-aged woman into a graceful, fearless dynamo. She plunged up and over the moguls with no hesitation, as if glorying in her skill.

Violet was surprised too. "I would never have believed Ann could ski like that," she said admiringly as she drew up beside Laura. "I don't think you have to look any further for lessons."

Laura laughed. "I couldn't stand the lectures that would come with them. Besides, I need to get to know the Murren ski instructor better."

They had two more wonderful runs, and then Laura suggested lunch. "After that breakfast, I didn't think I could eat even a cracker but now I find I could eat the whole box."

"Excellent idea," Violet agreed. She led Laura to a restaurant with three hundred and sixty degree vistas in all directions. It was noisy and crowded and had the nostalgic aroma of drying clothes and food Laura associated always with ski chalets. Sighing with pleasure, she selected a gourmet sandwich filled with exotic items that seldom made it into her refrigerator, like brie and bacon, while she gulped an energy enhancing cup of tea. Life didn't get much better than this. She must savor every moment.

Not all the people around her were equally thrilled by their wondrous setting, Laura noticed. Some looked dissatisfied, others bored.

"That's the Frenchman we saw last night at the café," she said to Violet, gesturing toward one of the discontented faces. "The one who had a young woman with him. Monsieur Guillard, I think Gustav called him."

"She's not with him now," Violet remarked. "He's with someone else, a good deal older but remarkably striking all the same. Could she be the wife?"

Laura contemplated the woman's arresting face. High cheekbones, plenty of lines as if the woman had spent her life in sun and wind and air and had no intention of disguising that fact.

"If so," she replied, "she isn't at all what I had imagined. No rejected wife there! She looks formidable."

The unknown woman proved her right. Glaring at her companion's jaded expression, she uttered an emphatic French expletive and a volley of mixed English and French. "Merde! Mais c'est magnifique ici!" she hissed. "Et tu, Henri, tu es *bored*! C'est disgraceful." Disgust was heavy in her voice.

Monsieur Guillard's only response was a dismissive gesture with his fork as he speared a piece of meat from his plate and transferred it to his mouth.

His eyes widened in surprise and his face went suddenly pale, then almost blue. He half rose to his feet, clutched at his chest with frantic fingers and slumped across the table.

CHAPTER FIVE

Laura and Violet moved at the same moment. Violet's long legs got her to the Frenchman faster. The room fell suddenly quiet as people at nearby tables noticed their abrupt gallop across the room, then amplified into a muted buzz as they passed on the news of the unfolding drama in whispers.

"Meat in his throat," Laura murmured in Violet's ear in case she hadn't seen what had happened. Violet nodded.

Wrapping her arms around the Frenchman from behind, she hauled him up and shoved hard with both fists into his chest, while Laura supported him. When nothing happened Violet repeated the maneuver.

The unknown woman's voice rang out dramatically over the subdued whispers rippling around the room. "C'est un veritable crise du coeur! Finalement, ze cold heart weel take its revenge. Un coeur froid cannot live, n'est ce pas? Is eet not so I ask you?"

Jumping up, she came to stand behind Violet and Laura and watched their ministrations with avid interest.

Violet paid no attention and tried again. A half-chewed piece of meat shot out, flew across the table and landed with a plop beside a plate at the next table. Its occupants shrank away from the offending morsel.

Monsieur Guillard sat down heavily, struggling to control convulsive heaves surging through his chest. He lost the battle, and the rest of his meal followed the chunk of meat. This time, however, the trajectory was less violent and only reached as far as his ski boots and the floor around them. Laura stepped discreetly out of the way.

Wrinkling her nose in distaste at the smell, Monsieur Guillard's companion took up a stand at the far end of the table. Her dramatic voice rang out again, but this time it was heavy with disappointment. "Ah! Quel dommage! A shame, n'est-ce-pas? Apres tout, not a crise de Coeur, only un piece de veau. Ah, it eez too bad, do you not theenk so?" The speaker shook her head morosely and looked up at Laura with sad eyes.

"I suppose that depends on your point of view," Laura replied, since the woman seemed to expect a response. Whoever she was, she clearly didn't think much of Monsieur Guillard and didn't mind sharing her opinion of him with the whole room. Laura rather admired her for it.

Some color had returned to the Frenchman's face but he still looked decidedly unwell. Laura was about to run to the counter to tell someone to call a doctor when two ski patrol medics, apparently summoned by an alert waiter, appeared beside Mr. Guillard.

"We will take him to the hospital to check him," they told the onlookers. "Does anyone know his name?"

"His name is Henri Guillard," the unknown woman told them flatly, giving the name a strong and breathy French emphasis.

She expelled a great sigh as the men carried the Frenchman away on a stretcher. "Do not try too hard," she muttered to their retreating backs. "He is not worth it." These remarks were uttered in excellent English that Laura suspected had originated in the U.S..

"I gather you know him and don't like him," she noted dryly.

"Those of us who are former wives share a dim view of Henri," her eccentric companion replied. Her entire face creased with mirth as she spoke, and Laura found the look irresistible. What a character!

"How many wives are there?" she asked curiously.

"Only two, at least as far as I know," was the answer. "I am the first but I divorced him because he was so dull, in matters of the bedroom especially. An Englishwoman was next, much younger and inexperienced, poor creature. He divorced her because she was dull in the same way, only far more so." She shuddered theatrically. "Can you imagine how deadly that must have been, night after night?"

The breathy sigh came again. "I am certain he had many mistresses as well but I do not know them. The most recent one is a medical student I believe, quite young and intelligent. I shall have to warn her. He is a bastard.

"It is not such a bad way to finance one's education – I would have done it myself had it been necessary," the woman went on, "but one must pick the man with care. He must be very rich so that no other paramour is needed to pay the bills. That way, one's own lover can be accommodated. But even more important is that the man must not be malicious and cruel, like Henri. Yes, I shall advise her. She must find another man." Her voice was serious now, and Laura thought she meant to do exactly as she said.

"Do other people share your views about Monsieur Guillard?" she asked.

"Many dislike Henri almost as much as I do, but many more are afraid of him. Henri knows how to inspire fear. That is his most compelling trait. Fear has made him a fortune which he should not have."

She smiled mischievously. "I have often dreamed of killing him myself," she confessed in a voice that was loud enough to carry across the room. "Execution style, the way the Mafia do. That would be fitting for Henri."

"Interesting," Violet murmured beside her.

"Very," Laura agreed, and decided it was time for introductions. She very much wanted to know this intriguing woman's name.

"I am Laura Morland and this is my friend Violet McLarty," she said politely.

The reply was disconcerting. "Ah, you wish to know who I am," the woman answered. "As you should," she added, nodding sagely.

"My name is Felicia Lamont. I came originally from the United States as I imagine you have guessed. That was a very long time ago. I have been an actress, a pilot, a hunter and let me think, an explorer, a journalist and a reporter I expect wraps it up, although I have also been a student of many disciplines and an advocate of many causes. And a psychic when the spirit moves me but I fear I am becoming too lazy recently.

"I was an heiress," she added nonchalantly. "That can make one lazy. I must discipline myself. It is too easy to play the eccentric as I did just now. I do not usually speak in such an atrocious mixture of tongues, but occasionally my theatrical tendencies overwhelm me. It is such fun. And I did command everyone's attention."

She compressed her lips thoughtfully. "Yes, it is time once again to take stock..." She broke off and surveyed the room as she pondered this statement. Her eyes widened with incredulity. "I do believe..."

She doubled over with laughter. "I do believe," she sputtered again when her laughter subsided, "that all three of us were here, in this room, to witness the indignity upon Henri's person. Is that not glorious? I am sorry you saved him but at least I can take my revenge by letting him know that the three of us and everyone else he knows were here to watch his humiliation. Oh, so undignified, losing one's dinner in such a public fashion. And the smell! Unbearable, my dear." Peals of laughter rang out again.

"But *who* is here? All three what?" Laura asked, bewildered.

"Why his two wives and the latest mistress. Except now that I see her again I wonder if she really is..."

"Who are they? Where are they?"

Felicia pointed to a table by a window where Ann Lawrence, Reginald and Karl Hoffman were sitting. "I am the first, and that woman, the English one who still does not understand what happened and promptly married a very dull Englishman and had a male child as consolation, was the second wife. Karl will have a go at her next, I imagine. He does that. It is his hobby."

Laura gaped. Ann Lawrence the young wife of such a man? It must have been an appallingly bad match. And was Karl Hoffman's habit of seducing women the reason for the undercurrent of tension in the breakfast room? She shook her head. That could be part of it, but she was certain there were other, deeper reasons that she knew nothing about.

"And there is the mistress, at that table by the door," Felicia told them. "Except as I say perhaps she is not after all. I shall find out."

Laura was less surprised this time when she saw the young woman who had been with Henri Guillard last night. She had a different companion now. The Braun's son Nicolas, Laura realized. As he had last night, he raised his head as soon as she looked at him. He was a very sensitive young man.

How intriguing that they were together – and unless she was very much mistaken they were together in more ways than simple proximity. She watched Nicolas gaze at his companion, his face unguarded now, and the long look he gave her spoke volumes. Yes, she was right. He was definitely in love with her, desperately in love. What would Monsieur Guillard think of that? Had he seen? Could that be the reason he had choked? A sudden intake of breath, in surprise, or jealousy or possibly rage…

Felicia's voice brought her back to the present. "I wonder," she mused aloud, "if perhaps that is why…"

She stopped abruptly. "You must excuse me please, ladies. I shall ski swiftly down to the hospital to torment Henri. This may be my only chance to see him when he is at his worst. He will hate that. I shall order him a new lunch and hope he chokes again when I tell him all of us were watching when he spewed out his dinner. It is too bad, really. We would all be better off without Henri." With a jaunty wave, she swept to the door, scarves and coat trailing but somehow looking glamorous rather than messy.

"A character," Violet pronounced. "And an interesting one who probably knows a great deal about what goes on in Zermatt. I am very glad we met her even if it was at the expense of Monsieur Guillard's dignity.

"And now, unless you require another cup of tea after our little drama, I suggest a few more runs."

Laura shook her head. "No more tea. Skiing will clear my brain better. How very astonishing that Ann Lawrence was one of the wives. Maybe that explains her difficult personality. What a trial for an innocent young woman!"

"Possibly an even worse trial for Monsieur Guillard," Violet observed tartly. "What a ghastly duo!

"Made a fortune by inspiring fear," she added, turning to Laura. "What does that bring to mind?"

"Extortion, blackmail and other nasty habits, and that it might be an excellent idea to look into his business dealings," Laura replied promptly as she snapped on her skis.

"Just what I was thinking," Violet agreed, and pushed off. Laura followed, and then forgot about everything except the exhilaration of being here, of hearing her skis crunch through crisp snow, even of landing face down in powder when the skis insisted on tripping her up.

They skied for another two hours, hardly speaking except to decide which run to take, and then went back to the hotel to change for the Braun's party.

"What's the dress like?" Laura asked. "All I've got is that dark green shift I always wear, and I found a beaded jacket in one of those marvelous English thrift shops that more or less matches and dresses it up a bit."

Belatedly, she pulled the garments out of her suitcase, which she hadn't had the energy to unpack the night before, and shook them out. Wonderful fabric, she thought, not for the first time. You could roll it into a ball and it just unwrinkled again.

"That will be perfect," Violet pronounced. "You'll see jeans and ski clothes and designer outfits and everything in between. I shall wear my African jacket, just to be contrary." She pulled out a long rust-colored cotton jacket that had been woven in an African village and was splendidly enhanced by stylized animals. Over black tights and turtleneck, it looked exotic.

When they arrived at the Brauns, Laura lingered in the doorway to survey the crowd in the big, high-ceilinged room. Violet was right. Every kind of dress was represented – grunge and chic, all mixed together. Bearded men in jeans and work boots, and young people in fleece-lined boots and bulky sweaters conversed amicably with conventional-looking businessmen in dark suits, while plump matrons in elderly cocktail dresses and pumps chatted with glamorous women in designer clothes and outrageously high heels, or jeans so tight Laura wondered how they ever got them on – or off, which was perhaps the point. Animated conversations in at least five languages bounced around the room in a deafening, though not unpleasing, cacophony of high spirits, and everywhere arms gesticulated.

Quite a few conference representatives were present. Makedu and Amina were easy to spot with their height and colorful robes; Sigrid was there, looking elegant but sensible in navy, so was Ann Lawrence who managed to look dowdy despite a fashionable pantsuit, and Karl Hoffman. His clothes were faultless; his eyes were everywhere. Even as he carried on a conversation with Ann and a woman with a remarkably bouffant hairdo, and contrived to be charming and attentive to both, his gaze roamed the room constantly as if in search of more promising contacts or perhaps more beautiful women. Only his square jaw gave him away. It seemed to have a life of its own, thrusting itself out critically or tightening derisively while the rest of Karl's face conveyed polite interest. After each innocuous interchange, it closed with a decided snap.

His lips gave him away too, she realized. That upward curve hid the disdain he really felt. Karl Hoffman didn't like women, except to bed them.

A familiar voice that carried easily over the din of conversations distracted her. "Murdered, mes cheris! Murdered, I tell you. Oh, quell dommage! Cette pauvre Madam! Pres de la gare, n'est –ce-pas? That one in Interlaken, you know. We shall all be afraid to sleep or to fair une promenade until les gendarmes discover le perpetrator. Une crime de passion, c'est vrai."

As before, some words were French, others English, and even before she spotted her Laura was certain the speaker was their eccentric acquaintance of the morning, Felicia Lamont. For this occasion she was flamboyantly dressed in a floating gold and scarlet skirt and top. A matching hat with a huge red rose clung precariously to her mane of gorgeous white-gold hair - allowed to go white naturally, Laura thought, but still shot through with the original gold.

The room became suddenly silent, one of those breathless silences that cut through a babble of talk and make all ears attentive. People stared open-mouthed; then, as abruptly as they had ceased, the animated discussions began again. This time yesterday's murder was the sole topic of conversation. Laura wasn't surprised. The morning newspapers had been full of it.

Felicia looked pleased, as if she had hoped for exactly this reaction.

Helga Braun, on the other hand, looked distressed. Perhaps she had hoped the subject wouldn't come up to spoil the mood of their party, as well as giving rise to a great deal of gratuitous speculation. The latter, she thought, when she saw Helga exchange a glance of commiseration with her husband. Giving her hand a squeeze, he shrugged his big shoulders eloquently before turning to greet an acquaintance. Helga nodded, resigned.

"Felicia certainly likes to stir things up," Violet murmured in Laura's ear. "I don't think our hosts are well-pleased by her outburst. This might be a good time to introduce ourselves."

Laura nodded. "Perhaps we can sympathize," she agreed. "And possibly get some information while we're at it."

The distress vanished from Helga's face as they approached, and she greeted them with a warm smile. She looked lovely in a long deep blue dress that matched her eyes. "You must be the friends of whom Hans spoke. I am glad you have come. But I am sorry this terrible thing has happened just as you arrived," she added with a grimace. "In this country we have few violent crimes, and it still has the power to shock."

"I imagine it does," Laura replied sympathetically. "I live near New York, where violence isn't unusual, but it still shocks most of us. Here, such events must be very frightening."

Helga sighed. "They are," she agreed. "It grieves us that even here in Switzerland, where we try to live in peace, such things should happen. Poor woman. It is so very sad."

"People are more likely to know the victim in a small country, too," Violet put in. "I believe the woman worked for one of the foundations in Switzerland, and that made me wonder if people at the conference knew her."

"Some of the representatives might," Helga agreed readily, "and perhaps some of the other people here. I shall ask. I did not know her personally," she added, "though I have met her sister, Anna. She runs a hotel in Lauterbrunnen. I must find out the address and write her a letter."

An unexpectedly helpful answer, Laura thought, and wondered if Helga had intended to give them information. Perhaps Hans had confided in the Brauns. If he had told them what she and Violet were really doing here, that meant he trusted the couple absolutely. Hans was not an idle talker.

"But let me introduce you to my husband, Ernst," Helga went on, turning to him. Another guest appeared at that moment and pulled her aside, so Violet and Laura introduced themselves. Herr Braun shook hands warmly, seeming genuinely pleased to see them. Laura liked him instinctively. His large features gave his face character, and his eyes were full of humor and a restless kind of intelligence that would suit a venture capitalist. She suspected Ernst would be willing to take chances in his business dealings and be bored if he couldn't.

"Thank you for including us," Violet told him politely.

"It is our pleasure," he answered. "Hans has a very high regard for both of you," he added, and Laura saw amusement, possibly admiration in his face. She wondered how much Hans had told him.

"Hans is one of my favorite people," she told Ernst. "He is so understated, as I think the British would say."

"He is indeed," Ernst agreed. "And I am glad he told us you were here. It is good to see new faces at our party. Here in Zermatt we are a small group and see each other often. I sometimes wonder what we still find to say to each other. All the same, as you can hear, we manage quite well."

Felicia came up to them then and greeted them effusively. "Did you know these are the heroines who saved Henri?" she asked Ernst. "With the Heimlich maneuver, I think it is called. I told them it was too bad, that we would all be better off if Henri had choked himself on that meat."

Ernst roared with laughter and gave Felicia a warm hug. "Felicia my dear, I am glad you said that since I could not," he whispered into her ear. He glanced at the door and his eyes brightened. "Especially because the subject of your remark has just come into the room. Did you time it that way?"

It was Felicia's turn to howl with laughter. Her whole body shook with it, disturbing the precarious balance of her hat. The rose fell disarmingly across one eye. "Oh that poor man; truly I have given him a hard time today," she confided in a low whisper, wiping her eyes as she unconcernedly propped the rose back in place. "I visited him in hospital and taunted him mercilessly because we all saw him – two wives and this new mistress and everyone else - looking such an unattractive shade of green, and all that vomit; my dear it was not pleasant. And the smell!"

Her face sobered abruptly. "Only I hope it is not so about the mistress."

"I too," Ernst agreed, and Laura noticed that his eyes strayed to his son, Nicolas. She also saw that the possible mistress had come in the door on Henri Guillard's arm, looking extremely lovely in red silk pant suit with a full blouson jacket that somehow contrived to emphasize her slenderness.

Ernst watched all three of them warily, as if preparing for trouble. Nicolas, however, didn't react, or if he did, he hid it well. Nor did he look at the couple or acknowledge their entry. They didn't look at him, either. His father let out a breath of relief but looked puzzled as well.

"Nicolas does not react," Felicia observed sotto voice. For a moment she too looked puzzled and then comprehension came suddenly into her eyes. "She plays a dangerous game, that one," she muttered. "Yes, I must talk to her soon. There is no time to waste."

Ernst turned sharply to look at her, a question in his eyes. As if to forestall it, Felicia turned quickly to Laura and Violet. "Now you must come with me and meet everyone," she stated firmly. "I shall take you around as my own special find. Is that all right with you, Ernst?" She favored him with a brilliant smile and a kiss on the cheek.

"Anything you do is always all right," he agreed, regarding her fondly. "But later I will make you explain yourself," he added softly.

"Felicia sees all and explains little," he informed Violet and Laura. "She is the sphinx of Switzerland."

Felicia laughed. "You are a fine man, Ernst," she pronounced, "and Helga a fine woman," she added as Helga turned to greet her affectionately.

Adjusting her hat firmly, Felicia bore Laura and Violet away. She led them first to Henri Guillard and his companion. "Bonsoir, Henri!" she said cheerily. "You are looking remarkably well after your undignified experience." Felicia sounded quintessentially British now, and Laura saw Henri's shoulders stiffen. He did look surprisingly well, though he was still pale.

"You are becoming a pest," he told Felicia coldly before turning to Violet and Laura. "I believe I should thank you for your help earlier today," he said, his voice expressionless. "It was good of you to come to my rescue." He bowed first at Violet and then at Laura. A spasm of pain passed across his face as he did so, and he straightened slowly. Violet's forceful treatment must have left bruises. Laura was reluctantly impressed. It must have taken considerable effort and willpower to get to the party – and to make such an entrance.

"Permit me to introduce my good friend, Mlle Veronique," Henri went on, giving a subtle emphasis to the *good.*

Veronica smiled at them gravely. "I am very pleased to know you." Her voice was soft, lilting, her accent impossible to place.

She was a lovely woman, Laura thought admiringly, tall and willowy and graceful, but her eyes were sad, too sad for someone so young. Dark blue eyes, she saw, so dark they were almost purple. And smoky lashes that she didn't think looked that way solely because of mascara. It was unusual coloring.

And then she saw the bruise – a livid bluish-yellow swelling on one side of Veronica's pale neck, barely visible under her jacket. How had she come by it? Surely not skiing. This looked as if it had been inflicted by a person. Henri?

Veronica adjusted the full jacket quickly, and the bruise disappeared from view. She must have worn the jacket on purpose because it hid her neck, Laura realized. Veronica's eyes flicked to Henri, and Laura was certain she saw a flash of fear. Then the near-purple eyes sought hers. There was anxiety in Veronica's gaze but mostly appeal. Please, the eyes seemed to say. Please don't remark on the bruise.

Laura nodded imperceptibly but she was suddenly afraid. Every instinct in her cried out that this young woman was in danger. As Felicia had said, there was no time to waste.

CHAPTER SIX

Laura glanced at Violet and saw the same recognition of impending danger in her eyes. An unspoken message passed between them. Before the party was over, they must find a way to talk to Veronica alone.

Henri immediately made that impossible. Clasping Veronica's arm tightly, he turned her toward the door. "We have a dinner reservation in a few moments, cheri," he reminded her. "We must leave now."

"If you will excuse us?" he said to the rest of them. His tone was polite but very firm. Wincing, Veronica tried to pull her arm away, but he didn't let go. Again, Laura thought she saw a flash of fear in the young woman's eyes. It was gone so fast that she thought she had imagined it until she saw Nicolas finally react. His fists clenched and he took a step toward Veronica, glowering. A pleading look from her stopped him. Still glowering, he turned away and almost ran out the door.

Recovering her poise, Veronica put a hand on Henri's restraining arm. "We must thank our hosts before we leave, Henri," she said. "It will only take a moment." She gestured toward Helga, who was talking to the Iranian delegate a short distance away.

Even the gracious Helga seemed to be having a hard time maintaining the conversation, Laura noticed. Dr. Nezam didn't reply to her remarks, but simply nodded impassively and waited for her to say something else. A deliberate tactic, she wondered, or was it because he didn't know English very well?

Karl Hoffman planted himself in front of Henri and Veronica before they could take a step towards Helga. "I have brought the American representative for you to meet," he announced with a well-practiced smile that lasted only a second. "This is Lindsey Steele, who is new to the conference this year."

Laura tried not to gape. The woman looked utterly out of place in this sophisticated setting. Her astonishing hairdo was held up by what smelled like a gallon of hairspray, and her face held a remarkable collage of make-up which was not skillfully applied. Her eyelids were bright blue, her lips crimson and both colors extended well beyond normal perimeters. Large jewelry and a shiny turquoise pant suit that emphasized her cleavage completed the ensemble.

Lindsey's gaze fastened on her. "Howd'ya do, M'am?" she said, sticking out her hand. "Ah'm tickled to de-ath to meetcha." The southern accent was so thick Laura could barely understand her. For non-Americans, it must be almost indecipherable. What an unlikely delegate!

Laura shook the proffered hand. Lindsey Steele's grip was unexpectedly strong. "Hello, Ms Steele," she replied, at a loss for further words.

"Oh deah, you must call me Lindsey. Just everyone does, even our fine President, did-je know that? And we can't stand on formalities in such a glorious party, now can we?"

Laura glanced at the others. They looked nonplussed, except for Violet who was having trouble controlling her twitching lips.

Laura's lips began to twitch in sympathy. Hastily, she introduced Lindsey to Veronica and Henri, last to

Violet, so she had time to recover her composure. Felicia had vanished from their side, though how she had managed it so unobtrusively in that colorful costume was a mystery.

"Oh my, such a doll!" Lindsey enthused as she shook Veronica's hand. "But you must excuse me, folks, will you'all? Where ah come from that's what we call a lovely young woman, but ah must break the habit here, mustn't I?" She beamed at Veronica, who gave her a startled look and a tepid smile. Karl Hoffman rolled his eyes and melted into the crowd, Ann at his heels.

"That is most kind of you," Veronica replied unconvincingly.

"An' now ah've offended her," Lindsey crowed, seeming pleased at this outcome. "But nevah mind. Now I want you to tell me all about yourselves, will you please? Ah'm the stranger here, and ah'd truly love to know."

She stared straight at Veronica, then at each of the others in turn, and Laura had the distinct impression that she meant to get an answer.

Surprisingly, Veronica took her up first. "I am a medical student," she said without inflection. "At the University of Zurich."

"All you girls are so brave these days, ah think it's grand! But we ladies mustn't forget why the good Lord put us here, must we, dahlin? Hearth and home and all that, remember? And those lovely babies befoh' it's too late?" Lindsey wagged a cautionary forefinger in Veronica's direction.

Laura almost choked. How appalling! Talk like that was entirely out of place at an international conference on empowering girls and women.

Veronica, to her credit, forbore to answer. An uncomfortable silence fell.

"I am a professor of gender studies in the U.S.," Laura said, partly to break the impasse and partly to see how Lindsey would react to her statement. "I teach and do research on male and female roles, both in the past and today."

Lindsey either didn't hear or wasn't interested. "Well now, isn't that grand?" she said blandly, and turned with a gracious smile to Henri.

"I am a businessman," he said shortly, irritation clear on his features. "And now if you will excuse us, we have a dinner engagement." Grasping Veronica's arm again, he steered her forcefully toward the door. Head down, Veronica allowed him to pull her away.

Lindsey watched them go, frowning. "Not a very conversational sort, is he?" Laura wondered if she ever said a sentence that didn't end with a question. No she didn't, she decided, when Lindsey continued.

"Now tell me all about yourself, will you Violet? Ah hope you don't mind my callin' you Violet, but it's such a pretty name, isn't it?"

"I'm just an ordinary tourist," Violet answered briefly. Lindsey's eyes were still focused on the door through which Veronica and Henri had disappeared, and Laura wasn't sure she had heard that either.

"Do you suppose ah really offended that lovely girl?" Lindsey asked anxiously. "Or maybe that father of hers? Men are so protective of daughters, aren't they?" Laura almost choked again.

Violet managed to turn a snort of laughter into a cough. "Yes," she replied, without specifying the question she agreed with. "I think we should take

Lindsey around and introduce her to some of the other delegates, Laura, don't you?" she added.

"Oh lord, I'm doing it too," she added in horror under her breath.

Laura repressed a smile. "An excellent idea," she replied, struggling to imagine what Makedu might find to say about Lindsey.

"That would be so kind of you, wouldn't it?" Lindsey smiled and followed them eagerly. Half way across the room she stopped like a balky horse. "Now if that isn't an old friend, right over there?" she trilled excitedly. "Ah simply must go say hello to her. It's been such ages. She was the aunt of a friend of mine, an Auntie Mame type. Remember Auntie Mame, Laura?"

Laura did indeed. Auntie Mame was the legendary American aunt who had taken her wide-eyed young nephew all across Europe, disregarding conventions, schedules, schooling and all other irritating strictures that hounded schoolboys. The nephew had adored her and so had every other child excited by travel and bored by school and routine. Someone had made a movie about her.

"I certainly do," she answered, following Lindsey's gaze. Her eyes came to rest on Felicia. "You mean Felicia?" she asked, startled.

"Why of course I do, dahling, haven't I known her almost my whole life long?" Lindsey looked triumphant.

"See you later, okay?" she added, and disappeared in determined pursuit of Felicia, who seemed to be edging toward the door. Clearly, she was not as eager as Lindsey for a reunion.

The crowd closed in and Laura lost sight of them. It was a relief to be rid of Lindsey but she wished she could have watched how Felicia managed the encounter. She suspected Lindsey wasn't easily defrayed from her purpose. Felicia wasn't either. Definitely an explosive combination.

"I wonder who appointed her," Violet remarked with a frown. "She seems so wildly inappropriate for a conference of this type."

"No doubt a political appointment considering our present administration," Laura answered. "Somebody important owes a favor and so we get Lindsey, courtesy of a big donor. Probably from the Texas crowd."

"I suppose," Violet replied, but she didn't sound convinced.

"I fear it happens all the time in American politics," Laura explained. "The results are often predictably dreadful. They certainly could be this time," she added. "Even without kidnapping threats, this conference isn't likely to be peaceful. We've already got one tactless if not bigoted representative and a dedicated womanizer; now we have a southern charmer who seems to have an anti-feminist agenda and for all I know an anti-birth control one as well."

"With steel underneath," Violet murmured. "Isn't that what they say about American southern belles? I wonder if she's as dense as she pretends to be. I really do sense steel underneath.

"And that is not meant to be a pun," she added hastily.

Laura grinned. "Lindsey Steele," she mused. "I wonder, too. She has a remarkably steely grip, did you notice? No pun intended there, either. Is it possible that all that southern belle charm is purposeful obfuscation?

"Excuse the questions," she added.

"Forgiven," Violet answered. "It seems unlikely, but I would still like to know why the American representative is new this year and how Lindsey Steele came by the job. It's worth checking anyway."

Laura considered the idea. Lindsey's ultra southern façade would make a superb cover. But why would the new American delegate need one? And why an American delegate in the first place?

"How were the delegates chosen for this particular conference?" she asked, suddenly aware that she had no idea. "Most of them aren't from the countries receiving the funds, as far as I can tell."

"Quite a few of them may be self-selected, thanks to a free ski vacation in Switzerland," Violet joked.

Laura laughed. "I can understand that!"

"More seriously," Violet continued, "many are here because they want to keep up with what's happening in the field of girls' education or because they will be involved in administering the funds and evaluating the outcome of this grant. Others were probably sent by countries with an interest in anything that happens near their borders or in their sphere of influence. Iran, for instance, and India. I don't know how the U.S. fits in, which makes Lindsey's appearance even more of a mystery."

"I see what you mean," Laura answered. "I'll send out some emails. Maybe someone I know will have information on her." She lowered her voice. "I want to know more about Veronica, too. I had hoped we could get her alone and talk to her, but Henri seemed determined to spirit her away. Did you see that bruise?"

"Yes, I saw it," Violet answered. "I also had the distinct impression that Lindsey saw it, and that was why she was so interested in Veronica."

Laura was startled. "That's strange. Lindsey acted so oblivious."

"We need to know more about both of them," Violet decreed. "Felicia might have information about Lindsey, and the Brauns might be able to tell us more about Veronica. Let's see if we can find them."

"And while we're looking, we might grab some of the delectable food," Laura suggested, eyeing a table full of hot and cold canapés.

"Excellent idea," Violet agreed. "Hans says the Brauns are known for putting on a good spread. As far as I'm concerned, that can be dinner."

"Me, too," Laura agreed, tucking in happily to shrimp and cheeses and hot sausages and all sorts of other delicacies in heated casseroles. Some were hard to transfer from plate to mouth without dribbling down her beaded jacket, which must look all right since quite a few people had admired it, but she managed her fair share and emerged from the feast without a stain.

Grabbing a few last bites, they began their search of the room, but to no avail. Felicia had disappeared, probably in an effort to elude Lindsey, who was holding forth to a baffled trio of long-legged young women in tight jeans and a bored young man who didn't bother to hide his yawns. The Brauns were easy to find, but too involved with guests to be questioned discreetly. They would have to try later, or call.

Two other delegates arrived, and once again they were caught up in introductions. A lithe balding man with a delightfully humorous face turned out to be the Pakistani delegate, and a gangly older woman with pure black hair and a bossy air named Dashka was the Indian one. She was also the accountant for various aid organizations and possessed an encyclopedic knowledge of programs that dealt with children and education. She lived part time in London, and seemed to know everyone well.

Discovering that Laura and Violet were new to the group, she took it upon herself to bring them up to date. She spoke crisply and very fast in a lilting accent so that the words seemed to blend into each other.

"We work with UNICEF, of course," Dashka began, "but our branch of the organization has a special mission to focus on girls and the opportunities they are given. That is why we are eager to take up this challenge and make it work. It could mean so much to these girls in countries where they are still excluded from schooling and careers. Still, it is uphill work and will remain so…"

Her voice sped on. Laura was interested and tried to be responsive, but her whole body had begun to droop with fatigue.

When a break came in the Indian delegate's efforts to educate them, Violet inserted an admiring comment. "Your knowledge is impressive, Dashka," she said. "I'm eager to hear more but now I fear that Laura and I must return to the hotel. We promised to meet some friends there for coffee."

She consulted her watch. "A bit late already I fear." The Indian delegate nodded politely and turned to educate someone else.

Laura grinned. "Coffee's new to me but it's a great idea. Maybe we should invite Felicia and Lindsey. That ought to produce some fireworks."

Violet's eyes danced. "Karl Hoffman might make an excellent moderator," she murmured mischievously.

Laura found a suitable repartee. "Just to enliven the party, we might include Ann Lawrence. Can you imagine the fireworks then?"

Violet laughed. "Let's see who we can find."

Laura's mind snapped back to more serious matters when she spotted the ski instructor standing at the door. How unexpected! What was he doing here? She had assumed he was in Murren by now.

She nudged Violet. "My ski instructor just came in the door."

They watched the ski instructor cross the room to greet Nicolas. They must be friends. Or were they? They looked as if they would just as easily punch each other as converse politely. Nicolas especially looked wary, even hostile. Laura saw Ernst move quickly to join them.

She and Violet moved unobtrusively closer, hoping to overhear some of the conversation.

"Damn you, Max," Nicolas hissed. "You treated her like…"

The rest of the words were cut off by Ernst. "Not the time or the place," he interrupted firmly.

The ski instructor paid no attention. "You were once my best friend," he said bitterly. He stared intently at Nicolas for a long moment; then he turned and strode out the door. Nicolas watched him go, his face suffused with anger.

"I wonder what that was about," Violet said curiously. "The ski instructor – Max - definitely seems to be a player in this drama, whatever it is. Once we get to Murren, we'll be able to find out more about him."

"Why not follow him?" Laura suggested.

Violet nodded. They thanked the Brauns as quickly as they decently could and hurried out the door. They were lucky. The ski instructor emerged from a bar, moving fast, as if he had a particular destination in mind.

Someone else was interested in Max. A woman, Laura thought, but it was hard to be sure since the person was dressed in a bulky jacket and ski pants, and a wooly cap and scarf hid most of the face. She or he stood immobile in a doorway, but the eyes followed the ski instructor. Laura and Violet veered that way, but as soon as they came close the watcher turned and went inside. The graceful movement reminded Laura of someone she had seen recently.

"Was that Felicia?" she whispered to Violet.

"Not sure," Violet hissed back. "But it could have been."

The ski instructor stopped and looked back, as if to make sure no one was nearby. Chatting amiably and keeping their heads turned away from him, Laura and Violet went past him and turned down a side street.

Max surveyed the street again for a few moments before he darted up a flight of stairs into a small but elegant hotel.

A few minutes later, they saw his figure appear against a lit window that faced the street. Henri Guillard stood beside him, to Laura's surprise. Max was talking and gesticulating angrily. Henri listened attentively but he made no comment. Then, in a gesture that seemed entirely out of character, he put an arm around the younger man's shoulders. His mouth moved, and it was obvious that whatever he was saying was conciliatory.

Laura frowned. That, she hadn't expected. Nor had she expected the next development. Veronica, now dressed in pants and a loose turtleneck sweater, came into the room. She nodded stiffly to Max but did not come closer to greet him. The tension in her body was palpable. He hesitated, then he approached her tentatively, arms outspread in a gesture of appeasement.

Veronica froze. Turning abruptly, she left the room. Max's arms dropped and Laura was certain he was swearing. His good looks obviously weren't enough to win over Veronica.

"Another baffling exchange," Violet murmured. "They all know each other, though, and that's interesting in itself."

"I guess so," Laura agreed dubiously, "though that might not mean much. Everybody here already seems to know everybody else. Still, those two – Max and Veronica, seem to know each other well enough to be at odds with each other. That doesn't happen between mere acquaintances. It looked almost as if they once had a close relationship but now they don't."

"It did indeed," Violet agreed. "And I think…"

She stopped abruptly and held up a hand for silence. Laura heard the sound too – footsteps. A moment later two men came into view. Laura was sure she had seen them at the Braun's party, well-dressed, prosperous-looking men. To distract herself from thinking about how cold she was, she memorized their physical characteristics as they came closer. The first man had a fleshy face with a bulbous nose, a slight paunch. His ears were unusually large. The best word that came to mind for the second man was leonine. He was slim with a narrow face, close-set eyes and black hair. Laura thought he could be the man who had loaded boxes onto the train and taken a shot at Thomas, but she hadn't seen him well enough then to be sure.

The men went quickly up the stairs of the hotel and a few moments later they appeared at the lit window, hands outstretched to greet Henri. It was a business-like gesture, not a cocktail party greeting, though how she knew that Laura wasn't sure. Perhaps the lack of wide-toothed smiles.

Henri's form reappeared in the window, facing them. He surveyed the street; then thick curtains swung across the window and the room disappeared. Laura and Violet waited, wriggling toes and fingers to warm them, in case someone else turned up for this meeting or whatever it was.

The front door opened abruptly and Veronica came out. She looked hurried and harassed, but purposeful. She glanced quickly up and down the street as if making sure no one was watching her. Apparently satisfied, or perhaps too impatient to wait any longer, she closed the door behind her with a decisive pull and set off down the street.

"Should we try to talk to her?" Laura mouthed.

"I'd like to see where she goes first," Violet said. "Let's watch for now." They followed, keeping in the shadows. They needn't have bothered. Veronica didn't look around at all but went straight to the doorway through which the watcher they had seen earlier had disappeared. She knocked once, the door opened a crack and she went through it.

Violet and Laura crept closer and waited for Veronica to reappear. She wasn't dressed for this, Laura lamented as her fingers and toes grew numb.

Violet called a halt to the vigil a few minutes later. "Maybe we should have grabbed her while we could," she said. "It's too late for coffee, so let's get to bed. We leave for Murren after lunch tomorrow, and I'm hoping we can get up early enough to have a few runs first. Okay by you?"

Laura nodded, repressing a yawn. "A few runs sound great if my knees still bend and my muscles don't seize."

They had most reached the end of the street when they heard footsteps behind them. "One of the men we saw with Henri Guillard," Laura whispered after a quick look. "The one with the fleshy face and big ears."

"Let's see where he goes." To their astonishment, he too knocked once on the doorway through which Veronica had disappeared and gained entry. Soon after, a thin man in a dark grey suit repeated the process. Laura assumed he was the second man they had seen with Henri, the dark one, until his hair gleamed blond as he passed under a streetlight. A stranger, then.

More footsteps sounded. "Max!" Violet hissed. The ski instructor knocked on the door in the same way as the others and disappeared inside.

"What are they all doing in there together?" Laura said, mystified. "And why one of Henri Guillard's business associates?"

"Certainly a strange combination," Violet agreed. "Veronica and Max weren't even talking the last time we saw them."

"Or Nicolas and Max," Laura remarked, and stifled a gasp of surprise as Nicolas plunged through the door at just that moment, as if summoned by her voice. His beautiful face was so twisted with fury he looked as if he might explode. His hands were shaking so badly that he could not zip his jacket. It flapped in the wind as he charged down the street.

They waited some more, too intrigued now to leave. A few minutes later the door opened again and Veronica came out. Max was behind her. He looked upset and frustrated. "You must!" he hissed, grabbing her by the shoulders. "It is the only way. They will kill you if you don't!"

Veronica's face crumpled. "Oh Max," she said. "Max, what are you really up to? Is it for me or is it for him?"

"It is for you," he said. "For you." Placing his arm gently around her shoulder, he urged her down the street.

"Look!" Laura whispered urgently, as a shadow detached itself from the building Max and Veronica had left. It materialized into the other man they had seen with Henri, the smaller, leonine one. Laura watched him creep stealthily after the two young people and shivered. He was stalking them, she thought, stalking them like an animal already salivating for its prey.

CHAPTER SEVEN

Laura's brain was still puzzling over the interchange between Veronica and Max when she woke up the next morning. The strange combination of people who had gathered behind that mysterious door was an even bigger conundrum.

Violet interrupted her thoughts. "Time for the slopes!" she decreed. Obediently, Laura switched her mind to the morning's skiing.

It was snowing lightly as they took their first run, miniscule flakes that wiped like feathers across Laura's cheeks. In this weather, she exulted, the mountains would be a joy. Others seemed to feel the same way, and many of the party-goers were also on the slopes. Karl Hoffman and Ann swept by them, skiing fast and purposefully. To Laura's surprise, she also spotted Henri Guillard ahead of them on the lift when they went up again. However much she might dislike Henri, she had to admire his stamina.

She and Violet had two magnificent runs, but by the third it was snowing hard. Skiing in lightly falling snow was a delight, but skiing in heavy snow was downright scary. The light was so flat that Laura could hardly tell what was up and what down, and the goggles that were supposed to help just got foggy. Laura tried to keep Violet's red jacket in sight to guide her, but every time Violet swept up and over a mogul it disappeared.

At the top of the next rise, Laura stopped to peer into the ever-flattening light, trying to relocate Violet. She finally spotted her waiting patiently at the edge of some trees on the other side of the trail. Wiping off her goggles - and freezing her hands in the process, Laura pushed her skis into the thick snow and began to traverse the slope.

She looked up in alarm when she heard a muffled boom from the woods, lost her balance and fell. Not an avalanche, she noted with relief. No snow was cascading toward her. Probably a tree dropping a heavy load of snow. Hauling herself up again, Laura continued her traverse.

"Laura, look out!" The horrified yell came from Violet. Laura whirled and saw a man above her, hurtling down the steep slope on his back like a rocket. He was heading straight for her.

Laura pushed forward with all her strength. She was just in time. The man slammed into her, but instead of hitting her full on, he only hit the back of her skis. The blow knocked her over anyway and sent her rolling down the slope. Digging in her ski poles, she managed to stop after a few feet, and when she wriggled limbs and arms and torso, everything seemed to work. Swearing under her breath, she got her skis under her again and stood. What was the matter with the man! Surely he could have done something to avoid her.

He wasn't moving at all now. That didn't look good. A heart attack? Laura scrambled up the rise and went over to him.

"Are you all right?" Even to her, the question sounded ridiculous. It was obvious that the man was not. He lay at an awkward angle, one side of his face pressed against the snow, arms akimbo, legs spread-eagled. He was intensely, frighteningly still. Surely, he couldn't be dead?

Alarmed, Laura sank down to examine him more closely. His hat had been pushed over his half-buried face, and she pulled it gently away.

Shock poured into her. The man was Henri Guillard, and he was indeed dead. The hole in the middle of his forehead made that abundantly clear.

****

Laura stared down at Henri, too appalled to move. The sound of Violet's skis crunching against snow as she crossed the slope aroused her.

"I think he's dead," Laura said helplessly when Violet joined her.

Violet didn't answer. Taking off her skis, she knelt beside Henri. She picked up an arm, felt for the pulse, dropped it again and pressed her fingers against his neck. "Nothing," she reported. "We need to get help. Blow that whistle."

Clumsily, Laura pulled out the whistle Violet had insisted she carry at all times during this trip in case she needed help. At first she couldn't blow it; her lips were too numb and her fingers too shaky but after a moment she managed to produce a piercing sound that careened across the hills. She blew into it again, and then once more, the trio Violet had recommended.

The snow was coming down thick and fast now. Violet brushed the flakes lightly away from Henri Guillard's face and continued her examination, her fingers quick and skillful as she looked for signs of other wounds or injuries. She was in detective mode now, not callous but emotionless because that was needed. Laura was glad she didn't have to do the examining. In death, Henri looked defenseless, no longer able to keep people from intruding on his space as she imagined he had very effectively in life. He looked older, too, as if his face already had collapsed. Henri would not have liked being seen this way, she thought with pity.

A skier appeared on the other side of the trail. He or she – it was hard to tell through the curtain of thick snow - peered in their direction and then set off again, gliding effortlessly over a steep mogul before disappearing. Another skier followed, taller this time. Probably a man, Laura thought. He too was a superb skier. Both sets of ski tracks were quickly obliterated.

Another skier came down the slope and stopped near them. "Do you need help?" he called out, first in German, then in English. "I heard the whistle."

"We need the ski patrol," Violet told him. "As quickly as you can."

The man nodded, pulled out a cell phone and gave crisp instructions, naming the slope and their approximate distance from the top. Laura was impressed. Their unknown Samaritan was both organized and efficient.

His face twisted with shock when he came closer and saw Henri on the ground. Not unknown, Laura realized. She had seen him at the Braun's party.

"But that is Henri Guillard!" he exclaimed. "What has happened to him? Has he died? Surely not… But his look is not good…"

"We will have to wait for the ski patrol to tell us that," Violet replied steadily, and Laura noticed that she had positioned the hat so that it once again hid that dreadful hole.

The man said nothing more, but Laura saw him turn away and repeat his call, more urgently this time. He glided off a short distance and stood at the edge of the trail, waiting to make sure the ski patrol would arrive.

Three more skiers appeared, hardly more than blurry outlines in the flat light. One of them skied down, and Laura saw that he was Ernst.

His eyes met Violet's and Laura's when he saw Henri. Without speaking, he knelt beside the body and performed his own quick examination.

"The patrol is behind me," he told them when he had finished. "I saw them with the sled at the top and wondered what had happened, so I came ahead. I fear, though, it is too late?"

Violet nodded almost imperceptibly. Ernst sighed, and stood up. "Helga is behind me. We will stay just above you and keep everyone out of the way unless there is something I can do here to help."

"Keeping people away would be a great help," Violet told him. "They tend to crowd around and I believe privacy is essential in this case." Ernest looked at her curiously but asked no more questions. Instead, he murmured a few words in German. Laura had the distinct impression that he had said a prayer. Even Henri Guillard deserved a prayer.

The ski patrol arrived and took over. A fast and efficient examination before they placed him gently on the sled told them he was dead, and why. Curious skiers kept gathering above them but Ernst's authoritative voice soon sent them on their way.

"Who found him?" one of the ski patrolmen asked.

"I did," Laura answered. "He fell and almost slid into me."

"Then I came to join her," Violet interjected. "I have some training in first aid and hoped I could help."

The patrolman nodded. "We wish to talk more to both of you," he stated in excellent if stiff English. "Please follow us down to the aid station."

They strapped Henri in tightly and started straight down the slope in a deep snowplow. Probably the best way, Laura realized, considering the burden they had to balance behind them. Violet did the same, apparently effortlessly. Laura arranged her skis in the spread-eagled plow position and pushed off, but her thighs were soon screaming for relief. After that she did her best to make slow turns but her legs were shaky, her toes and fingers numb, and it seemed to her she spent more time prone than upright. By the time she got to the bottom, she could hardly stand.

Violet propped her up and they went thankfully into the warmth of the first aid station, where the patrol people were already dialing hospital and police numbers. One patrolman took pity on them and brought mugs of steaming hot chocolate. After that, Laura felt better able to answer the questions fired at her by both ski patrol and police for the better part of an hour.

Finally, after what seemed like fifty explanations and a signed statement detailing who they were, who had been nearby at the time, how they knew Henri and what they had seen and heard – especially the booming sound that Laura now realized had been a shot - they were permitted to leave, with strict instructions not to go anywhere except to Murren as planned.

Violet led them into a small bistro and ordered tea. "You look dead on your feet. Whoops! Sorry. Just an expression."

Laura grinned weakly. "I do feel a bit shaky. It's not much fun having a dead man ski right into you, especially one you know. Being grilled like that isn't either."

"No, but I fear there will be more of it. The questions, that is."

"No doubt they wonder why we were so conveniently on the scene both times disaster struck Henri," Laura said with a sigh. "It isn't as if I like disasters or dead bodies," she added. "It's just that I seem to come across them with depressing regularity."

Violet laughed. "I'm glad your sense of humor is intact," she commented. "Now, how about a bowl of thick soup to warm you up the rest of the way? I had some here the first day and it's excellent."

"Wonderful. I wasn't sure I could eat anything after that, but soup sounds just right. Meantime, something's been puzzling me. How did the killer get a bullet right into the middle of Henri's head? I'm assuming he was shot by an unknown killer hiding in the trees while he was skiing across the slope, fell immediately and slid down into me. But maybe…" She let the sentence dangle, trying to picture alternate scenarios.

Violet considered. "You're right. It's hard to get a bullet smack into the middle of a man's forehead when he's in motion, especially if you're hiding in the trees at the side of the trail. The bullet would go in at an angle unless the victim was coming straight across the slope at the shooter."

"Or unless the shooter was directly below him," Laura put in. "But the shot came from the trees, so that can't be. Here's another problem: if Henri was skiing across the slope, why did his body change position and slide down the hill instead of continuing in the direction of his velocity? Could someone have given him a push in my direction once he was down?"

"I doubt it, but it's still an excellent question," Violet replied. "I have others. First, why wasn't there a hole in Henri's hat? It's the kind of hat that's usually worn low over the brow, so why didn't the bullet go through it? And why didn't Henri have goggles or any kind of glasses on a day like this? And how would the shooter know he was coming that way?"

"Maybe he had pushed the hat up, and the goggles fell off when he slid," Laura suggested. "But I can't figure out the second part. The person who shot him couldn't just camp out in those woods, hoping Henri would come by some time soon. The killer must have known Henri was about to ski down that trail and had time to get himself or herself into position."

"Or the killer might have been skiing with him and gone ahead," Violet noted. "Which makes me wonder about the man who phoned for help. He was on the slope where Henri was shot. Probably just coincidence, but he was in the right place at the right time."

"So were the two people I saw while you were examining Henri," Laura said. "They skied across the slope a few minutes later. I think the first was a woman, the second a man, but I couldn't see them very well. They were both excellent skiers, for what that's worth.

"I imagine the police will find out who they were," Violet said. "However, I'm not sure any of our scenarios is right. Henri's killing has a professional look to me. That hole in the middle of the forehead smacks of an execution, done by an expert, though we still have to figure out how the killer managed it. We also need to know what type of gun was used and how much expertise was needed to fire it accurately. I imagine the police are already out there looking for it, just in case it was left behind, which is unlikely."

"St. Bernard dogs could sniff around," Laura suggested.

Violet nodded. "They'll be up there soon I'm sure. In the meantime, we're in a good position to find out who held a grudge against Henri, was afraid of him or being black-mailed by him, or had just got in his way somehow."

"With Henri, that could be a long list," Laura remarked wryly. "I'll get busy right away overhearing conversations."

Violet regarded her apprehensively. "Don't forget there have been two murders already," she cautioned. "Be careful!"

Laura grinned. "I always am," she answered blithely.

Violet looked skeptical but she didn't argue. "We also need to keep our primary agenda in mind, which is to prevent the delegates' children from being abducted," she reminded Laura. "Four more have arrived, and I'm counting on you to help keep an eye on them once the conference starts."

Laura groaned. "I'll do my best, but I hope they're not all as superior as Reginald or as hyper as the twins."

"I'm sure you will handle them admirably," Violet said with a certainty Laura didn't share. "Right now, however, we have to get ready to leave for Murren. The trip is fantastic and I urge you to keep your mind on the scenery and not even think about Henri. If anything can distract you from a murder, this will. You may never see anything like it ever again."

She was right. By the time they reached Murren, the traumatic events of the morning were fading from Laura's mind. In Switzerland, she decided, simply riding trains was an enthralling adventure – even more impressive than all those postcards she'd seen over the years. A series of them, all perfectly timed, carried them past row after row of stunning, white-crowned peaks with charming villages nestled below them, over gaping chasms that yawned under the train and over bridges that looked built into the sky. Finally, they came to a stop in a small town that was literally backed up against a long expanse of perpendicular cliff. The wall of stone rose so high that Laura couldn't see the top even when she craned her neck up as far as it would go.

"That's where we're going," Violet explained laconically, pointing to the top. "Murren is on top of the cliff. It's quite dramatic up there."

Laura gaped. Getting up there looked impossible – there was no visible road, nothing but the broad rock face that went straight up and a huge frozen waterfall. "But how? Surely, we don't go up on ropes with our suitcases?"

"No problem for the Swiss," Violet replied. "They can find a way to get up anything, and they have. It's quite a miracle of engineering. We go up the cliff in a funicular and then we transfer to an electric railway."

Porters swarmed around them, busily loading their luggage onto an open cart at the back of a series of carts that looked like the cog-railways Laura had seen in amusement parks. She was glad the snow had stopped. Otherwise, all her clothes would get wet in that open cart. Expensive suitcases might be waterproof, but she doubted her Walmart rollers were.

She and Violet snagged a seat in the last row of one of the small wooden cars, which gave them a fantastic view of the cliff, the scenery below and all around them. The train ascended at a near-vertical angle, clanking and jerking noisily on its metal cogs. Laura was entranced despite feeling dizzy every time she looked at the drop below. The train really was going straight up! She held on tightly lest gravity alone send her tumbling back down again.

The Pakistani delegate, his wife and two children were in the rows ahead of them. The little girl, who looked about six, squealed in delight in a mix of English and her native language as the car rose higher. Her brother, about ten, was more interested in the workings of the train. He leaned over, trying to see what was beneath the car, and then up at the cables overhead.

"How do they make it work?" he asked his father. Laura was surprised to hear him ask in English – and relieved. Keeping an eye on children who spoke a variety of languages she didn't know would be a challenge. So far, all the ones she'd encountered spoke English.

She understood when his mother introduced the family. "This is my husband, Hassan Masood, and I am Eileen Masood," she said with a smile. "Our daughter is Parveen, our son Jafar." Both father and children politely shook hands. "I am American by birth, but I have lived in Pakistan most of my adult life," Eileen continued. "Still, I have always spoken English to the children so they will be able to talk to their grandparents and other relatives."

Violet and Laura introduced themselves; then they all lapsed into silence as the views became wilder, more mesmerizing. It was enough just to watch.

Kjersti and Kristin, who were in the car ahead of them, were much less restrained. Their exclamations of undisguised enthusiasm carried even over the noisy clanking of the train. True to form, Reginald tried to be blasé, especially since a third girl was with them. She was a few years older than the twins and impressively gorgeous. Reginald seemed to feel the full effects every time her glossy dark hair brushed his cheek as the bumpy train sent her tumbling into him. He even grasped her arm protectively when she gasped in alarm at the train's angle. Kjersti and Kristin alternated between looking scornful, giggling and turning so boisterous that Laura feared they would fall out of the car.

"Trouble there," Laura murmured to Violet. "Who is she?"

"And maybe more trouble coming," Violet answered. "That's Zaina, the Indian delegate's daughter, though how Dashka managed to produce such a smashing girl defies comprehension. The Iranian delegate has a son about the same age. So far, Reginald looks stunned and can't stop ogling Zaina, and the Iranian boy exudes sex appeal." She gestured to the car behind them.

Laura half turned and saw a boy who looked as she imagined Lawrence of Arabia might have looked – thick brown hair and flashing green eyes, with broad shoulders and long legs. He was very different from his self-effacing, hook-nosed father. This boy had an air of confidence and maturity about him, as well as being classically handsome. He probably also had a lot of experience with young women. For the first time, she felt sorry for Reginald.

She rolled her eyes. "Definitely problematic. I'd hoped two boys the same age would keep each other harmlessly busy competing on skis. I fear instead we'll have a pair who would just as soon choke each other."

"At least they'll be competing under supervision," Violet assured her. "While their parents attend meetings, we've arranged ski lessons for them with instructors who have been told to watch them carefully. Most afternoons, we have arranged some sort of excursion for everyone. It's the night I worry about most. That's when kids prowl."

Laura was reminded of Violet's prophecy that night, when scratching noises on the door of their balcony woke her. Blearily, she wondered if Kristin and Kjersti would be dumb enough to try climbing from one balcony to the next, as she and her brother had done during a particularly dull family vacation. There, however, the balconies had been low and there was soft turf beneath them. Here, the stunt was extremely dangerous since the balconies literally hung over the precipitous cliff. One misstep and the explorer could land at the bottom in the town below, even slide helplessly down that incredible frozen waterfall. Surely the twins wouldn't be that reckless!

Grumpily, Laura got out of bed and went to the balcony door to look. Her eyes widened, and she gasped. Pressed against the glass, staring at her in wild-eyed panic was Catherine.

CHAPTER EIGHT

"Catherine!" Laura exclaimed in horror. "Catherine, what's wrong!" Even as she asked the question, she knew. Thomas – it had to be Thomas. He must be in some kind of trouble, or worse...

Fumbling for the door handle, she opened it wide and pulled Catherine into her arms.

Violet was beside her in seconds. She didn't ask questions, just helped Laura support Catherine over to the bed. She was shaking so hard she could barely stand.

Violet checked her quickly. "Just exhaustion, I think, and cold. No injuries that I can see."

"Hot chocolate," Laura said, pointing to the small electric kettle in one corner of the room. "Works on Catherine the way tea does on me," she added, trying for humor to defray terrifying thoughts about what had gone wrong. Was Thomas badly injured, even dead? Why hadn't she said she would marry him when she could? He had asked her often enough! How independent did she need to be? Surely it didn't matter that she was a year or two older...

Violet filled the kettle and switched it on, tearing open one of the packets of chocolate as she moved. By the time Laura had wrapped Catherine in one of the down duvets and settled her on the chair, the hot chocolate was ready. Laura helped her take a sip.

"First, tell me if you're all right, aside from being cold and probably underfed and exhausted as well."

"I'm okay," Catherine muttered through clacking teeth. "It's my Dad! You've got to help me find him... Oh, Laura, this afternoon he just vanished, and I don't know where he is... he was right beside me and then he wasn't... You've got to help me, please!"

"Of course I'll help you," Laura soothed, grasping at the comforting fact that Thomas had at least been alive when Catherine had last seen him. "Just get yourself warm so you can talk and tell us what happened. And keep sipping that hot chocolate. Remember how it revived you in that pub in England? You were practically starving!"

Catherine tried to smile and took a big sip, then another.

Laura turned to Violet. "This is Catherine, daughter of Thomas the art detective, about whom you've heard quite a bit even if you haven't met him. You certainly ought to have met," she added. "You'd get along marvelously."

"So I gathered," Violet replied. "Your other detective friend." She grinned. "Not that we're necessary. You seem to find crimes and criminals all on your own. Or maybe they find you."

Catherine giggled, and then hiccupped. A great improvement, Laura thought, and sent Violet a grateful glance.

"And Catherine, this is Violet, who as you may know, is also a detective, though of a different sort than your father. She specializes in children."

Catherine looked intrigued. "I wouldn't mind doing that," she said, hiccupping again. "Art's not all that interesting, but I really like kids and I don't like to see them get hurt."

"Catherine's a whiz with them," Laura confirmed. "You should have seen her handling a six year old girl improbably named Angelina who could swear in French as well as in English – and face down belligerent cows."

"She's a whiz at climbing up balconies too," Violet observed.

"And vines," Laura commented. "She scrambled up and down one the last time we were together, when we set out to rescue Thomas from the nasty fate the villains had planned for him."

She frowned. "Even so, climbing up to a balcony that hangs over a cliff wasn't such a great idea, even for you, Catherine."

"I only did what you did, Laura, the time you had to climb down that slick stone wall in the Roman Baths," Catherine said innocently. "Remember? You told me about it on the phone. So I just knotted my sweater and my jacket together, threw them over the lowest rung and climbed up on them. That's one reason I'm so cold. They're still out there.

"Besides, they lock all the doors at night," she added, taking another sip. "This hot chocolate is great. Warms down to the toes."

"A worthy addition to our group," Violet murmured, "once we find Thomas, of course. Do you know what sort of case he is on?"

"I don't know much about it," Catherine answered. "He doesn't want me to know, in case the criminals try to get information out of me. But he did say that his job might be connected to what you and Laura are doing here and that we were going to come so he could check it out. He'd already bought train tickets and given one to me. That's how I got here.

"And, of course, he wanted to see you, Laura," she added with a grin. "He likes to surprise you."

Laura grinned back. "He does indeed," she agreed, "and he already has. He turned up on the train from Interlaken, and I certainly didn't expect that." She decided not to mention the possible shooting episode. Catherine was worried enough without that.

"Typical," Catherine said. "My Dad loves stuff like that." Her face sobered. "Anyway, we were in a museum and he just vanished. He wasn't at our hotel when I went to look, and he hadn't left any messages. He always leaves a message if he's all right. The strange thing was that his suitcase was gone but some of his clothes were still in the closet."

"Was there any sign of a struggle?" Violet asked.

"Not really," Catherine answered, "but the room had been searched, not messed up with things thrown around like you see in movies, but I'm positive someone had gone through my suitcase because my clothes were in different places. My Dad's pockets were cleaned out too. He always has junk in them."

She sighed. "I should be used to it by now but I never am. Anyway, I talked to everyone I could think of, but no one knew anything. So then I wondered if you might have heard from him again. Besides, I needed help, so I came to you. I was sure you could think of something. You always do."

Laura blinked hard, touched by Catherine's faith in her. She had better figure out fast how to live up to it and find Thomas – as well as keeping four teenagers and two children from being abducted.

"We'll come up with a plan to find your Dad," she promised confidently, wondering what on earth it was going to be. "In the meantime, keep in mind that your father's talent for getting out of tight spots is surpassed only by his ability to get into them. He can dream up the most ingenious ways to escape practically anything."

"That's true," Catherine agreed with a reluctant smile.

"Now, on to that plan to find him," Laura continued. "First, tell us anything else you can think of about what your father was doing in France. If we both remember everything we can, we might have a starting point."

"He said something about paintings being stored in Switzerland during the war, in caves or some kind of shelter they built," Catherine told her.

"Bomb shelters," Laura inserted. "He wanted me to find out everything I could about bomb shelters here. He said there were thousands of them."

"They're all over this country," Violet agreed. "Every family had to have one in case of nuclear war. Most are still stocked with food and water. They built underground bunkers in the mountains, too, with all kinds of weapons stored in them. I imagine they're all around here. They even had underground airfields. The Swiss like to be well-prepared for anything and everything."

"It had to do with the Nazis, he told me," Catherine put in. "They stole a lot of paintings I guess. He also said the case couldn't possibly involve any danger because it all happened so long ago, so that's why he thought it would be fun if I came to France too. And now look what's happened!"

Her face fell. "I'm sure he said other things, but I can't seem to think any more, not since he disappeared... Oh Laura, where do you think he is?"

"I don't know, but we are going to find out," Laura said with a firmness that belied her doubts. "After all, people really don't disappear."

"He did, though. One minute he was beside me in this museum and then he wasn't. I was staring at a painting that was pretty cool, and out of the corner of my eye I saw him go into the next room; you know how they have all those rooms in museums for different kinds of exhibits, but when I followed him he wasn't there. So I looked in all the rooms and even got someone to look in the men's restroom, and I tried calling his cell phone but there wasn't any answer, just that horrible voice mail person."

Laura visualized the scene: Thomas walked innocently into the next room, and someone who had been watching saw that he was alone for the first time and took a chance, pressed a gun hidden in his pocket against Thomas's back and escorted him out of the museum... it was a scenario that looked like a bad movie, over-dramatic and all the rest, but that didn't mean it couldn't happen – especially to Thomas. But why?

Because Thomas was getting too close to information that someone didn't want him to have – information that must be connected to hidden paintings in Switzerland. But what kind of paintings? He must have had some materials on them, have left some clue...

"Did you and your father check backpacks at the museum?" she asked Catherine. "Usually, they make you check any bags you're carrying so that you can't knock things over or stash anything away in them."

Catherine's head came up hopefully. "Of course. I forgot. I had to check my backpack and Dad checked a briefcase, but first he took some papers out of the case and put them in his pocket. I remember seeing him do it."

"Did you get the pack and the briefcase back when you left?"

"I got my pack, but I didn't see my Dad's briefcase there. I asked about it, but they didn't know if he'd picked it up or not. I wish we could find it. It's bound to have some clues about what he was doing. His computer, too. I didn't see it the whole time I was with him, and that's odd. He's never without it."

"He told me on the train that it had been taken," Laura put in. "That's why he wanted me to do the research – he couldn't."

"I'll have the briefcase checked out," Violet said. "What was the name of the museum?"

"Musee des Beaux Arts in Lyon," Catherine supplied.

"Some of the other things Dad said are coming back to me," she added. "There were missing paintings – there always are – and it had to do with being taken by Nazis and secretly brought to Switzerland for storage until the war was over and the Germans could get them back, only of course, they didn't belong to the Germans, but to the people they put in concentration camps or stole them from. I remember him talking about Dutch painters, too."

Laura jumped up and began to pace. "I remember Thomas saying once that the Nazis had stolen over seven hundred thousand artworks. They hired experts to pack the paintings so they wouldn't deteriorate and to find safe storage places for them. One of those underground bunkers would certainly qualify – a lot better than a musty cellar in an ancient castle."

"They'd be a great place to store stolen art," Violet agreed. "Some of them are huge, with a lot of rooms – kitchen, bedrooms and so forth, all made of reinforced concrete. They're temperature controlled and well-ventilated - though how air was supposed to get in without also letting in gasses from a nuclear explosion was never explained, at least not to me."

From outside the window they heard a muted buzzing. Catherine leaped to her feet, discarding the duvet. "My backpack - quick! It's my phone in my backpack, outside the door."

Violet got there first, hauled the pack inside and handed it to Catherine, who fumbled for the cell phone and snapped it open. Her shivering had abated, but her fingers were shaking.

"It's how he tells me he's okay when he can't talk. He just makes it buzz." She stared at the screen. "That's his number. So at least we know he's out there somewhere.

"I'll text him that I'm here. Then at least he won't worry about me," she added. Nimbly, she punched in a brief message: *In S w L,* Laura saw. *In Switzerland with Laura.* Clever. Only Thomas would know what it meant.

"He'll understand that even if he's only got a few seconds to look," Catherine said with satisfaction. "Maybe he'll text back."

No message came, and her face changed again. "Why can't he send anything? And why can't he talk?" she wailed.

Probably, Laura thought, because someone had a gun to his head and all he could do was press numbers through his pocket. Thomas must have very skillful fingers. He did, too. Long fingered, nimble in all sorts of sensitive places. But this was not the moment to daydream about things like that.

Instead, she listed all the other possible reasons. "It probably just means he's in an impossible situation for talking, like a noisy room or a place where there's not much reception, or he has his phone put away."

It wasn't a very convincing list, but Catherine looked reassured. She had learned to take advantage of any comfort that came her way, Laura thought with a spurt of pity, because going around in a constant state of tension didn't work. Or perhaps it was just her nature. Catherine was astonishingly resilient. For that matter, so was Thomas.

Catherine's next comment made her resilience clear. "I'm starved," she said. "Do you suppose I can get breakfast here? I can pay."

Violet let out one of her wonderful guffaws. Catherine grinned sheepishly; then she shrugged. "My Dad is never *not* in trouble, one way or another, so you learn to live with it. Anyway, now I have Laura to help and you too, Violet, so that makes it much better."

"Definitely a good addition to the team," Violet murmured again. "But," she added in a louder voice, "if we're going to help find your father, you need to know what Laura and I are here to do, which is keep the children who have come to a conference with their parents from being abducted. There have been threats, very vague ones, but we can't afford to ignore them."

"Wow! I'll help with that," Catherine said enthusiastically.

"I'm sure we can use your help," Violet said. "The first thing I need to emphasize - and it is extremely important - is that the conference members don't know what I am really doing here, and I don't want them to know. I can do my job a lot better if people aren't aware that I am a detective and that Laura's helping me."

"What's the conference about?" Catherine asked.

"It's on making sure girls in all parts of the world get the same chance to go to school as boys do. In some places, girls aren't allowed to go to school, or their parents can't afford to send them as well as their brothers."

Catherine, who had thus far eschewed "boring" school or college for a backpack and travel and camping in the woods in England, looked surprised. Then she laughed. "If someone had told me I wasn't allowed to go to school instead of forcing me go to one I hated, I'd have been mad!"

"In some countries where it's hard for girls to go to school, they literally risk their lives to get an education," Laura inserted, unable to resist the chance to make a point. "Girls younger than you do it every day."

Catherine looked thoughtful. "Maybe I would too," she said, "if someone said I couldn't."

Laura didn't take the lesson further. One point at a time.

"So that's the main thing," Violet concluded. "You mustn't give us away. We haven't told the parents about the threats, either, at least not yet. We don't want to alarm them. Instead, we have told everyone that Laura and I are old friends on a ski vacation together. Can you handle that?"

Catherine nodded soberly. "I'm used to it," she said with a dramatic sigh. "My Dad and I are always going off on vacation together that's really only part vacation, so I know how to keep my mouth shut and how important it is."

"Thank you, Catherine." Violet grinned. "Now they'll be told that Laura's niece – that's you - has decided to join us, so keep that in mind too."

Catherine laughed. "I make a great niece," she assured them.

"Now, on to logistics," Violet pronounced. "We'll need a third bed, for starters. Plenty of room in here. On second thought, maybe I'll book an extra room for the eventual arrival of Thomas."

"Do you really think he'll get here?" Catherine asked, forlorn again.

Laura answered for Violet. "Yes," she said firmly. "And before I forget, I've got to check my dratted cell phone. It never seems to be working and we might really need it now. For all I know, Thomas has tried to call it."

"It isn't working," Catherine confirmed. "I tried to call it earlier but one of those voices said it wasn't in service or something. I'll have a look at it. I'm good at cell phones."

"I bet you are," Laura agreed. "But first I want you to check inside your backpack. It's just possible your father managed to stuff those papers he took out of the briefcase into it when he was leaving the museum."

Catherine's face brightened, then fell again. "I looked in it quite a few times on the train coming here, getting out money and stuff, and didn't see anything. Still, I'll check again."

"Where did you come from?" Violet asked.

"From Lyon, in France. It's only a few hours away from Geneva by train," Catherine answered as she rummaged in her pack. "I got the last train. That's why I'm so late. My Dad told me where you and Laura would be."

She peered into an inside zip pocket and pulled out some papers. "Look," she crowed. "Oh Laura you are so brilliant. Why didn't I find it before?

"But what is it?" she added in bewilderment, opening the thin document. "I thought it was a letter, but it looks like an article from a magazine or a newspaper. Written a long time ago... Here, one of you take a look."

Violet reached out a hand. "Aha!" she said, her face breaking into a grin. "Now that really is a find. A few of the puzzle pieces may be coming together. Laura, can you guess who wrote this article?"

Laura frowned. "I don't know any journalists, do I?"

"You met one, or a person who was one, two days ago," Violet prodded.

Laura stared at her as the faces of people she'd met paraded through her mind. "Felicia!" she breathed. "Felicia Lamont."

Violet handed her the article. *An Aladdin's cave of art stolen by the Nazis and stashed away in Switzerland is reputed to be worth billions of dollars in today's markets*, she read. A description followed of efforts to locate the art, estimate how much of it there was, the amount still missing, where it might be hidden, and its possible value. That amount of money must have attracted a lot of unscrupulous collectors, Laura thought. Probably it still did, and that was why an old case had turned dangerous.

Violet was muttering to herself. "I can see why Thomas, an art detective, would be carrying around an old article by Felicia Lamont about Nazis stashing stolen art in Switzerland and where it is now, but what does that have to do with a conference on educating girls in the developing world?"

"Boxes," Laura pronounced. "Boxes being stolen – that's a start. I'm sure boxes come into this somehow. The trouble is, I can't figure out how – unless some of the paintings are stored in them."

Violet was dubious. "Would paintings fit into boxes like the ones you saw?"

"Some of the Dutch ones would," Laura answered. "They can be quite small. I saw more than my fair share of them when Catherine and I and Thomas were in the Cotswolds. So maybe that's the connection."

"While we're on the subject of boxes, I'm told there aren't any in the Castle Chillon cellars," Violet informed her.

"But I saw them!" Laura objected. "And I saw Max unloading more."

"I have no doubt you're right," Violet agreed. "I'm beginning to believe that it's all a matter of timing."

Before Laura could ask what she meant, Catherine interrupted. "Here, Laura, I've fixed your phone," she said, holding it out. "And would you two mind telling me what this box stuff is all about before I starve to death? It's past seven o'clock. I thought skiers always had an early breakfast."

Laughing, Laura took two fast steps and opened the door with a flourish for Catherine, almost knocking over the maid who was standing directly in front of it. The young woman let out a gasp of surprise. Thrusting some towels into Laura's hands, she scuttled away.

"She was listening," Catherine hissed indignantly. "I know she was."

"I believe you're right," Laura agreed. "But of her own volition or someone else's?"

Violet looked thoughtful. "I saw her yesterday with Karl. He didn't see me, and I'm quite sure he was handing her money - which could of course be a tip, but now I wonder. I'll find out what her name is."

"I don't think she speaks English," Laura said. "I tried to talk to her yesterday, without success."

"That's what is so odd," Violet answered. "She was talking to Karl in English, but when she caught sight of me, she switched to rather fractured German. I really do wonder what Karl Hoffman is doing here besides chasing women and chairing a conference."

"I wonder about Lindsey, too," Laura said as they sat down to breakfast. "She doesn't make sense."

"Who's Lindsey?" Catherine asked.

"The woman with all the blond hair." Laura tilted her head toward the American delegate, who was sitting at a nearby table.

Catherine took a look at Lindsey and laughed. "I know who *she* is," she said. "I live in Virginia, you see, with all the people who work in Washington. Nobody knows exactly what she does, but the rumor is that she's with the C.I.A. What's she doing here?"

CHAPTER NINE

"Laura Morland?" Laura looked up. The young woman who had tapped her shoulder was dressed in hiking boots, a ragged pair of jeans and a shirt that reached almost to her knees. A red bandanna was folded across her forehead and tied at the back of her head, 70's style, and her smile was brilliant. She had to be American, Laura thought, with those gleaming teeth.

"A guy named Tom handed this to me at the train station after he heard me talking about coming up here to ski. He said please give it to Laura Morland at the Alpina Hotel. He said it was important and told me to read it so I would remember it in case it got lost. I did, and it sure doesn't make much sense. But maybe you'll know what it means." She grinned. "Seems to be about a cat, and what you can do about the guy's cat from up here, I have no clue."

"A cat?" Laura was baffled, but only for a moment. *Cat* was Catherine's childhood name. She read the scribbled note quickly. *pls keep cat. Find in big shelter nrst u. OK. Thx.* She glanced up at Catherine, who had jumped up to read over her shoulder, and then passed the note to Violet.

"Yes, actually I do," she assured the young woman, "and thank you so much for bringing me the note. I've been worried about the cat's owner, so it's a relief to hear from him. Where did you see him? What station?"

"I saw him yesterday in Lauterbrunnen," the young woman said, offering a hand to shake. "I'm Barbara, by the way. Sorry I didn't get the note to you earlier. Great party down there, and you know how it is."

"I'm glad to meet you, Barbara." Laura put out her own hand and felt it enclosed in a remarkably hearty grip. This was one strong woman! "I'm Laura Morland, as you know," she said. "Will you be skiing around here?"

"Up at Schilthorn. I'll probably climb part of the way up. Saves money."

"That's a rigorous undertaking in the snow!" Laura was impressed. No wonder Barbara looked so fit.

"Not so bad, when you get used to it. Well, I'm off to pick up some food. Enjoy the rest of your dinner. See you on the slopes maybe."

"Can I treat you to dinner?" Laura asked impulsively. "It's a way of saying thanks. We only ordered a minute ago, and we would enjoy having you."

Barbara hesitated. "Are you sure? My place has a communal kitchen, but this sure looks a lot better." She eyed the lavish plates around them hungrily.

"Laura means it," Catherine assured her. "She likes feeding people."

Barbara laughed. "Your Mom, I guess," she ventured. "Thanks." She sat down beside Catherine.

"Actually, my aunt," Catherine corrected. "One of those venturesome aunts that you read about. And the lady sitting beside her is Violet. They do adventures together."

"Hi, Barbara," Violet said. "We've been a bit worried about our friend Tom. I wonder if you got any sense of how he was feeling."

"He looked kind of anxious to me. He didn't like the man he was with, that's for sure. He even ran away from him just before he talked to me. The man caught up with him, though. I have to admit, I wondered if maybe…"

Her voice trailed off in embarrassment.

"If he had some kind of mental problem?" Laura asked gently.

"Yeah. I mean, he did act a bit crazy. He kept talking about his cat, how someone had to look after it, and he didn't like those shelters. He seemed so upset about it, more than people usually are. Kind of noisy."

Laura almost laughed. She could imagine Thomas in the role. Probably he'd been trying to draw attention to himself so people would remember that they had seen him, which made his trail easy for her and for Catherine to follow.

She frowned. That didn't make sense. Attracting attention meant anyone could follow him. And what were they supposed to find in the big bomb shelter nearest them – Thomas or something else?

There was no way to know. They would just have to find the shelter, and Thomas, and let him explain.

"He can act sort of crazy sometimes," she admitted. "But he wasn't injured or physically sick or anything like that?"

Barbara shook her head. "Not that I could see. Just over-anxious, sort of babbling. But maybe that was because the guy he was with was real mean-looking. Wouldn't want to meet that one in a dark alley."

"What did he look like?" Violet asked.

"Sort of dark and oily. Little eyes, close together. Like that actor – what's his name? Peter somebody. He plays criminals and psychos."

Once dinner was over she left after repeated but heart-felt thanks. Violet waited impatiently for the door to close behind her. "Would you two mind explaining what that note means?" she asked. "I thought I was pretty good at deciphering clues but I'm stumped!"

Catherine laughed. "I was called Cat when I was little. My Dad's saying for Laura to keep me and that he wants us to find him or something in the nearest big bomb shelter. And that he's OK. It's pretty clever," she added. "No one but us would know he's not talking about a shelter for cats."

"You're right about that," Violet agreed. "I certainly didn't."

"I'm going to look for big bomb shelters near Murren on the computer," Laura announced, relieved that she had something definite to do after a whole day of feeling useless. The conference had officially started this morning and she had tried to distract herself from worrying about Thomas by going to Karl Hoffman's opening speech. It had been superb – eloquent and moving enough to bring tears to a few eyes. Laura was impressed but she still wasn't sure Karl had much interest in girls' education, that he had other unknown reasons for being here. She wished she knew what they were.

After that, she had attended a session on educational policy, but neither Ann nor Lindsey seemed willing to concede even minor points. Laura wasn't surprised by Ann, but if Catherine was correct about Lindsey's identity, why was she being such an obstructionist? Maybe she just wanted to block foreign intervention of any kind. More likely, Laura thought, considering the current administration, she was a rabid conservative who would block any program for girls and women lest it include birth control education and even the possibility of abortion, whether to save a mother's life or not.

Her search for information about large bomb shelters in this area was equally frustrating. She found one in a tunnel a few miles away, but did that constitute *nearest u*? It had three floors of living space, operating and exercise rooms and even a prison. She hoped Thomas wasn't locked in that.

She also learned that the Alps had been turned into a veritable fortress during the war. An estimated three to four thousand bomb shelters and gun emplacements - even some air strips - were scattered across the mountains, in houses or built into hillsides and barns. The idea that this glorious scenery was bristling with guns was a shock. And how could they find the shelter Thomas meant among so many? Even if they did, how would they open the door? They were made of steel and concrete and weighed thousands of pounds.

Catherine, who was looking through stacks of the hotel's brochures, had better luck. "Here, Laura," she called excitedly. "I found a brochure about a bomb shelter that holds a lot of people near here. Let's see if we can get in and look around. How about tomorrow morning?"

She handed Violet the brochure. "This could be the right one. It's dug into a hill near somebody's barn, and it's quite close."

"Don't forget we're having an early breakfast at the Piz Gloria restaurant on top of the Schilthorn tomorrow," Violet reminded them. "It's the big treat of this trip."

She studied the brochure's map closely. "It looks as if the shelter is on the way down. We could ski there and scout it out. Actually, skiing may be the only way to get to it. There aren't any roads, just a track."

"How early do you mean?" Catherine asked. She liked her sleep.

"Very early, like up at 6 AM," Laura told her. "But once you're there, even you will admit it's worth every un-slept minute. First, it's a chance to look for your father; second, it's one of the most the most incredible vistas you'll ever see. The Piz Gloria restaurant revolves, so you get a constantly changing view of three of the biggest mountains in the world and the whole landscape around them. Third, that's where Her Majesty's Secret Service, with James Bond, was filmed. Just come with us and you'll be very glad you did."

She was right. Catherine was up and ready in time and after that she was so enthralled that she almost forgot to eat. The brilliant yellow, gold and rose spectacle of the sun coming up over the snow clad peaks of the Jungfrau, the Monk and Eiger was unforgettable – the maiden on at one end, the ogre at the other, and the monk standing guard between them, the old legend said. They stared and stared as the restaurant revolved, providing an ever-changing view so compelling that at times the entire restaurant fell silent.

Laura sighed, replete, though she wished Thomas was here to see all this.

She stood, stiff-necked from looking up so much. She looked down instead, to the ground below the restaurant, and gasped. There he was! Could thoughts conjure people up? And was he all right? He looked very pale.

Another man was with him, and it didn't look like a voluntary duo. The man was standing right next to

Thomas, and every time Thomas moved, he edged close again. He was the bigger of the two businessmen who had come to see Henri Guillard, Laura realized, the one they had also seen going into the door after Veronica. There was no mistaking the fleshy face and big nose, even without the ears. But why did he have a gun on Thomas?

"Your Dad," she said quietly to Catherine. "Don't draw attention to him. I think someone may have a gun on him. But he's down there, and all right. He's on his feet – his skis, that is, at least."

Showing commendable restraint, Catherine neither yelled nor gestured in her father's direction. "Who's the man with him?" she asked tensely.

"I think he's a man I saw in Zermatt," Laura answered.

"Thomas doesn't know me, so he won't react," Violet said in her ear. "Stay here and keep an eye on him. I'll go down and see if I can get closer."

Laura and Catherine waited, nerves stretched to the breaking point. A few moments later, they saw Violet approaching the duo on skis. She accelerated as she came closer, and then suddenly seemed to get out of control. Before she could stop herself, she had crashed into the man with Thomas. He fell heavily, with Violet on top of him. Laura saw Violet mouth words to Thomas and grin as she began to extricate herself. He looked up at the window, saw them and waved a jaunty salute. Then he was off, skiing down the hill as if his life depended on it, which perhaps it did.

Laura and Catherine grabbed their packs and bolted for the door. By the time they reached the scene, Violet had disentangled herself from the man and was apologizing profusely in French and English.

"I believe we met at the Braun's party," Laura said when he was upright again, apparently unhurt.

"I believe so," he replied politely. "Forgive me, ladies, I must hurry on and go after my companion. He appears to have left without me."

Before Violet could stage another accident, he took off down the slope at a furious pace. He was a superb skier despite his bulk, and Laura's heart sank. Unless Thomas was equally good, he didn't stand a chance.

"Is your Dad a good skier?" she asked Catherine.

The answer was not reassuring. "No. He's only skied a couple of times as far as I know. I'm better than he is, and that's not saying much."

"Well, thanks to Violet, he has a head start at least," Laura said, trying to conceal her anxiety. "That was a great tackle," she added to Violet.

"Let's hurry and go after him," Catherine urged. "He's bound to fall and then the man could catch him again."

"True," Violet agreed. "But he can't do nearly as much harm without a gun." She patted the suspicious bulge in her pocket.

Catherine's eyes lit up. "Cool! Did you actually manage to get it out of the man's jacket without him knowing? I'd like to know how to do that."

"Slowly, very slowly," Violet advised.

"Our best bet," she added, "is to take the cable car one stop down so we can make up the time difference. That's what the hotel recommended anyway since the top is the steepest part."

Fortunately, there was no line, and they descended quickly. All the way down they looked for Thomas and his pursuer, but they only got occasional glimpses of the trails. They looked incredibly steep.

The rest was also steep, Laura discovered when they started down again on skis. She and Catherine slid on their backsides most of the way, but the snow was so soft, the weather and scenery so beautiful that despite her fear for Thomas and the fact that she fell constantly, Laura began to feel a touch of euphoria. Skiing experiences like this didn't come every day.

"The shelter should be near here, so let's start looking for it," Violet said, checking the map. "I think Thomas will go there if he got away."

In fact, they didn't have to look at all. The shelter was obvious, due to the fact that the metal door caught the sun's rays and almost blinded them. To Laura's surprise – and relief, it was propped open. They peered into the dark space beyond, but it was impenetrable after that brightness.

"Seems odd that the door's open," Violet said with a frown. "We'd best be as quick as we can and not draw attention to ourselves. Let's hide our skis in those trees and use as little light as possible."

When the skis were concealed, they crept into the cavernous opening, trying not to use their flashlights for more than a second or two. This was the living space, Laura conjectured after a flick of her light. It had a big kitchen with commercial fittings at one end of the room, tables and chairs and living room furniture for at least fifty people at the other. A card table was set up, and a deck of cards was spread on it, as if someone had just been playing.

"This place is creepy," Catherine whispered. "Actually, I hope my Dad isn't in here. I don't think he is, either. It feels empty."

It did, Laura agreed. "Thomas, are you here?" she called out softly, but no answer came. The deathly silence was unnerving.

They went on into the darkness beyond. Another quick flash revealed a bedroom with rows of bunk beds and chests of drawers. A bathroom of the kind found in large athletic clubs was next, causing Laura to wonder what the plans were for sewage for all these people.

Violet was already in the next room. "Laura, can you and Catherine go back and stand at the front door?" she called softly. "We need to know if anyone is coming." There was a warning in her voice.

It came too late. Laura had already looked in and even in the dark it was obvious that the elongated shape on the nearest bed was a man. The elation she had felt earlier vanished as if a switch had been turned off, and fear turned her insides to jelly. What if that was Thomas? It had taken at least an hour to get here. A lot could happen in an hour...

Catherine came up behind her. "Laura," she whispered in anguish. "Laura, could that be my Dad?"

2.

"Caught up to you finally, darling!" a familiar voice said behind them. Laura whirled and saw Thomas. Her first impulse was to slug him for causing them so much anxiety. Her second was to take him to the hospital. He was so pale his skin shone white in the darkness. He looked ready to faint, and unless she was badly mistaken, he was in a lot of pain. One sleeve was empty and the arm was bound protectively against his chest;

the other arm reached out for Catherine, who was trying hard not to cry. Too many shocks too fast, Laura thought with sympathy. She felt like weeping with relief herself.

Thomas tried to smile at her; then a surprised look came over his face and he did faint. Catherine and Laura crouched over him.

"Dad! Dad, please say something," Catherine begged. Thomas's eyes opened briefly. "Okay," he said. "Tired."

"Your shoulder?" Laura asked. Last time they had been together in the Cotswolds, Thomas had dislocated his shoulder. It had popped back into place again when a brute she didn't like to think about had grabbed his arms and tied them behind him.

"Bloodier this time, I fear," he said. "But the same arm."

Violet was already beside him, unwinding the bandages that bound his arm to his chest. "Someone's been taking pot shots at you," she observed. "Did your pal at the top do this?"

"You must be Violet," Thomas said with an attempt at a grin that turned into a wince as Violet probed. "No, someone else did it."

"Do you know what he looked like?"

"Narrow face, dark, eyes close together, thin," Thomas supplied. "He escorted me here on the train, or tried. Calls himself Ludwig. I ditched him but he spotted me again long enough to take a shot at me. He missed that time but not the next. Then the other one turned up."

Laura's eyes met Violet's, who nodded slightly. Laura went into the second bedroom. The other man

128

who had been with Henri Guillard lay on the bed, the dark leonine one with eyes that were too close together, just as Thomas had said. Like Henri, he had a hole in the middle of his forehead.

That made two. Would the man they had seen with Thomas at the top meet the same fate? Or was he the killer of the other two men?

"The man who shot at you is in the next room, dead," she told Thomas when she returned.

"Then we've got to get out of here!" Thomas tried to stand but collapsed. "I was seen with him on the train - I made sure of that - and the police already regard me with grave suspicion. And him, I'm glad to say."

"Is that why you acted crazy?" Laura asked, unable to resist the opening. "To draw attention to *him*?"

Thomas nodded. "Nasty guy, Ludwig. I wanted the police to notice him, hopefully haul him in for questioning. I can smell criminals sometimes, and he was one. Didn't want him after you or Catherine."

"I bet that's why he took the boxes off of the train and stayed behind," Laura said triumphantly. "You had spooked him. He was probably afraid the police would be waiting at the other end."

"Sounds plausible," Violet agreed. "In the meantime, however, Thomas is right and we've got to leave as fast as we can. Being found in the vicinity of a second body would really blow my cover, so let's go.

"Catherine, I want you to go to the door and alert us if anyone is coming. Laura and I will support your father and get him out. I don't think we have much time. Someone might already have called the police."

Only a moment later, Catherine yelled from the door. "Snowmobiles coming. Better hurry!"

"Catherine hears like an owl," Laura grunted as she and Violet struggled to get Thomas to his feet and moving. "I can't hear a thing. Can you?"

"Barely audible," Violet answered. "Hearing gets middle-aged fast."

They made it into the trees across from the shelter and ducked down into a hollow just in time. Two snowmobiles roared up, holding four police officers. Without speaking, they approached the shelter, guns drawn.

"I didn't know the Swiss police carried guns," Laura murmured.

"A lot of Swiss men do too," Violet told her. "They all do military service and they keep their guns. The Swiss also do a lot of hunting."

So it wasn't just the mountains that were bristling with firearms, Laura mused. The people were too. How unexpected in this neutral country.

"I wonder who called the police?" Violet asked. "And why that person left the body unguarded until the police arrived."

"The murderer could have called and then left so we'd take the blame," Laura said grimly. "And maybe the body wasn't unguarded. Maybe the killer or an accomplice was watching us the whole time we were in the shelter. He, or she, could be accusing us of Ludwig's murder this very minute."

"Good thing we left," Catherine observed, snuggling up against her father's good side. They waited nervously while the police examined the crime scene. Finally the four men emerged from the shelter, carrying the body. Once they had loaded it into a snowmobile, both vehicles roared back down the trail.

When their noise ceased, Thomas fell asleep, or at least Laura hoped he was asleep. He might have passed out. Catherine's eyes were closed, too. Her tear stained face made her look terribly defenseless, although Laura knew she wasn't. Catherine was a tae-kwon-do champion.

"Thomas needs a hospital," Violet said quietly. "He could be hit in other places that I haven't seen."

"How do we get him there?" Laura asked. "If the police are suspicious of him – and of us - we can't ask for their help. Do you think we can patch him up enough so he can ski as far as the hotel?"

"I doubt it. He's lost too much blood," Violet answered. "It's no wonder he fainted. I'm amazed he got this far." She frowned, mentally assessing her resources. Laura was amazed there were any in this isolated spot.

"Let's see who I can conjure up," Violet muttered finally, pulling out her cell phone. A brief call ensued in some kind of code. Violet looked satisfied when she hung up, and that satisfied Laura, too.

Violet rose. "I'm going to look around up there while the door is still open to make sure we didn't miss anything significant. I'll be as fast as I can."

Laura nodded. "I'll watch here." Settling herself against a tree, she began a mental list of unsolved problems, starting with why Rosa had been killed, why Max had unloaded boxes at Castle Chillon, who had killed Henri Guillard...

Her eyes closed involuntarily. She jerked them open, again they closed and then she gave into the impulse to doze, just for a moment.

"Do not move," a steely voice said. Laura opened her eyes and saw a gun pointed at her face. The man who had been with Thomas at the top of the mountain had crept up on her, unheard.

"If you move, I shoot her," he warned Thomas in a deep, expressionless voice. "You shot my good friend, so I intend to do the same to you."

"Not me, I fear," Thomas drawled. "You'll have to look elsewhere. I don't shoot people. Don't even own a gun or know how to use one."

Which was true, Laura knew. Thomas hated guns. He was far more likely to get shot if he carried one, he insisted. Thomas disarmed people with charm and unsettled them with persistent questions and distractions. Mostly it worked.

Laura decided to try the tactic herself. "Was your good friend the man who was left behind when the train started up again?" she asked suddenly.

He looked surprised, but his eyes remained firmly fixed on Thomas. "What do you know about that?" he asked.

Laura shrugged. "I was on the train. I saw him outside unloading boxes. Then he took a shot at my friend." She gestured to Thomas. "He missed that time but not the next."

The man hissed through his teeth but he didn't answer.

"Why was he unloading the boxes?" Laura persisted, wanting confirmation. "And why was he left behind when the train started up again?

"He had his own reasons," the man said shortly.

"What was in the boxes?" she asked innocently. "Was it medical supplies?"

Confusion showed this time on the man's face, but he didn't answer.

Laura fired another question. "What were you doing with Henri Guillard in Zermatt? Did you and your friend Ludwig have a deal with him?"

That question provoked a fast answer. "I do not do business with men like Henri Guillard," he said flatly.

Laura tried to think of more unsettling questions as she scanned the trees for Violet. How long had she been gone? And how long had she, Laura, slept?

Suddenly she realized that Catherine was missing. Where was she? Had she been abducted? Was it possible to sleep through an abduction?

Another thought struck Laura with greater force. Where had the man got his gun? Violet had taken it from him, but now he was holding it. Had he killed Violet to get it, maybe Catherine too?

Horror swept into her but it was swept aside by fierce and overpowering rage. Jumping to her feet, Laura shook her fist in the man's face.

"What have you done with them?" she screamed. "What have you done with Catherine and Violet?"

CHAPTER TEN

Three things happened simultaneously. The man recoiled, too astonished at her sudden attack to shoot, Laura supposed. Then a dynamo that was Catherine in full Tae-kwon-do readiness, enhanced by rage at anyone who threatened her father, landed a forceful blow on the side of the confused man's neck, and Violet came charging at him with equal intent to do harm but instead only caught him as he fell. His gun flew into the bushes and discharged.

"Well," said Thomas, his lips twitching. "I don't know why I ever bother to defend myself. There's no need at all with you three keeping watch."

To her eternal mortification, Laura burst into tears. "I thought you'd both been killed or at the very least abducted," she wailed. "I mean, Catherine had vanished, and Violet had the man's gun, so when he had it…"

"You've never burst into tears when I was abducted and possibly killed," Thomas observed.

"All I did was get up to go to the bathroom," Catherine apologized. "I guess I should have told you first."

"I wonder what gun he had?" Violet asked, patting her still bulging pocket. Her face cleared. "Of course, he took his friend Ludwig's gun. That's why there wasn't one on the body.

"I'd like to know who this one is, and what he's up to," she added, bending over the fallen man. She pulled some papers and a thick wallet gently out of his pocket and examined the contents. Sliding the wallet back, she handed the papers to Thomas.

"Here, Thomas – this should interest you," she said wryly. He scanned the papers and began to laugh, and then, suddenly, they were all laughing without knowing why. Laura's stomach ached with it.

Thomas stopped himself with a gasp. "That hurts!"

"Snowmobile's coming!" Catherine warned. The laughter stopped as fast as it had begun. After a minute or two, they all heard the snowmobile laboring up the hill. Laura hoped it wasn't more police, looking for them this time. She waited tensely, trying to dream up legitimate reasons to explain whey they were hiding in the woods with a wounded man, a stunned one, and laughing hysterically. She couldn't find any.

Finally, the snowmobile came into view. As if in answer to a prayer instead of a coded call from Violet, Gustav, the waiter from Zermatt, emerged from the driver's seat.

Violet went out to meet him. Laura watched them exchange a glance that had all sorts of meaning, and understood why he was there. Gustav was one of the "helpers" Violet had mentioned at the café.

"I'm glad to see you again, Gustav," Laura said. "Very glad."

"I am happy to help," Gustav replied, surveying the scene with interest. "it looks as if you have been very busy up here."

He knelt beside the stunned man. "This is Maurice Flambert. I have seen him with Henri Guillard, and have long wanted to speak to him."

He turned to Thomas, now looking extremely uncomfortable and in danger of fainting again. The bout of laughter hadn't helped him.

Catherine watched over him like an anguished chick. "He's really wounded this time. Usually, he makes a fuss if anything hurts but this time he isn't, and that means he *does* hurt. We shouldn't have let him laugh."

"Laugh?" Gustav looked astonished.

"I'll explain later," Violet promised. "As you say, we've been busy."

"We'll take him to the hospital right away," Laura assured Catherine.

Thomas sat up straighter. "No hospital," he yelped. They'll put a guard on me. Or put me in jail."

"Just as well," Laura said. "Otherwise, who knows what you'll do."

"Find a doctor," Thomas said. "There's bound to be one who will come to the hotel. Think of all that lovely money from Americans who can't go for more than a day without a doctor telling them what to do or how to eat."

"I'm a doctor, or a doctor in training," Gustav said mildly.

"Oh, please look at him," Catherine begged. "There's blood all over his arm and some on his chest. Violet is worried about him too. She didn't say so, but I could tell."

"You seem to know him quite well," Gustav commented as he bent over Thomas. He had actually brought a black bag, Laura saw, as he pulled out a stethoscope. Shades of the old days when doctors came to patient's bedsides, except they were in the woods instead of a house.

Catherine looked puzzled. "Of course I do. He's my Dad."

136

"Ah!" Gustav seemed satisfied, and Laura wondered what that interchange was really about. Had Gustav been instantly attracted to Catherine and wanted to know what her relationship was with his patient? How unexpected!

Except it wasn't really, she thought, regarding Catherine objectively. She was an astonishing looking young woman, with a heart-shaped face, green eyes enhanced by black lashes, and a mane of dark hair that glinted chestnut in the sun - without benefit of a bottle, Laura knew for sure. She had admired that hair, even unwashed for weeks, when Catherine was camping in a stable among the horses. And a pair of dogs almost as big as horses.

Concealing a smile, she waited to see what would happen next.

"Your father is fundamentally healthy, I would say," Gustav reported, "but he has bullet wounds in his arm and shoulder. They are only flesh wounds but we must make sure they don't get infected."

Catherine, who had watched his examination with avid attention, looked impressed with the concise diagnosis. "Could you do that if he was at the hotel? I mean, come in every day to check him? I can change bandages. I've done it on a lot of horses."

Gustav looked impressed in his turn. "If you can handle a horse, you should be able to handle a person."

"Horses are easy compared to my Dad," Catherine told him. "You just talk to them and they stay still. My Dad jumps around a lot."

"He will not jump much for a day or two," Gustav predicted. "Antibiotics and pain medication should take care of that."

He turned his attention to the other man, who still hadn't stirred. "What happened to this one?" he asked. "It looks as if he had a hard blow to the side of his neck. His pulse is all right, though."

Catherine looked embarrassed. "I guess I hit him harder than I meant to," she apologized. "I was too mad to check myself."

Gustav looked stunned. "You did that to him? What else can you do?"

"Well, I ride horses, and I like climbing," Catherine confessed. "Rocks and walls mostly."

"And balconies and vines," Laura inserted.

Violet intervened. "You can check out each other's accomplishments later. At the moment, we need to remove ourselves from the vicinity of a crime before the local police make another visit.

"We've left enough evidence of our presence to get us all arrested," she added gloomily, looking at the trampled snow around them. "Blood spots, boot prints, body prints. I just hope they don't bring up dogs!"

"I'll come back later and clean up," Gustav promised. "By the time I've finished the police will think we were sheep or goats.

"I'll take Thomas first and then come back for Maurice," he added, since the snowmobile wasn't large enough for all of them.

They loaded Thomas onto the snowmobile, with Catherine in attendance. "Take him up to our room," Violet instructed, handing Gustav a key. "I don't care how you get him up there, just try not to let anyone see him until he gets cleaned up. I doubt the hotel thinks much of shot-up guests."

138

"Maybe we can hoist him up to the balcony," Catherine suggested. "I know how to make rope pulleys."

"Easier said than done with a wounded man," Gustav replied. "Is there an elevator?"

"Great idea," Catherine agreed. "I'll distract anyone who is in the lobby while you get him into it. We can say he had a skiing accident."

"Instantaneous rapport," Laura murmured to Violet as the snowmobile roared to life.

"You can almost feel the magnetic vibrations," Violet agreed.

They both whirled, suddenly aware of movement behind them. Taking advantage of their momentary distraction, Maurice Flambert had crawled to the bushes and retrieved his forgotten gun.

He rose shakily to his feet. "Once again, I shall have to leave you, ladies," he said, rubbing his neck with his free hand. His eyes were on Laura but he spoke to Violet. "Do not pull out your gun. Mine is already pointed at your friend and will go off before you can reach it."

Without taking his eyes off Laura, he backed out of the trees and onto the road. As soon as he was out of sight, Violet went after him. She was too late. He had already stepped into his waiting skis and taken off down the slope at breathtaking speed. Laura listened for the sound of a crash, sure it would come, but she had underestimated his expertise.

"Damn!" Violet said explosively.

"Maybe not," Laura said pensively. "I wonder about him. I'm not sure he really meant to shoot anyone. I think he's playing a role because he doesn't know who's on what side. I could be completely wrong, though."

"What makes you think that?" Violet asked.

"His face when I screamed at him, asking what he'd done with you and Catherine," Laura answered. "He was appalled that I thought he had killed anyone. He could easily have shot me then, too, but he didn't."

"Rather a risky way to find out," Violet observed dryly. "And maybe he was horrified because he saw Catherine flying at him and me right behind her."

"I suppose," Laura conceded. "The other thing, though, is that he was so polite at the top and when he left: *please excuse me ladies* sort of talk. And that business of *you killed my good friend, so I intend to do the same to you* sounded like something he'd heard in a movie. Also the way he answered about not doing business with Henri Guillard. I thought he was telling the truth."

"Interesting," Violet murmured. "Definitely worth checking out. For all we know, he's looking for his family's long-lost treasure stolen by the Nazis.

"Is that why Thomas laughed when he read that paper you got out of Maurice's pocket? Was it something about stolen art?"

"It was a copy of Felicia Lamont's article, the one Catherine found."

Laura laughed again. "I can definitely see the humor. The article would also make him a natural ally of Felicia's," she added, "which would explain why he was included in that mysterious meeting in Zermatt after the Braun's party."

"If the first person we saw going in was Felicia," Violet pointed out.

"I'm pretty sure it was," Laura said. "What else was in that wallet? It looked quite hefty."

"A lot of money, mostly Swiss Francs, and some ID. His name *is* Maurice Flambert, he is a Swiss citizen, and he appears to be a psychologist."

"Doesn't sound like a killer, but one never knows," Laura observed. "He doesn't look like one, either, unlike the mad psychiatrist we ran into last year. At any rate, now that we don't need to watch him, maybe we should search inside the shelter. We didn't find anything earlier – except of course, the body. But I don't think that's what Thomas had in mind."

"Good idea," Violet concurred. "Your blood-curdling screams brought me back before I had time to do much looking. But I did find a storage room that was full of boxes. We can start there.

"Grab your skis so we don't have to go back for them when Gustav comes," she instructed. "We'll leave them by the shelter door this time, so if anyone comes to close it they'll look inside first."

Propping the skis beside the entrance, they made their way to the storage room. Laura shivered. The cavernous space looked even darker and felt even creepier this time, despite the fact that the body was gone.

"This place makes me claustrophobic," she muttered. "I wonder if the Swiss planned for mental problems from being locked in here? They'd have to carry me out on a stretcher."

"They couldn't, if there was a nuclear attack," Violet pointed out. "On a more practical note, I wonder what kind of lighting system they planned. It wouldn't be as claustrophobic if we could see what's around us."

Laura aimed her flashlight at the wall nearest the door. "No switches that I can see. But where would they get the electricity anyway?"

"Haven't thought that through," Violet admitted. "Here's the box room. Let's take turns going to the door to listen while we tackle a few boxes."

She shone her light around. "That looks like one of the missing boxes. It's the right size and shape, and the identifying label, *medications for children,* is still on it." Dropping to her knees, she pried it open, revealing dozens of packets of a powdered medication.

"Oral re-hydration packets," Violet said. She opened another box, which contained the same thing. She sat back on her heels, puzzled. "These really do look like the missing boxes. But why steal boxes from a warehouse in Interlaken and bring them up here instead of just ordering them from the supplier?

"Since they weren't ordered from a supplier, there's no paper record to follow," Laura hazarded. "Maybe that's why they were stolen."

"I can see that," Violet answered. "But there must be other ways -"

She stopped abruptly. "I hear voices - children's voices I think. You go see while I close these up. If it's Gustav, send him in. Anyone else, stall them."

To Laura's astonishment, the twins ran up to her as she emerged into the daylight. "It is Maman! She needs help!" Kjersti said, grabbing her arm. "You must come with us and help.

"We are so glad to find you," Kristin said, her eyes filling with tears. "Maman has fallen over a cliff and she is just lying there. Oh, please…"

"I'll come right away," Laura assured them, grabbing her skis.

A moment later, Violet emerged. "Show us where your mother is," she said calmly. Her composure was contagious, and the twins, who had been reduced to sobs, began to tell what had happened as they made their way laboriously back up the slope.

"We were skiing down," Kristin said, "and we came to this cliff, quite a big one, so we went around it. We thought Maman would follow in our tracks but then she suddenly went right over this cliff and she fell very hard. We couldn't wake her but then she woke up and said she would get up in a minute. We had seen you down here so we said we would get you to help…"

Kjersti interrupted. "But there she is!" she exclaimed, her voice a mix of astonishment and relief. They looked up and saw Sigrid, making her way slowly down the slope. Laura noticed that one arm hung by her side.

"I am so happy to see friendly faces," she said when they reached each other. "Thank you, girls, for finding Laura and Violet. Oh, such a morning we have had. So glorious to start, and so bad after!"

"Maman, you should not be skiing," Kjersti objected. "You are injured."

"Only my wrist and aching head," Sigrid said. "I am glad it was not worse."

"I will call for a snowmobile to take you down the rest of the way," Violet assured her, taking out her cell phone. "I know just the person. His name is Gustav, and he is a roving waiter and medical rescue team member."

"Let's wait for him here," Laura suggested when they reached the shelter. "We'll bring out a chair so you can rest while you tell us what happened."

"Excellent," Sigrid agreed. "I am a little dizzy from the fall. It stunned me for a few moments, and I should very much like to sit down."

Laura recruited Kjersti and Kristin to help her carry chairs out into the sunshine while Violet examined Sigrid's wrist.

"What is this place?" Kristin asked, wrinkling her nose as they went in. "It smells strange, as if no one has been here in a long time."

Kjersti shivered. "I would not like to be locked in here," she said. "It's... I don't know the English word for when a place makes you feel a little scared."

"Creepy?" Laura suggested. "That's how it feels to me. It's a bomb shelter, actually. There are bedrooms and bathrooms and lots of other rooms."

"Can we explore?" Kjersti asked, her face eager again.

"Not until we have your mother settled in a chair and have asked her if it is all right," Laura replied. "She's most important right now."

"Yes, that is so," Kristin agreed, with a disapproving look at her sister, but she too went eagerly into the shelter once Sigrid gave her approval.

"Only explore the first three rooms," Violet said firmly as they left. "No further. It is a big place, and it is too easy to get lost."

"Now, tell us how you came to go over that cliff," Laura said when the twins were out of earshot. "I can't think you did it on purpose."

"No," Sigrid agreed. "That is what is so strange. I had my skis ready to turn away from the cliff so I would follow the girls' tracks, and then I felt a push." She frowned. "It really felt as if someone gave me a push, but surely that is impossible!"

Violet asked the obvious question. "Did you see or hear anyone near you?"

"I was not aware of anyone close to me," Sigrid replied, "But there was a big mogul behind me, so I would not see anyone who was behind it."

"Did you see other skiers anywhere around?" Laura asked.

"The only ones I saw were Karl, Ann and Reginald. They were just above me, so I suppose they could have skied fast and reached me. But surely none of them would push me. They would not do that."

Actually, Laura thought, any of them might have given Sigrid a malicious push – Reginald because he didn't like her authority over him, Karl because she was resistant to his charm, and Ann because Sigrid would never agree with her. Or were there other, less trivial reasons that she didn't know about?

"Please do not say anything about them to Kjersti and Kristin," she added. "They dislike Reginald already and would be quick to blame him for this."

"We will keep it to ourselves," Laura promised.

Sigrid's brow furrowed as another recollection came. "I think, though I am not sure, that I also saw the Iranian delegate above me, Dr. Nezam. But I do not even know if he skis. Or if his son does."

"Nor do I," Violet said, sounding interested.

"His son does, I think," Laura said. "Or at least he's taking lessons."

Gustav's arrival precluded further discussion. If he was surprised at the disappearance of Maurice and the arrival of still another casualty, he didn't show it. Sigrid, however, remarked that Gustav's appearance exactly when they needed him, while welcome, was an interesting coincidence.

"When the girls were small, we used to play a game called w*hat is wrong with this picture,*" she said as the twins followed Gustav to the snowmobile. "I had much practice, so is not hard for me to see that something is wrong with the picture presented all during this conference. When you are ready, I would like to know what it is."

Before they could answer, she took her seat beside Kristin and Kjersti and the snowmobile started up. "Back as soon as I can," Gustav shouted over the noise of the engine and squeals of pleasure from the twins.

Laura wasn't surprised. Sigrid was too intelligent to miss the accumulating signs. "Sigrid would be a good ally," she said. "Can we recruit her?"

"I'm not sure we have much choice," Violet said. "I don't want her investigating on her own."

"I bet she's already done some unobtrusive sleuthing," Laura replied.

Violet grunted reluctant agreement. "This is getting out of hand," she grumbled. "We need answers. Let's go back to the boxes. I'm going to take some of them to the hotel with us when Gustav returns, too."

As they opened the next one, Laura noticed that there was an extra space at the bottom of the box under the re-hydration packets. "Maybe something is down here," she suggested, gently pulling off the bottom layer of cardboard.

146

She was right. A thin container like a pizza box, except much sturdier, was revealed. Laura pried off the top, and her eyes widened in triumph.

"I imagine this is what Thomas is looking for," she said exultantly, pulling out an oil painting protected by a simple frame and sheets of polyurethane paper. She shone her flashlight on it. "It looks like one of the Dutch paintings I was talking about. I'm no expert so I can't tell if it's a real one, but I think that polyurethane is the kind of wrapping that's used to store valuable paintings."

"I'm beginning to see how art thefts and boxes stolen from a warehouse are connected," Violet said, "but it's a stretch to figure out why anyone would steal a box of children's medications and hide a valuable painting inside it."

"A handy way to transport stolen art," Laura conjectured. "No one would think to look for paintings inside a box clearly marked children's medications."

"Sounds a bit far-fetched," Violet commented. "There must be easier ways." She shook her head in frustration. "I'm missing something, but I can't think what. Maybe I'll find it in the other boxes. I'll pick out some to take with us while you get the painting into your pack so Thomas can look at it."

"Good thing I brought my biggest pack," Laura remarked as she wrapped the painting in its polyurethane covering, placed it in the box and maneuvered the whole into her pack. Just as she finished, they heard still another voice.

"Busy place!" Violet observed. "Sounds like Felicia this time. I wonder what she's doing here. I thought she was in Zermatt."

"So did I," Laura agreed. "I'll see what she wants while you clean up." Not bothering this time to use her flashlight, she started back towards the door. She had done this so many times now that she didn't need light.

She froze as the shadowy form of a person moved along the wall ahead of her and slithered into the next room. Laura crept after it, holding her flashlight in front of her so she could snap it on quickly to see who it was.

Felicia was suddenly behind her. "The door to the shelter is usually closed," she remarked curiously. "Do you know who opened it, or why?"

Startled, Laura spun around and saw Felicia looking over her shoulder. How had she crept up so silently? And how long had she been in the shelter?

A long time, Laura thought. Felicia moved easily through the chairs in the sitting room, as if her eyes were already well adjusted to the darkness. That meant she could have been listening to them talking about medications and paintings – might even have seen the painting.

"I don't know," Laura answered. "Violet and I didn't expect it to be open, either, but when we saw that it was, we decided to have a look."

It occurred to her to wonder if the shadowy person she had just seen had opened the door. If so, he or she could close it again at any moment.

"It might be a good idea to leave while the door remains open," she added. "I'll call for Violet to come too. She's poking around in here somewhere."

"An excellent suggestion," Felicia agreed, and made her way to the door.

"I'm glad to see you, Felicia, but surprised," Violet said when she caught up with them. "I assumed you were in Zermatt."

Felicia, dressed this time in a stunning gold and black ski suit and a bright gold scarf with black tassels, pulled off her gloves and hat and sank wearily into one of the chairs they had pulled outside for Sigrid. Under her tan she looked ill, Laura thought with concern. No amount of flamboyant dress could hide her pallor.

Her tone, however, was as dramatic as ever. "My dear, we are all here," she said. "No one could stay in Zermatt, when we knew she might have come here. Helga and Ernst are here, and many others from Zermatt. Even Max is helping, and Nicolas, though they are currently not on the best of terms..."

She broke off. "But that is not what matters now. It is an emergency, and when that is so, we must focus only on the search."

She frowned. "I do wonder if this is connected to Henri's un-lamentable death. That is the terrible thing, because it could put her in danger from so many, and it is so hard to know where to look first. When I saw the door open I hoped she might be here, but she is not..."

Violet interrupted the confusing barrage of words. "Felicia, what emergency are you talking about? Who are you searching for?"

Felicia's eyebrows went up almost comically high. "Why haven't you heard? Veronica, of course. She is missing! No one has seen or heard from her since the night of the Braun's party."

CHAPTER ELEVEN

Despite misgivings, Laura agreed to keep an eye on the children for the afternoon. Their ski instructors had been recruited to help search for Veronica, a full schedule of seminars was planned for their parents, and Violet was going to Lauterbrunnen to meet with Rosa's sister. That left only Laura.

"I'm sure you will think of something creative to do with them," Violet said cheerily, seeing Laura's consternation. "Or Catherine will."

Laura brightened. "Excellent idea."

"Let's explore Gimmelwald," Catherine suggested without hesitation. "It's a neat little town. The kids will like it, I think. We can walk down and then take the train back up. All the kids need is boots and warm clothes, which is great because some don't ski very well yet and all that equipment is a pain with little kids anyway. They're always falling out of it. And snacks."

"Catherine, you're a genius," Laura proclaimed. "Let's check on your Dad and then we're off." She was worried about leaving Thomas for too long, not because he was worse but because he was recovering almost too fast, and she was afraid he would soon insist on joining the action. She hoped Gustav, who should arrive to check him in an hour or so, would rein him in.

"You're not allowed out until tomorrow," she reminded him sternly.

Thomas grinned. "Seems a shame not to do some poking around, as you call it," he said. "There's a computer downstairs, or I could talk to some of those nice young people waiting on tables. They see a lot."

Shaking her head in exasperation, Laura left him to it.

She found Catherine downstairs explaining the revised plans to the kids. Reginald looked unimpressed until Zaina, the Indian delegate's daughter, expressed enthusiasm. The Iranian boy, whose name was an uncomplicated Ben, to Laura's relief, was willing, so were the two Pakistani children, Jafar and Parveen. The twins, as always, embraced the idea with gusto.

"We'll bring sleds," Catherine said, in case anyone wants to try sledding on the way down or wants a ride. Little Parveen looked relieved.

They stopped to buy snacks, a noisy and time-consuming process that got them off to a late start, and set off. The trail was well packed down, easy to follow though steep in places. It should take forty to fifty minutes, Laura had been told when she enquired at the desk, which sounded just right.

She hadn't counted on the multiple distractions of snowball fights, efforts to sled down the road which inevitably ended in a snow bank accompanied by peals of excited laughter and laborious attempts to extricate the occupants of the sleds from deep piles of snow. Good-natured shoves and rough-housing that pushed them in deeper followed until finally the group moved forward again. Laura was pleased that everyone was having such a good time, but they weren't getting anywhere very fast. Almost an hour had passed, and they still hadn't come to Gimmelwald.

The sky darkened suddenly, and she glanced up. Ominous-looking clouds were fast obscuring the brilliant blue of the sky. The man at the desk had assured her that it would be clear and sunny all afternoon. Obviously, he had been wrong. It really did look like snow.

Maybe they should go back. Impossible, Laura decided. That meant climbing, which would be even slower. There was no option but to keep going and take the lift back up to Murren.

Then, without even a few flakes of warning, thick show began to fall. At the same time, the clouds descended so rapidly that in moments they were enveloped in fog. Laura could make out the children's shapes, but that was all, and the light was so flat that she could barely tell up from down.

"Stay together," she ordered. "Until the snow eases, link hands with each other, like a chain. Catherine, you take Parveen on one side and Jamal on the other. All the rest of you, take the nearest hand and hold on tight."

Everyone obeyed, intimidated by the suddenness of the storm and its power to turn a perfect day into a test of fortitude. Silent now, they crept down the slope one step at a time, struggling to stay upright in the ever-flattening light. Parveen was shivering so hard she couldn't stand. Catherine picked her up and transferred Jamal's cold hand to Laura.

"I think I see a cabin," Ben called out suddenly. "Perhaps we can go there until the snow stops." Laura hadn't heard him speak more than a few words before and was startled at the depth and resonance of his voice.

She peered through the thickening fog and made out the shape of a cabin on stilts. A summer cabin, probably, but it might have a wood stove so she could warm everyone up – if she could figure out how to get it going.

"Thank you Ben," she said gratefully. "We will go there. At least we'll be out of the snow and if we're lucky, the cabin will have a woodstove. Does anyone know how to make a woodstove work?"

"We do," the twins chorused. "We have one at home."

As they got closer, however, the evocative scent of burning wood made it clear that a stove or fireplace was already in use.

"Someone must live there in winter, too," Catherine said. "It's one of the summer places people use when they bring the cows into the mountains.

"Those wide rocks on top of the stilts keep rats and mice out," she explained to the others. "Even the rats can't climb around them."

"I am glad of that," Zaina said with a shiver. "I do not like rats. There are many, too many in India."

Laura went to the door, noting a pair of skis propped up beside it. They were wet with melting snow. Someone must be here. She knocked, hoping that whoever it was wouldn't mind an unexpected invasion of children.

There was no response. She knocked harder, then pounded. Still silence, not even the sound of footsteps. Catherine came up beside her. In her arms, Parveen was weeping quietly, tiny sobs that wrenched the heart. The child looked half-frozen, and her mittens were soaked. Jamal was trying to comfort her, but she just kept sobbing.

"We've got to get her into the warmth," Catherine said, "or her fingers are going to end up with frostbite."

Laura gave another loud knock and when there was still no answer, she tried the door. To her surprise, it gave way. A rush of heat came out at them.

Too much heat, surely. Laura took a few steps into the room and gasped. The wood stove had been turned up as high as it would go. It blazed furiously.

Kristin took a step toward it. "It burns too hard," she said. Holding her scarf over her face, she turned a knob on the front of the stove with mitten- covered hands, then backed away and ran for the cooler air at the door.

Kjersti imitated her sister. Scarf over face, mittens on, she turned the knob again. "It should be better now," she said confidently from the door.

She was right. The fire subsided, and cold air from the door quickly cooled the room to a reasonable temperature. Everyone trooped in.

"Where are we?" Zaina asked, her large brown eyes round with curiosity. "And is someone here, do you think?"

"Someone has been here," Ben observed. "I see food on the counter."

"Maybe someone fell asleep and forgot the fire," Laura suggested. "And I think we're on the outskirts of Gimmelwald, though I can't be sure.

"See if you can find a way to make us all a hot drink while I look in the other rooms," she added. "Hot chocolate if there is any. That will comfort Parveen. She loves hot chocolate."

The children eagerly set to work, and Laura heard exclamations of triumph as first a kettle, then some tea and biscuits and packets of hot chocolate were discovered, and even powdered milk to make it thicker.

Good. That should keep them busy while she did a quick exploration.

She didn't have to look far for the occupant of the cabin, or for the reason the stove had been left on high. A woman lay face down on a bed in the next room. She was utterly still, much too still….

Laura's heart dropped to her stomach. Surely not another body…

Closing the bedroom door so the children wouldn't look in, she went closer. A small sound and the slight movements of breath going in and out reassured her. Laura's tension eased. "Hello?" she said tentatively.

There was no answer. She leaned over the woman. She was young and tall, very slender. Was it possible? No. This woman had dark hair; Veronica was blond. But who was it then, and why was she so deeply asleep that even the noisy laughter from the next room hadn't woken her?

Laura shook the woman's arm gently. "Hello!" she said again. "I need to know if you're all right."

The woman made no answer, but she turned over in her sleep. Laura's eyes widened with shock. Dark-haired or not, this woman was Veronica.

****

Laura took in the details, the classic face and high cheekbones, the slender build, and most telling, the bruise that hadn't yet faded completely. A woman could fool people at a distance by dyeing her hair, but not up close.

She pulled out her cell phone to call the hotel and tell them Veronica had been found. To her dismay, there was no signal, not even a glimmer of one. The phone looked completely dead. She stared at it, disbelieving. It had worked well since Catherine had fixed it. Could it be the storm?

"I see you recognize her." The deep voice was just behind her. "She is safer this way for the moment, but it cannot last." He sighed. "She is like a daughter to me, but I cannot protect her forever."

Laura whirled. The man who had been beside Thomas at the top of the Schilthorn, the one Catherine had felled with Tae-kwon-do, stood facing her, hands outstretched in a conciliatory gesture. Where had he come from? The bathroom that opened off this room, she realized. She should have searched it.

The bedroom door opened a crack and Catherine crept in, hand raised to fell him again. The man seemed to sense her presence and turned.

"You are very good at that," he said, smiling at her, "but there is no need to do it again. I think that now it is better to talk."

Catherine looked inquiringly at Laura. "I'm not so sure about this," she said dubiously. "He really did threaten to shoot…"

"Your father," he supplied. Catherine stared at him, nonplussed.

"Yes - it is time to talk," Laura agreed, "but I need to ask some questions first. Most important is why Veronica is sleeping so deeply. Did you drug her?"

He shook his head. "I did not, but she has been drugged. I am merely watching over her until the drug wears off, but since I do not know what she was given or who gave it to her, I do not know when that will be. She would be better in hospital," he added, "where they cannot get at her."

156

"You were one of the last people to see her before she disappeared," Laura said, trying to provoke him. "You went into a house with her after the Braun's party," she added for clarification.

He looked surprised but answered readily. "That is true," he agreed. "But I not drug her or kidnap her. Someone else did that."

"Max?" Laura hazarded.

He shook his head vehemently. "Max and Veronica do not always agree," he said, "but Max would not harm his sister."

Laura hid her surprise at the revelation by asking another question. "Would he hit her?" She gestured at the fading bruise. "Or was that Henri Guillard?"

He sighed. "Perhaps. Henri was not a good man. Or perhaps it was…"

He broke off to bend over Veronica and stroke her arm gently, leaving Laura to wonder what name he had been about to say.

"If you look closely," he continued, "you will see the mark of an injection on this arm. It is quite recent, I believe. The spot of red blood at the site indicates that."

"If it is recent, why is she already so deeply asleep?" Laura asked sharply. "Most drugs take time to have such an effect."

"I imagine it is not the first injection, that someone wishes to keep her sedated for a time," he answered patiently. "My arrival about five minutes ago may have interrupted the person who sedated her, and he or she left abruptly through the bathroom window. That is why I did not come to the door. I feared that person was returning, this time with more lethal intent.

"It is quite warm in here, is it not?" he added, mopping his brow with a handkerchief. "The person who preceded me did not stop to turn down the stove before exiting so precipitously."

The handkerchief was immaculate, Laura noticed, a well pressed square of linen with initials in one corner. "M.F.," she said. "Maurice Flambert. And what brought you here, Monsieur Flambert?

"Has it anything to do with stolen art?" she added impulsively, thinking of Felicia's article and the painting she and Violet had found.

He laughed, a rumbling noise even deeper than his voice. "You are full of surprises," he said. "Or perhaps the article that mysteriously disappeared from my pocket provides a clue. But tell me, what brought Dr. Laura Morland, an American professor of gender studies, to Switzerland to investigate criminals and murders – as well as herd a group of children on a ski trip?"

"You are well-informed," Laura said dryly. "Unfortunately, I cannot speak frankly about my reasons for being here at the moment. The children in the other room know nothing of what has happened."

"I understand," he replied. "Perhaps instead, you would introduce me to these young people. I would be very interested in speaking with them, and no doubt they are curious about the man in the other room who failed to let them in or turn down the stove.

"They are a lively bunch," he added, as crashing sounds followed by uproarious laughter sounded from the living room.

Laura hesitated. She wasn't enthusiastic about taking Maurice Flambert into a room full of children for

158

whom she was responsible, but short of locking him in the bedroom - futile anyway since he could leave through the bathroom window - she had no choice but to keep him with her.

"I will speak freely about why I am here if they wish to hear my story," Maurice said quietly, seeming to intuit her reluctance.

It took only a moment for Laura to agree. She badly wanted to know more about this man, and he didn't look dangerous, only amused for some reason. He also seemed genuinely concerned for Veronica.

"In that case," she said, "perhaps you would like to join us for tea and biscuits? I am aching for a cup of tea."

He laughed again, delighted at the idea. "That sounds excellent," he agreed, and followed her into the other room.

"I see you found the person who lives here," Ben said smoothly as they entered. His eyes were unusually perceptive for one so young, Laura thought. She would have to keep her wits about her with Ben listening – and his father, so unlike the son but for their reticence. Neither of them gave anything away.

The children greeted Maurice politely, but their faces were guarded. Was that because they had seen more of the world than less cosmopolitan children or was there something about this man in particular that they didn't trust?

Jafar was the first to speak. "If you were here, why did you not answer the door?" he accused. "My sister was crying with the cold."

159

"I am sorry about your sister," Maurice answered, his face creasing in what looked like genuine sympathy. "Is she all right now?"

"My fingers still hurt," Parveen answered, holding them out for inspection.

The big man took them in his and rubbed them gently. "I am so sorry that I did not let you in. I was asleep, like my daughter, who is sick with a fever in the other room," he answered. "I heard the knocking but thought it was a dream, as one does sometimes when one is deeply asleep."

"Why did you leave the stove up so high?" Kjersti asked.

"That was a bad mistake," Maurice said penitently. "I am not usually so careless but I have been distracted recently. You see, my daughter and I have lost something of great value to us, and we can think of little else."

"Did you come to Switzerland to find it?" Kristin asked.

Maurice nodded. "I shall take a drink of the tea Mrs. Morland has so kindly made for me, and then I will tell you the story of what we have lost."

"I like stories," Parveen said, sitting down beside him. Jamal took a seat on the other side, and Kjersti and Kristin perched nearby, their faces eager.

He had definitely charmed the younger children, Laura thought with reluctant admiration. She wasn't sure about the older ones. Reginald always maintained a mask; Ben was always watchful. Zaina of the round dark eyes was the ingénue. Or was that a pose too? Her eyes flashed a message to Reginald, and for an instant both their masks dropped. Her face showed suffering,

160

and his showed warmth. Laura was touched. Those two had a bond of some kind. And maybe there was another side to each of them she knew nothing about.

Maurice put his tea cup back on its saucer with a little clink. All eyes turned to him. His face was sober, almost a mask of tragedy.

"I am a Swiss Jew," he began bluntly, and Laura saw the children's bodies stiffen. "My family has lived in this country for many, many years, as your ancestors have lived in your homelands for many years. There are some who blame Jews for all the world's ills, but I assure you that all of us – Jews, Muslims, Christians alike, are responsible in equal measure. There is plenty of blame to go around.

"As you know, Jews were persecuted all across Europe when the Nazis were in power. Unfortunately, my family was living in Germany at that time. My parents believed that our Swiss nationality would protect us, but they were wrong. We were evicted from our home, all our possessions were taken, and we were left with nothing. My father was killed; my mother and I went to the concentration camps. What kept her alive during those terrible years was the knowledge that we had a Swiss bank account where we had stored valuable possessions that no one could take from us. But when the war was finally over and we returned to Switzerland, she discovered that the documents proving our ownership of the bank account were missing, and so were its contents. My mother had survived the camps, but that shock killed her."

His lips compressed in remembered grief. "I was only six years old then, but I made a vow to honor my mother by finding and taking back what had been stolen from my family. That is what I am doing now, that is why I am here." He sighed heavily. "But as you also know, mine is not an unusual story. Some of you may have one like it."

"It is the story of my father's family," Zaina said in a voice that trembled with sadness. "They were Palestinians. They lost everything because of the Jews. Jewish soldiers killed my father and his father and one of my aunts, only because she tried to save them. She was a nurse and they…they..."

She buried her face in her hands.

Reginald came to stand beside her and placed a comforting arm around her shoulder. Kristin and Kjersti exchanged astonished glances; then their gaze went back to Maurice to see what he would do. They were uncharacteristically silent, awed by the gravity of the discussion.

Maurice nodded. "Yes, Jews are guilty too, especially the Jews of today, who should know better. I am sorry for what they did to your family.

"We have much in common," he added.

"No," Reginald said forcefully. "Jews have money and power, the Palestinian people do not. Even their land has been taken from them."

"That is very terrible," Maurice agreed. "To have your land stolen, the source of your livelihood, is unforgivable."

Jamal stood to face Maurice, his small body rigid with tension. "My family has suffered too. My uncle was killed and his wife and all their children."

Maurice looked down, and Laura was almost certain she saw tears in his eyes. Who was this man, and why was he doing this?

"Who killed them?" Maurice asked gently after a moment.

Jamal shook his head. "I do not know. No one knows."

"Someone who hates," Maurice said, his voice vibrating with emotion. "Hatred is the enemy, embedded in those who are unhappy enough to embrace it. Sometimes they are Jews, sometimes Muslims, or they are Christian. Hatred unites them, though they do not know it."

Parveen began to cry, aware that the people around her were sad even if she didn't understand the words. Zaina was struggling to contain tears, too.

Maurice's face filled with contrition. "Look, I have made this child weep! That is wrong, too." He wiped her eyes with his handkerchief, his big fingers gentle. "We have had enough of this gloomy conversation," he decreed. "Now we must speak of the good things that have happened to us. Let us start with Parveen. Tell us, child, what has happened recently to you that was good."

"Riding up on the train," she said immediately, her face brightening. "We have no rides like that in Pakistan."

"Did you enjoy that too, Jamal?" Maurice asked.

Jamal shuffled, uncertain still whether to trust Maurice. His curiosity about all things mechanical got the best of him. "I would like to study how the trains work," he said. "My father said he would show me."

Maurice nodded his head gravely. "You will be a fine engineer," he said. "A brave one, too, I think." Jamal smiled at him tentatively.

Maurice turned to look at Ben, the only one who had not spoken. "And you?" His deep voice was very soft, almost mesmerizing.

Suddenly there was rage in Ben's eyes. "I have nothing to say," he stated. Opening the door, he went outside.

"He is a cipher, that one," Maurice murmured. "Too old for his years."

"I will go after him," Zaina offered. "I think he has lost someone too."

"Thank you, Zaina. You are merciful to all, I believe."

Zaina glanced back at him in surprise as she went to the door. "That is what I wish to be. I am training to become a nurse."

"Excellent!" Maurice answered. *"The quality of mercy is not strained. It droppeth as the gentle rain from heaven..."* he quoted softly.

"The Merchant of Venice," Laura said. "Portia, pleading for mercy from Shylock, the Jewish moneylender."

"Yes. She was the true heroine of Shakespeare's tangled story, as young Zaina will also be one day."

"She is so beautiful," Laura said, feeling curiously chastened. She had misjudged many of these children even after knowing them for many days. Maurice had seen right through them in a matter of minutes.

"Beauty can blind one to other qualities," Maurice observed.

"Yes," Laura agreed. She stood. "I too will go out and see if Ben is all right and if the snow has stopped so we can make our way back to Murren."

She didn't provide her real reason - to see if her cell phone would pick up a signal outside. She was impressed with Maurice's ability to understand young people and wondered if that was his specialty as a psychologist. All the same, she had only his word for it that he hadn't kidnapped and drugged Veronica. That deep, sonorous voice was a pleasure to listen too, but did it tell the truth?

There was no way to know until she could check his statements. In the meantime she had to get Violet or the police here to guard Veronica.

She jiggled the phone. Still no signal. What was wrong with it?

Catherine came out, holding out her cell phone, just as Ben and Zaina walked up the path. "Mine has a signal, if you need to call about where we are or anything else," she offered.

Laura wanted to hug her but thought it might be inappropriate with Zaina and Ben watching. "Catherine, you really are a savior," she said fervently.

"Gimmelwald is only a few minutes from here," Ben told her. He looked less angry, if not happier. Laura wondered what had enraged him. Probably she should ask Maurice, she thought with a spurt of unwarranted irritation. He seemed to know everything.

Aloud she said: "That's good to hear. Thank you, Ben. You are all such a help. And while I'm on the subject of help, I would appreciate it if you three would check on the younger children while I make a phone call to let your parents know where we are. They'll be worrying."

When the door closed behind them, she punched in Violet's number. To her relief, Violet answered on the first ring.

"I found Veronica," Laura said. "She's in a summer cabin on the left about five minutes short of Gimmelwald. She's drugged but her breathing seems all right. Maurice Flambert is watching over her. I don't think he drugged her but I could be wrong. I don't want to leave her until you come."

"Unbelievable," Violet said. "No doubt you also know who *did* drug her and put her there and why."

"Not quite," Laura said, and briefly described what had happened.

"Stay where you are until I get there," Violet instructed. "I'll let the search parties know about Veronica. They'll come and get her, probably take her to hospital. I'll also commandeer snowmobiles for you and the younger children. I'm back in Murren so it shouldn't take long."

"Be sure to let the parents know the kids are all right," Laura put in.

"Will do," Violet agreed. "They're beginning to worry."

"What about Maurice?" Laura asked. "We can't very well charge him with anything without giving away our own agenda - and dragging Thomas in."

"True." Violet sighed. "This is becoming too complicated. I'll think about what's best to do while I'm chugging along."

Maurice took the matter out of their hands when he came through the door and took down his skis. "I told the children I must go to Lauterbrunnen to buy food for my daughter, who will be hungry when she wakes," he said quietly.

"To you, I give a slightly different explanation. I am aware that other plans will be made for Veronica. I am happy for that, so long as she is in safe hands. As I said, a hospital would be best, one with a guard at the door. I myself shall leave. I cannot do my work from inside a jail, if that is where the police decide to put me on suspicion of drugging her."

Laura didn't argue. She had no means of keeping him here anyway.

"We still need to talk," she reminded him. "If some of what your family lost was paintings, you may also wish to talk to the man you threatened to shoot. Who, incidentally, has never been known to use a gun, even for target practice," she added, "lest he accidentally shoot himself."

Maurice looked embarrassed. "That was a mistake. I am not skilled at thinking like a criminal. Nor am I skilled with a gun," he admitted sheepishly. "It is a good thing I did not have to use it. I too might have shot myself."

Laura tried not to laugh but failed. Maurice laughed with her.

"We are staying at the Alpina Hotel," she told him when their laughter subsided, "but you probably know that already."

"I do," he agreed, clipping on his skis. "I will contact you again. I do not know when but it will not be too long. Unless…. Well, I will do my best," he finished.

"Are you in danger?" Laura asked.

He regarded her gravely. "It is always dangerous to try to take back what one has lost," he said, "especially if it is exceedingly valuable."

"How valuable is exceedingly?" she asked.

Maurice began to slide away. "When last I checked, an undisputed Vermeer was worth about one hundred million dollars," he called back cheerfully as he gathered speed. "Think of all the good deeds one could do with that! Think, too, what a *pair* of Vermeers might fetch!"

CHAPTER TWELVE

Laura sat down abruptly on the porch step, feeling light-headed. Was she carrying the equivalent of one hundred million dollars in her battered old backpack? She never had shown the painting to Thomas. In the alarm about Veronica, she had forgotten all about it.

She jumped up again frantically. Where was her backpack? It must be in the house. Surely, she hadn't left it back at the hotel…

It was leaning against the kitchen wall. She peeked into it surreptitiously. The painting was still there, undisturbed as far as she could tell. It might be a fake, she thought, trying to reassure herself. She didn't succeed.

She raised the backpack gently onto her back, vowing not to take it off again until she had a safe to put the painting in, better yet a vault.

Shoulders tense, she went into the bedroom to make sure Veronica was all right. Catherine followed her. She sent Laura a quizzical look as they bent over Veronica, who was breathing normally. "You okay?"

Laura nodded. "Just a bit frazzled."

"Sorry to frazzle you even more, but your phone didn't work because it had been disabled," Catherine said quietly. "Not sure what they did to it, but it sure was dead."

Laura stared at her. "You mean someone disabled it on purpose?"

"Seems like it," Catherine replied. "I think I've fixed it, but you might have to get a new one. Whatever, you'd better keep it with you from now on. Have you left it in the room recently or maybe in your pack where someone could get at it?"

"Probably," Laura answered glumly. She wasn't used to being sabotaged. At least it hadn't been in her pack at the same time as the painting. It had been in her pocket. So whoever disabled it had done it earlier – which meant almost anyone could have done it.

Another shock awaited them when they got back to the hotel. Their rooms had been searched, carefully, methodically, thoroughly. The room Thomas was in had been searched too, while he was downstairs.

"A professional job," Violet said glumly. "I think they were looking for something specific, not just for information about us."

Laura sat down abruptly. "The painting," she breathed. "They might have been looking for the painting." Sliding it out of her pack, she handed it to Thomas. His jaw quite literally dropped, she noted, when he took it out of the protective sheath. She had never seen that happen before.

"What is it?" Violet asked.

Thomas took a steadying breath. "It looks like a Vermeer," he said, "but that doesn't mean it is. He almost never signed his paintings, which makes identification difficult. All the certified Vermeers are in museums, but the historical records describe up to ten paintings that are missing. Rumors that the Nazis – even Hitler himself - stole or bought some of them and stashed them away in Switzerland have been around for a long time.

Violet looked impressed. "We had better find a bank vault and take Gustav and a few other guards with us when we deliver it!"

170

"The banks have already closed for the day," Laura said nervously. "We'll have to think of a good hiding place for tonight."

She shuddered. "It's a good thing I forgot to give it to you earlier, Thomas. What do you suppose would have happened if it had been in the room?"

"I prefer not to think about it at all," Thomas stated flatly. He pulled himself to his feet. "We've got to go back to the shelter right away, while the door is still open. If Maurice really did have a pair, the second one could still be in there. We might never get this chance again."

"Already closed and locked," Violet said. "The police had it closed as a crime scene soon after we left. But Gustav knows the farmer who owns the barn and he'll let us in again in the morning."

"Someone else might persuade – or bribe - the farmer to open up before we get there," Thomas warned. "I never did find out why the door was open when we first got there, but it implies that other people can open it."

"Maybe the person I saw in the shelter when Violet and I were there earlier opened it," Laura said, and described the shadowy person she had seen when she went to intercept Felicia. "If so, he or she could get in again."

"Do you have any idea who this shadowy person is?" Violet asked.

Laura shook her head. "I didn't use my flashlight, so all I saw was a shadowy form against the wall. It went into the next room, but I couldn't follow it because just then Felicia came up behind me. I think she'd been in the shelter for quite a while before she called to us, which means she could have seen the person too. She could also have heard us talking about the painting or even seen it. For that matter, so could the other person."

"Your shadow person might not have had time to get out again before the police locked up," Thomas noted. "If so, he or she might try to sneak out when no one is watching."

"Gustav is watching," Violet said with a satisfied smile. "He is in the woods across from the shelter, and he will let us know immediately if anyone tries to go in our out. In the meantime, we will be watching the delegates here. They have all been invited to gather on the sundeck for drinks at six o'clock – on hand-painted cards created by one of the staff members, no less. The recent meetings have been fractious, to put it mildly, and the party is an attempt to bond. It also provides us with a perfect opportunity to see who comes, who is absent and if anyone leaves."

"Do I detect your devious mind behind the party?" Laura asked.

Violet grinned. "Perhaps." She glanced at her watch. "We have half an hour before it starts and I'd like to catch you up on some of the information I've received. First, no sign of your briefcase or computer, Thomas. Second, Rosa's sister. No surprises, just that she thinks Max used Rosa and that Rosa had been nervous recently. She has no ideas about who killed her. She knows Veronica too. Likes her, but worried that she's keeping bad company. We may be able to find out more tomorrow at Rosa's funeral in Lauterbrunnen.

"The reports on Henri Guillard are more interesting. First, he runs an import-export business that has warehouses all over the world. That puts him in a great position to peddle drugs, legal and counterfeit, and art - and to fiddle with orders. The gun report is helpful, too. He was shot with a high-powered rifle that takes an experienced hunter to shoot accurately, but not necessarily an expert. Henri may also have been killed earlier and somehow brought to the slope. Quite a trick, if it's true."

"That would explain why there's no hole in the hat," Laura commented.

"What hat?" Thomas was baffled. "And who's Henri Guillard? And Rosa?"

Laura laughed. "I forgot you don't know any of this. Rosa is – was – the woman I saw out the train window. I told you about her. She was killed soon after that. And the hat belonged to Henri Guillard, a really nasty man who knocked me over when his body slid into me. It was a very steep slope."

Thomas put his head in his hands. "Do you ever go anywhere without running into dead bodies?" he asked rhetorically.

"I didn't run into Henri – he fell into me," Laura noted, and launched into the rest of the story from the time she had seen Thomas in the train until he found them in the shelter.

"Speaking of the train," Violet added, "no one knows why it stopped. Nor do they know anything about the boxes, only that a man loaded quite a few boxes into the train in Interlaken that subsequently disappeared.

"Now, let's have a quick look in the boxes we brought from the shelter before we leave for the party."

She knelt down and pulled them out from under the bed. "Not the greatest hiding place, but the best I could do on short notice."

"Definitely not a great hiding place if we find another painting like this one," Thomas commented wryly. His eyes roved around the room. "Sometimes the best hiding place is the most obvious one."

He looked carefully at the framed prints of stiffly conventional roses that hung over each bed. "About the right size," he said. Lifting one of them down, he took out a sharp penknife and neatly sliced off the backing. He removed the flower print, laid the suspected Vermeer, sans frame, behind it, and put both of them back against the glass, flower print showing. Reattaching the backing with a few drops from a tube he found among the jumble of objects in his pocket, he hung the print back on the wall over Laura's bed.

"That should do until we find a more reliable place," he said, regarding it with satisfaction. Laura wasn't so sure. The idea of sleeping with a hundred million dollars over her head was just as daunting as carrying it on her back.

Violet was already examining the contents of the boxes. "Let's take a look at this," she said, "or rather a taste." Opening one of the re-hydration packets, she stuck in a damp finger and tasted the powder delicately.

"Re-hydration powder tastes sweet, and this doesn't," she commented.

Laura did the same. Her lips puckered in distaste. "Ghastly stuff," she said. "Could it be cocaine?"

"I don't think so," Violet answered, "but I am no expert. I'll send it to the lab tomorrow for analysis."

"Let me try," Thomas said, pressing some powder against his lips. "I don't think it's cocaine either," he pronounced. "That makes your lips feel numb and this doesn't. I wonder if it could be a different medication, maybe a more expensive one that could be sold for even bigger profits."

Laura decided not to ask how he knew so much about cocaine. He grinned at her. "No," he said. "I'm not an expert, either."

The door opened and Catherine came in. "What's that?" she asked taking note of the granules on her father's hand. "Are you three snorting coke? If you are, can I join the party?"

"We are *not* snorting coke," Thomas said sternly.

Uncowed, Catherine helped herself to some of the grains. "Not coke," she said positively after tasting it carefully.

"How do you know?" Thomas asked, his voice dangerously quiet.

Catherine looked at him scornfully. "If you think anyone can go through high school without knowing that stuff, you are more out of it than I thought you were. Why do you think I left? The kids were either drunk or stoned half the time. Not exactly a healthy environment."

"Any idea what it is?" Violet asked.

"Probably one of the designer drugs," Catherine decreed. "But it could be an explosive, considering how many terrorists are hanging around. Or maybe that stuff you need for nuclear bombs? You know – uranium?"

Laura was horrified. "Are you joking?" she asked.

"Look!" Violet had pulled something else out from beneath the bed, a small machine that looked like a tiny tape recorder.

Laura stared. "What is it?"

"A listening device," Violet said. "Quite a sophisticated one. Now who would put that there?"

"Lindsey?" Laura speculated. "Catherine said she was with the C.I. A. If I was a C.I.A. agent, I would investigate us. Or try."

"I'd say the person who did the search put it there," Thomas commented.

They were interrupted by a knock on the door. Laura went to see who it was and found Sigrid. "May I come in?" she asked politely. Her eyes moved from one face to the next, seeming to see right through each of them; then she took in the packet of tiny white granules, their powder-whitened fingers and palms, the open boxes of medications and the small device in Violet's hand.

That look could make any miscreant nervous, Laura thought - or anyone who was trying to hide something – like them. She needn't have worried. Sigrid's sense of humor was well-developed.

"It needs only a glance to confirm that my suspicion was right," she said with a chuckle. "Something is very wrong with *this* picture, so I hesitate to imagine what is wrong with the conference."

Always the gentleman, Thomas made an effort to stand when Laura introduced him. Sigrid waved him down again. "You had a skiing accident, I am told," she said, eyeing the bandages around his chest and shoulder skeptically. "That is an unusual place for a skiing injury.

"I wished to speak to Violet or Laura," Sigrid continued, "but I can come back later." Laura and Violet exchanged a glance of tacit agreement.

"You can speak freely to all of us if that's all right with you," Laura said. "Thomas and Catherine are old friends."

Sigrid nodded, and her face became serious. "Then I shall be blunt. I am aware that something is very wrong about this conference and I would like to know what it is. From what I see here – she gestured at the medications and the listening device, I suspect that it could involve drug trafficking. I also think that Laura and Violet are not here just for a holiday."

"You're right. Something is wrong at this conference," Laura agreed. "We are here to find out what it is. As for me, I am who I said I was – a professor of gender studies in the U.S., but I am also here to help Violet."

Violet took up the explanation. "My sister really did organize our housing and travel," she began, "but I am also a detective who specializes in protecting children. I was asked to attend the conference because vague threats had been made against the children who came here with their parents, so we arranged to have them protected. We now believe the real purpose of the threats was to prevent the conference from taking place at all. At this point, they seem aimed at disrupting the proceedings more than harming the children. However, we continue to watch them carefully, with Laura's help. I also recruited Gustav, the man who brought you back here. He has experience in detection as well as medical matters."

"Thank you," Sigrid said. "Gustav's appearance at just the right moment did seem too fortunate to be mere coincidence. But have you any idea who is responsible for the threats, or the illegal drug activity?"

"We're overwhelmed with ideas, but we haven't pinned pin down the criminals," Violet replied honestly. "Your help will be much appreciated."

Sigrid nodded. "Yes, I can see that. So many people at the conference seem to have motives that are not related to the subject matter."

She turned to Thomas. "And your role?"

Thomas, usually able to rise to any occasion, for once looked stumped. Maybe his injuries were slowing down his brain, Laura speculated. Or maybe he just didn't know how to explain his relationship with her. She wasn't sure how to explain it either.

"Thomas is Catherine's father," she explained, coming to his rescue. "She calls him an art detective. We worked together last year when I inadvertently became embroiled in a mystery in England that involved counterfeit paintings, which is his field. We were rather at cross purposes for a time. That is, I thought he was the villain and he thought I was."

Sigrid's eyes twinkled. "I can see the difficulty, though you seem to have straightened it out.

"Yup," Catherine said. "With my help. Someone had to stop them from arguing all the time. It was like they were on stage."

"We were, in that old manor house," Thomas agreed. "So was everyone else." He turned to Sigrid. "I came here because I realized that the case I am working on, which involves art stolen by the Nazis, is connected to the case Violet and Laura are working on. I had something of a mishap along the way."

"Ah - the skiing accident," Sigrid said with a straight face.

"Well, not exactly," Catherine said. "But it's awfully complicated, and this stuff" - she regarded her finger critically – "complicates it even more."

"I image it does," Sigrid said with a laugh. "All of you seem to lead an adventurous life," she added with what sounded like a touch of envy.

"That's what so great about it," Catherine enthused. "When Laura and my Dad get together, sparks fly and so do murders. They seem to attract them. I don't know what it is about them."

"I can see I have a lot to catch up on," Sigrid said dryly. "I had no idea art was involved and certainly not cocaine, if that's what it is. But let me tell you what I have noticed among the conference participants, and some of the people who work here. Perhaps it will help.

"First, I am interested in what Violet said about disrupting the conference. I believe some participants are doing just that. Ann is one, as you know, the American delegate is another. Karl may be a third. He is a good moderator normally, but in this case his efforts seem designed to stir up discord, so that we cannot move on. I do not think that is accidental."

"I noticed at the first meeting that there's an undercurrent of tension in this group that has little to do with girls' education," Laura put in.

"So much tension we cannot think well," Sigrid said. "It is as if all the delegates are tangled up with one another in ways I cannot understand. They may also be spying on one another – or someone else is, perhaps someone they have hired. Kristin and Kjersti have become acquainted with some of the girls who work here, and they joke about how they are spying on delegates. It is like a game they are playing. One of the girls - I think she's called Nina - boasts about how good she is at spying on people without being seen."

"That's the girl who was listening at our door," Violet contributed.

"Yes," Sigrid agreed. "I have noticed her loitering outside people's doors.

"I wonder if Karl started the game," she added. "He is clever at using people – especially girls. As for women, he goes after first one, then another, so that they too turn against each other. I saw him with Amina recently, and he was acting just as he had with Ann. I am sure he has made a conquest of Ann, so he turns to the next, and Ann is angry. So is Makedu."

"And Amina?" Violet asked.

"She seems uncertain how to stop him. She is young, and young women in Africa are expected to be submissive or at least polite to older men. Perhaps she has not yet found a strong voice."

Laura sighed. Girls were expected to do what older men told them to do, which was why so many were raped by their teachers. She was surprised, though, that Amina retained such inhibitions, with Makedu as a mother.

"I imagine Makedu will correct that without delay," she said. "If I were Karl, I would back off quickly. An angry Makedu sounds formidable."

"I wouldn't want to face her," Catherine said fervently.

Makedu's enraged voice in the hall seemed perfectly timed to corroborate her words. "That was unforgivable!" she screamed. "How could you do such a cruel thing to her?"

Sigrid yanked the door open and they ran into the hall. Makedu was holding Karl by the shoulders and shaking him forcibly. Beside her, Amina moaned, a low animal sound that was pitiable in its distress.

"Look what he has done!" she cried, holding up her magnificent robe so they could all see. It had been slashed from top to bottom, as if someone had taken scissors or a knife and cut through the fabric with vicious swipes.

Amina collapsed on the floor, holding the robe to her face. "My beautiful robe that was given to me by my parents when I finished my studies," she sobbed. "No one can make it right again." Sigrid went to her and took her in her arms, crooning to her as if she were a child.

"I did not do this!" Karl protested scornfully. "I would not."

"Then why were you in our room?" Makedu demanded, shaking him again. The power of her anger drained the blood from his face. "What were you doing in our room?" she repeated, her vice a low growl now.

Karl wrenched away from her and strode furiously down the hall. Laura saw that despite his effort at self-control, he was trembling.

Makedu looked after him, her eyes narrowed, her face thoughtful. "He did not do the cutting," she said after a moment. "I know who is the real culprit, but that does not mean Karl is not involved."

She helped Amina to her feet. "Now we must see what can be done to fix this terrible damage," she told her in a practical tone. "Perhaps we could stitch the edges together, so the robe has many seams and thus floats like the wings of a bird." Murmuring about repairs, she led Amina into their room.

"I must go to Kjersti and Kristin," Sigrid said soberly when the door closed behind them. "Such a vicious act will upset them badly."

"Ann?" Violet asked when they were back in their own room.

"Probably," Laura agreed. "I suspect she can be vindictive and she may be jealous as well."

"That was an unexpected development," Violet said thoughtfully. She looked at her watch again. "Let's clear up here as best we can, and then it will be time for the drinks party. I imagine Amina and Makedu will be late, but they will come. Makedu will be watching for the guilty person as a lion watches for its prey. Amina will be there too, to save face and to watch with her mother, and perhaps to seek revenge. In her own way, she is just as formidable. Karl will be there, too, to regain his dignity in their presence."

Violet nodded her head, more to herself than to any of them. "Yes," she said, "I believe this could be a very interesting party. Someone is becoming ever more desperate to get us out of the way."

CHAPTER THIRTEEN

Thomas elected to stay in the room during the party, fearful of leaving the painting unattended. Instead, he planned to watch from the window, which overlooked the sundeck – so named because it faced the afternoon sun and had heat lamps that allowed guests to linger even after the warmth had gone.

Karl was pacing restlessly with his fingers tightly clasped behind his back when Laura and Violet arrived. He didn't see them at first and kept on striding back and forth along the deck. Laura watched as he thrust out his square jaw aggressively while his lips moved to express an unspoken thought, then closed it with an audible snap as if to prevent the words from ever emerging.

She wondered again what he had been doing in Makedu and Amina's room. A listening device there too perhaps?

She shook her head. Karl would get someone else to do his dirty work. He liked to keep his perfectly manicured hands clean - which made his presence in the African women's room even more puzzling. It also meant that he probably hadn't killed Henri Guillard or Ludwig, which was a shame. He would make a good villain.

"Good evening, Karl," Violet said, and he turned sharply to face them. He didn't offer a handshake as he usually did, and Laura wondered if his hands were still shaking too hard. Uttering a few perfunctory words of welcome, he made a visible effort to regain his normal cheerful and in-charge expression. He didn't succeed. His jaw was still too tight.

Squeals of delight came from the nearby playground as Parveen careened down a siding board into the safety of her father's arms. Jamal sat on a swing, kicking his legs valiantly in a futile effort to make it move. Seeing his dilemma, Catherine demonstrated the mechanics of pumping. Then she pushed him until he had enough momentum to pump for himself. His face lit up with delight at what was apparently a new skill for him.

"I'll watch the children for a while," Catherine offered when Jamal was well launched.

"Thank you, Catherine," Hassan said, and came to join Eileen, who was chatting with Laura and Sigrid.

"The children cannot play like that in Pakistan," Eileen said wistfully. "They must be watched carefully all the time, so they don't learn to pump swings or ride bicycles the way American children do."

"Security?" Laura asked.

Hassan nodded. "It has been worse recently," he admitted. "There have been some kidnappings, and even paying the ransom money does not guarantee the children's safety."

"It's hard for me to imagine," Laura said. "Would it be better, do you think, if the Americans weren't involved?"

Hassan considered. "People for whom violence has become a way of life would probably find other reasons to carry out kidnappings and bombings if the Americans were not there. Education is the only answer, especially for girls, and a way for women to make some money. My colleagues and I have built twenty schools for girls and women and we are building more. They have been very successful but we must often keep them secret."

"But it is not just the violence," Eileen said. "It is a very different culture. Maids and dogs are examples. The children are served, their clothes picked up, and no matter how many times I tell them it is their job to care for themselves, they become accustomed to service. I would like them to have a dog too, but in Pakistan dogs are considered vermin, not to be touched. The maids say that dogs like to eat small children, so they are terrified of them."

She stopped, embarrassed by her outburst. "I should not complain about these problems, which are not serious compared to safety," she apologized. She smiled sheepishly. "It is because you are American," she told Laura. "Only an American can really understand what I mean about maids and dogs."

Laura laughed. "I do. I will say, though, that my children never had maids but they still dropped their clothes on the floor."

"Mine, too," Sigrid admitted, with a rueful glance at the twins.

Kjersti and Kristin smiled half-heartedly, but Laura could see that they were still upset by what had been done to Amina's robe. Their faces cleared when they saw Parveen and Jamal in the playground. "We'll help!" they cried, and ran to join them. They alternated between helping Catherine push and catch the younger children, and playing on the equipment themselves. They were like a pair of monkeys, climbing and swinging and sliding fearlessly, with no sign of self-consciousness.

"That is just what they needed," Sigrid said. "They have had to deal with problems they never encountered before in Switzerland, and they are growing up fast.

When that happens, it is good to play again like a child."

"They are so fearless, so agile," Eileen said, and they all heard the longing in her voice. "I wonder if my two will ever be like that?"

"Yes," Hassan said, taking her hand. "We must think very hard about how to accomplish that."

Laura wanted to find out what he meant, but the arrival of Dr. Nezam and Ben interrupted the discussion. Not much of a relationship there, Laura thought as she watched Ben shy away in distaste when his father accidentally bumped his arm. Dr. Nezam froze and pointedly moved a few steps away. Laura could almost feel the wall between father and son, and wondered what caused it. It seemed important suddenly to know, as if it held a vital clue to whatever was going on at this conference.

Hassan followed Dr. Nezam and asked him a question Laura couldn't hear. Dr. Nezam answered readily, but the expression on his face didn't change. He was like a poker player. Perhaps people in that part of the world had to be. The point of the game was to hide one's real goals by pretending to have opposite ones, even as the player gained full knowledge of what was in an opponent's mind – and hand.

Ann bustled in, looking officious and pleased with herself. She went straight to Karl, said something privately to him, and then moved away again, her face flushed. Reginald stayed at her side, almost as if he were attached with an invisible cord.

Another dysfunctional parent/child relationship, Laura mused. Ann clearly doted on her son, but what did Reginald think of his mother? Probably a mix of emotions – embarrassment, disdain, grudging affection or at least caring, but love? She thought not. So why was he always with her?

Karl had regained his composure and was circulating, handing out glasses of wine and soft drinks to the delegates, with a pleasant word to each. The talk became general, and it seemed to Laura that people were having a good time. She heard laughter, joking and cheerful dialogue instead of the rancorous diatribes Sigrid had described in the meetings. Maybe the party would turn out to be a bonding experience after all.

Karl had just handed a glass of red wine to Ann when Amina made her entrance. There was a low dais at one end of the sundeck for musicians, and Amina mounted it, slowly, majestically. She wore her damaged robe, and she had elected to wear it exactly as she had found it after it had been so viciously slashed. Beneath the robe she wore skin-tight pants and top in a vivid shade of deep red. The effect was electrifying. Each time she moved, the red tights became blood smeared on her legs and thighs, her breasts and belly, and the jagged slits in her robe turned into gaping wounds that shouted their presence and could not be ignored.

All conversation ceased as the delegates watched her, mesmerized by her tall, commanding presence and the desecrated robe. Back and forth Amina paraded, head high, spine straight, as imperturbable as the queen she played in this drama. Makedu, dressed all in black, her face covered by a black veil, walked behind her daughter, head bowed in sorrow and grief.

The sound of shattering glass broke the silence, as loud as an explosion. The glass had dropped from Ann's hand, and wine the color of blood spread out across the deck.

Someone gasped; then there was silence again, as if they were all frozen in place, barely able to breathe. Laura tried to think, to move, perhaps get a napkin to mop up the wine, but it had already soaked into the wood. All she could do was look, see what was in the faces. Shock mostly, and then a slow realization. One at a time, all the heads turned toward Ann. Oblivious of their scrutiny, she gazed steadily at Amina. For an instant, there was an expression of utter satisfaction on Ann's face.

Reginald suddenly moved a few steps away from his mother. His eyes went to her, then to Amina's robe, then back to his mother. Four times they went back and forth. Then he turned sharply and almost ran into the street. Laura thought she could feel something snap inside him, and the pain that went with it. A bond had broken, leaving behind it an aching hurt. She looked for Zaina, hoping she would go after Reginald and comfort him, but Zaina wasn't there. Dashka wasn't either. Where were they?

Ben went instead. He ran lightly after Reginald and walked beside him, close enough to make it clear that he was there if he was needed, but not so close that he intruded. No one else moved.

A discordant voice broke the spell. "Ah'm so sorry, folks, just forgot the time down they-ah, didn't I? Couldn't pull my old self away from all those delectable shops, with all those goodies..."

The distinctive drawl stopped suddenly as Lindsey recognized that the silence around her was unnatural. "Oh my," she said with religious fervor. "Ah think the

Good Lord is tellin' us somethin', ah really do!" Her eyes scanned the faces, then came to rest on Amina's robe. "Oh, my!" she said again.

Abruptly, everyone moved at once, a few steps to relieve the tension, but still no one spoke. Ann started toward the street as if to call Reginald back, but he was already out of sight. She shrugged and turned to Karl. Irritation was clear on her face.

"Boys can be impossible!" she complained loudly. "Reginald never tells me anything any more and he just disappears all the time." Laura thought she was about to stamp her foot, like a petulant child.

All eyes turned to her again, shocked anew at her total lack of perception. Didn't she know that slashing Amina's gown was a despicable act, that Reginald had left because he believed she had committed that act? But if she didn't know, why had she dropped her glass?

A shrill scream of panic broke into Laura's thoughts. A dog, a huge St. Bernard, had broken free from its leash and gamboled into the playground. It headed straight for Parveen. She screamed again and again, insistent high-pitched shrieks that seemed impossibly loud, coming from so small a child. She stood petrified, still screeching in terror as the enormous animal galloped toward her. Eileen and Hassan leaped up, but they were too far away to reach her in time.

Catherine sprinted across the playground, but Jamal got to Parveen before her. His face bleached of color, he stood in front of his sister. The dog leaped at him playfully and knocked him over. Then it placed a huge paw on Parveen's shoulder and licked her face, knocking her over too in the process. She fell like a rag doll, as if terror had robbed her body of substance.

Catherine pulled the St. Bernard away, handed the remains of its leash to Kristin and Kjersti, and knelt beside the children. Parveen was silent now, so frightened she seemed unable to breathe. Murmuring a soothing flow of words, Catherine rocked her like a baby with one arm while holding Jamal with the other. Tears were running down his face, of mortification that he had not kept the dog away from his sister, that he too was horribly afraid.

Hassan arrived and gathered the boy into his arms. Still murmuring soothing words, Catherine handed Parveen to her mother. The child had relapsed now into gulping sobs, but at least she was breathing again.

Energized by the excitement, the dog was impossible to hold. The twins were straining, and Sigrid ran to help, with Violet and Laura behind her. The dog's handler, a ski patrol member, finally came too.

"I am so sorry," he said, grabbing the dog's collar. "I was training the dog and then it dashed away. I do not know how it could do that. The leash is very strong."

Sigrid, who had been examining the leash, held up one end of it. "The leash has been cut," she said flatly to Laura and Violet. "Someone cut the leash almost all the way through. That is why it snapped."

****

The day's traumas were not over. Thomas had left the room briefly to get some food from the ever-willing kitchen staff, who adored the injured hero – the role he was currently playing for their benefit. Laura wondered what he had told them but dared not ask. It would probably be outrageous.

He had taken the flower cum Vermeer painting with him, just in case, as he put it. His caution was rewarded. When he returned, he found boxes scattered all over the floor, emptied of medications. Fortunately, Violet had secreted the ones she wanted to send for testing in the big purse that was always with her. The second painting had disappeared, too, and someone had rummaged through all their belongings, even through the bedding.

Thomas had also seen Lindsey while he was getting food. "She was in the hotel all during the party," Thomas said, "and I'd like to know why she didn't go down until she made that appearance right at the end."

"She told us she had been in Lauterbrunnen. *Couldn't pull my old self away from all those delectable shops,*" Catherine said in a fair imitation of Lindsey's drawl. "I wonder what she was really doing all that time? Searching the room?"

"It could have been someone else," Violet pointed out. "Any of the people at the party could have gone inside while we were in the playground. No one would have noticed with all that drama."

"True," Laura agreed, "but Lindsey definitely has some explaining to do. She sounds more and more like the person who searched our rooms, which suggests she really is a spy – but a spy for who?"

Thomas had more revelations. "My view from the window produced another intriguing piece of evidence," he told them. "I saw the man who works at the desk here chatting with a ski patrol member with a big St. Bernard on a leash. He really seemed to like the dog. He was bent over him for the longest time, practically slobbering over him. I assumed that he just found dogs irresistible, but now I wonder."

"I also wonder if he overheard Eileen saying the children were terrified of dogs," Violet commented. "Someone must have, and he's a good candidate. Seems to me he was on the deck earlier, helping with drinks and food. I'll see what I can find out about his background."

Catherine shuddered. "Targeting children like that is horrible!"

"It is," Violet agreed. "I have already been to see Eileen and Hassan to tell them what we're doing here and that it might be better for them to take Jamal and Parveen away. I felt I had to after the attack. I just can't guarantee the children's safety any more."

She sounded discouraged and angry, and Laura wished she could speed up the investigation. Getting information about Lindsey would be a start. Both she had Violet had sent queries to people who might know more about her but so far no replies had arrived. Not surprising, Laura realized. She had only sent the messages a few hours ago. It seemed much longer. A year's worth of shocks had been crammed into today.

And now Thomas, improbably, was teasing her by making what she termed *come hither* signals under the table. She felt his hand on her knee, rubbing gently, and he batted his eyelashes – longer than any man's should be – at her in a way that he probably thought no one else would decipher.

He was wrong. "Dad! You're still wounded," Catherine reminded him. "If you do anything *active* – she stressed the word active – you'll open up those wounds and bleed all over the furniture."

He grinned at her, unembarrassed. "You're a hard minder," he told her, referring to their standing joke that he needed her to look after him.

Laura glared at him and hoped she wasn't blushing. Granted, it had been a long time, but this was not the moment even without his wounds.

"Have you forgotten that you fainted this morning?" she asked severely.

Thomas grimaced. "No, unfortunately I haven't," he said mournfully. "I just wanted to remind you of my eternal undying devotion. *Your beauty stuns the eye and warms the heart,*" he declaimed as if he were on stage.

"I just made that up," he added with a grin.

Catherine laughed. Laura maintained her glare until Violet laughed too, and then she gave in to the smile that was twitching at her lips.

"Well, I lightened the atmosphere, didn't I?" Thomas said. "All of you looked glum after that debacle on the sundeck, so I thought we could do with a laugh. As Shakespeare's fool said – what was it, Laura? I've forgotten."

"Better a witty fool than a foolish wit", Laura quoted with a smirk. It wasn't exactly the quote he meant, but it did seem apt.

Thomas raised an eyebrow. "Here's another," he said. *"A fool thinks himself to be wise, but a wise man knows himself to be a fool."*

Laura was astonished. He must be reading up on his Shakespeare. Probably so she couldn't have the last word, or quote, if that was what they were arguing about. Bantering was a better word, she decided.

"Oh what fools we mortals be," she countered.

Thomas frowned. "Doesn't sound quite right. I shall have to look it up in that handy quote book I've taken to carrying around with me." That produced another round of laughter; then they separated to get ready for bed.

Violet's mood changed back to grim as she tried to think what to do next. "I expected something unusual and hopefully revealing to happen at the party that would give me a sense of direction, but it didn't," she said disconsolately. "All it did was terrify two innocent children. If I had known how ghastly it would be, I would have called the whole thing off."

"I thought I detected your hand behind the party," Laura said, concealing a smile. "And we did learn something - that the desk clerk could be a suspect; Lindsey too, and that Ann may be even nuttier than we'd thought.

"You shouldn't blame yourself, either," she added. "You couldn't have known then about Amina's robe, or an over-friendly loose St. Bernard whose leash had been cut."

"No," Violet agreed, "but it is still my responsibility. Somehow, I've got to set things right again. That's harder than ever since almost everyone at the conference probably knows who I am and what we're here for by now."

"Call a meeting," Laura suggested. "Or make a surprise appearance and announce that you are a detective when the delegates gather in the morning. Some people know that already and the conference is in shambles anyway, so why not? I'll watch faces. We might learn something from them."

"You may be right," Violet agreed. "We have a good idea of what's going on, and we even have some idea why. It's the location, not the subject matter. Now what we need to do is tease out who is doing it, and why."

"It could be both," Laura suggested sleepily. "Some delegates may object to the idea of educating girls, at least in those places, and some of them are stashing drugs and art nearby and want us gone."

Violet sat up in bed, looking astonished. "Of course! That's it. I've been trying to put all the incidents into one package and there could be up to three groups involved - one for paintings, one for drugs, one for fundamentalism and sheer obstinacy about women's place in this world. Maybe one group doesn't know what the other is doing. Or maybe one person is manipulating two sets of criminals for another unrelated reason."

"Sounds extremely complicated," Laura answered. "It could also get very dangerous – which might explain why Henri and Ludwig were killed – probably Rosa too."

"But so far, no one from the conference has been killed," Violet observed thoughtfully. "Just pushed over a cliff, clothes slashed, or children terrified out of their wits. Nasty but not lethal."

Laura yawned. "I'd like to nail the nasty ones, but we should probably go after the lethal group first. Maybe your announcement will smoke them out."

"Or frighten them away," Violet answered. "That's the problem. It isn't easy to tell people who are guilty of murder – or anything else - what you're up to without scaring them away. That may prevent further violence, but it doesn't tell us what's going on."

"Look at the bright side," Laura ventured as she closed her eyes. "Maybe each of the groups will do the job for us by telling us about the nefarious activities the other criminals are engaged in. It's a great way to divert attention from their own even worse pursuits."

Her words proved to be prescient.

CHAPTER FOURTEEN

The day started off at a furious clip. A knock on the door aroused them half way through Laura's morning wake-up tea. Eileen stood there.

"I will be quick," she said. "First, Hassan and I are grateful to you, Violet, for confiding in us. You and Laura, Catherine too, have helped us to come to a decision we have been pondering for months, that the time has come to leave Pakistan. Our children's safety is more important to us than anything else. I am leaving with Parveen and Jamal today for the U.S.. Hassan will follow as soon as he can turn over his duties to the man who assists him, a man he trusts. The schools will be left in good hands."

She smiled and held out her hands. "So, I have come to say goodbye." She hugged each of them, and then hurried off to pack.

Laura was genuinely sorry to see them go, but her major feeing was relief that Jamal and Parveen would no longer be targets for people who felt no compunction about hurting the most vulnerable members of the group. Who in this normal seeming group was that cruel? And who would be next?

Not Kjersti and Kristin at least, she learned when Sigrid informed them that her husband was flying to Switzerland tomorrow to ski with them so they could both watch the girls. "I am concerned for them," she said simply. I think it is better if they are kept busy with us for the rest of the conference."

Laura hoped that tomorrow was soon enough. She felt as if a hurricane was brewing, and she was waiting for its violent resolution. She scanned the faces in the breakfast room and thought they all felt the same anxiety. Some menace they couldn't name was all around them, and they felt helpless to defray it.

Their next visitor was Helga Braun. She beckoned Laura and Violet into a small meeting room for a final cup of coffee. She got right to the point.

"First, I wish to thank Laura for finding Veronica. We were very afraid for her. We had looked in Gimmelwald but had not found her.

"I have been to the hospital to see her," she continued. "She told me that she had decided to go away for a few days to think. A man came up behind her and dragged her into a car as she walked to a hotel in Bern, where she had booked a room. From then on, she was kept sedated. She says she didn't know her captor and probably cannot identify him since she was always drugged.

Helga shook her head sadly. "Max and Veronica have had a hard life. Their mother died when Max was born. Their father remarried but then he was killed in a car crash. Many people, including Veronica, think his death was not an accident, that he was killed because he fought political corruption. Veronica was also sure that Henri had been involved in her father's death. She decided to investigate him any way she could. Max did not agree. Henri had befriended him and Max may have seen him as an influential man who could be helpful. At the same time, Max was afraid for Veronica and kept trying to convince her to leave the whole thing alone. In retrospect, he was right."

She looked down at her hands, a way of hiding the sadness that had come into her eyes, Laura thought. "Nicolas tried to dissuade her too," Helga went on. "He and Veronica have loved each other since they were children. They planned to marry. Nicolas begged her not to become involved with Henri, but Veronica is as determined as her father to fight for what is right. Nicolas is very sensitive and can be emotional. I think he had not realized how... how *fierce* Veronica can be when she takes on a cause. Perhaps he should not have..."

She stopped abruptly. Someone else had stopped in the middle of a sentence about Nicolas, Laura recalled. Felicia, perhaps, or Maurice?

"Well, that is not important," Helga resumed quickly. Laura's curiosity about Nicolas grew. Was it possible that he had inflicted that bruise?

Her eyes met Violet's. Time to find out more about Nicolas. He was clearly over-sensitive, but what else?

They had to find out more about Max, too. How close had the relationship between him and Henri been? Close enough for Max to work for Henri?

"I thought that knowing more about Max and Veronica's background might help your investigations," Helga said, sounding composed and in control again. "I may also be able to provide a few insights about the delegates I know."

She smiled faintly. "Yes, Hans did imply that you were here not just for the skiing, a secret that is safe with Ernst and me."

"What about Ann Lawrence?" Laura asked. "She is not easy to work with, or to like."

"She is disturbed," Helga said immediately. "We all sense it, especially Reginald, though he never says anything. It is hard to know what to do."

"Disturbed in what way?" Violet asked. "Do you think she would kill?"

Helga hesitated. "I don't know," she said slowly. "And I hope we never have the opportunity to find out."

An interesting statement, Laura thought. Intentionally or not, it implied that Ann had not killed *yet*, which meant she probably hadn't shot Henri or Ludwig. Why would she, anyway? And could she? Ann seemed too undisciplined, almost childish in many ways.

"Who do you think shot Henri?" she asked impulsively. "Could Karl have done it? Was he involved with Henri?"

Helga's lips tightened, and Laura sensed that she didn't want to answer the question. "Karl could have been involved with Henri," she replied finally. "He is both arrogant and greedy, essential traits for working with Henri. But I do not think he shot him. He seems to me to lack the nerve.

"As for the others, the Indian delegate, Dashka, seems sincere, but from time to time I sense unease in her. I cannot think it is easy to represent India. Too much money changes hands without being accounted for in that country, which makes her vulnerable."

Another fascinating comment, Laura thought. Dashka, too, was deserving of scrutiny. Where was she? She hadn't come down to breakfast, or to dinner last night. That was odd. Dashka always came to meals. She liked her food. Zaina had been there, though, sitting with Reginald and Ben.

"Rosa?" Violet asked. "Did you know her?"

"Only a little," Helga replied, "but one hears things from time to time. I am told she did not have good judgment in her choice of men."

"What did Max want of her?" Violet asked bluntly.

"I wish I knew," Helga replied. "Women fall in love with Max, and he knows it and probably uses it. But Rosa was all wrong for him, so he must have had some other reason to cultivate her. I think it had to do with her job, but I am not sure. I have never known him to do that before -"

She broke off, frowning. "I wonder if I am wrong, and Max was trying to protect Veronica by finding something that would implicate Henri," she said slowly. "If he did that, he might stop her from investigating and putting her life in danger. Max is younger than his sister, but he feels very protective of her."

"Max hides his feelings well," she added, "but they are there."

A very different and more complex picture of Max, too, Laura thought. The more she heard of him, the less he sounded like a villain.

"Have you met Lindsey, the new American delegate?" she asked.

Helga laughed. "I have not met her but I have certainly seen her. She seems to want to be seen and remembered. I wonder why that is?"

She looked at her watch and stood. "I have kept you long enough. But before I leave, it has come to my attention that some of the young people who work here have been spying on the guests. That is disgraceful. Employees who betray the trust of their employers must be sent away. I shall discuss the issue with the owners of the Alpina and see that it is done. Indiscretions in a hotel are bad for business, bad for Switzerland, and must not be permitted."

Laura was impressed. This was Helga the businesswoman with a reputation for toughness talking.

"I will speak to the owners now," Helga continued. "Then I plan to come to the morning meeting to hear what Karl has to say and some of the others. After that, I must go to Lauterbrunnen to help Felicia and Rosa's sister prepare for the funeral. A great many people will be there, Felicia tells me, so perhaps you will learn something if you come. Felicia has organized it all, and asked me to invite both of you especially."

"I will be there," Violet agreed, "barring unforeseen complications from the announcement I am about to make."

Helga raised a curious eyebrow. "I am glad I will be at the meeting to hear it, then," she said, and turned to Laura. "Will you be at the funeral too?"

"I would like to go," Laura answered, "but I have offered to stay here and deal with any of those unforeseen complications that I can handle."

In fact, she was glad of an excuse not to go. She had been the last person to see the dead woman, except for her killer, and she hadn't looked forward to fielding questions about Rosa's emotional state in her final moments.

As soon as Helga left, she and Violet, accompanied by Gustav and a few other men, delivered the painting to the bank, then hurried back to be in time for the meeting. Thomas waylaid them in the hall.

"Package delivered?" he asked.

"Excellent," he replied when Violet nodded. "Sitting around here guarding it doesn't suit my plans for the next few days."

"What plans are those?" Laura asked suspiciously, wondering what he was up to now. Whatever it was probably involved risks he was in no condition to take. To her annoyance, Thomas was saved from answering by the arrival of Makedu and Amina, and then by the clock.

"Time to get into the conference room," Violet announced. "I want to watch faces as people come in."

A number of delegates were missing, Laura noted, as she took her place at one side of the room. Sigrid had taken the twins to the airport to meet their father; Hassan was helping Eileen pack, and Dashka still hadn't made an appearance. Helga was there though, and to Laura's surprise, Felicia was sitting beside her. Her pallor struck Laura again forcibly, and she reminded herself to ask Helga if Felicia was all right when she had a chance.

When everyone was seated, Karl opened the meeting. "We have two changes in plans today," he told them. "First, I will attend the funeral in Lauterbrunnen for the woman who was killed a few days ago, so I will not be here for the afternoon's activities. Second, Violet McClarty, whose sister organized the hospitality for us, has asked if she could say a few words before our meeting begins."

Violet rose and went to the podium. Her face was serious as she surveyed her audience. A long moment passed before she spoke, and Laura watched to see who fidgeted or looked nervous. Ann looked jumpy and irritable, but Karl was the most obvious. His jaw went in and out, and the hands lying on his lap twitched involuntarily. Laura noted that Dr. Nezam was watching Karl too. His face didn't change but his hooded eyes were critical. Lindsey was also studying Karl, far more astutely than Laura expected.

Once again, Zaina was there despite her mother's absence, flanked by Ben and Reginald. Laura wondered why they had come. Normally, they skied with their instructors in the mornings. Zaina's eyes were red, her face strained. Something must have happened. To Dashka?

Laura saw Catherine join Zaina and the two boys. She must have noticed Zaina's distress and wanted to help. Kids that age were always more willing to talk to each other than to an adult, and Catherine knew she could pave the way for further confidences if the three young people had any information.

Violet's voice broke into her thoughts. "I am an investigator with a well known international company, as well as the sister of the woman who made your travel arrangements," she said baldly. "I am here because various threats have been made to disrupt this conference. My colleagues and I are also aware that for some of you, the conference interferes with other, possibly illegal activities. If any of you have information about these activities or suspect someone is involved in them, or have seen or heard anything that could be relevant, please let me know as soon as possible. Your cooperation is essential to everyone's safety, your own included. Three deaths and a number of accidents which were not accidents have already occurred; the next one could happen to you."

Violet let another long moment pass while she leaned over the podium and examined each member of the audience in turn. Her yellow-brown eyes were hawk-like as they probed the faces. Laura had seen the effect of that intense gaze on guilty people before and hoped it would flush out them out again.

"I apologize for deceiving you but it was essential to our work," Violet continued. She paused again to look at her audience, and when she resumed, she spoke slowly and softly, stressing each word. "I cannot emphasize strongly enough how important it is that anyone with information come to me. Your own safety may depend on it. Our investigation has reached a critical point, and withholding information could be very dangerous. We need to hear from you. I will be in my room until lunchtime."

The silence that fell was electric. Laura scanned faces. A spasm of fear crossed Karl's face but was quickly replaced by indignation that Laura was sure was put on. Ann looked resentful, Makedu looked furious, Amina stunned. Dr. Nezam's eyes narrowed but his face remained impassive. Zaina's face, oddly, was suddenly hopeful. Lindsey seemed skeptical, but when she saw Laura's eyes on her, surprise took over. "Well ah never!" she exclaimed softly. "Who would have thought?" Her tone was unconvincing.

Violet provided her cell phone number and her room number in the hotel. Then she stepped down, gesturing to Karl to take over. Laura saw Reginald scribble on a piece of paper and hoped it was one of the numbers.

Violet left, but Laura lingered in case anyone wanted to talk. She and Violet had agreed that anyone with information might be less intimidated by her than by a professional investigator. In fact, no one paid much attention to her. They were all talking at once, and Karl rapped his gavel in vain.

Laura saw Catherine and Zaina and the two boys slip out a side door and hoped that meant Zaina had agreed to talk about what was bothering her.

Ann's voice rose loudly over the babble. "That woman had no right to come here under false pretenses! She has nothing to do with our conference. She is entirely an outsider." A revealing reaction, Laura thought. Ann sounded like an offended adolescent who resented the presence of a new person in her group. No one paid any attention to her. Grudgingly, she subsided.

Makedu's reaction was more surprising. She bore down on Laura and told her forcefully what she thought of Violet's deception. "To deceive friends is unpardonable," she said angrily. "Amina and I were your friends. We trusted you and Violet, and you have not trusted us. Why did you not confide in us? We could have helped. We know more than you, I assure you."

Laura apologized profusely, trying simultaneously to convince the furious woman to lower her voice, that their silence had been essential, and to start helping now by telling Violet what they knew. Somewhat mollified, Makedu agreed and swept away, head high.

Amina waited a moment before she followed. "Maman is spectacular when she loses her temper, is she not?" she said with a grin.

"She is indeed!" Laura agreed, smiling back. No doubt a daughter had often been at the receiving end of a tirade like that. Her mind flashed back to Sigrid's comment that Amina didn't have enough confidence to repel Karl's advances. That was hard to believe now. A young woman who could deal equitably with her mother's explosive temper could surely handle an aging lothario. So why had Amina hesitated to do so? Could she be afraid that Karl would exact some kind of revenge on her mother?

Relations between mothers and their offspring, Laura mused. That theme came up over and over again. Dr. Nezam and Ben, Ann and Reginald, Makedu and Amina, Dashka and Zaina – maybe even Helga and Nicolas. If she could get to the bottom of those conflicts and fears, it seemed to her that she would also get to the bottom of this seemingly impenetrable mystery.

Karl's gavel finally had an effect. "I am sure you are as surprised – even shocked - as I was by Violet McCarthy's announcement," he said when finally there was silence. "I suggest we postpone the scheduled topic and meet informally to discuss this development."

He sounded aggrieved now, which Laura suspected covered fear. She was probably right, she thought, when despite his announcement he left the room without pausing to talk to anyone. She wondered if he would go to the bomb shelter. If he had anything illegal hidden there, he would want to remove it as quickly as possible. He would get a surprise if he tried. Gustav and his helpers were once again waiting nearby.

Dr. Nezam left the room behind Karl. To follow him or to confer with him? Laura was about to trail them and find out, when Lindsey confronted her.

"Ah'm so sur-prised, Laura," she chortled, drawing out the words. "Just so sur-prised about Violet be-in' a detective and all. She just bowled me over. It's so exciting, isn't it? Our little conference a hotbed of intrigue? Just imagine that!"

Ann came up behind them. "It's disgraceful!" she said loudly. "Simply disgraceful. I'm surprised at you, Lindsey, to think it's amusing."

Without waiting for an answer, she huffed off. Lindsey watched her, and Laura saw that her lips were twitching with amusement. It was the first sign of normal humanness she had seen in Lindsey.

"Rather an ass, isn't she?" Lindsey muttered under her breath. Her voice sounded completely different, and Laura had the strong feeling that Lindsey was either laughing at her too, or giving her a signal of some kind. Whichever it was, Lindsey clearly wasn't what she seemed to be.

"See ya'll later," Lindsey said in her usual tone, and darted off in the direction Karl and Dr. Nezam had taken. Laura wondered if she intended to follow them. She was tempted to follow Lindsey following Karl and Dr. Nezam, but decided she should check in with Violet first.

As she passed Thomas's room, she heard the murmur of voices. To her astonishment, Maurice was with him. Laura was relieved – to find Thomas still in his room and not out endangering himself, and because she had worried about Maurice. She had even wondered if he was still alive, with the police after him on one side and various sets of criminals on the other.

The two men were so absorbed in their conversation – about art, Laura assumed, that they only nodded a greeting. She left them to it and went across the hall to see how Violet had fared.

Violet looked satisfied. "Quite a few people rose to the bait. Karl arrived first. He pounded up here to scold me on behalf of the organization for my disgraceful deception, but what he really wanted to say is that Dr. Nezam is involved in an illicit enterprise but he doesn't know what it is. Dr. Nezam came in moments later to say that Karl is involved in illegal activities but he doesn't know what they are. It's the first time I've heard him speak more than a word or two. So it was just as you predicted, each incriminated the other and I have no doubt that we will get more information from both men as they compete to convince us that the other is the villain.

"Karl also told me that he thought Makedu and Lindsey were behaving suspiciously and that one or both of them could be blackmailing delegates. Makedu came next to report something similar, once she stopped berating me for deceiving them. There's a blackmailer at work in the hotel, she said. She thinks Karl is being blackmailed, and is too terrified not to pay up, and maybe Dr. Nezam. He's not a sensible choice, she said, since the person is more likely to get a bullet to the brain than money. I suspect she's right. Dashka could be another victim, she thinks, considering her unexplained absence."

Violet grinned. "Makedu and Amina make a great pair of detectives. They see everything! They're not out skiing or detecting every day like the rest of us, so they watch the hotel staff as well as the delegates. The man at the desk, for instance, is Iranian by birth, Makedu tells me, and my inquiries confirmed it. That makes me wonder if he's connected to Dr. Nezam. Makedu agrees that he probably cut the leash of the St. Bernard."

"He is also the person who assured me that it would be sunny all afternoon when the kids and I got caught in that snowstorm," Laura said crossly, recalling the incident. "I wonder now if he did it on purpose as a way to disrupt the conference. It wasn't as destructive as cutting the leash, but it was still a horrid thing to do."

She frowned. "I wonder how Makedu found out he's Iranian? Do you suppose he told her?"

Violet laughed. "I doubt it. More likely, Makedu has been doing some spying on her own. I certainly wouldn't put it past her."

"Makedu is a law unto herself," Laura agreed.

"One of the women who cleans the rooms is the Iranian clerk's girlfriend, according to Amina," Violet continued, "and she's helping him. I suspect she's the maid you caught spying on us when you opened the door so fast. Makedu and Amina think she's sadistic and that she, not Ann, probably slashed Amina's robe. While we're on the subject of maids, Makedu also says that from time to time, Lindsey can be seen making beds with a freshly scrubbed face, no make-up and a bandanna tied around her head, Swiss style."

Laura was chagrined. "I never thought of that! One doesn't look carefully at maids, and I of all people should know better after last year's experiences."

"Ah, yes," Violet said with a grin. "The chauffer with the cap. One tends to ignore people in a uniform."

"At one's peril," Laura agreed. "That oversight cost me dearly.

"I also wonder how Makedu knows about the possible blackmailer," she added. "I've been thinking that Amina's reluctance to repel Karl might have more to do with fear of reprisal against her mother than with a lack of confidence, and that leads me to wonder about Makedu's past. Is she blackmail material too? Is that how she knew about it?"

"If so, I imagine she sent the person packing," Violet said tartly. "But I'll see if I can find anything about her early life."

"Not if the blackmailer targeted Amina instead of her," Laura countered. "That would explain why Amina was reluctant to tell Karl to get lost. Maybe he went after Amina because she was next on his list of conquests and he knew she would be too afraid for her mother to complain publicly. That's blackmail."

Violet's lips twisted in distaste. "I'm not sure even Karl would stoop so low," she said reluctantly. "I really don't like that man. I wish he was the killer but I think Helga is right. He doesn't have the nerve."

"Sadly, I don't think he does, Laura agreed. "But I known he's guilty of something besides seducing women and I'm determined to find out what it is."

"I'll second that," Violet agreed.

"A few more interesting facts from Makedu and then I want some coffee. She and Amina have hired a snowmobile so they can explore the area." Laura had an instant vision of Makedu and Amina whipping around the town in their snowmobile, robes and scarves flying in the wind, eyes and ears alert.

"They're becoming a common sight in Murren, I hear," Violet continued. "They watch everything and everyone, including skiers. I asked them about Dr. Nezam and they report that he is an excellent skier – remember we wondered if he skied at all when Sigrid said she'd seen him above her on the trail? Well, she probably did. Ben, on the other hand, is a beginner, which is   interesting. The father's an expert, the son a beginner."

Laura nodded. "Normally, the son soon gets better than the father if they ski together. There's something very wrong with that relationship but I haven't been able to figure out what," she added, frowning in frustration. "That little fact makes me wonder if those two are actually father and son, or if they are, how long they have known each other. Or doesn't that make any sense?"

"As much sense as anything else in this puzzle," Violet said glumly. "It all seems like a big tangled ball of sticky twine at the moment. Maybe the coffee will clear my head. Let's go get some."

They almost bumped into Catherine at the door. She looked desperate with anxiety. "Dashka's been missing and she just got back. She's been beaten up so badly she can hardly walk, and she's bleeding all over the place. I've called Gustav and he'll be here as soon as he can. Hurry!"

She shot out the door again and ran down the hall. Laura and Violet were right behind her.

CHAPTER FIFTEEN

Catherine continued her rapid explanation as they hurried down the hall. "Zaina's too frightened to tell me why they beat up her mother, but I finally got her to tell me what she's so terrified of. It's because she has four younger sisters. Dashka rescued them from an Indian brothel and adopted them. The men who beat up Dashka threatened to kill them or take them back to the brothel if she talks. I don't know about what. But we've got to find out or we can't help, and I know Zaina will clam up again if we don't get there fast."

Laura tried to digest the information on the run. That was potent grounds for blackmail – but what was Dashka doing for the blackmailers to ensure that her daughters were left alone? Not money, surely. Dashka looked as if she didn't have any to spare.

Dashka looked frail and helpless lying on the bed. Her face was bruised and bloody, her body stiff with discomfort. All her bossiness was gone, and she was only a small battered woman who was horribly afraid. She lay still, her eyes downcast, her lips clamped tightly together, whether to endure the pain or to keep herself from talking Laura wasn't sure.

Zaina sat beside her, holding her hand. Laura noticed that the girl's skilled fingers were taking her mother's pulse even as tears ran down her face.

Laura bent over the bed. "Dashka," she said. "We can't help you unless we know what's wrong. Please can you tell us who did this to you and why?"

"They wore masks so I do not know who they were," Dashka answered.

She looked up at them, her eyes pleading for understanding. "I cannot tell you more," she said helplessly. "The children..."

"They threatened to harm my sisters and take them back to the brothel if my mother said anything," Zaina told them. "They said they would take her job away, too, and then we could not live."

Violet came closer. "Dashka, would it help you if I arranged to protect your children? Would you let me do that? Then, when you know they are safe, you might be able to tell us what's wrong."

Dashka looked doubtful, but Zaina's eyes lit up with hope. "Could you?" Her face fell. "But how can you? They are not here, they are in London. My mother's sisters are looking after them while we are away."

"If they are in London, I'm quite certain we can," Violet assured her. "If they were in India it might be more difficult, but the company I work for has many people in London."

Tears oozed from Dashka's eyes. "Then maybe it is possible. I am so afraid for them... Please, if you could make them safe..."

"Zaina, I will need the names of your mother's sisters, your address in London, and a telephone number," Violet said briskly. "Then I will call the London office and arrange it right away."

Zaina nodded and wrote them all down, her tongue sticking out between her teeth as she concentrated on getting the names right in English. It wasn't her first language, Laura remembered. She spoke it well, but writing it might still be harder.

When she had finished, Zaina handed the paper to Violet and knelt by her mother again. "Do you think we should call your sisters first so they know it's all right to let the people Violet sends into the apartment?"

"We have told them not to let strangers into the house," she explained to Laura and Violet. "We are afraid for the children even in London."

Laura could have wept for them. How terribly sad to be always afraid.

"Yes, we must call them," Dashka agreed, "though I do not want to." Her lips twisted convulsively as she fought back tears. "It makes me so ashamed to tell them what has happened, that I have made this necessary. But you are right. They will be frightened and suspicious if we do not."

"If my children had been threatened, I would have acted as you did," Laura assured her. "I am sure your sisters will understand."

"One of them will; the others will not," Dashka said bluntly. The irritation in her voice made Laura suspect that she rather enjoyed being the superior sister, and that this revelation would impinge on her status.

She turned back to Zaina. "We had better talk to Perpetua, Zaina. She is the most sensible," she said resignedly.

"My mother has three sisters," Zaina told them. "One of them is very good at cooking and reading books to the children but has no idea how to manage in the city or deal with strangers. The second sister is very emotional. That is why we leave Perpetua in charge. She knows how to do everything."

The phone call was placed and fortunately the sensible sister was there to take it. Zaina's relief was transparent when her mother hung up.

"You see, Maman, I was right. These terrible things can be fixed," she said, kneeling by her mother again. "There are good people who can help us."

She turned to Violet. "When you said you were a detective -" Her voice broke, and she squeezed her eyes tight shut before she resumed.

"We have been so afraid these last days... But then you said you were looking for the people who do these bad things at the conference, and then I thought maybe we might be all right..."

Dashka put out a shaky hand and smoothed Zaina's hair. "Yes, you are right. It is good that we let them help us, even if it brings shame on us for what I have done." Her voice was infinitely weary, her face still drawn with sorrow. She, more than Zaina, understood that the battle was not yet won. She might still have to fight for her job, for the means to support her children.

One brave woman, Laura thought, and wondered how long she had been victimized this way. A long time, she realized, when Dashka spoke again.

"I tried to make up for it by helping as many of the children as I could," Dashka said, looking up at Violet with tired eyes.

"What did they make you do?" Violet asked gently. "Did you have to alter one of the agency's orders and financial records?"

Dashka looked surprised. "I know nothing of that, only of how people at the agency in India procure girls for the brothels. It is very profitable, which I saw on the accounts. I went to the managers to report what I had learned, and that is when it started. If I spoke, they threatened to come after Zaina and I would lose my job. They said no one would believe me, a mere woman, anyway."

Tears rolled down her cheeks. "And so I could not tell anyone what they were doing, what they are still doing... all I could do was to go to the brothel and rescue as many as I could, but it is not nearly enough..."

Raising her hands to her face, she sobbed. "How can one woman stop such abuses? Tell me that!"

"You did your best. That is all any of us can do," Violet soothed her, and left the room to make the necessary calls.

When she returned, she told them that a policewoman with experience in cases like this would stay with Dashka's family as long as she was needed. "She will be there day and night to make sure the children are safe. She can have reinforcements there in minutes, too. So try to stop worrying.

"We will investigate the agency," she added, "but we will not let anyone know it was you who provided the information."

"Thank you," Dashka whispered. She looked utterly exhausted, and neither Laura nor Violet had the heart to question her further.

Zaina went to Catherine and hugged her. "This happened because of you," she said, teary-eyed again. "If you had not encouraged me, I would not have dared to speak, and then we would still be afraid."

Catherine hugged her back. "Zaina," she said stoutly, "you deserve all the help you can get, and it's a good thing I was here to get things going."

217

A knock on the door heralded Gustav. He and Catherine exchanged a look that conveyed volumes. Definitely an understanding was brewing there, Laura thought, and wondered how Thomas would react.

Violet took Gustav aside to exchange a few words with him; then Gustav bent over his patient and Laura, Violet and Catherine left.

"If Dashka didn't alter the orders for the agency, who did?" Laura asked. "And did she do anything besides hold her tongue?"

Violet shook her head. "I just don't know. I do know, however, that Dashka isn't telling us something. She's holding it back. I can just *feel* it."

"Maybe it's something she doesn't want to admit to Zaina," Laura suggested. "I'll try asking her again when Zaina isn't there."

"Thanks." Violet looked at her watch. "I must leave for the funeral in a few minutes, so I'll just grab a sandwich from the buffet and run."

"What were you and Gustav talking about?" Laura asked curiously.

"How best to guard Dashka and Zaina," Violet answered. "It's not just the children in London who could be in danger. Dashka knows too much and that makes Zaina vulnerable, too. Gustav will post someone at the door."

"Maybe we should have asked why the blackmailers suddenly turned on her now," Laura said with a worried frown. "Was it something she did?"

"I think I know already," Violet said gloomily, "and I don't like it one bit."

"What?" Laura asked.

"Us," Violet said bluntly. "They went after Dashka because *we* are here. You write about girls being forced into prostitution in Indian brothels; I am a detective who breaks up prostitution rings. The criminals must have decided it was time to reinforce their message, so they beat Dashka up. Trafficking of girls is a highly profitable business, and they didn't want her or anyone else interfering with it.

"And to make things worse for her, I just announced publicly that we came here to investigate criminal activity at the conference, which should really stir them up," she added as she stuffed a sandwich into her oversized purse and hurried out the door.

"Sure will," Catherine agreed. "There's bound to be another crisis soon."

"At least we've got Dashka and Zaina settled for the moment," Laura said philosophically, "so let's get some lunch while we can.

"Thanks, Catherine, for getting this started," she added. "Dashka would never have talked if you hadn't persuaded Zaina that we could help. Your efforts really made a difference."

Catherine looked pleased. "I like Zaina at lot. She's kind, and there aren't many kind people around these days. She's had a hard life, too. Her father was killed and her mother died in the refugee camp, so she didn't have any family. Dashka found her at the camp and took her in."

"So Zaina is adopted too," Laura commented. "I had wondered."

Catherine nodded. "Dashka loves rescuing people. She's pretty good at it too. She literally raided that brothel to get Zaina's sisters out and ran off with them.

They came from Nepal originally. Zaina says they bring busloads of stolen Nepalese girls to that brothel in India because they are beautiful and have pale skin. Sometimes they're only seven or eight years old."

"She's right," Laura agreed. "In some Nepalese villages no girls are left because the procurers took all of them. Sometimes they're stolen, but some parents sell them for money or for things like TV sets or a new roof."

Catherine shuddered. "That's unspeakable!"

"Yes," Laura agreed. "It is shocking, though I suppose the parents think it's all right. In that part of the world, girls are considered a liability."

""Don't the girls try to escape from the brothel?" Catherine asked.

Laura shook her head. "They don't speak the language, there's nowhere to go, and the brothel owners beat them up or kill them if they try. They usually give the girls drugs to keep them passive anyway. Most of them are there for life unless someone like Dashka rescues them. It's a ghastly fate."

"Dashka really is brave," Catherine observed. "I hope she doesn't lose her job because of what she's done. So many people depend on her, and not just her family. Dashka spends a lot of time in refugee camps helping children."

"I hope so too," Laura said, but she wasn't optimistic. Once the managers of the agency in India realized that they were being investigated, they would get rid of Dashka as soon as possible.

Catherine looked at her, suddenly wide-eyed. "Drugs," she said. "You said they give the girls drugs. Do you suppose that's the connection with Henri's business, that the brothel owners got the drugs from him?"

"Of course!" Laura was appalled. Why hadn't she thought of that before? Was that what Dashka didn't want to tell Violet? And did Zaina know?

Thomas joined them, noted their serious faces and took it upon himself to distract them with an amusing description of Maurice wriggling and grunting as he forced his large body through a small window. "It was quite a sight," he said, "and I fear I was laughing so hard I was no help at all."

Laura was mystified. "Why was Maurice going out the window?"

"He's doing his best not to be noticed," Thomas explained, "so he eschews public entrances and goes out the window instead of the door when he can. Good thing, too. I think he may be the owner of the painting, which means a lot of people would like to see him disappear permanently.

"Which doesn't necessarily mean it's a genuine Vermeer," he added. "A lot could have happened in the intervening years."

"He hinted that there could be two of them when I talked to him in Gimmelwald," Laura said.

"Which makes Maurice a bigger target still," Thomas noted. "I tried to persuade him not to leave at all, but he's hot on the track of something – he wouldn't say what, and there was no stopping him."

"How did Maurice get down after he went out the window?" Catherine asked curiously.

"He went down the fire escape, I believe, or I hope he did. The only other means of egress would be to slide down a drainpipe."

221

Catherine looked chagrined. "I wish I'd known about the fire escape when I got to the hotel! I had to climb up to Laura's and Violet's balcony to get inside. It was really late – way past midnight. I was freezing!"

Laura frowned. "I hadn't thought to ask until now how you got to Murren in the middle of the night. I didn't think trains or gondolas operated after about eight PM. Surely you didn't climb up the cliff!"

"There was an unscheduled gondola going up," Catherine explained. "The guys who were loading boxes onto it let me ride along. They didn't even charge me. Good thing, too. I didn't have any Swiss money."

"Boxes?" Laura asked, dumbfounded. "Did you say boxes?"

Catherine nodded. "Just supplies for the hotels, I guess. It's the only way they can get stuff up here."

Laura clapped her hand to her forehead. "Why didn't I think to ask that question before? I wondered how they got the boxes up here without attracting the attention of…

"Was anyone else in the gondola?" she asked abruptly.

"No. Just me and the guys -" Catherine too stopped in mid-sentence and her eyes widened. "One of the guys was the man at the desk, at least I think he was," she added excitedly.

She closed her eyes, concentrating. "Yes, I'm almost sure it was. He looked different because he was in work clothes. Only he didn't come to the hotel like I did. He and one other man put some boxes in a snowmobile and went off in the other direction, probably to the bomb shelter. Does that help?"

Thomas looked horrified. "You mean to say you came up here in the middle of the night by yourself? Why didn't you wait until morning?"

"Because I was so worried about you, Dad," Catherine explained patiently. "I mean, you'd been abducted, and I had to do something. Besides, you said to go to Laura if anything happened to you.

"Just following orders," she added innocently.

"I'd better find another business," Thomas muttered.

"Don't do that!" Catherine was appalled now. "Then I wouldn't have any excitement in my life. Laura wouldn't like it either, I'm sure."

"You have to admit," Laura put in, "that Catherine's pretty resourceful."

"Too resourceful," Thomas grumbled. "One of these days, Catherine, you'll get yourself killed. Why can't you marry some nice guy and lead a normal life?"

"Just like my mother," Catherine teased.

Laura tried to think of a way to change the subject lest they begin a futile discussion about the merits of marriage. Despite the fact that he led a wildly unconventional life, Thomas was astonishingly conservative in some respects. According to Catherine, he'd never in his life had an affair until he met her, and since he intended to marry her that made it all right. "So you might as well give in and marry him, Laura," Catherine had finished with a grin.

Laura decided to put that subject off for future consideration. "Does anyone know the desk clerk's name?" she asked.

"He says it's Joe," Catherine replied, "but I'm not sure it's his real one."

Gustav appeared in the doorway and Catherine leaped up to go to him. Thomas raised an inquiring eyebrow.

"Gustav's been ministering to Dashka this time," Laura said hastily, and explained what had happened.

"I wouldn't be surprised if Henri Guillard and his cronies were involved in prostitution too," Thomas observed. "Henri is dead and so is Ludwig, but who knows how many other people around here are also mixed up in it?"

"So now we have three illegal businesses to figure out all at once," Laura said glumly. "Art, drugs and prostitution – trafficking, I should say."

"An unholy trio," Thomas agreed. "Some of these people have their tentacles in all three at once."

"Yes," Laura agreed. "Which is why I shouldn't be surprised that trafficking in girls seems to follow me wherever I go. It's the most profitable business in the world except for arms. It's everywhere, including the U.S. Our recent Super-bowl in Texas was also billed as the Super-bowl of sex trafficking. Thousands of prostitutes, many very young girls, were brought in."

Thomas winced and changed the subject. "Catherine's changing, isn't she?" he asked as he rose to his feet.

"Yes, she's much more mature," Laura agreed. "I think you may be surprised at what happens next."

Thomas grinned. "Or I might not," he said, without elaborating.

"I'm off," he added nonchalantly. "Have an appointment to do some research on the art front that I've been putting off." Whistling a jaunty-sounding tune, he headed for the stairs.

"The computers aren't up there," Laura pointed out.

"Research comes in many forms," Thomas said obliquely, and stopped to blow her a kiss from the landing.

Laura smiled at him, but she was suspicious. Thomas only blew kisses when he was up to something he didn't want to tell her about, which was invariably something potentially dangerous. She had better keep an eye on him.

She sat on, however, feeling too lazy to do anything but sip her tea and survey the room. Who among the people here would have beaten Dashka or arranged for her to be beaten? She suspected Dr. Nezam would. Karl wouldn't do it himself, but he might arrange for it to be done. So would Lindsey. There was a strong element of ruthlessness in Lindsey, Laura decided, watching her elbow her way from the buffet with a plateful of food.

An unexpected thought jumped into her mind. Lindsey had searched their room. Maybe it was time to search hers. She would be here for a while, with all that food. Maybe Thomas would help, if she could find him. The plan would have the added bonus of distracting him from his investigations.

Abandoning her lunch, she hurried upstairs and found Thomas just coming out of his room, jacket in hand. She explained hurriedly.

Thomas grinned. "The pass key the maids use to get into the rooms is kept in the laundry closet," he told her. "I'll grab it. And Lindsey's room is above mine. She hasn't got a balcony or the desirable view, either," he added, "which probably means she decided to come at the last minute."

"Interesting deduction! You're really good at this, aren't you?" Laura complimented him as she watched him fit the key deftly into the lock.

"I'll check closet and drawers, and you look for papers," she added.

The first drawer she opened produced a startling result. Lying on top of a pile of scarves was a red bandanna folded to be worn across the forehead and tied at the back of the head, 70's style. Laura stared at it, trying to think where she had seen it before.

A picture clicked into her brain. "Barbara," she breathed, Barbara of the red bandanna and the firm handshake, like Lindsey's. And a red bandanna that could also be worn Swiss-style by a cleaning woman...

"Barbara was Lindsey," she whispered to Thomas. "That's how she knew who we were. She's a cleaning woman too. *She's* the one!"

Thomas looked horrified. "You mean that girl I gave the note to? She looked so honest and hearty!"

Laura nodded. "That's her. And she knew exactly what your note meant all the time."

****

Laura hurried back to the dining room to reclaim her lunch. To her relief, Lindsey was still there, eating salad. Laura took a bite of her own salad without tasting it while she pondered the implications of their discoveries. Other items had confirmed Lindsey's double – maybe triple – identities, like wigs and gaudy jewelry and, surprisingly, a dark grey man's suit. Could buxom Lindsey really impersonate a man? Still, she was surprisingly slender otherwise.

Thomas hadn't found any papers that revealed Lindsey as a CIA agent or that referred to any of her other identities, which told them only that she was careful. Once he had locked up again, he really had left, citing an appointment for which he was already late. Laura tried to decide if she should follow him and try to keep him out of danger, or follow Lindsey to see what she did next, if she ever finished her lunch.

Zaina came into the room, distracting her. Ben and Reginald jumped up to greet her. It was remarkable, Laura thought, how Zaina had brought them together. Normally boys that age competed fiercely over a beautiful girl. Instead, they had become friends.

Zaina perched beside them to bring them up to date; then she sprang up again to fill a plate with food to take back to the room. "You can bring tea if you want," she said to Reginald and Ben. "My mother loves tea. India tea if they have it, and lemon." The two boys jumped up to comply as Zaina left the room carrying a plate for her mother.

Catherine reappeared. "Gustav wants to put Dashka in the hospital," she said, "But Dashka doesn't want to go. She's too worried about Zaina."

"Maybe Zaina could be cajoled into acting as Dashka's nurse," Laura suggested. "If the hospital will permit, that is."

Catherine looked doubtful. "They're both pretty stubborn," she observed. "Zaina looks compliant, but she's not that easy to persuade."

"She just went up with a plate of food for her mother," Laura said. "Did you see her go by?"

Catherine looked puzzled. "No, I didn't. Maybe she took the elevator."

"I guess she must have," Laura agreed.

Reginald and Ben passed them holding a pot of tea covered in a towel for Dashka, and an extra cup for Zaina in case she wanted some.

"Have to keep it hot," Ben explained. "Reginald says people who live in England like their tea really hot."

"Do you know where my Dad is?" Catherine asked Laura when the boys had left on their errand of mercy.

"He left," Laura answered, "wearing his coat, which is worrying."

"Uh oh," Catherine said. "He thinks he's recovered from those wounds, but I doubt he is. Maybe we'd better grab our coats and go look for him."

Laura nodded, glad to have the decision made between following Lindsey and Thomas. Lindsey hadn't even tackled the desserts yet.

She and Catherine were on their way downstairs again with their jackets and packs when Ben and Reginald charged past them.

"Have you seen Zaina?" they called out as they ran by. "We can't find her. Dashka's up there but Zaina isn't. And Dashka never got her lunch."

Laura and Catherine ran down after them, asking everyone in earshot if they had seen Zaina in the last half hour. No one had. Finally, they went outside. Ben and Reginald were already there, shivering coatless in the cold. Ben came up to them, white-faced.

"Zaina's gone," he said. "She was seen getting into a snowmobile about fifteen minutes ago," he said, "and then she disappeared."

CHAPTER SIXTEEN

"Who took her?" Laura asked.

"No one saw who was driving it," Reginald answered. "They just saw Zaina get in. People notice Zaina," he added desolately. "She's so beautiful."

"Are those the people who saw the snowmobile?" Laura asked, pointing to skiers sipping hot drinks at an outdoor table.

When Reginald nodded, Laura asked them which way the snowmobile had gone. "Toward the train station and the Schilthorn," they answered.

"That route goes past the bomb shelter, so let's look there first," Laura told the boys. "Get your jackets and anything warm you can find. Catherine, see if Gustav is still around. We need his big snowmobile."

The boys didn't question her but ran to obey, as did Catherine. Laura tried to control her shaking hands while she punched in Violet's number, but there was no answer. She left a message instead.

Fortunately, Gustav was still in the building. He and Catherine appeared with the snowmobile just as Ben and Reginald came running out.

"We brought the duvets from the beds," Reginald said as they piled onto the machine, "and scarves and mittens."

"Good thinking," Laura told him. "Zaina will be cold." Further conversation was impossible as the motor roared to life. When it eased a little, Laura tried to call Violet again, but there was still no answer.

"I'll text her," Catherine offered, and sent a two word message: *bomb shelter*. "I'll try my Dad too."

Laura sighed. "You can try your Dad, but I doubt he'll answer. I have a strong suspicion that he went to the bomb shelter too, and if I'm right, he won't be able to get a signal."

"Why do you think he went there?" Catherine asked.

"Because he's aching to find that other Vermeer, because he was so eager to get away without us earlier, and because he had a long conversation with Maurice this morning," Laura replied. "I'd be willing to bet they agreed to meet up there."

"You're probably right," Catherine agreed. "If he and Zaina are both in the same place, it makes things easier for us," she added, trying to be practical. Laura wasn't so sure. Thomas had a way of complicating things.

Gustav lowered the motor to a purr and turned off the lights as they got closer to the shelter. "No point advertising our arrival," he said, cutting the power and drifting to a stop a short distance away.

"This could be a trap," Laura warned him. "It's not an easy place to search, either. There are so many rooms and all sorts of hiding places."

He nodded. "It could. I'll do my best to make sure no one threatening is waiting for us before the rest of you go in."

"The door is closed," Catherine said in alarm. "How will we get in?"

"I know how to open the door," Gustav assured her. "The farmer has also revived a rather antiquated lighting system at the behest of the police. I don't know how well it works, but I will try to turn it on. I have brought extra torches too, in case we need them."

He turned to Ben. "Could you look in the bag under your feet and hand out a flashlight to everyone who needs one?"

Ben seemed to shake himself out of a trance. "Yes. Yes, I will," he replied, rummaging in the bag. Laura really looked at him for the first time since Zaina had disappeared. He looked dreadful – terrified for Zaina, but even more, as if an unbearable conflict raged inside him.

Gustav asked all of them to wait until he had the door open and the lights on, if he could make them work.

"Thomas could be in there," Laura warned him, "and Maurice Flambert may be with him. He's the man Catherine felled during your last rescue mission. He turns out to be a Swiss Jew looking for art stolen from him by the Nazis. So don't knock him out again. He's actually very nice."

"I'll take your word for it," he said. "But if he has a gun…"

Ben's deep voice interrupted. "He won't use it even if he has one," he said. "He's a pacifist and he doesn't like guns."

Laura wondered how he knew that, but his eyes gave nothing away. Had he met with Maurice again? He must have, she thought, to say that about him with such certainty.

Gustav regarded Ben curiously but didn't ask questions "Thank you," he said. "I will be back as fast as I can." He ran lightly to the door at an oblique angle so he wouldn't easily be seen, inserted a key in the lock and pressed some buttons. Slowly, the door swung open, but the lights didn't come on. Gustav disappeared into the darkness.

He reappeared after a few minutes. "We'll have to search by flashlight. The lights don't work. I'm not sure why. Do any of you have experience in fixing electrical systems?

Ben nodded. "When I first saw an electric bulb I thought it was a miracle," he said. "I was eight years old, and I decided to learn all about it. I can fix most problems."

The remark stunned Laura. It seemed so unlikely that the son of a very wealthy man should have been without electric lights during his childhood. Poor Iranian families might not have access to electricity, but rich ones did.

"I know a little too," Reginald volunteered. "I'll help."

They filed in, blinded by the sudden darkness. "Over here," Gustav directed the boys, aiming his flashlight at a fuse box.

Leaving them to see what they could do, he hurried back to Catherine and Laura. "I'll go ahead and look first," he said. Ignoring his offer, Catherine fell into step beside him, so Laura went too.

They shone their lights around the living area, the first bedroom, the bathroom. Laura's heart began to beat hard as they approached the second bedroom, where they had found Ludwig.

She aimed her light on the bed for just a second, but that was enough to show Gustav already bending over a dark form on the same bed. Laura's heart seemed to stop. Was it Zaina, or would it really be Thomas this time?

She went closer. It was neither. Instead, it wasn't anyone at all.

****

It's just a bundle of blankets," Catherine said indignantly.

"Better than a body," Gustav pointed out.

"Apologies," Thomas said from behind them. "I thought you were the villains returning. We were trying to stall them."

This time, Laura almost did slug him. "You scared me half to death," she accused, putting a hand to her heart to slow down its pounding.

"And me!" Catherine said. "I was sure it would be you or Zaina."

"No, she's right here." He waved his flashlight like a magician, and Zaina appeared beside him. She was shaking with either fear or cold, but she didn't look injured. Laura realized that she too was shaking, no doubt with shock. The last few hours had been extraordinary - never mind the days before.

"They put me in here," Zaina whispered, "and then they closed the door. It was so dark… and I didn't know where I was, but then…

Suddenly, blindingly, the lights came on. Laura slapped her hands over her eyes. Why had they chosen such atrocious fluorescent lights?

Ben and Reginald appeared, looking pleased. Their faces changed when they saw Zaina. They rushed to her, and Reginald, who was still carrying the duvets, wrapped one around her shaking shoulders.

Overcome by the small gesture of comfort, Zaina began to cry. Laura led her over to the other bed and rocked her in her arms. Catherine sat down beside them,

Gustav beside her, while Reginald sat on the bed across from them. The relief in his eyes was touching. Ben knelt and bowed deeply in what Laura assumed was the direction of Mecca before he sat. Perhaps it was his way of giving thanks that Zaina was all right.

"Don't get too relaxed," Thomas warned. "We need to leave. The men who abducted Zaina will be back, probably with less pleasant reinforcements."

Zaina looked up. "That was the strange thing," she said, wiping her eyes. "They didn't hurt me or even threaten me. They just drove me here, led me inside, and the minute Thomas appeared, they vanished."

"It was quite flattering," Thomas said. "They took one look at me and ran. I felt like Superman. That doesn't happen very often."

Zaina smiled tentatively, but then panic suffused her face. "We need to call my mother and tell her I'm all right. She'll be terrified."

Catherine jumped up. "I'll go outside where there's a signal and do it right away. The rest of you follow as quick as you can."

"I'll go with you," Gustav said.

They ran for the door; the others followed more slowly. They had almost reached the door of the first bedroom when the lights went out again.

"I'll go fix them," Ben offered.

Thomas stopped him. "Zena's abductors might have turned them off," he whispered. "We'll be harder to find in the dark. The rest of us should stay together to protect Zaina, too. She's the one they want."

"Why?" Reginald asked, his voice agonized. "Why would anyone want to harm Zaina? She's never hurt anyone in her life."

"Let's go back to the other bedroom and barricade the door," Laura suggested. "That will slow them down." They tiptoed back into the second bedroom, but the sound of voices and the gleam of flashlights told them they were too late to start hauling beds and bureaus against the door. Instead, they waited and listened.

"Did you two forget to close the door when you left?" That sounded like Joe, the desk clerk, Laura thought.

"No. We closed it when we left her here earlier. I'll close it again." One of the men who had brought Zaina here, Laura surmised. She heard the door close with a soft thud.

"In there," a different man directed, and Laura felt Ben stiffen beside her. Was that his father's voice? She hadn't heard it often enough to know. But why would Dr. Nezam come here?

They heard shuffling noises, like something heavy being dragged across the floor, then a soft thump from the other bedroom. To Laura's admittedly over-stimulated imagination, it sounded like a body being lowered onto a bed. Too heavy for Catherine. Was it Gustav? Where were they?

Footsteps came toward them. Instinctively, they clustered protectively around Zaina.

Dr. Nezam came into the room. He stood in the doorway, regarding them impassively as his flashlight moved from one face to the next. His expression didn't change until the light reached Ben. Then his jaw tightened and Laura saw a gleam of fury come into his hooded eyes.

"You!" he spat. Ben said nothing but his eyes expressed his feelings. Laura thought she had never seen such rage.

Three men were behind Dr. Nezam. One was the desk clerk, as Laura had suspected; she didn't know the other two but thought she had seen them in the gondola station. One of them was hardly more than a boy, a frightened one. She saw him look anxiously at Zaina, and wondered if he might make an ally.

"Who is in the next room?" Thomas asked blandly.

"I imagine you already know," Dr. Nezam replied evenly. "I believe he intended to meet you here." His voice was a bit shrill, higher than Laura had expected and with less authority than his son's. Did that rankle?

"Ah, you found Maurice. I imagine you know him quite well too, at least by reputation," Thomas observed. "He's a fascinating man, isn't he? His field is art, I believe, and the workings of the human mind."

He frowned. "I find it difficult to understand how such a man can be a threat to you. Have you taken up the study of art, perhaps as a collector, as well as indulging in various less savory activities? But of course, you are here as a delegate to the conference. One tends to forget that as one nasty incident after another occurs. I wonder if you are the instigator or perhaps Karl?"

His voice held a teasing note, and Laura knew he was trying to unbalance Dr. Nezam with provocative remarks designed to compel an unguarded answer. So far, the Iranian hadn't risen to the bait. His face remained expressionless, so she decided to help with some probing questions of her own.

"You've been watching me ever since you saw me on the train, haven't you," she asked, looking him in the eye. He didn't like eye contact either, she realized, when he flinched almost imperceptibly.

"What do you want with Zaina?" she continued, still staring at him.

"That is none of your business," he shot back, his face flushing with anger. His eyes shifted away from her and fastened on Reginald.

"What is he doing here?" he demanded of the desk clerk Joe. "I thought I had made it clear to his mother that she was not to let him interfere."

The remark implied that he had power over Ann, Laura thought. Were they working together? If so, on what?

"My mother has nothing to do with you," Reginald said defensively.

Dr. Nezam didn't answer, nor did Joe. No one else spoke either. The low moan from the next room sounded loud against the silence.

"Maurice," Zaina said, and started for the door. "I must tend to him."

Dr. Nezam blocked her way. "You will stay where you are," he ordered. Zaina paid no attention, but brushed past him as if he didn't exist.

"We will all go," Laura said, and walked past the Iranian into the next room, followed by Thomas and the boys.

Maurice was lying on a bed, and a woman Laura didn't at first recognize was bent over him, a small knife in her hand.

The young woman looked up, startled, as they came in, and Laura saw that it was Nina, the desk clerk's

237

girlfriend. Had she used that knife on Amina's robe? And was she about to use it on Maurice?

Zaina stared at Nina, then at the knife, and horror filled her face.

"Leave him alone," Ben ordered. Nina hesitated and looked to Dr. Nezam for guidance. He nodded, and she put the knife away.

Dr. Nezam took a deep breath. Their indifference to his authority had unsettled him badly, but Laura saw that he was even more unsettled by the fact that they were all watching him, waiting to see what he would do next.

"We will leave now," he said stiffly to Nina and Joe. Turning on his heel, he headed for the door. The others trailed behind him.

Ben's commanding voice stopped them. "Did you have someone do that to my father too, before you killed him?" The scathing hatred in the accusation was powerful, and Dr. Nezam flinched again.

"Your father disobeyed my orders," he said stiffly.

Ben's rage exploded. "You had no right to give him orders," he thundered, leaning toward Dr. Nezam with clenched fists. "My father was the leader of our village, respected by all who knew him and many others. But you - you had no respect from anyone. You had only men you paid to do what you did not have the courage to do for yourself."

"You are without gratitude," Dr. Nezam answered shrilly. "I took you and your mother into my home and gave you everything you needed."

"You stole my mother because you lusted after her and wanted her for your wife, and you took me because you had no son of your own and you saw that I was strong," Ben replied, his tone heavy with loathing. He had an extraordinary voice, Laura thought, capable of expressing every nuance of his emotions.

"Perhaps that is why you killed my father, so you could get both of us," Ben continued, and now his voice was steely with hatred.

"You had never known even running water before I took you in," Dr. Nezam shot back. "You would have grown up uneducated, unable to be anything but a penniless herder like your father."

"My father had self-respect," Ben said, and the sudden softness of his tone made the words even more compelling.

Dr. Nezam shrugged. "No woman is happy with only that," he said. "Now that she is *my* wife, she is surrounded by luxuries."

"You gave her nothing of value," Ben retorted in a tone that dripped with contempt. "For all your luxuries, she is not happy. She loves my father still, and mourns him, but she has no love for you. How could she love a coward? For you she has only scorn." The effect of this remark on Dr. Nezam was powerful. His face went a dull red, and his mouth twisted into a grimace.

Ben barely noticed. A reminiscent smile was playing around his lips. "My mother was happy until you came," he said softly. "She and my father knew happiness together, and I knew happiness with them."

"Then you were fools," Dr. Nezam snapped. "I could make you a leader in our country, so that you have power over all who oppose you."

Ben laughed, a ringing laugh that filled the room with his disdain. "So I too could intimidate people as you do, as Henri Guillard did? So I could take bribes and blackmail others, pay and bully my way into power, and buy loyalty? Or execute innocent people if they got in my way?"

He shook his head emphatically. "No. That is not for me."

Dr. Nezam's lips tightened and he shouted a furious reply. Laura didn't hear it. A slight movement from the desk clerk Joe had caught her attention. She watched him draw a gun out of his pocket and raise it slowly. No one else had seen the movement, she thought. They were all too intent on the drama being played out between Ben and Dr. Nezam.

Laura drew breath into her lungs. Maybe this was the moment to put all those lessons to work. Joe was right in front of her, about the right distance away. She let out the breath, drew in another, and lunged up with her knee. Her blow caught Joe exactly where she had intended. The gun flew out of his hand and he dropped to his knees, howling in pain. Thomas picked the gun up, then stared at her in astonishment.

"You really did learn to do that, didn't you?" He grinned. "I guess I don't have to worry about you any more."

Laura rubbed her leg. "Takes a toll on the leg, never mind the nerves," she said, and sat down hard on the next bed. "Now, let's let Zaina get on with nursing Maurice."

"That would be nice," Maurice said faintly, trying to sit up. "I congratulate all of you. I shudder to think what would have happened if you had not come."

"Stay still," Zaina advised as she bent to examine him.

"Thank you, Maurice," Thomas said affably. "However, all I have done so far is watch. In that capacity, I observed that the target of our attention has stolen away while our eyes were on Laura's remarkably effective attack.

"To redeem my record," he added, "I shall go after him."

Laura stood up again, wincing as a sharp pain shot through her knee. "You aren't in any shape to do that," she protested to Thomas.

He grinned. "Neither are you, from the look of it," he replied, watching her limp a few steps.

"No need anyway, Dad," Catherine said from the door. "They're all taken care of. The two hapless helpers came out with their hands up, so they were no problem. Gustav went for Joe, but Laura had pretty well disabled him anyway so he just helped Violet handcuff him. That was a great move, Laura. I saw it from the other room," she added.

"Thanks," Laura said. "That's a real compliment from an expert like you."

"I tackled Dr. Nezam," Catherine continued, "but he didn't put up much resistance. I should have gone for Nina instead. She really is a fighter. She came at me with that knife of hers, but I managed to step out of the way and she got Dr. Nezam in the arm instead. He gave her a look that would have terrified me out of my wits. She was so appalled at what she'd done that she just gave in. Gustav is binding up the arm."

"Sorry, Ben," Catherine added. "I don't mean to be disrespectful of your father."

"He is not my father," Ben said firmly.

Catherine nodded and refrained from asking questions after a quick look at his flushed face. "He never seemed much like it," she agreed.

"Nina cut my mother, too," Zaina said suddenly. "*He* must have told her to do it." She pointed in the direction of Dr. Nezam. "I know because Maurice has the same kind of cuts I saw on her. They're not deep, just painful and -"

She broke off, squeezing her eyes tightly to force back tears. When she spoke again, her voice had a strangled sound. "Painful and *cruel,* that is what they are; Nina is cruel, and so are the men who killed my father and my aunt, and the men who abuse little children and the women who run the brothels and let them do it, help them even. I saw what they had done to some of the girls. To become rich from the bodies of little girls, as the brothel owners do, is the cruelest of all. No one should be cruel like that."

Sobbing, she collapsed on the floor beside Maurice. He took her hand in his and caressed it softly until her tears abated. "Most of us, most of the people you know are not cruel. Remember that."

"The man who called himself my father is cruel." Ben's tone was implacable, filled with hatred. "Men like him do not deserve to live."

"My mother is cruel too, too." The words sounded as if they were being forced from the depths of Reginald's throat. "Maybe she didn't slash Amina's gown, but she was glad it was destroyed. I don't know what she does for Dr. Nezam, but she probably does something," he added bitterly. "I tried to watch to keep her from doing things but I couldn't watch all the time…"

He looked at them helplessly, and Laura wanted to take him in her arms as she had Zaina. He was only a boy, after all.

Maurice did it for her. He beckoned to Reginald and drew him down on his other side. "To speak of your mother as she is took great courage," he said. "I am proud of you." Reginald's eyes glistened with tears.

"It is hardest of all to have a parent, or someone who calls himself your parent, who is cruel," Maurice went on, talking to all of them now. "But look around you. Laura is not cruel, or Catherine or any other others gathered here. That is what we must do, those of us who are not cruel, who abhor cruelty. We must gather together to help each other. That is how we find the strength to move past our bitterness and our sorrow.

"Already," he added, "you three have begun to do that, have you not?"

Zaina looked at Ben and Reginald. They glanced at each other and nodded sheepishly.

"One thousand acts of kindness," Maurice said softly. "For every act of cruelty we witness, we who are not cruel must perform one thousand acts of kindness. In that way, we balance the horrors of our world and preserve our sanity."

No one spoke. No one could speak after such a message, Laura thought. The silence was peaceful.

****

Maurice finally broke it. "Well then," he said in a practical tone, "perhaps someone can help me up and we can get out of this horrible place."

"We're all ready for you," Violet said from the door. "Sorry to be late, but you seem to have tidied everything up without me. All I had to do was to have them taken down to the station for questioning." She grinned. "If I keep this group around, I shall soon be out of a job.

"I'm not quite sure yet what to charge them with," she added, frowning, "but we'll think of something."

"I know." The emphatic words came from Zaina, startling everyone. "At least I know for Dr. Nezam." She went to stand beside Ben, as if to lend him strength. "It is worse," she said gently, looking up at him with eyes that knew far more than they should. "I saw him, you see, meeting with the men in India who find children for the brothel. He – Dr. Nezam, who calls himself your father, owns the brothel and many others. That is why he is so rich. I did not want to tell you this before because I knew it would hurt you so much. But now I think it is all right, even if it is very hard to bear."

Ben stood stiff as a board as shame and revulsion joined the rage in his face. "Yes," he muttered. "Yes, it is worse. He is a monster." He closed his eyes, absorbing the pain. "I did not know... I did not know..."

Zaina put a hand on his arm. "I am sorry," she said. "So very sorry." She turned back to the others. "I must say the rest, I must..."

She too closed her eyes, and the words came out in a rush. "My mother knew that Dr. Nezam was a brothel owner, too but she did not speak because if she did, she could not afford to rescue the children from the brothel and bring all of us to London to live in a place where we might be safe. She had to get the money from him first..."

Her voice broke, and she buried her face in her hands. "She only took it for the children... Always, it was for the children..."

She looked up again, her brown eyes liquid with pain. "You do not know how hard it was for us in India. No one will speak to girls who came from the brothels, they hit them and spit on them, and will not let them go to school, and always someone is looking for them to take them back... But we are still not safe, not in London, not even here in Switzerland until he is gone, until he cannot reach us at all, so now we must speak. He would have killed me to teach my mother a lesson or made the others kill me if you had not come, if all of you had not been here..."

She broke down completely. Laura took her in her arms again and rocked her slowly back and forth. No child should have to bear witness to such horrors.

Ben came to stand beside them. "You were right to speak," he told Zaina. "He must be stopped."

He turned to Violet. "I will help in any way I can," he told her. "I will find out more. I know who to talk to."

Violet shook her head. "Let us do it, Ben. Give us the names, and we will do it. You are needed here. It will not help anyone if you are killed."

Maurice spoke. "Violet is right," he told Ben gently. "You are needed here. All of us need you. Most important, your country will need you. One day, Iran will be ready for a courageous leader who is not tempted by corruption. Only in you have I seen the bravery and determination that might restore the greatness that once made Persia the envy of the world."

It was both a compliment and a reminder of responsibility. Laura saw Ben's shoulders straighten. "Yes," he said. "I understand."

Maurice turned to Zaina. "Let me see your face, child," he said. Laura released her, and she came to stand beside him.

"In all my years, I have never seen such courage as I just saw in you," he told her. "You are an example for all of us. We are proud of you."

Zaina leaned down to kiss his cheek, leaving marks of her tears on his skin. Maurice touched them reverently; then his voice became practical again.

"Good," he said. "Now, let us go back to the hotel. I shall see if I can book a room." He patted his stomach. "I am eager for some sustenance, too. No one thinks well on an empty belly. Shall we go?"

Gustav came to help him up. "I'll take Maurice and the three kids in the big snowmobile and the rest of you can come with Violet," he told them.

"Are you sure you can walk, Maurice?" Zaina asked, looking worried.

"I am all right," he assured her. "They just hit me over the head, the way criminals always seem to do. Very few of them have much imagination."

"True," Thomas agreed. "But when a criminal *does* have imagination, look out. I suspect we are dealing with one of them here, as well as a bewildering array of ordinary types. The trouble is, I don't know which one it is. None of them quite seem to fill the bill."

Laura took that as a challenge. The conference would end in a few days, so she had better hurry up if she wanted to figure it out first. There were plenty of candidates, but as Thomas said, none of them felt quite right.

"Maybe we need to cast a wider net," she mused aloud, and wished she hadn't when Thomas raised his eyebrows thoughtfully.

Violet reached into her pocket for the snowmobile keys but came up with some sheets of paper instead. "I finally got that lab report on the drugs," she explained, "but I haven't had time to read it yet. Shall we take a quick look at it before we leave?"

"Definitely," Catherine said. "I'm aching to hear what that powder we licked was especially."

Violet skimmed the report, read it again, and began to laugh helplessly. Catherine and Laura and Thomas watched her, bewildered. What could be so amusing about a lab report?

"You'll never, ever guess what the powder really was," Violet said when she could talk again.

Laura's mind raced over possibilities, without success. "No, we never will," she retorted. "We're all too tired to think. So hurry up and tell us before I burst with curiosity."

"Viagra!" Violet sputtered, doubling over again. "Heavily diluted Viagra, you'll be happy to know, but Viagra all the same. I wonder whose idea that was."

CHAPTER SEVENTEEN

Laura rummaged in her closet for an outfit that would hide her identity and be acceptable in an après-ski café. She settled on a one-piece ski suit she had bought in hopes of being instantly transformed into a graceful skier, and clunky fleeced-lined boots that were all the rage among young people. Over it all, she donned a fat down vest that made her look a lot plumper than she really was. Hard on the vanity, but good for disguise.

The only way to cast a wider net, she had decided, was to spy on as many of the people she had met in Switzerland as she could find. Fortunately, most of the Zermatt group was in Murren, thanks to Rosa's funeral. Helga and Ernest were staying at a nearby hotel noted for its après ski café. Felicia was there too, and presumably Veronica. Even Max might put in an appearance.

Turning to her face, she applied a layer of dark foundation that turned her skin positively swarthy, added a coat of coral lipstick that went just over the edges of her lips, which made her look as if she'd recently had a lip-enhancing injection, lined her eyes, and brushed mascara liberally on her lashes.

She frowned at her reflection in the mirror. She was beginning to resemble Lindsey, but maybe that wasn't all bad. Still, she didn't want to overdo it, so she toned down the lips and the mascara. Her hair was the real give-away. Pulling it into a tight bun, she covered it completely with a bulbous but stylish beret she had found on sale while prowling the streets earlier.

Her nose, still too pert, and her over-high cheekbones were next. Recalling the Grand Dame's methods, Laura made a gooey paste of face powder and oil, filled in the bridge of her nose and the sides of her nostrils and cheeks, then covered it with the dark foundation. Now she didn't look like anyone she had ever seen before, she noted after another glance in the mirror.

Satisfied, she pulled on gloves, stuffed necessary items into a waist pack in lieu of the backpack too many people might recognize, ran down the back stairs and out a door to the now-deserted deck. Since Thomas was once again closeted with Maurice, Violet was in Lauterbrunnen interviewing Dr. Nezam, and Catherine was with Gustav, no one who knew her well was likely to see her anyway, but she didn't want to take chances.

The noise level increased as she came closer to the town center. Good. Music and conversation were what she needed. Murren wasn't a big town, so there weren't many night spots to choose from. The most popular was in the hotel where the Brauns were staying, so she decided to go there.

She saw Max right away. His blond head shone almost white when he bent it toward the dim lamp in the middle of the table. They were the only lights in the café, which suited Laura. She would look pretty terrible in harsh light.

She stood in the entrance, trying to think how to get closer to Max, who was surrounded by three admiring young women. Interestingly, he looked bored rather than flattered by the attention.

Laura edged in his direction. The couple at the next table were signaling for the bill and getting ready to leave. Could she just sit down? Belatedly, she wished she had brought someone with her. A single woman at a table stood out a lot more than a duo.

"Care for a drink?" Laura looked up, startled. The tall man behind her was unkempt, a kind of rakish ski bum. He had a straggly beard, and even stragglier hair that poked untidily through an ancient wool hat that was coming unwoven and looked as if it hadn't been washed in a decade. It had fallen down on his forehead, covering his eyebrows. Even his eyes were almost invisible.

Laura took a step back; the man took a step closer. To her horror, he leaned over as if to kiss her, and for the first time she saw his eyes.

She pointed to her cheek. "How did you know who I am and that I was here?" she hissed when he was close enough. Ignoring the cheek, Thomas kissed her lightly on the lips. That, Laura realized, she would know anywhere.

"I was pretty sure you would do what I was about to do," he answered with a grin and a shrug. "Which shows how remarkably compatible we are. And I knew you because I saw you sneaking out of the hotel.

"You look dreadful," he added. "It's really quite a good disguise."

"I can definitely return the compliment," Laura said, trying not to laugh.

"Shall we sit?" Thomas politely pulled out a chair for her, belying his image as a bum. The waiter who approached the table looked dubious, however – or he did until Thomas pulled out a wad of cash. "White wine for the lady, a good Riesling might be best, double scotch for me," Thomas said, surprising Laura. She hadn't known he drank scotch. "And perhaps some of those delicious-looking sandwiches like the ones on the next table."

His accent was pure English, and his manner had suddenly turned into Lord of the Manor. One of those eccentrically wealthy Englishmen, the waiter would no doubt conclude.

The coterie of bubbly young women with Max apparently came to the same conclusion, and were regarding them with ill-concealed disdain. Laura looked harder and saw with astonishment that one of them was Lindsey in her Barbara identity. She must be spying too, which suggested she really was still CIA.

Laura put up a hand to shield her face. Her disguise wouldn't bear expert examination. For one thing, her make-up felt as if it was melting. So was she, for that matter. Could she take off her vest?

The young women returned their attention to Max. Thomas mouthed words at Laura, which annoyed her until she realized it was good cover for listening. She mouthed words back, listening hard. The conversation at the next table was hardly scintillating, however, mostly the trio teasing Max with allusions to his attraction for the women in his classes. That *must* be boring, year after year, Laura thought sympathetically - stultifying, in fact.

Finally, the two other young women got up to leave. Lindsey didn't waste time. She leaned closer to Max. "I hear there's some shenanigans going on up at the bomb shelter that you're involved in," she said baldly. "I'm interested, and I pay, but I don't talk. Know anything about it?"

Max stared at her. "Who are you?" he asked.

251

"I work for an international newspaper," she answered, pulling out some bills. "I never reveal my sources and I don't point fingers."

Max shrugged. "Keep your money. I do not know anything about it, and if I did, I would not talk about it. Now, if you will excuse me?"

"I think you do," Lindsey said as he rose. "If you don't, why did I find this in the old bomb shelter?" She pulled out a picture of Max and Veronica standing in the open door of the shelter. They were smiling and holding hands.

"I have no idea," Max stated, but Laura was certain he was upset by the photograph. "Now I really must go." He took a step.

"I hear that Veronica is your sister," Lindsey said.

"What of it?" Max replied irritably.

"I also hear she *isn't* your sister," Lindsey said, emphasizing the negative.

"You heard wrong," Max snapped. Tight-lipped, he made his way through the tables to the door.

"Your young man stood you up?" Thomas asked in his clipped accent.

"Touchy bloke," Lindsey replied, in full Barbara mode. "Guess I'll see if I can track him down again." She too made her way to the door.

"Interesting exchange," Laura said. "I wonder where Lindsey heard that they weren't brother and sister?"

"She might have made it up just to get a reaction," Thomas answered, "or maybe she really knows something, or just assumed it from the photo. Where did you hear that Max and Veronica *are* brother and sister, and do you know that with certainty?"

Laura shook her head. "No. I don't. Helga told us they were, and so did Maurice. I'd be surprised if they were lying. Why would they do that?"

"No idea," Thomas replied. "But I saw Helga and Ernest in the lobby and wouldn't be surprised if they come in here quite soon."

He turned to the waiter who had just plunked down their drinks. "That Max fellow who just left is one of the ski patrol members, I hear," he said.

"I believe so," the waiter replied in stilted English.

"He has a sister named Veronica, I think?"

"That I do not know," the waiter answered, and moved away to clear the table Lindsey had just vacated.

It didn't stay empty for long. To Laura's combined trepidation and delight, Helga and Ernst and a group of friends took it. Laura turned her face away and leaned closer to Thomas. "Do you really think I'll fool them?"

"Just don't talk." Thomas grinned. "Let's look madly in love, lean close and murmur to each other, sotto voice. That should do it.

"Laura my beloved," he began, but Laura cut him off.

"Don't use my name!" she hissed. "I'll be... Melissa, how about that?"

"Awful. I'll never get it off my tongue. How about Candice?"

Laura shuddered. "Then you're Cuthbert." Thomas laughed inaudibly, which shook his beard so badly that Laura was sure it would fall off.

"Cuthbert and Candice it is," he agreed when he could talk again.

One of the women with Ernst and Helga was looking at them, Laura noted, and not with approval. Probably it was Thomas's ghastly hat.

"Maybe you ought to take off that horrible hat," she advised.

"My hair would fall off at the same time," he said, which triggered her own bout of helplessly inaudible laughter.

The group at the next table began an absorbing conversation about Rosa's murder, which had the felicitous effect of holding their attention and quelling Laura's laughter since she wanted to hear. To her relief, they spoke English, probably in deference to an English couple among them.

"A madman, no doubt," the Englishman pontificated.

"Oh no dear, it's all mixed up with some boxes that were taken," his wife contradicted. "She worked at one of those places they store them, you know, to be sent to poor countries when there are emergencies. I heard she had threatened to expose them, so they killed her. A gang, I guess."

"Is that the rumor going around?" Ernest looked intrigued.

"I believe there's some truth in it," another man said in accented English, and Laura recognized the man who had called the ski patrol in Zermatt. "There has been another murder in the old bomb shelter on the way down from the Schilthorn. A bullet through the head, execution style, like Henri. It makes one fear that some kind of international criminal organization is involved. I dislike the thought of that happening in Switzerland."

In contrast to her husband, Helga looked almost sick. "I think we should not repeat all those rumors," she said quietly. "We must let the police do their work and then tell us what really happened."

Ernst wanted to know more, however. "What could boxes being stolen have to do with the murders?" he asked, ignoring Helga's warning look.

"Drugs, darling," the well-preserved woman next to him said. "It's always drugs, isn't it? They are everywhere these days, especially at the U.N."

"And then the mafia types get involved," someone else said.

Oddly, Ernst looked relieved. "I suppose that's it," he said, and changed the subject to the day's skiing.

His guests were more interested in gossip. "Wasn't it miraculous the way that woman found Veronica so quickly?" one of the women marveled. "Such a fuss – all of us out looking, and there she was all the time."

"We were very relieved," Helga agreed. "And she seems fine now."

"Is she talking to Max again?" another woman wanted to know. "I wonder what that spat was all about."

"I am sure she is." Helga's voice was patient but her face was strained.

"I never was sure if those two were brother and sister, the way they said," a sunburned man mused, "or if they were closer than that."

"Where did they come from? Does anyone know?" another asked.

"They grew up just across the border in France, a small town across Lake Leman. They still have family there." This time Helga's tone was firm, a clear signal that they had gossiped enough about Veronica and Max.

The two women took the hint, though Laura was sure they were frustrated. Women with the tantalizing scent of scandal in their nostrils were relentless.

"How is Nicolas?" one of them asked. "I haven't seen him recently."

"He is in Germany completing his studies," Helga answered, and once again her tone didn't invite further comment.

The woman looked surprised. "I had no idea he was studying there. When did he leave?" she asked, unable to resist one more question.

"It was a recent decision," Helga answered, her tone even firmer. "He has become very interested in psychology, and this is the best place."

"I see," the woman answered, but Laura heard the doubt in her voice. She suspected Helga heard it too, but she gave no further explanation.

The men were slower to pick up the signals. "I always thought Nicolas and Veronica had something going. Everyone did, didn't they?"

The other man nodded. "I was certain of it."

Ernst answered this time. "Oh, you know how they are, these young people. First it's one, then the other." Firmly, he changed the subject again, this time to the political scene.

Laura and Thomas exchanged a glance. "How much do you know about Helga and Ernst?" Thomas whispered. "And Max and Veronica?"

"Not much," Laura mouthed. They wouldn't learn much more here, either, she thought. The subject had been firmly closed by Helga and Ernst.

"Google them, for a start?" she suggested.

Thomas looked dubious. "I doubt it would tell us much, but we can try. "Internet café down the way." They left as unobtrusively as they could, considering the impossible hat that no one could fail to notice.

"Why did you wear that thing?" Laura asked when they were back on the street. "It's hardly inconspicuous. Everyone will remember you."

"Not me," Thomas pointed out. "They will remember the crazy man in the hat, accompanied by a lady of uncertain repute."

Laura was shocked. "Is that what I look like? I meant to look…"

"Like a sophisticated woman of the world?" Thomas supplied. "The odd thing is you should, but when you don the make-up, it seems to go awry."

"I guess it takes the Grand Dame's talent to pull it off," Laura lamented. "And that's not very flattering after I tried so hard."

Thomas grinned. "I'll help by getting rid of some of that lipstick." Pulling her into a secluded area behind a hotel, he kissed her hard and long. Laura pulled away long enough to wipe her lips with a Kleenex and then returned the kiss. It had been too long – much too long.

"It's been almost two whole days since I got shot," Thomas whispered. "I'm sure I've healed. Maybe we should go back to the hotel instead."

Laura was astonished – not by the suggestion but by the two days. "Is that all it is really? It feels like a week at least."

"More like a year," Thomas said mournfully. "Why is it that every time we get together, one or the other of

257

us is recuperating from damages inflicted by some unfeeling villain?"

"Look at the bright side – we're never bored," Laura countered.

"True," Thomas agreed. "Quite a lot does seem to happen during our brief interludes together. But for now, how about hot coffee and then the hotel?"

Laura grinned. "We can always try it and see what happens."

Thomas kissed her again. "It's a bargain."

"Maybe nothing will happen for the whole night," Laura said wistfully. "I could do with some peace and quiet."

"I hope *something* will happen," Thomas objected.

Laura laughed. "I meant nothing that has to do with guns or violence or abductions. Other forms of activity will be welcome."

They were about to emerge from their secluded spot and go back to the hotel when English voices on the sidewalk made them pause.

"I wonder what's really going on with Nicolas," a woman said. Laura recognized the upper-class accent of the Englishwoman at the Braun's table.

"Follow," Thomas mouthed. "Lovers." Draping his good arm around her shoulders, he led them into the street. Laura clung close, lover-like.

"Something fishy," the husband replied, "and not just with Nicolas. I want to know what Ernst was trying to get at with all those questions about boxes. I hear a lot of his venture capital projects have gone south recently."

"South?" His wife was puzzled.

"Slang term for losing a lot of money," he husband translated. "I've helped to fund some of them and I'm getting worried."

"Oh dear, that doesn't sound good. I wonder what he's invested in now?"

"Something to do with art stolen by the Nazis and mysteriously turning up again, is what I heard. Sounds a bit risky. Lots of money in it if it works, but what if the real owners show up?"

"I shouldn't think they would after all this time," his wife said. "And even if they did, how could they prove it was theirs?"

"That's a point," he answered, sounding relieved. "Most of the records are long gone. Really quite a creative project when you come to think of it. The big mystery is how he got hold of art like that, after all this time."

"Felicia?" Laura mouthed.

"Or Maurice," Thomas mouthed back.

The English couple went into their hotel, so Laura and Thomas ducked into the Internet café, hoping now to find material on Ernst's reputed venture. The cafe yielded great coffee but no information on the new enterprise.

"I need to put some of our investigators onto this," Thomas said. "I'll send out queries in the morning. Someone in the art world must have heard of it."

They came out into the street again and almost collided with Catherine and Gustav. "Sorry," Catherine said politely, and walked on a few steps. Then she spun around. "Gustav – that was my Dad! But who's he with?"

"How did you know?" Thomas said grumpily when she confronted him.

"The way you walk," she said promptly. "Is this your date?" Hands on hips, she examined Laura. Her lips twitched. "Hi, Laura."

"I wouldn't have known," Gustav assured her. "You don't look like you."

"Thanks, Gustav. Right now, though, all I want to do is take it all off," Laura said. "We're on our way back to the hotel to do just that," she added. "How about you two?"

"We're going back to Gustav's place," Catherine told her. "We'll come by in the morning and see if anything dramatic has happened. See you!" Taking Gustav's arm, she sauntered away.

"There goes my daughter," Thomas said, looking bemused. "I've always wondered how I'd feel when she announced she was spending the night with some fellow or other, but at this particular moment, I can only say that I am heartily glad. The only company I want right now is you."

"My feelings precisely," Laura agreed. "Maybe if we hurry we we'll get there before anything else happens," she added. "I've got this prickling on the back of my neck that I get when…"

Someone smacked into her, running hard. Laura fell against Thomas, and he fell against the fence that ran along the road to protect visitors from the precipitous drop on the other side. The fence gave way, and they might have tumbled all the way down the vertical cliff to Lauterbrunnen if strong hands hadn't reached out to pull them back.

Laura looked up, expecting to see Catherine and Gustav but saw Lindsey instead, or rather, Barbara. "You okay?" Barbara asked.

"I think so," Laura replied, and looked around for Thomas.

"Right here," he said. He was already on his feet, apparently uninjured. "I didn't fall that hard," he said. "But I could have, if someone had done a better job of weakening this fence. I guess they ran out of time."

"Guess so," Barbara agreed, examining the damaged fence. "Somebody really doesn't like you two."

"Did you see who it was?" Thomas asked.

Barbara shook her head. "All I saw was a crouched over person running fast who disappeared behind that building. If I were you, I'd watch my back."

"Good idea," Laura agreed. She stood up and flexed her arms and legs to make sure everything was all right.

"Looks like it all works," Barbara observed. "I move along, then."

"Thanks," Laura said belatedly. "Good thing you were nearby."

Barbara laughed. "That's because I was following you. I thought it was you in the café, but I wanted to check it out." Putting her head to one side, she examined Laura critically from head to toe. "If I were you, I would go ultra-sophisticated next time. I'd be happy to give you a hand if you want.

"See you around!" She went on down the street.

"What do you suppose that was all about?" Thomas asked.

"The attack or Lindsey?" Laura asked.

"Pretty clear what the attack was about," Thomas answered. "I meant Lindsey – whose side is she on, do you think?"

"No idea," Laura answered. "However, she didn't threaten us, do anything violent or show any murderous intent. Instead, she saved us from a very nasty fall or worse. For all those things I am profoundly grateful because I can put off figuring it out until morning and I'll still be alive to do it – that is, if we hurry."

"My sentiments exactly," Thomas agreed. Grabbing her hand, he jogged up the rest of the street to the hotel. Without pausing, they sprinted up the stairs and collapsed onto the bed. After that, they hardly said anything at all.

CHAPTER EIGHTEEN

"This case makes me think of three interconnected spider webs," Laura mused when they gathered to talk the next afternoon. ""Karl is the spider of the smallest web, which persuaded delegates and other people to sabotage the conference, presumably for the benefit of one or both of the other webs. Henri Guillard was the spider at the center of the next web, the drug trade. He lured in greedy investors, and thousands of victims got caught in his traps. Dr. Nezam is the spider at the center of the biggest web, the prostitution one. He found unscrupulous people to finance his brothels, one of them probably Henri, and trapped millions of helpless victims in his web. He may also have bought drugs from Henri to sedate the girls.

"Now what we need to know is which suspects got lured into which webs, or maybe into all of them."

"A large order," Violet said dryly. "But I like the image. Here's another. Henri is dead, as is his second in command, Ludwig, and I believe we are seeing evidence that his web is collapsing. Dr. Nezam has been apprehended and one of his brothels is being investigated, leaving his web vulnerable. Karl has called in sick and the conference has come to a halt, which suggests that he – and his web – are breaking down too. Now – what happens when three interconnected, overlapping webs begin to collapse?"

"Spiders panic," Thomas answered. "So do the people who were helping them. They try to salvage what's left and then run in all directions."

"Exactly," Violet agreed. "I think it will soon be panic time at the shelter and that we should be on hand to see what happens."

Let's go!" Catherine said enthusiastically. "I'll call Gustav."

"He's on his way," Violet told her. "We'll follow soon. But first I need to give you an urgent update on Dr. Nezam. He is pleading diplomatic immunity, which means we can't charge him, only expel him. We held him overnight, but we had to let him go this morning. That leaves Dashka and Zaina vulnerable if he wants revenge. I've had a special guard put on both of them.

"I also suspect Dr. Nezam will go back to the bomb shelter before he leaves. I think he heard, probably from Nina or Joe, that valuable art might be stored there and he wanted to find it. That's the only reason I can come up with to explain why he had Zaina abducted and brought to the shelter, and then Maurice. He knew that if Nina started cutting Zaina up, Maurice would talk. And what does Maurice know about? Art. Dr. Nezam also knew that Thomas, another source of information about art, was meeting Maurice there. For all I know, he had planned to abduct Catherine along with Zaina to get even more leverage."

"That is diabolical!" Catherine was outraged.

"Good thing you've been sticking close to Gustav," Thomas told her. "I recommend you stick even closer until Dr. Nezam leaves."

Catherine grinned. "Will do," she agreed.

Laura laughed. "Dr. Nezam must have been appalled to find all the rest of us up there, even Ben. For once, we foiled the bad guy's plans."

"In terms of sex trafficking, we haven't," Violet said grimly. "Dr. Nezam will keep right on procuring girls and get away with it. We can't prosecute him here, and I doubt he'll be prosecuted in Iran. You can tell us more about that."

"Human trafficking is illegal in Iran but it still has one of the worst records in the world because no one prosecutes it," Laura explained. "The Iranians might decide to make an example of Dr. Nezam to curry international favor, but I doubt they'll bother."

"I doubt it too," Violet agreed. "So our next job is to keep Dr. Nezam from tormenting Dashka and Zaina any more, but I can't think how to do it."

"I've got one idea," Catherine said immediately. "Let's threaten to expose him as the person who ordered the Viagra because he was in desperate need of it unless he leaves Dashka and her family alone."

"Catherine!" Thomas looked shocked. Then his face changed and he began to laugh. "Actually, that's quite brilliant," he conceded. "Dr. Nezam would die of embarrassment. Especially if he knows all of us will hear about it."

Violet grinned. "I'll have a cozy chat with Dr. Nezam before he leaves," she said. "Let's hope it works."

"What about Dashka?" Laura asked. "Will she be charged? Extorting money is a crime, which is probably the reason she didn't tell us about it."

"She was just asking for money from a friend so she could move to a safer place," Violet said innocently. "If I were her lawyer, that's what I would say."

"In Dashka's case, I would cheer," Laura said. "She deserves a break."

"So does Zaina," Catherine said fervently.

"I'll try to make sure they get one," Violet promised. "Now, before we leave, does anyone else have information to report?"

"Thomas and I do," Laura said, and described what they had overheard last night about Nicolas and about Ernst's new art venture.

"We also saw Lindsey as Barbara, posing as a reporter and questioning Max about Veronica. Barbara said she'd heard they weren't brother and sister, and so did the people with the Brauns. Max looked shaken."

"Intriguing!" Violet replied. "We'll have to dig into that. I wonder if there are church records somewhere, of birth or marriages."

"Helga said they grew up in a small French town across Lake Leman where they still have relatives," Laura reported. "We can ask Helga for the name of the town and send someone there to ask around."

"I'll check it out," Violet agreed. "I want to hear more about Ernst too."

"I've sent out inquiries about his art venture, and I should get back some information soon," Thomas told her. "What I most want to know right now, however, is the location of all those paintings Ernst hopes to sell. We know large numbers of paintings stolen by the Nazis ended up in Switzerland, far more than the two Maurice wants to find. My sources say they are near here. I can't believe they are all hidden in fake bottoms of medication boxes, so where are they?"

Laura heard the frustration in his voice. "The shelter is the logical place to look for them," she said resolutely, "so we just have to look harder."

"Right," Violet agreed. "We'll do a thorough search when we join Gustav."

"Meantime," Thomas said, "Ernst needs money to get his venture off the ground. He may well have asked both Henri and Dr. Nezam to invest. As far as he knew then, neither hadn't done anything illegal, but it would put him in bad company. We have to keep that in mind."

Violet nodded. "Ernst is a risk-taker, so it's possible.

"I wonder if there's an art web too," Laura mused.

Thomas looked thoughtful. "Two master spinners and one caught in the web," he said enigmatically.

He cleared his throat. "Speaking of art, I believe I may be able to cast light on one item that Dr. Nezam and possibly others were looking for," he said in a low undertone. He held up a small package wrapped in brown paper.

"Guesses?" he mouthed, holding it aloft. "But whisper please."

"The other Vermeer," Laura breathed. "Does Maurice know?"

"I'm keeping it to myself for the moment," Thomas whispered back. "It's safer. Maurice and I had agreed to meet at the shelter to look for it, but then Dr. Nezam got word of our plan. Nina of the ever-ready ears, no doubt. Dr. Nezam intercepted Maurice but to my enormous relief, he didn't find me, so I had time to look around.

"I haven't checked for listening devices and I don't trust the walls, so we had better not talk about this any more, even in whispers."

"Lindsey," Catherine said. "I'm sure she's the one who put in the listening devices. Where does she fit into these webs? My guess is that she's the one master-minding all of them. She seems to know everything."

"So does the Zermatt group, as I have taken to calling Felicia and Helga and Ernst," Thomas observed. "I haven't even met them, but they strike me as ubiquitous. It's as if they are on a collective mission working toward a goal we haven't yet deciphered. We don't know if it's a worthy goal, either."

"Or whether Lindsey is part of the group," Laura mused. "Which reminds me - I forgot to say that Lindsey also saved Thomas and me from going over the cliff last night. I don't think anyone meant to kill us," she added, describing the incident. "He or she just wanted to scare us, as usual."

Violet looked exasperated. "You'd think our various opponents would have given up those tactics by now, but I guess not."

"Lindsey may have administered the push herself," Thomas remarked. "Then she played the hero and saved us."

Laura blanched. "I hadn't thought of that, but it is possible. And then she had the temerity to warn me to watch my back – and to give me advice on my next disguise!"

Violet laughed. "I can't figure out whose side she's on. Instead of being mastermind, as Catherine suggests, Lindsey could be master infiltrator of all three webs in her role as spy."

"Or both," Catherine proposed. "Kind of like the Grande Dame.

"Or like the Zermatt group?" Thomas suggested.

"We seem to be surrounded by them," Laura commented wryly. "But back to Lindsey. "I finally got some replies to my queries about her this morning, but I'm not sure they help. Lindsey was with the CIA but no one seems to know if she still is. Apparently, she got *born again* – the religious conversion kind. That put off a lot of her colleagues. They didn't want to use her any more because she was always trying to convert them or other people."

"But neither we nor they know if she got *born again*, as you put it, because that makes an invaluable cover," Violet pointed out.

"Cover," Catherine said positively. "She's not for real. I'd bet on it."

"She certainly knows how to act," Thomas agreed. "She had me fooled in her Barbara persona. Do you suppose she's someone else as well?"

Laura's eyes opened wide. "The man in the grey suit!" she exclaimed, and described the scene she and Violet had witnessed in Zermatt after the Braun's party. "We think Felicia was in the house, and we know Veronica, Nicolas, Max and Maurice were. We also saw a man in a grey suit go in, and I found a grey man's suit in Lindsey's room. I didn't realize its significance until now, and I still wonder how Lindsey can dress as a man with her over-endowed figure."

"That's just push-up bras," Catherine explained. "Even flat-chested women can look like Dolly Parton, or almost, with the right bra."

Laura grinned. "I hadn't realized. Maybe I'll get one for my next disguise." Catherine laughed, and Thomas looked interested.

"Time to leave," Violet said, standing up. "We can speculate forever, but right now we need to act. Our spider webs are collapsing and I want to watch what happens – *and* I want to be there if Dr. Nezam makes a return visit."

"I bet all our suspects go there," Catherine said. "Which means Gustav has his hands full, so let's move right along."

Thomas held up the painting again. "Too late to take it to the bank. Any bright ideas about where to hide it?"

"You'll have to bring it with you," Violet said. "I don't dare leave it here, even in the hotel safe. Who knows who has access to that."

Violet had a snowmobile waiting for them. It was almost dark now, and very cold. Laura shivered despite her down jacket and the blankets they had brought for warmth. The ride seemed interminable, and with every mile, her fears about what could happen at the shelter grew stronger. Her small band of unarmed companions was setting out to do battle with unscrupulous criminals who would kill to get what they wanted, and three of the people she cared for most were with her. It was a terrifying thought.

****

Violet doused the lights and stopped the machine well before they got to the shelter. They plodded up the road, their boots squeaking against the hard-packed snow. Their progress was audible to anyone within earshot. Laura looked around nervously.

Violet gave a low whistle, which Laura assumed was a signal when a man came toward them out of the trees. "Gustav's inside with two other people," the man said. "I'm not sure what they're doing, but Gustav said to come in quietly, without torches. He's in the box room."

The door was already open, and they slid in noiselessly. At this point, Laura thought, she could almost find her way with her eyes closed.

They crept toward the box room, helped by a low but steady light that emanated from it. A small lantern, Laura saw, peering inside.

The scene that confronted her was so absurd, almost comical, that she had to press a hand against her mouth to keep from laughing. Karl was crawling awkwardly among the scattered boxes, frantically opening one after another, while Makedu stood over him like an avenging angel, brandishing a decoratively carved stick over his back.

"What did those evil people tell you about my beautiful Amina? Tell me," she shrieked. "And keep finding those packets. They will all go down the toilet, every one of them. Men are bad enough as it is and Africa has no need of that! Shame! Do you know who they use it on? Little girls, that's who! Even babies!"

She took a step closer, holding the stick high. "Now speak and keep on speaking until you are so embarrassed you will never speak again, never chase after a woman again. We are weary of your lecherous womanizing!"

"They said she..." Karl couldn't go on, and Makedu raised her leg as if to kick him in the derriere. "They said she wanted it, wanted a man who... a man like me, who... who could stay..."

"Oh God," he moaned. "I cannot tell you the rest..."

"Say it all!" Makedu bent over him, her eyes fiery.

Karl gulped and tried again. "They said it was because... because..."

Makedu smacked him with the stick. Gagging, Karl pushed out a stream of almost inaudible words. Pornography and Dominatrix and bondage were the most prominent. So that was what Karl liked. Laura felt physically sick.

Karl seemed to as well. Still gagging, he forced out more whispered words as Makedu prodded him with her stick. Not until he had collapsed on the floor, gagging uncontrollably, did she relent and change the subject.

"How many of those packets have you found? And how many are there?" she demanded. "And why did you come into our room?"

"I don't know how many," Karl said miserably. "I've haven't counted... And I came because they said she was waiting for me. They said..."

Karl looked up, saw the stick move. "They said that she was interested in me, that she was a woman who liked to do..."

Makedu's outraged shriek interrupted him. "Who told you such despicable lies?" Karl hesitated, and Makedu gritted her teeth. "You are going to tell me because if you do not, I will force all those packets down your miserable throat. I will do it, I tell you! You will choke on them!"

Karl winced as she waved one of the offending packets in his face. "They all did – Henri Guillard and Ludwig and then..." He gulped.

"Tell me!" Makedu loomed over him, her hands poised to open the packet. "Tell me or you eat this!"

"Nina and Joe, and... and Dr. Nezam, though he never said it directly."

"Ah! Now we get to the ones who are alive," Makedu crowed. "Tell me, which of them killed Henri and Ludwig?"

"I don't know," Karl groaned. "I don't know, and you can ask me forever but I still won't know."

"Was it Dr. Nezam?" Makedu shook a threatening fist in his face but Karl just kept shaking his head hopelessly. Laura thought she had never seen anyone look so crushed, and she felt almost felt sorry for him. Gone was his charm, the easy patter that made him amenable to so many people. Karl was like a worm crawling along the floor now – the worm that he was, she knew, but she still wished Makedu would stop taunting him.

Makedu wasn't willing to give up yet. "Then was it the girl? That desk man who calls himself Joe but comes from Iran?"

Karl frowned. "Maybe they all did it together," he mumbled, as if thinking of the answer for the first time.

"Ah! So they were all working together." Makedu sounded triumphant. Karl relaxed slightly, but Makedu wasn't willing to let him off the hook yet.

"Who is the boss of this criminal organization," she yelled, waving her stick like a warrior about to strike. "Tell me or..."

"Henri. Henri Guillard planned it all." Karl's reply came quickly this time. "Ask anyone; it is true. He got Ludwig. I don't know where Dr. Nezam came from or... But I had nothing to do with it, nothing at all."

"There is another person," Makedu growled. "I can hear it in your voice. Who is it? Hurry! I am holding this packet ready..."

Karl blanched. "I only saw him once... I don't know, really..."

"Saw him where?" Makedu snapped. "Who, where?"

"Ernst," Karl whispered, his face puzzled. "I don't know why he was here."

"Here, in this abominable place?" Makedu pressed.

"Yes," Karl answered, but now he was babbling defensively. "But they all come here – Felicia and Ernst and Max and Veronica. They know the farmer who owns it, and that must be why Ernest was here. Ann comes too sometimes. I've seen them all. It doesn't mean anything. None of them have anything to do with this, what Henri and the others were doing. I have nothing to do with it either, except for the... the..."

"Viagra, I believe it is called," Makedu said caustically. Abruptly, her voice dropped to a sibilant whisper, and she wrapped her arms around her body, as if to comfort herself. "Viagra, one of the greatest curses ever to befall Africa," she whispered, "almost as great a curse as the men themselves. And it is the women and children who suffer the consequences. Always, it is the women and the children, the girl children who suffer...

"How do you think they like it when the men go on and on and on," she screamed at Karl, her voice harsh and accusing. "They are only babies..."

Her dark eyes were moist with unshed tears, and her face was suffused with agony, an agony too deep and painful to be borne. "Why do men make us suffer this way?" she howled in a voice that vibrated with the depths of her torment. "Our only sin is to be born female. Why, I ask you, why must you make us suffer so horribly? Why do our men in Africa treat us like slaves, use us and rape us and beat us, keep us on our hands and knees for their pleasure... Why do you rape our innocent daughters, our babies...

"What is the matter with the men of Africa?" she cried out desperately. "I ask you, what is the matter with these men?" Again and again she screamed the question, loud primeval howls of anguish that seemed to fill the shelter with images too horrible to be seen. Laura wanted to cover her eyes with her hands, and she felt everyone around her shrink back, as if the words had hit them physically and made them smaller.

Karl's crawling body went slack with shock, and Laura wondered if he was weeping. Makedu was, she saw, when the howls finally stopped.

Makedu herself broke the long silence that followed. She sighed heavily and wiped her eyes. "But that is not fair," she said in her normal voice. "It is not just the Viagra, and some men at least are good.

"Some of them are here," she added slyly, giving Karl a tiny kick. He jerked to his feet, his face contorted with embarrassment.

Gustav and Violet stepped into the box room. Karl stared at them, aghast. Then he saw Laura and Thomas and Catherine. His mouth opened and closed, but no words emerged. His humiliation was complete, Laura thought, and decided to give him a break. "Good evening, Karl," she said politely.

Karl didn't answer. Making a pathetic effort to regain his dignity, he ran his fingers through his disheveled hair and straightened his clothes. Without speaking, he pushed past them. Violet's voice stopped him.

"I need to ask you a few questions," she said calmly.

Karl bristled. "I have nothing to -"

The deafening report of a gun going off behind them cut off the rest of his words. An instant later, the big door clanged closed. The sound was louder than usual, as if someone had pushed it hard.

They raced toward the sound of the shot, confused now by competing reverberations from both gun and door. The entryway was empty, but the acrid scent of smoke from gunshot was strong.

Violet put out a hand. "Stay here," she commanded. Gesturing to Gustav to accompany her, she crept through the living area into the first bedroom. Laura heard their footsteps stop and then go on again.

The bed in the second bedroom. She knew they were there, that they were looking down on… On what? Another body or a bundle of blankets?

"You can come now," Violet said. Her voice brimmed with weariness.

Laura went in, with Thomas on one side, Catherine on the other, and forced herself to look. Dr. Nezam lay face up on the bed. He had a bullet hole in the middle of his forehead.

CHAPTER NINETEEN

"I need to report this right away," Violet said resignedly. "I can't say I'm sorry Dr. Nezam is dead, but I don't appreciate having him killed right in front of our noses, or our backs in this case."

"I'll go outside and call as soon as we've had a good look around," Gustav offered. "I'll turn the lights on too."

"Thanks." Violet examined the body again and frowned. "Actually, Dr. Nezam couldn't have been shot while we were in the storeroom. We would have heard him and his killer come in. He must have been shot earlier, like Henri, and brought here."

"We would have heard him being carried in," Laura pointed out, "so he must have been brought here earlier, too."

"I don't see how," Gustav replied. "I looked at the bed when I first got here and all I saw was a bundle of blankets. I suppose he could have been hidden under them." He sounded doubtful.

"Maybe that's it," Violet agreed "That way, all they had to do was fire the gun from the door, close it and run."

"A dead man is hard to carry, which suggests more than one person could be involved," Thomas thoughtfully.

"Remember that Agatha Christie play? The whole group did it." Laura said. The Orient Express, I think it was."

"That," said Violet, "is a very interesting idea."

Gustav looked horrified. "Spare me! We could end up trying to arrest some of Switzerland's most important citizens."

Shaking his head, he went off to deal with the lights. Laura listened to his receding footsteps and felt an overwhelming urge to go after him and run out the door into the open air, air that didn't smell of gun powder and wasn't contaminated by still another death. She turned to follow her impulse, but Gustav returned before she had taken more than a step.

"The door won't open," he said briefly. "I'll keep trying, and see what I can do with the lights. I wish I had Ben here."

"You don't, actually," Thomas reminded him, "considering that the man he lived with, father or no, just got shot."

"Right you are." Gustav shook his head as if to clear it. "I'm getting muddled with so much action."

"Do you suppose we could go into the other room to talk?" Catherine asked plaintively. "Dr. Nezam isn't a pretty sight even in the dark."

Violet took a last, searching look at Dr. Nezam, memorizing his position, the direction of the shot and other details, and then went off in search of Karl. Laura used her flashlight to look again herself. There was something subtly different about this murder, she thought, struggling to think what it was. Not the bullet; it had gone straight in, just as it had with Ludwig and Henri. What was it then? The answer wouldn't come.

Shuddering, she went into the living area. Makedu was already there, sitting quietly on a couch. She looked exhausted.

"Dr. Nezam was a cruel man," Makedu said. Her voice was hoarse, rasping in her throat from all her shouting. "Perhaps Karl will be next. I think he is very afraid." She pointed toward the box room. "He is cowering in there."

Laura sat down beside her. "You were amazing," she said sincerely. "Poor Africa – what a burden you carry, the women I mean. Will it ever change?"

"There is a woman from your country who is training African women to lead their countries," Makedu replied. "They are all women who have been raped and abused and forced to flee from their homes. With this woman's help, they built a village with their own hands. They call it *The City of Joy,* and that is where they learn to be leaders of their villages, learn to train others to be leaders of their villages and cities, and then to be leaders of their countries. Yes, one day Africa will change. The women will see to it."

Thomas sauntered in. Examining their faces, he let the silence linger and then managed to cheer them up in his own indomitable way.

"This isn't so bad," he said cheerfully, sitting on Laura's other side and caressing her hand. "Nice and dim, just right for an intimate chat. Laura and I aren't all trussed up like chickens waiting to be slaughtered the way we were on our last adventure, either – until Laura managed to get hold of that knife and then drop it in full view of the nasty pair who had tied us up while trying to decide how best to kill us."

Makedu laughed. "What happened then?" she asked.

Thomas launched into a vivid portrayal of the charming art galley where he and Laura had been tied back to back on a pair of very uncomfortable chairs. He had just finished a description of their crab-like gait as they shuffled across the room to retrieve the much-needed knife from Laura's backpack while still tied to the chairs, when the lights came on.

Makedu, who had been smiling broadly, put her hands over her eyes. "Oh such brightness," she groaned. "At least in Africa, it is not bright in this way. Why is sunlight so different?"

Violet came back, with Karl trailing behind her. "Karl has information I think all of you should hear," Violet said. She looked at him expectantly.

Karl sat down on the chair furthest from them and with the least light. He didn't look at them as he began to talk in a dull monotone.

"Henri Guillard was in the import/export business. He had warehouses all over the world to store legitimate and counterfeit drugs. He had contacts with pharmaceutical companies, and that's how he got the drugs. He bribed people in them to do what he wanted, or maybe he invested in the companies. He invested in any business that would make money for him. He did not care if they were ethical. We were all afraid of him. I don't know who shot him but I am glad he is dead. I got some... some Viagra from him to sell to others. From then on he made my life a misery. He always wanted more, and he threatened to talk about me if I did not make the via - the drug more profitable. He would have, too... I was afraid... I am still afraid. Perhaps I will be next..."

His voice trailed off, then resumed again in a defensive mode. "I did not do anything illegal. I only sold a drug that is already on the market but that some people cannot get. That is all. I have not killed anyone. Henri made Ludwig do his dirty work. Maybe Ludwig shot him. I don't know. I don't know who shot Ludwig either, or Dr. Nezam. He got drugs from Henri, and Henri had shares in the brothels. I don't know anything about the art.

"Someone has been blackmailing me, but it stopped," he added suddenly. "I don't know who it was." He stared at Makedu. "Maybe it was you."

"Or maybe you were blackmailing Amina, so she wouldn't repel you as she wanted to," Violet suggested. "What is it you know about Makedu?"

Makedu laughed. "Probably he knows that I killed a man in Africa," she said. "That was no crime. He deserved it. I found him trying to rape my niece, so I pulled him off and did what needed to be done to make sure he would not rape a girl again, but unfortunately, he died as a result. Perhaps Amina was worrying about that. She should not have. I am proud of it.

"I would do it again if I had the chance," she added, looking hard at Karl. His face blanched and his hands went down to his lap protectively.

"I will not stay in the same room as this woman any longer," he stated, and went back to the box room.

"I wonder who was blackmailing Karl?" Laura asked. "And why it stopped?"

"Possibly because the blackmailer was dead," Thomas suggested.

"Perhaps," Violet agreed, "although I have another idea." She refused to elaborate, saying she had to talk to someone first.

The lights went off again, and Laura shivered. "I don't like those lights but this place is even creepier without them. Hard to search, too. We need to find that art."

"I might as well catch you up on some of the other reports that have come in while we wait for Gustav to fix them," Violet said philosophically. "First, a man resembling Joe was seen in the area where Rosa was killed. It's suggestive that she was killed on a Friday, Joe's day off."

"Makes sense," Laura agreed. "Ludwig was on the train the whole time."

Violet nodded. "Thomas was right, though, that Ludwig shot him. The bullet Gustav dug out of his arm matches Ludwig's gun. I think Dr. Nezam was shot – executed might be a better word- with a high-powered rifle like Ludwig and Henri, but we'll know more when I get help up here. I have no idea who shot him, though. Seems to me all the obvious suspects are already dead.

"Now – on to the lab report, which might at least have the benefit of amusing you. I spent most of the morning figuring it out. Briefly, all the stolen boxes I have examined so far contain powdered re-hydration packets because they can be easily mixed with illegal drugs that are also in powder form. Each packet now contains one of the counterfeit drugs heavily diluted with lactose powder or baking soda and some re-hydration salts. Henri made his money by getting at least ten doses from each single dose of a drug.

The drugs include ecstasy, a name that describes what buyers think it will do for them; a potent tranquilizer that is normally used on horses whose name I can't recall and a concoction called the White Powder of Gold, or *the elixir of life.* It has a large group of remarkably naïve followers who believe it confers immortality, so they pay handsomely for it. Then there's the Viagra, which was ordered separately by Karl. I note with interest that Europe is his biggest market, mostly via the internet. He had it sent out in discreet boxes."

"Speaking of boxes, Henri had a streamlined transportation system from here to his warehouses all over the world, where the counterfeit drugs were re-labeled and sent to buyers. Most of his business was legitimate, though, which made it easy to get away with an illegal sideline. He knew that boxes labeled children's medications from a reputable agency wouldn't be challenged, and I doubt anyone would have paid attention to them if Laura hadn't come along. The changes in the agency's orders might not have been noticed, either, if Max hadn't asked Rosa to check on them."

"Max! How did he know about them?" Laura was astonished.

"I'm not sure yet. Either because he was working for Henri or because he was investigating Henri. I only learned about it yesterday at the funeral, when Rosa's sister told me that Max had asked Rosa about the boxes. Apparently, Rosa herself had increased the number of boxes being ordered. She assumed the aid agency wanted more and thought no more about it. It hadn't occurred to her that the extra boxes went missing until she sat down with the records and put it all together – and was killed as a result."

A wave of sadness washed over Laura. Such an unnecessary death. She wondered if Max felt guilty about his role in it, and was surprised to think he might. On the other hand, she reminded herself, he might have set Rosa up to be killed because she knew too much.

The lights suddenly came on again, and Gustav and Catherine reappeared. "The door must be locked from the outside," Gustav told them. "I don't think we can open it from here."

"Definitely a dilemma," Violet said, eyeing her unresponsive cell phone.

Laura was less sanguine. Being trapped in here was a nightmare come true. "There has to be another way out," she said shakily, hoping certainty would keep a creeping sensation of claustrophobia at bay.

"You're right," Catherine agreed valiantly, after a quick glance at Laura's face. "The people who built the shelter must have planned an emergency exit. Let's search for it now, before the lights go out again."

"Stay together, or at least in pairs," Violet warned. "This is a big place and whoever shot Dr. Nezam could still be here, hiding somewhere. If you get into trouble blow a whistle. If you don't have one, scream."

"I will watch the door," Makedu offered, "and I will make that coward Karl join me. If I tell him the murderer is loose, he will come in a hurry. He knows what I can do with my stick. He can hide under the table if he wants."

Brandishing the stick, she went to get Karl. Gustav and Catherine set off to search the box room for doors; Laura and Thomas and Violet went into the bedrooms to search the area beyond them. Laura took another quick look at Dr. Nezam, hoping to spot was what different; then she concentrated on looking for doors she hadn't been able to see in the dark.

Beyond the second bedroom was a large area filled with the machinery that kept the shelter habitable – a water tank and heating system, and a ventilation system.

Huge metal coils sprouted from it that Laura assumed transported air. They disappeared into the ceiling, and presumably outside.

"They're wide enough to crawl through," Thomas said thoughtfully.

Laura felt her stomach clench painfully. Twice, she had been forced to creep through narrow tunnels and she didn't want to repeat the experience.

"All yours," she muttered. "Tunnels aren't my thing."

Violet gave her a quizzical look. "I doubt it will be needed," she said. "The shelter was built to protect people from contaminated air from nuclear fallout, so why would the ducts go outside?"

"Maybe they take air from outside and filter it," Thomas pointed out. "See that machine? It's a huge filter, I think. Besides, there's nowhere else to get air, unless they recycle what they have endlessly."

"Makes sense," Violet agreed, causing Laura's stomach to clench again. Still, if it was the only way out she supposed she could do it. At least ducts wouldn't smell of mold and have spiders and snakes inside them.

That assumption was quickly dashed. "I'll be curious to see what sorts of creatures have taken up residence inside them," Thomas remarked. "Snakes in particular have a liking for holes that go into the earth. Mice, too. I've found whole colonies of them in pipes." And where there were mice there were usually rats, Laura thought with a shudder.

"Is that really true?" she asked suspiciously. Thomas liked to make up stories like that to disconcert her.

"No idea," Thomas answered blithely. "I've never crawled through a pipe, but I guess we'll find out." Laura glared at him and he grinned.

Catherine and Gustav saved Laura from attempting the experimental exit strategy, at least for the moment.

"We found a locked door," Catherine said excitedly. "It could be a way out, or the art could be behind it."

"I think the lock could be picked," Gustav added. "Anyone good at locks?"

"I can probably do it," Thomas offered.

They trooped after Catherine and Gustav to the box room again.

A door Laura hadn't seen before at the back of the room was open. "It was covered with boxes and we saw it when we moved them," Gustav explained. "They were empty so it wasn't hard. They have labels on them, though."

"Not Surprising. Rosa said hundreds of labels that identified the boxes as children's medications were also missing," Violet told them.

Thomas rummaged in the pockets of his jacket came up with a tiny set of tools. He peered closely at the lock, pulled out a tool and twisted gently while concentrating intently on the feel of the tool in his hand. When the first tool didn't work he inserted a slightly larger one. After two tries, the lock yielded.

"A cautionary tale," he warned. "People have no idea how easy it is to pick locks they've been told are foolproof."

"I want one," Catherine said. "Where do you get them?"

Thomas looked uneasy. "Not a good item to have in your pocket if you're picked up by the police," he warned.

"No problem," Catherine replied. "I'd just say I have it so I can get into my house if I forget my keys. The police think women are always forgetting their keys or locking them in their cars. They almost never think we're thieves."

"The hazards of being male," Gustav murmured. "We're never supposed to lose our keys so we must be thieves." Opening the door cautiously, he peered inside. "Not art or exit," he said. "Medication diluting."

The room was large, with a low ceiling. Rows of long tables stood at regular intervals. They were covered with boxes, some empty, some with half filled packets; others ready to be closed up. Empty packets were scattered about.

"Looks like the place where they mix the powders," Violet agreed. "I guess they divide the re-hydration salts among ten packets, add a small dose of the drug, some baking soda or lactose powder, whichever one best matches the drug's color and texture, and them close them up again."

"All the packets look alike, so how do they tell which is which?" Laura asked. "Henri wouldn't want his sedative orders to get mixed up with ecstasy or the white powder of gold – or Viagra."

"There's a tiny mark on the top," Violet answered. "An initial, it looks like. I guess that's how they tell which is which."

Catherine laughed. "Getting Viagra when you thought you were getting a sedative would be a shock, at least for men."

Thomas looked at her askance, and Laura knew exactly what was going on in his mind: how had his innocent little girl morphed into a young woman who knew all about drugs and Viagra?

"Would they notice the difference with heavily diluted drugs?" she asked.

"The placebo effect is pretty powerful," Gustav replied. "If they thought it was Viagra it would act like Viagra, I imagine.

"Which makes me wonder where the real drugs are." His eyes lit on a locked metal cabinet on the far side of the room. "That must be it."

Thomas went to work on the second lock, while Violet examined boxes.

"We need to take some back for testing," she told Gustav. Together, they carried a selection of boxes, each with a difference initial, into the storeroom to be put into the snowmobile when they finally got out.

Laura picked up the last one. "I'll take it and check on Makedu at the same time," she said. "Not too much more I can do here."

She found Makedu sound asleep in her chair. The stick had fallen out of her hand. Laura smiled. Makedu deserved a rest after that bravura performance.

Karl was nowhere to be seen. She had better locate him, Laura thought resignedly. They were responsible for him until the authorities came.

She went back toward the bedrooms, thinking that Karl might have decided to lie down. A whiff of fresh air tickled her nostrils as she entered the second bedroom. Where had it come from?

The scent was gone almost as soon as she had detected it. Maybe she had imagined it – a side effect of claustrophobia perhaps?

She examined the room again, alert to anything she hadn't noticed before. A big free-standing closet with tall double doors, the kind Europeans often used in lieu of closets, caught her eye.

Pulling the doors open, she looked inside. The smell was stronger here, as if it had been trapped behind the doors. Could there be an exit behind the cabinet? Maybe Karl knew about it and had left that way.

Excited now, Laura tried to push the tall cupboard out of the way, but it wouldn't budge. Karl couldn't have pushed it either, she realized. She would have heard the noise, and anyway, it was much too heavy.

Shining her flashlight on the back of the closet, she felt along the edges with her fingers. Without warning, the back of the closet slid to one side. Laura jumped backwards in surprise. How had that happened?

She stared. Behind the panel was a tunnel – quite a large one, big enough to walk easily. It didn't even smell musty. Excitement gripped Laura again. She had found the way out! What a triumph it would be to go outside, come around and unlock the door for everyone else. The smell of air was strong, which meant the outside couldn't be far away...

She took a few tentative steps into the tunnel, shining her flashlight ahead of her. It wobbled in her hand, she noticed. The realization sobered her. Maybe she shouldn't be doing this alone. Karl could be in there, waiting to hit anyone who came in. He had a flashlight, she was sure, a heavy one. He might even have taken Makedu's stick. Had it been on the floor beside her?

Laura took a deep breath, tantalized by that elusive scent of fresh air. Then, reluctantly, she turned to go back and get the others.

She sensed more than saw something behind her and ducked instinctively. Out of the corner of her eye she saw a figure, a crouched-over figure whose head was hidden. She whirled to confront it, but before she could even raise her flashlight as a club, the figure barreled into her and hit her hard in the belly, knocking the wind out of her. A scream making its way up Laura's throat was cut in half; the rest came out as a croak. Her eyes streamed with tears from the force of the blow. She blinked hard, desperate to see who had hit her, but the cascade of tears blinded her.

Hands dragged her further into the tunnel and dropped her. She lay where they left her, choking and gasping in an effort to draw breath. She heard the panel slide closed again, heard running feet going down the tunnel away from her. Again, she smelled fresh air, and then it was gone. Laura closed her eyes as blackness began to swirl around her.

****

Pounding noises roused Laura. Someone or something was hitting the panel forcefully. Makedu's stick? Certainly that was Makedu's voice behind the thuds. With every blow she swore vengeance on Karl. "Wait until I get my hands on that bastard, that creeping worm. He will be sorry he was ever born…"

Laura wanted to laugh but her throat was too sore from all the coughing and choking. But at least she was breathing again.

"Press along the edges," she croaked.

Sudden silence followed her instruction. "Praise the Lord!" Makedu cried. "Halleluiah! You are alive!" The pounding resumed, harder now.

"No!" Laura tried to yell but couldn't. Still, this croak came out louder. "Push around the edges," she repeated.

The pounding stopped and she heard softer noises of hands against the panel. After a moment, it slid open. Makedu burst into the tunnel, brandishing her stick. Her eyes opened wide with fear when she saw Laura on the ground.

"What has he done to you?" she moaned. "What has that bastard done…"

"I'm all right," Laura assured her. "Just winded."

"Winded?" Makedu looked puzzled.

"Whoever it was barreled into my stomach," Laura explained.

"Ah. So you had to fight him. That is not good. He is a big man. Well, we shall see." Grunting with the effort, Makedu lowered herself to the ground next to Laura. "Let us see what has happened," she said, reverting to her practical tone. "Can you see my fingers? How many?" She held up three fingers.

Dutifully, Laura told her, and Makedu gave her a great smile. "Now, can you get up? Or if you are too dizzy, can you sit? Or hold up both your arms?"

Laura grimaced. "I could do all three, but I would be sick all over you if I did," she confessed.

Makedu laughed triumphantly. "Then you are not so bad. That is the test I always do when people have been in a fight, you see. That way, you know if their brain has been affected. I am glad to see that yours works."

A voice came from the living area. "What is all the racket about and where are you?" Violet this time. She didn't sound alarmed.

Makedu's answer was indignant. "Here in the escape route. It is a good thing I was watching and listening. He might have killed her if I had not heard her scream. None of you paid attention."

"We didn't hear," Violet protested.

"Who screamed and what escape route?" Catherine this time.

"Why Laura of course. He trapped her in here. She is alive, but she cannot get up just yet. We are in the big cupboard."

Abruptly, three heads appeared at the back of the cabinet and peered out at them. Violet, Catherine and Thomas stepped into the tunnel.

"Good heavens!" Violet exclaimed. "How did you find this?"

Thomas reacted differently. His face went whitish-green when he saw Laura on the floor. "I shouldn't let you out of my sight," he said shakily.

"I'm all right. I really am," Laura assured him. "I just feel sick."

"No thanks to that monster," Makedu asserted.

"You need food, that's your trouble. And tea," Catherine diagnosed. Rummaging in her pack, she handed Laura a cracker.

"Yes," Laura agreed weakly. "But I found the way out. And I don't think it was Karl who barreled into me. Whoever it was wasn't tall enough."

"Not Karl?" Makedu frowned. "But then where is he?"

"Here," Gustav said. "He was in the bathroom." Karl's head appeared at the back of the cabinet; then he disappeared again.

"Any idea who did barrel into you?" Violet asked.

Laura shook her head. "None. The person was doubled over and I think had a hat pulled low, so the head was hidden. Great big jacket that covered up the shape. Strong, that's all I know. My best guess is that it's the same person who ran straight at me a few nights ago, except from the front this time."

"Well, at least you found a way out, if the air I smell is any indication," Violet replied. "That's quite a feat. I gather there must be a sliding panel at the back of that big cupboard?"

"Yes," Laura answered as she nibbled the cracker. It did make her feel stronger, so she decided to get to her feet. Thomas helped her on one side, Makedu on the other. She managed not to throw up.

"If you didn't hear me scream, we might not have heard Dr. Nezam being carried in," she pointed out when she was standing.

"Good point! I'll check the exit door to see how far it is," Violet said, striding down the tunnel. Catherine was right on her heels. After about ten feet, the tunnel forked. Violet took the right fork, Catherine the left.

Violet's voice came first. "Not far at all," she called back. "The exit comes out behind the hill so you can't be seen from the road. That must be how they brought Dr. Nezam in."

"Dad! "Dad, you've got to come!" Catherine's voice was shaking with suppressed excitement. "I think we've found it! Dad, this has got to be it!"

CHAPTER TWENTY

Unanswered questions buzzed around Laura's brain. She wished she had someone to talk to, but Violet was at the police station, Thomas and Maurice were talking about paintings and Catherine, as usual, was with Gustav.

Laura made a mental list. Maybe that would help. They knew a lot now about the various criminal enterprises and the men who had run them, and they might even have found the missing art. Catherine's excitement had been warranted but premature since they couldn't open the big steel door she had found. Presumably, the art was in the room it protected, but no amount of lock picks would get them in. Two specialized keys like the ones used in bank vaults as well as the combination for the large padlock-type instrument on the door's panel, were needed to open it. Good for the art, Thomas noted, but frustrating for them. Still, it was a marvelous discovery. So was the room where the drugs were mixed. The locked metal cabinet where they assumed the full-strength drugs were kept had been emptied out, though, by unknown hands.

The person or persons who had killed Henri, Ludwig and Dr. Nezam were also unknown. The only circumstances the three men had in common was that they were executed with a high-powered rifle, were involved in enterprises most people would consider criminal but were unlikely to be brought to justice. Laura wondered if that had anything to do with their deaths.

Confusing the picture further, Ludwig had been shot in the shelter with a single shot, but Henri and Dr.

Nezam had been killed, carried to the places they were found, and then another shot had then been fired to make it seem that the murder had just happened. In Henri's case, the killer had skied away from the scene before he or she could be apprehended; in the other cases, the killer could have escaped on a snowmobile. That was all they knew, and the list of possible suspects was fast diminishing.

The other persistent and thus far unanswerable questions, apart from the missing full-strength drugs, had to do with relationships between parents and their children. Laura understood the reasons for Ben's hatred of his father, and for Reginald's gallant attempts to keep his mother from doing nasty things, even Zaina's and Amina's fears because their mothers had something to hide, but Helga's reluctance to talk about Nicolas remained a mystery. Was she trying to hide something about her son?

Relationships between the young people, particularly Max and Veronica and Nicolas, were just as puzzling. Max and Nicolas had once been best friends, or so Max had said, but now they mistrusted each other. Was Veronica the cause? Nicolas was clearly in love with Veronica, but was she in love with him? Helga's assertion that they had loved each other since childhood and planned to marry could be wishful thinking. They *planned* to marry, she had said, not they *plan* to marry. Was that a clue? And what about Max and Veronica? What were their feelings for each other and how could she find out?

She might not be in a position to solve the murders or track down the missing full-strength drugs, Laura mused, but she could find out more about the people who might provide clues about them. Murren was a small town where everyone knew everyone else, and Max and Veronica apparently spent quite a lot of time here. And what did most people in Murren do on a blustery, snowy day like this when the skiing was unpleasant? They went to a coffee shop with a friend, that's what they did.

Grabbing her jacket and a big scarf, Laura went out to prowl the streets for a likely coffee shop. She peered into the windows of each one she passed. On her third try, she grinned triumphantly. The Englishwoman was sitting inside with one of the other women who had been with the Brauns. Perfect! They were inveterate gossips who had been very frustrated when Helga had cut off discussion about Max and Veronica and Nicolas. The odds were good that the two women would talk about them again.

The tables around the Englishwoman were full, but a small balcony that overlooked the room was almost empty. Laura snagged a table just above the two women. Their English stood out against the background chatter of German, and she leaned towards them, listened unashamedly.

"Henry and I were talking about Nicolas just last night," the Englishwoman was saying. "He was such a charming child, but he's gone moody suddenly. And I can't imagine why they sent him to Germany to study psychology."

"I cannot understand it either," her companion agreed. She paused, and then seemed to come to a decision. "I have never talked about this before, so please don't repeat it. But the truth is that I have always been curious about Nicolas. Perhaps you don't know this, but Helga and I grew up together, and I came to her wedding. Both she and Ernst were eager to have children, but for many years they did not. Then, which she was about thirty, Helga went to the U.S., Colorado in fact, to look for investments in the ski industry. She was there for almost a year, and when she came back she had Nicolas. Of course Ernst visited her quite often, but I still wonder…"

The Englishwoman's eyes opened wide. "Well," she ejaculated. "That is an odd turn of events. What do you suppose happened?"

"My dear, one can only guess," her friend replied. "What was even more interesting is that Felicia came to visit Helga in Colorado that same year. She had been in Europe somewhere, writing those articles about art, and the man she had been living with – he was a revolutionary, fighting communism in East Germany I think, was killed. Felicia came home – she was originally American, you know, and one of my friends saw her in the airport in New York, before she went to join Helga. She said Felicia was quite plump – a bit of a belly, she put it. Felicia was always so thin. She was well over forty by then of course, but still, such things do happen. One cannot help but speculate…"

The Englishwoman's skimpy eyebrows went up almost to her hairline. "I certainly do! What if Felicia was pregnant? She was much too old to handle a child for the first time and anyway, she couldn't take it on, not the way she lived, traveling all over the world. But for Helga -"

"Yes. A perfect solution for both of them, one would think." The Swiss woman sighed. "Still, we will probably never know if that's what happened. It seemed too intrusive to ask Helga. She is a very private person and does not like to talk about herself."

"No. Probably we won't ever know." Disappointment was evident in the Englishwoman's voice, but she quickly found a more tantalizing topic. "I have always wondered about Max and Veronica too," she confided, "especially Veronica. She is such a lovely girl, but she doesn't look at all like her mother, the first wife who died. She looks like her stepmother, practically a carbon copy of her. Max looks like the first wife though, and like the father who was killed - the image of him, I'd say. I wonder what that means?"

"Two wives," the Swiss woman said dismissively. "Not much mystery there. The first one died when Max was born, so he got another before he was killed."

"But that doesn't explain why Veronica looks so much like the second wife and Max looks like the first, which is backwards since Veronica is the oldest. It doesn't explain why people keep wondering if they really are brother and sister, either. They don't act like it, at least to me."

"They are unusually close," her friend agreed, "which also makes me wonder why they have been so angry with each other recently."

She looked at her watch. "I must leave," she said reluctantly. "But I have some friends in the village where Max and Veronica grew up. I'll give them a ring. They might know something."

"I should leave too," the Englishwoman agreed. "But be sure to tell me what your friends in that town say.

"Do you know anything about the art venture Ernst is involved in?" she added as they gathered up their coats.

"I doubt it will succeed," the Swiss woman said. "My husband thinks the murders we keep hearing about might be connected to it, too. That gives it a bad reputation, which won't help."

The rest of the conversation was lost when the women moved away and the waitress brought Laura's coffee. A young woman like her might know Max, Laura thought, and asked.

"The waitress laughed. "Everyone knows Max," she said in accented English. "But no one knows Max. He keeps his thoughts to himself."

Laura asked if she knew Veronica, and her face clouded. "She never mixes with people like me who live here. She is always studying books. That is good, but she does nothing else. She does not know how to have a good time."

Laura heard resentment in her voice, which wasn't surprising. Veronica must seem arrogant to young women without her aspirations.

She paid the waitress and tipped her, a habit she found hard to break, and sat on with her coffee, trying to work out the implications of what she had heard. Nicolas might be Felicia's illegitimate son by an unknown rebel fighter – could that be what Helga wanted to hide? Or was the whole story a fabrication created by the overworked imaginations of two gossips? On reflection, Laura thought it probably was, but even if it was true, what possible connection could it have with the murders?

The gossip about Max and Veronica, on the other hand, had a ring of truth. Both Helga and the Swiss woman had said that Max's mother had died when he was born, leaving his father with an infant son. But did that mean the father was also left with Veronica, the older child? Or could Veronica have a different mother, one who had also been widowed- or deserted - and left with a child, and who had subsequently married Max's father? If so, Veronica would have a different father as well as mother. And that meant Max and Veronica had grown up as brother and sister but they weren't, and then Nicolas, a boy who was Max's best friend and who had loved Veronica since childhood and as an adult wanted to marry Max's sister who wasn't his sister...

Laura shook her head, bemused. This was straight out of Shakespeare. Not exactly incestuous, but certainly tangled. A quote came into her mind: *What tangled webs we do conceive, when first we practice to deceive...*

But why would anyone try to deceive? And who *was* Veronica's father if not the one who had been killed? Her stepmother was still alive, but would she talk? Women often didn't want to admit to past relationships, especially if a child had been conceived out of wedlock. That would explain why everyone had been told that Veronica and Max were brother and sister – to protect the mother's reputation and give Veronica legitimacy. People in rural Switzerland were still very conservative, and at the time of Veronica's birth, illegitimacy must have been a matter to hide if at all possible.

But if all this was true, what did it have to do with the larger picture, the murders and criminal activities

300

taking place at the shelter? Instinct told Laura they were connected, but she needed more than instinct to prove she was right. Downing the rest of her coffee in a gulp, she hurried back to the hotel to find Violet. It shouldn't take long to locate Veronica's mother; persuading her to talk might be more difficult.

Violet had already returned and was holding a formal gold and ivory invitation in her hand. She looked up, puzzled.

"Felicia has invited all of us to a gala party at the Castle of Chillon, of all places," she said. "I wonder what that's about?"

Laura smiled. "I hope," she said, "that it might be about answering some of our remaining questions."

****

Felicia's invitation also specified that the remaining delegates, as well as Violet and Laura and the rest of their group, would be driven to the castle and back in cars she had hired for the occasion. Laura was astonished – that was a big expenditure all by itself, never mind renting the castle for an evening and feeding and entertaining them.

She tried to work out the number of people and came up with at least twenty, even after the murders and arrests. She listed them: herself, Violet, Thomas, Catherine, Gustav, Sigrid, Sigrid's husband Lars, Kjersti and Kristin, who were determined to be included despite their parents misgivings, Ann, Karl, Reginald, Dashka, Zaina, Lindsey, Makedu and Amina, Helga, Ernst, Max and Veronica and Nicolas, if he came back for the party. Sadly, Ben would miss it since he had accompanied Dr. Nezam's body back to Iran for burial. He was the head of the family now, and all its responsibilities would fall

301

on his young shoulders. He would live up to the task, Laura thought, remembering how regal and handsome he had looked in the white robes of his tribe when she had said goodbye to him.

The cars Felicia had ordered were more like limousines, Laura discovered when they arrived at the hotel. Only once before had she been in a limousine, when a friend in a large investment firm had offered her a ride to the airport since they were on the same flight to London, though not the same class. The drive had been memorable. Hot coffee, newspapers, TV to watch, a chauffeur to hand her in and out and carry her suitcase. Laura had adored it. Luxury didn't come her way often and she appreciated it when it did.

This car was even grander, offering a chilled bottle of champagne instead of hot coffee. Laura and Violet debated whether to drink it. They had to keep their wits about them. This was, after all, a murder investigation.

They compromised and decided to limit themselves to one glass, to be followed by a big cup of coffee when they arrived at their destination.

Thomas expressed no such intentions. Opening the champagne, he landed the cork neatly in Catherine's lap, to her delight, poured them each a glass and took an appreciative sip of his own.

Catherine watched the bubbles rise in her glass. "Haven't had much of this stuff before," she confessed. "Too expensive."

"This one is," Thomas agreed, and provided an impromptu education on the impeccable vintage of this particular bottle. Gustav followed the flowery language with pleasure.

"Used to serve this from time to time but it seldom made it to my lips," he remarked, sniffing the champagne and rolling it gently in true gourmet fashion. Then he took a slow, lip-smacking sip.

"Does go to your head, however," he warned.

Perhaps, Laura thought later, that was why the trip to the Castle of Chillon was forever after engraved in her mind like the pages of a book, as if she was turning them over one by one. First, the drive along snowy, twisting roads that wound up and down, the night black around them but for the blur of twinkling lights in villages they passed; then brighter city lights made hazy and ethereal by falling snow, then the approach to the castle. It looked as castles always did in fairy stories - beautiful and remote in its island setting but also sinister, as if any kind of monster could lurk inside its hulking walls. Or perhaps it was only forbidding in her mind, because of its long and often brutal history. Laura never was sure. All she knew was that a sense of unreality pervaded her from the time she went into the door until she came out again.

It was snowing heavily by the time they arrived, adding to the fantasy. The flakes came down so fast they could hardly see as they made their way up the long entrance path, and only the gleam of snow atop the covered bridge ahead told them were they were going. On one side of the bridge, Laura saw the dark hulks of boats, their seats covered with a thick white layer, their hulls rocked by black water lapping insistently against them; on the other side was the old moat, almost hidden by tree limbs weighed down by a burden of ice. Once a drawbridge had protected the moat, Laura knew. She imagined it dropping with a thunderous clang.

Snow hit them again in the open courtyard on the other side of the bridge, but here light was everywhere – from bulbs strung around doors and windows, from torches and flares stuck into flower beds and huge pots that in summer held massed blossoms, from inner windows where candles and lamps glowed, from decorative outer lights on trees and bushes and walkways. Distorted by the thickly falling snow, they had the look of cobwebs in morning dew, a kind of Halloween illusion. The effect was mesmerizing.

Kristin and Kjersti came up behind them, breaking the spell. Ignoring the display of lights, they headed straight to the ancient wooden door that led to the catacombs below. Pushing it open, they darted in. Laura and the others followed. Immediately, they were plunged into darkness. Kjersti gave a little squeal, and her eyes were like saucers. As their sight adjusted, Laura saw a single muted light glowing somewhere in the rooms beyond. It had been aimed toward the ceiling, she deduced, because the wonderful arching beams that supported the rooms above were faintly lit, but the walls of the dungeon remained exactly as they might have been when men were manacled here, perhaps for the rest of their lives. Had Felicia arranged it this way? Or were there no lights down here ever?

They crept around with careful steps and peered into dark corners, through openings hacked into the stone and made secure by iron bars. By day, they let in light, but at night all that came through was the unnerving sound of restless water. Laura felt the chill of moist stones against her hands as they guided her through the dimness, saw that in some places, the massive boulders had been rubbed almost white by captive palms through the centuries. Depressed by the thought, she couldn't wait to leave.

Violet had other ideas. "Boxes," she whispered. "We need to look for boxes." To Laura's alarm, she plunged straight through a small opening between two rocks into total darkness.

Laura felt Thomas take her arm. "Courage," he whispered. "This place is worse than the shelter. Even if more atmospheric."

Together, they followed Violet. She was on the floor, flashlight in hand, examining boxes. "I think Max has been here today," she said.

"Maybe tonight we can finally find out what his role is in all this," Laura said hopefully.

"I intend to ask him," Violet said grimly. She put a few packets from the boxes into her purse, and after ensuring that Sigrid and Lars were with the twins, they went out into the open courtyard again.

Catherine and Gustav scampered up the stairs to the covered ramparts that stretched all along the inner walls. "A push from here would split a skull," Catherine remarked ghoulishly, looking down at them. "Come on up. We can go all the way up to the lookout tower. Better do it now. We won't later."

Catherine was right, Laura thought. Better do it now. Besides, the castle was a whole different experience at night, especially in the snow. Never again would she see it like this, lit up, snow-covered, fantastical.

The ramparts led them to steep flights of narrow stairs, back outside again and then up more covered flights, the last one so steep Laura wasn't sure she would make it up. Finally, they emerged breathless onto a balcony that gave a bird's eye view of the castle grounds, the lake, and all of Montreux.

A pair of moving figures approached the covered bridge below them. Max and Veronica, Laura saw. Their heads were almost touching, as if they were engaged in an intense discussion. Abruptly, Max pulled Veronica against him and kissed her long and passionately. Laura looked away. It seemed intrusive to watch such a personal moment. Still, it was a clue. That wasn't brotherly love she was witnessing. Or sisterly. Veronica's response was ardent.

They sprang apart as other people approached. Dashka, Zaina and the boys, Laura saw. Had they too seen the embrace? Maurice was with them. Good; she was glad he was here. Maurice had a way of making her feel that everything would come right. He kissed Veronica on both cheeks and wrung Max's hand heartily. Did that mean he didn't suspect Max? Or was he bluffing?

"You saw that kiss too," Violet asked in a low voice. Laura and the others nodded. "Hard to convince me that they aren't lovers," Catherine said. "They seem right together, even if they were brought up as brother and sister."

That summed it up, Laura thought, but it didn't absolve them of guilt. Max was clearly involved, and Veronica had wanted vengeance on Henri.

She shivered as an icy wind sprang up, flinging frozen snow drops into their faces. "Time to go inside," Thomas urged, and led the way down the five flights of steep stairs. The others followed.

"I hope they have heat going," Laura said as they climbed yet another set of stairs to the main door.

"Otherwise, I'll be wrapped up in my ski jacket all evening and won't get a chance to show off my one long dress."

To her relief, light and warmth flowed out as they went through the door to the main rooms. Lamps were lit, and heat blasted from space heaters and ancient radiators. The deep windows were almost covered by heavy curtains, shutting out the cold and blackness. All that could be seen between their folds was a glimpse of tiny leaded panes and candles gracing each window sill.

Within moments, they were warm enough to leave their jackets and snow boots in the cloak room. They paused briefly to rearrange clothes and hair and don dressier shoes; then they were ushered into the banquet hall, a long room with beautifully decorated walls.

"That is an impressive scene," Thomas remarked, regarding the rows of crimson-covered tables that were elegantly set for dinner with multiple wine glasses. Each was decorated with wide-branched candelabra filled with deep red candles, and tall vases of fresh flowers. "Felicia has done herself proud."

"I wonder where she is," Laura said. "Does anyone see her?"

"Maybe she wants to make a dramatic entrance once everyone is here," Violet suggested with a grin. Laura suspected she was right.

A waiter materialized, carrying a tray of drinks. Laura saw cocktail glasses with unknown concoctions, more champagne, white and red wine, and on a table against the wall were bottles all kinds. So much for coffee, she thought, selecting a glass of wine. It seemed rude to ask for it, with all these choices.

Another waiter followed bearing canapés. At least she could eat with her wine, Laura thought. That ought to help.

They wandered through other rooms, appreciating the beautifully carved chests, the well set-up bedrooms and even the plumbing. While rudimentary, it was efficient - and communal. A long row of toilet seats, about two feet apart, emptied into the lake. Laura tried to imagine rag-clad servants and elegantly dressed courtiers seated side by side with their pants down, and failed. There must be another privy, probably outside, for the low-born classes.

The armory was next. It was a vast, echoing room with flagstone floors and walls of large roughly cut stones. They were covered with weapons, antique lances and swords and guns, and on one wall, modern rifles. Laura's stomach flipped. Had one of them been used to kill Henri and Ludwig and Dr. Nezam?

Violet took a rifle down from the wall and examined it, pulling back the clip to make sure it wasn't loaded, Laura assumed. The conjecture reminded her forcefully of their reasons for being here. What if someone had put bullets in one of the guns ahead of time?

Violet apparently had the same thought and took each of the guns down to be examined. When she set the last one back on the wall, Laura saw a gleam of anticipation in her eyes. She wondered what it meant.

They heard the chatter of more guests arriving and returned to the banquet hall. First, Makedu and Amina burst through the door, faces ruddy with the unfamiliar cold. Their brilliantly colored robes seemed made to order for this elegant setting, as did Dashka's golden sari. Zaina wore a sari too, in turquoise that complimented her dark coloring. She looked young and innocent, like a girl attending her first party. Possibly it was, Laura thought with a pang of pity. Reginald came in with her. He looked older than his years in his formal dark suit, and remarkably handsome. Perhaps in a few years the twins would reassess their view of him, Laura thought hopefully. Or maybe they already had. They too had donned party clothes, or their version of them, which was peasant skirts and vivid blouses. They made a bee-line for Reginald, seemed unable to think of anything to say, giggled nervously and then burst into excited chatter. Reginald actually smiled at them.

Ann and Karl came in together. She had done her best with a slightly crumpled skirt and top, but Laura wished someone would give her lessons in how to dress. Maybe Karl would do it. He certainly knew how. Despite his recent humiliation he was in full party mode, always a flattering remark, eyes everywhere, a smile that wasn't a smile but only a twitch of lips. Laura had felt sorry for him after Makedu's tongue-lashing but she didn't now.

Sigrid, statuesque in high heels, appeared at her elbow, with her even taller husband Lars behind her. "I have not had time to introduce you properly to Lars," she said to Laura. "He is a professor of Middle Eastern Studies with a particular expertise on Iran. He and Ben had many fascinating discussions."

"We did indeed," Lars confirmed. "Ben is an unusually intelligent young man, just the sort of person Iran needs right now. I was honored to make his acquaintance and will stay in touch with him. The situation is unstable in Iran right now, and it is good for Ben to have friends abroad.

Laura was delighted. "I didn't know that. This has been a very hard time for Ben, and I am glad you were there."

An absorbing conversation on the state of the world ensued, and Laura realized that it was almost the first time since she had come to Switzerland that she had talked about anything besides the case.

Sigrid's next remark brought it back. "Let's hope there is no running to do tonight," she said with a smile. "I would not get ten feet in these."

Lars laughed. "Then I shall carry you," he said gallantly.

"Thank you, darling, we could try that, but just in case I have brought these," Sigrid replied, pulling a pair of battered ballet shoes out of her small purse like a conjurer. "I always bring them. My toes do not like high heels but sometimes it is enjoyable to wear them anyway."

"I wish I had thought of that," Laura said, eyeing her own heels, which weren't so high but were still entirely unsuitable for running.

More people came; Laura recognized some of Helga and Ernst's friends, and suspected others were associated with Felicia or with the castle's staff and donors. Soon the room was filled with animated conversation.

Violet appeared at Laura's elbow. "I think everyone is here now," she said, "so Felicia may make her entrance soon."

Laura surveyed the crowded room, looking for faces she hadn't yet seen. "Not everyone," she answered. "I still haven't seen Lindsey. Have you?"

Violet shook her head. "No. Maybe she's not coming."

"She will come," Laura answered and wondered why she was so sure. Perhaps, she thought, because Lindsey always seemed to turn up, usually in unexpected place and guises, rather like Thomas.

Lindsey's warning flashed into her mind. *Watch your back*, she had said. Laura vowed to do just that despite the festive surroundings. Three murders had been committed already, possibly by someone in this room, a killer who could even now be planning a fourth.

Watch your back, and watch people, Laura told herself. *Watch carefully and never, ever, let down your guard.*

CHAPTER TWENTY ONE

Laura heard a commotion at the door as Felicia made her long-delayed entrance. She was dressed in a tight black body suit covered by a full-length jacket of creamy satin that covered her from head to toe. To Laura it looked almost like a shroud. It hung on Felicia's slender frame, making the fragility beneath it shocking. Her skin was so pale it looked transparent, except for a patch of feverish red on each cheek. Her eyes were brilliant, still full of fire.

She really must be ill, Laura thought. There was even a nurse hovering in the background. Only when this realization had come to her did she see that Helga and Ernst, who were standing just behind Felicia, were poised to support her if that was necessary. Helga looked exhausted, and Ernest had unfamiliar lines of strain on his face.

"Greetings to all of you," Felicia said, and her voice at least still had strength. Seeing their shocked faces, she waved a bone-thin hand dismissively. "Yes, I am weaker than when you last saw me, but it will pass. It is a disease with a name like a wolf, and it comes and goes with the stealth of a wolf."

Lupus, Laura thought, one of the autoimmune diseases. But could it cause such fast and dramatic loss not just of strength, but of weight? Only a week ago, Felicia had seemed strong and vigorous.

Felicia smiled wryly. "The disease is made worse by stressful events, and they have been plentiful recently, as some of you know. But we will not speak of that now. Instead, let us enjoy our evening in the Chateau Chillon."

Helga whispered something to her. Felicia nodded. "Helga tells me the waiters are signaling that dinner is served," she announced. "Please take a seat. The charming people in the kitchens here have prepared a delectable feast for us that I am certain you will enjoy. And so shall I.

"If you will be so kind, Ernst, please sit on my right. Helga is on my left and Maurice is beside her. Everyone else, please take any seat you wish."

Felicia gestured to the nurse, a dark-haired woman wearing a simple blue dress. "You must sit too, my dear, perhaps beside Helga." Removing her cap, the nurse obeyed. Her hair fell limply around her face.

When everyone was seated, Felicia raised her glass. "Now, let us drink a toast to your health and happiness," she said to the guests. "My blessings to you all." She uttered a long sigh of satisfaction as she took the first sip of wine. "Ah! That is very good."

She smiled at them mischievously. "The doctors tell me I should not drink this, but it is good to be merry with one's friends, is it not Maurice?"

Maurice raised his glass to her. "To the bravest woman I have ever known," he said. Turning, he raised his glass to the whole group. "Enjoy yourselves, all of you, please. That is what Felicia desires. As she says, the cuisine and wine experts at the Chateau Chillon have provided a memorable repast and superb vintages, so we must pay them due respect by taking pleasure in every bite and sip, as will Felicia."

She did, too. Laura watched Felicia eat at least a part of every dish that was put in front of her with enjoyment, saw her sip each wine appreciatively. What kind of willpower did it take to do that, she wondered? Surely, Felicia didn't feel as well as she pretended.

Suddenly aware that feeling healthy and hungry was a blessing and not an automatic right, Laura decided to emulate Felicia and appreciate every bite and sip. It wasn't hard. The food was wonderful, not heavy servings but an array of small, beautifully presented dishes, each with it own distinctive wine, in the French style. As they poured, the waiters told them about each vintage and explained why it had been chosen for this dish. Thomas was enthralled, as was Gustav -and, surprisingly, Violet. Laura decided she had better educate herself on wines as well as African queens when she returned.

By the time coffee was served at the end of the meal, almost two hours later, she found it difficult to focus on the warning she had uttered to herself. It seemed all wrong to be thinking of murders as people chatted and laughed and toasted each other. The guests had definitely taken Maurice's injunction to heart and were paying full respect to the chefs and vintners by enjoying the food and the wine. It was indeed a memorable evening.

When the last plates had been cleared away, Felicia tapped on her glass with a spoon to get everyone's attention.

"Ladies and gentlemen, please feel free to explore the castle's magnificent interior if you have not had a chance to do so before. Be sure to see the grand collection of travel chests, the lavatory, another popular site, and the armory. I have also arranged to have the museum's shadow play presented for those who would like to view it. The staff here will be happy to assist you."

"For those who have come by car from Murren, I have asked the limousines to pick you up in about thirty minutes," Felicia continued. "It is still snowing, and the drivers want to make the trip before the roads become too difficult. So far, all is well, I am glad to say."

Felicia leaned over to exchange a few words with Maurice, who nodded, then Ernst and Helga helped her to her feet and they left the room. The nurse went with them. She was a rather mousy young woman, Laura thought, with an indeterminate-looking face and lank dark hair that badly needed a cut.

Maurice came to their table. "Felicia wishes all of you" – he gestured to Violet, Laura, Thomas, Catherine and Gustav – "to stay for a short time after the other guests have left. She has something to show you. A few delegates who have been involved in your investigations may also wish to stay. I do not know exactly what Felicia has in mind, but I am sure it will be interesting."

"Thank you, Maurice," Violet answered. "Do you know if Veronica and Max will also be staying on?"

"I am not sure," Maurice said, and Laura noticed that he didn't look at Violet as he spoke. Maurice was a bad liar as well as a bad shot.

"Though in one sense, they will be," Maurice added, and now the familiar twinkle was back in his eyes.

Laura wondered what he meant, and also how she would manage to get through the next thirty minutes. Her brain seemed to have snapped back to attention, and the tension of waiting to see what Felicia wanted to show them was excruciating.

"Let's tackle Max immediately then," Violet said, "and Veronica. I hate to break into a budding romance, but we've got to find out what they know and how they fit into this case." Her eyes roamed the room, but neither Max nor Veronica were anywhere in sight.

"Maybe we should look in the dungeon," she said. "Max could be there."

Laura shuddered. "How about looking in beds instead?" she quipped. "After that feast, it seems to me beds would have more appeal."

"Indeed they would," Thomas murmured, appearing at her elbow. Laura blushed and changed the subject.

"Lindsey," she said. "Let's look for her instead. I know she's here. I can *feel* her. Has anyone spotted her?"

Catherine laughed. "She's here all right. I talked to her a while ago."

"Where is she?" Laura asked, surveying the room again.

"That can be your challenge while we wait for the other guests to leave," Catherine teased. "Find Lindsey. It reminds me of that book, Find Waldo, you used to read to me, remember Dad? You had to find this little skinny guy with a green hat on every page of the book. Sharpened your eyes a lot."

Laura sighed. At the moment, her eyes didn't feel very sharp. Still, she set off to walk the room and look at every face. After two circuits and a number of embarrassing confrontations due to her prolonged examination of each visage, she was prepared to swear that none of them belonged to Lindsey.

"I can't find her!" she said in frustration when she located Catherine again.

"You will," Catherine said. "Believe me, you will."

Another warning flashed into Laura's mind, one she had uttered to herself last summer when she had failed to spot the villain under a chauffeur's cap and again on this trip when she had failed to spot Lindsey as maid. "*Never forget to look at people in uniforms*, she had berated herself.

Had she looked at the waiters and waitresses? No, she hadn't. Wearily, she set off on another circuit, but that too proved useless since most of the staff had vanished into the kitchen except for a few who were still serving drinks and coffee, none of whom were Lindsey. Laura snagged another cup of coffee to help keep her wits about her, and admitted defeat. At least, though, she had made it through thirty minutes.

Violet came in, brushing snow off her hair. "I made a quick trip to the dungeon. Max wasn't there but Lindsey was," she said. "Tell you later," she finished hastily when Felicia appeared in the doorway.

"I am sorry to keep you waiting, but it was necessary," Felicia told them. Her face was somber now, more serious than Laura had ever seen it. Oddly, though, she looked stronger, as if she had made it through some challenge and had benefited from it.

"We have prepared a show for you in the armory," Felicia continued. "It is self-explanatory and I believe will answer some of your questions concerning the events of the last week. I must speak to the performers now, but the nurse will escort you to the armory. She knows the way."

Slowly, she walked away, followed by Helga and Ernst.

The small group trooped after the nurse silently. The atmosphere had changed from one of gaiety to one of trepidation, almost fear. Laura felt as if someone had splashed a glass of cold water in her face.

The others seemed to feel it too. Catherine was holding tightly to Gustav's hand, and even Maurice, usually so calm, looked tense and watchful. Sigrid, who had elected to stay while Lars escorted the twins safely back to Murren, looked troubled, as did Makedu and Amina, who had also stayed. Oddly, Ann was still here too. Laura wondered why.

Thomas, on the other hand, looked expectant, as he always did when he was on the brink of solving a case, and Violet's amber eyes gleamed with the scent of victory. Laura found their optimism hard to share but hoped they were right. The investigation had dragged on long enough. It was time for closure.

The armory felt cold and forbidding after the warmth and cheer of the banquet hall. Laura shivered and wished she had brought her jacket. The room seemed ominous now, not just because of its history, but because an act of violence might still occur. There were places to hide – the tall pillars that ran the length of the room were wide enough to conceal a person, and the corners were swathed in deep shadow. There were plenty of usable weapons too. The guns might not be loaded but the lances and swords were still sharp enough to kill. There were smaller guns, too, that she hadn't noticed before.

She took her seat in the rows of chairs that had been set up to face one of the walls. On the opposite wall was a filmy curtain, and behind it Laura saw stealthy movements, as in a stage setting before the curtain went up.

The lights in the room went out as soon as they were all settled into chairs. They waited silently in the darkness, tense and expectant. A sensation she had experienced once before crept up on Laura, that she was only a puppet being manipulated by unknown hands, that she had come here by someone's design, would watch what was coming by design.

A low spotlight behind the gauze curtain came on, lighting up the stone wall in front of them. The shadows of two tall pillars bracketed the stage. A slender black shadow figure, crouched over and holding a rifle, slid into place at one end of the wall. Trees, represented by poles with sticks attached, were all around the figure. There was no sound, only stealthy movement against the rough stone wall. The effect was extraordinary.

Laura drew in her breath sharply. A shadow play; that was what they were seeing. Not the usual shadow play, the one performed for tourists, but one that would answer their questions.

A second figure, taller, appeared at the other end of the wall. That person seemed to be looking around, as if watching for a companion.

The first figure stood, put the rifle to its shoulder and fired. The sound was muffled, but there was little doubt in Laura's mind that it had been a shot. The second person dropped. Someone gasped.

More people appeared, many of them, lumpy in big jackets. They leaned over the fallen man, examining him. For it was a man, Laura knew, and the person with the rifle was a woman. Together, they loaded the man onto a sled and pulled him away from the trees into a clear area. Releasing him from the sled, they pushed. He was whisked away from them as if he were in free fall, limbs akimbo, sticks that seemed attached to his feet falling with him.

Henri Guillard, falling into her. Laura felt suddenly sick.

The spotlight went out but within moments it returned. The figure – the woman - with the rifle appeared again, this time in a clearing. Another figure came, another muffled shot was heard, and the second person dropped. Laura watched the group carry him, this time through what seemed to be a doorway into a room. They strained to lift him up, laid him on a bed. They melted away, leaving him there. Ludwig.

The spotlight went out. Laura waited tensely for it to come back but hoped it wouldn't. She didn't want to watch the third murder. Besides, the theme of the drama was clear already. Felicia was saying that she was the murderer, the executioner, for Laura was sure now that the woman with the rifle was Felicia, and she didn't want it to be true.

Inexorably, the show began again. The woman – Felicia - reappeared, the rifle on her arm. Another man strode up to meet her. They seemed to exchange words and then the man turned away. The woman made a sharp movement and he whirled to face her. She mouthed more words, but he shrugged disdainfully and made no answer. Slowly, the woman raised the rifle, aimed, and pulled the trigger. Dr. Nezam.

Bleak sadness washed over Laura. She didn't want to believe, couldn't believe, but maybe it was true.

Felicia had wanted Henri dead. *I have often dreamed of killing him, execution style,* she had said.

The spotlight dimmed and went out. The audience sat in stunned silence. Not until the overhead lights came on and dispelled the darkness did they begin to stir uneasily, but still no one spoke.

****

Ann suddenly leaped to her feet, breaking the spell cast by the electrifying performance. Her face was purple with rage, her fists clenched into tight balls. Her eyes were wild.

"No! None of it is true," she screamed. "Who does she think she is? That's a lie, a lie, I tell you! She didn't kill them. I did. I, the woman none of you take seriously, joke about. I, frumpy opinionated Ann, have fooled you all. I killed them. I hated Henri, hated him. I got drug orders for him but he never said a word of thanks. He just took me for granted, dismissed me like a slave. And I hated Ludwig, the sneaky little man who thought he was so important. I was the one who told him what to do, but he would never admit it. He tried to ignore me too. So did Dr. Nezam. No matter what I said to him or did for him he would not take me seriously."

Her lips twisted into a grimace. "He was a monster!" Ann spat the words out so hard that moisture sprayed the air in front of her. "He deserved to be killed most of all. He was arrogant, cruel, and he would not listen to me. He would not listen! None of you listen to me. You make fun of me, but I am the smartest of all of you. I planned this, I carried it out. I know where the art is, I know how to get the drugs, I knew who to give them to, how to deliver them, how to use them for my own purposes…"

Her eyes narrowed and her voice dropped to a malevolent hiss, then rose to a roar. "They had to be killed, all of them had to be killed before they did more damage, so I killed them. *I* killed them, not her. Not her, *me!* She always wants to be the one who is most important, but all the time it was me. *Me,* I tell you! Me!"

Her voice cracked and she had to stop. Maurice came to her and took her arm. "Come," he said quietly. "I will give you something to calm you."

"No!" Ann yelled at the top of her lungs. "I don't want to be calm. I want you to believe me!"

Shoving Maurice out of the way, she raked the faces in front of her with malicious eyes. "I want to ram it into all your stupid heads that I am the one who arranged all this, I made it happen, I planned it all… I learned to shoot; I was always the best in the class. The instructor told me that. He said I was the best shot he had ever taught. I could hit anything…"

She began to sob, great hulking sobs that seemed to come from deep in her belly. Violently, she wiped at her eyes. "No!" she howled to herself, "stop that bawling. You are the one who is important now."

Violet was suddenly in front of her. "Show us," she said, handing Ann a rifle she had taken from the wall. "Aim at that light." She pointed at one of the lights at the far end of the room. "Can you hit it?"

Ann stared at her, her eyes unfocussed; then she seemed to comprehend the question. "I can hit anything," she said proudly.

Wiping her eyes savagely again, she pushed her hair out of her eyes and lifted the rifle to her shoulder.

Her hands were steady as she aimed at the light and fired. The bulb broke into tiny fragments.

She handed the rifle back to Violet. "Now do you believe me?" she said. There was an expression of utter satisfaction on her face, the same expression Laura had seen after Amina's robe had been destroyed.

CHAPTER TWENTY TWO

Before any of them could react to Ann's demonstration, Max burst into the room. He looked frantic with worry. He whispered something to Maurice that Laura couldn't hear. His next words, though, were faintly audible: "Helga and Ernst, where are they? I must tell them."

"Steady," Maurice said, putting a hand on his arm. "They are with Felicia, behind the curtain. Come, we will find them. But it is no use trying to hide this any longer, at least from those who are still here."

Helga and Ernst emerged from the curtain before Max and Maurice reached it. Helga looked ready to collapse, but she faced Max squarely. "Maurice is right," she said quietly. "We cannot keep it from them."

"Tell us what happened," Ernst said.

Max took a deep breath. "He must have got away from the hospital. I had not known how bad it could be. I am sorry. I did not understand."

"Go on." It was a command from Ernst.

"Yes." Max straightened his shoulders. "He came here because he knew he could get the... get what he wanted here. He has passed out. Veronica is with him. She says he is alive but he does not move, does not speak."

So that was what Helga and Ernst were hiding, Laura realized. Nicolas, their Golden Boy, was addicted to drugs. How terrible for them!

Another thought followed immediately. Had they been afraid that Nicolas had committed the murders while under the influence of drugs? He had hated Henri and had an explosive temper. Was that the real reason for the shadow play, to throw the investigators – herself and Violet - off the scent?

"Did you put the drugs there?" It was the nurse speaking this time. Laura was astonished. Her voice had authority, not the meekness she had expected. It also had a trace of a southern accent.

Laura shook her head, mortified. Catherine was right. She would find Lindsey. It wasn't hard - just a matter of never, ever making assumptions about people in uniforms.

Max looked surprised too, but he answered readily. "Yes. I wanted to know what the drugs were so I could report them to the authorities and stop Henri. I had to. They would have killed Veronica."

"Why were you in the dungeon just now?" the nurse – Lindsey – asked. Laura wondered what her role was now. She seemed very much in charge.

"Getting the samples," Max answered, sounding impatient. "We went there as soon as the play was finished. That's why we found Nicolas. Otherwise he might have been there all night."

"We will check your story," Lindsey replied brusquely. She turned to Helga and Ernst. "We will bring Nicolas here, into the warmth. As soon as we can, we will take him to the hospital for observation."

"Thank you," Helga said faintly. "I will prepare a bed."

"We will need help to carry him," Lindsey told Max and the other men. "Best to fetch your jackets and boots. It's a mess out there. The snow is coming down harder than ever.

"Will you come too?" she asked Violet.

"I must deal with the other matter," Violet said. She gestured toward Ann, who had slumped onto a chair, once again forgotten. "She's volatile and needs to be watched. That wasn't a real bullet, by the way," she added.

Lindsey raised an eyebrow. "Volatile is an understatement. Ready for the loony bin, if you ask me. Great trick you pulled off, though.

"Do you suppose she really did it?" she asked in a whisper.

"We'll see," Violet said enigmatically. Laura noticed that she still had the rifle pointed at Ann, bullets or not. She also seemed to know why Lindsey was suddenly taking charge, or at least she hadn't questioned it.

"I'd better keep Gustav here too, just in case," Violet told Lindsey. "Ann looks harmless now but I can't depend on it."

She did indeed look harmless, Laura thought. Ann's face was blank, as if some part of her wasn't there at all.

Lindsey laughed. "I leave that one to you. Drugs are more my thing. DEA, drug enforcement administration," she added for Laura's benefit, flashing a badge that had been hidden under the blue dress.

Catherine looked triumphant but refrained from saying *I told you so.* "I'll go with them," she said instead, and went to get her jacket. Laura was about to join her when she saw Felicia emerge from the curtain. She looked as if the last of her energy had been sucked from her, and Laura decided she was needed here more than in the dungeon.

"Please, please dah'ling Felicia, will you lie down now?" Lindsey urged. The southern accent was back in full.

She turned to Laura. "She is so darned stubborn, this lady! Cain't make her rest no mattah what."

"You put on a good show," she told Felicia. "Real convincing, too, so long as no one but me knew you couldn't hit the side of a barn from two feet."

Laura stared at her. Was that the truth? And how did she know?

"Sure you'll be all right until I get back?" Lindsey asked as she went out.

Felicia sighed. "My niece is over-protective," she said to Laura. "Yes, I will be all right," she told Lindsey snappishly. "I'm not an invalid yet.

"And I'm an excellent shot," she added for Laura's ears alone. "I can't imagine where Lindsey got the idea I was not. Nor can I understand why she turned up as a delegate or DEA agent, or why she's suddenly so concerned for me. I haven't seen her for years.

"She was a pest as a child and she still is," she finished with panache.

Laura hid a smile. At least some of Felicia's old spirit was still there. She sympathized. Lindsey in large doses would be a trial, even without the bouffant hairdo and exaggerated accent. Possibly she had acquired her larger-than-life talent for showmanship at her aunt's knee.

But which of them was telling the truth? She hadn't the faintest idea.

"I'll find Felicia a place to lie down," she called after Lindsey. "I might even ask someone in the kitchen to make her a cup of tea."

"That would be wonderful." Helga this time. "I will take Felicia into the sitting room while you ask about tea. It is just down the hall, and we will be more comfortable there."

The temporary staff had been sent home, so only the permanent people were left. They knew Felicia well and were more than willing to provide tea for her and her guests. "We call Mrs. Lamont the angel of Chillon," one woman confided in lightly accented English. "She is very generous with her gifts and she always makes sure we have everything we need to put on a real feast for the trustees and donors. She pays for it too, and she even comes in here and helps us herself sometimes."

Tea and biscuits soon arrived. Helga drank a cup gratefully. "I'll get a bed ready," she said when she had finished. "The tea has revived me."

Helga still looked tired, Laura thought, but most of all she looked relieved. Not surprising. Thanks to Ann, Nicolas was off the hook, and so was Felicia.

"It revived me too," Felicia agreed. "The play was rather exhausting to perform, but I also found it stimulating. It went quite well, I thought." Unlike Helga, Laura noted with interest, Felicia didn't look relieved. Instead, she looked like the proverbial cat that had swallowed the canary.

Laura was puzzling over possible reasons for Felicia's smug look when another staff member rushed into the room. He looked frantic with worry. "Mr. Braun asked me to call for an ambulance, but it cannot get here," he told them. "The roads have been closed. No one can go anywhere.

"I thought I heard a shot," he added, almost in a whisper. "I hope that is not why he wants an ambulance?"

Two things happened before anyone could answer. First, Catherine came in. Her face was pinched with cold. "They're on their way," she said, propping the door open so they could bring Nicolas in.

At the same moment, an unearthly cackle that made the hair on Laura's arms stand straight up emerged from the armory. A moment later, Ann rushed into the room brandishing a small handgun. She cackled again.

"You thought you could keep me in there, didn't you?" she taunted Violet and Gustav, who ran in behind her. "But I am still too clever for you."

She smiled mischievously. "I can shoot little guns too," she teased her audience. "Even better."

Playfully, she aimed the gun at each of them in turn.

****

Gustav and Violet leaped toward her, but Ann forestalled them. "If you come closer to me, I will shoot," she said casually. "This one is loaded. I always like to have one with me, just in case."

Ann was enjoying herself, Laura thought incredulously. She was playing the lead role in her own drama and loving every moment of it.

"Stand in front with the others," Ann ordered Violet and Gustav. "I'll take her out first," she added, pointing the gun at Laura. "She irritates me. Too nosy and thinks she's so smart." That really did sound like lines filched from a TV drama, Laura thought nervously, and wished she knew how it had ended.

"Hurry," Ann snapped when Gustav and Violet hesitated. They had no choice but to comply.

"Don't make things worse for yourself, Ann," Violet said with commendable calm. Seeing the sudden rage in Ann's face, she tried another tactic.

"Ann, why don't you tell us how you did it? I didn't think a woman would be strong enough to move Henri or the others. But they were moved, we know that. Did you do it all by yourself?"

Ann seemed to swell. "Of course I did! It wasn't hard. I told Henri that I had information for him so we took the first chair lift up with the staff. No one can overhear on a lift. We often do it so he didn't suspect anything. We skied into the woods. I was ahead of him and when we came to the place where I had the gun I told him to stop so we could talk. He did, and so I shot him."

The cackle of laughter came again. "He looked so surprised. Then I got a sled I'd put nearby the day before, brought it to Henri and rolled him on to it. I was in the ski patrol once so I know how. I waited until the slope was empty, hauled him into the middle and sent him flying." Ann put a fist into her mouth to control another burble of laughter. "He slammed right into her." She pointed at Laura with her other hand. "That was the best of all."

"Then why wasn't he wearing a hat?" Violet's question was sharp.

"His hat?" Ann snapped back into seriousness. "He snagged it on a branch. I found it and covered the hole with it, but I couldn't find his goggles."

"And the others?" Violet somehow contrived to sound impressed with Ann's achievements, and Ann responded instantly.

"Ludwig was easy. He was already in the shelter. When I told him what I was going to do, he turned around and looked at me as if he didn't believe me so I just shot him. He really was surprised, even more than Henri. All I had to do then was put him on the bed. I took my time with Dr. Nezam, though. I wanted him to know what I thought of him. Everyone hated him," she said righteously, "but I was the only one who dared to get rid of him."

She giggled. "You didn't know he was there, did you? I had to fire again to make you pay attention. That was stupid of you."

Laura held her breath. Makedu was making her way noiselessly from the armory into the room, her stick raised. Despite her size she moved like a cat. She was barefoot, Laura noticed. Sigrid, in her ballet shoes, was right behind her, a high heel in her hand as a makeshift weapon. Amina was beside Sigrid clutching an ancient spiked club. Ann had her back to them, but she was so intent on playing her role that Laura wondered if she would see them anyway.

The door from the outer hall opened and Maurice walked in, distracting Ann. Immediately, she found a new target for her venom. "You had no right to interfere with Reginald," she shrieked at Maurice. "He used to listen to me but you ruined everything by getting him to listen to you instead. He won't do what I tell him to do any more."

Like blackmail Karl, Laura thought sadly. Was that why the blackmail had suddenly stopped – and why

Violet had hesitated to name the person she suspected of being the blackmailer?

"I'll kill you too," Ann added maliciously. That's the easiest, isn't it?" She shifted her position to point the little gun at Maurice, a move that gave Makedu just enough time to reach her. Makedu's stick hit Ann's wrist before she could pull the trigger, and the gun flew out of Ann's hand. She yelped with pain. Gustav twisted her other arm behind her back and held on.

Violet had just grabbed the gun when Lindsey and the three men struggled through the door carrying Nicolas. Veronica was at his head, supporting it. Nicolas looked supremely happy. Ecstasy? Laura wasn't sure.

Only when they had lowered Nicolas onto a table did they take in the scene. Thomas glanced at Laura, a question in his eyes. "Ann had another gun," she said in a low voice. "She got away. She's unpredictable."

Max and Veronica looked puzzled. Of course, Laura realized. They had been in the dungeon when Ann had made her extraordinary confession. She took them into the hall and explained what had happened. Veronica looked as if a weight had been taken from her as she turned a tear-stained face to Max. The relief in their eyes mirrored Helga's.

Ann made a sudden movement. Violet held the gun steady on her, and Gustav tightened his grip. Amina raised her club. Lindsey drew out a gun she apparently had hidden in her jacket and aimed it at Ann, too.

"I just want to see who it is," Ann said irritably, and glanced at the table. She cackled again. "Oh, it's Nicolas. I thought he would make a good customer. I can always tell the ones who'll get addicted quickly."

Laura flinched. Ann was fiendish! The next moment, she was less sure. Ann might be a fiend, but did she really know what she was doing?

She was looking down now, rummaging in a pocket of her voluminous skirt with her free hand. "Where is it?" she demanded. "I put it in here. I know I did. Someone must have taken it. I want it back!"

She stared furiously at them, as if unaware that the gun she had secreted in the hidden pocket had been knocked out of her hand. Laura felt a spurt of unexpected pity. It evaporated fast when Ann spotted the gun in Violet's hand and tried to lunge for it. Gustav handcuffed her and hauled her to a chair.

Ann went limp, and slumped down. The blank look was back on her face, as if she had forgotten them again. Laura doubted she really had. Probably she was just waiting for another opportunity to catch them off guard.

Violet was taking no chances. "It really is loaded," she whispered as she handed the small gun to Gustav. "Watch her for me. I don't trust her.

"I'll ask Maurice to prepare a sedative," she added.

It was the wrong thing to say. "No!" Ann screeched, leaping up again. "I don't use drugs. I just give them to other people." The cackle came again but it was a weary one now. "I'm tired," she said. "I would like to lie down."

Maurice appeared with a glass of water. Laura suspected it contained more than water, but Ann drank it thirstily.

Lindsey darted out of the room and reappeared with her nurse's cap pinned to her hair and her gun hidden behind her back. "Now, Ann," she said bossily, "it's time for you to rest. You're one of our best students and we don't want you getting too tired. Come along." She sounded exactly like a school nurse scolding a student.

To Laura's amazement the ruse worked. Ann went with the nurse like a docile child. She didn't seem to notice that Violet and Gustav, the people who had taken her gun and handcuffed her, were right behind her, just as she hadn't seemed to notice, or care, that it was Maurice, the man she had just tried to kill, who had brought her the water.

"I really am pretty smart, aren't I?" Ann agreed complacently. "I'm a lot smarter than the others. I wish they would stop making fun of me and ignoring me, though. That makes me mad."

Mad, Laura thought, was precisely the right word.

CHAPTER TWENTY THREE

Catherine stood up shakily and then sat down again. "Good grief," she said fervently. "I honestly did not know anyone could be that loony."

"She certainly appears to be," Thomas agreed. He looked preoccupied, and Laura wondered what was on his mind. She wondered even more when he left the room, announcing that he was going to check on the weather. For Thomas, *checking the weather* was a euphemism for indulging in unexpected types of investigation.

She was about to follow him when Veronica spoke. "He was so unhappy," she said sadly. She was looking down on Nicolas, and her eyes were tragic. Maurice came to stand beside her.

"Nicolas will recover," he said, and put a fatherly arm around her shoulder.

An idea popped into Laura's mind, an idea so preposterous that she blurted it out before she could stop herself.

"You're Veronica's father, aren't you?" she said, staring at Maurice.

Maurice looked dumbfounded. "I am," he agreed. "Proudly so. But how did you know? I only found out myself a few days ago."

"You mean all that time you never knew?"

Maurice sighed. "Perhaps it is time for me to tell the second half of my story. It is Felicia's story too, but I think she might like to rest before we begin. The scene we just witnessed was disturbing." Felicia was indeed pale, Laura saw. Her eyes were closed, her skin waxen.

"It was quite horrible," Felicia agreed weakly. "I do not ordinarily like to rest but perhaps this is a good time to reconsider. The staff has a small room where they relax between events. I can lie there for five minutes."

Maurice helped her to her feet and took her into the room. "Felicia is not as well as she pretends to be," he observed when he returned.

"No, I fear she is not," Helga agreed sadly. "It is not just the lupus this time, you know. But she will improve once everything has settled down. This has been a very difficult time for her."

Laura felt tears spring to her eyes. She hadn't believed Felicia's insistence that she was all right; she was too changed for that, but the confirmation that she was truly ill, probably dying, was still hard to bear.

"It has been a hard time for everyone. For us as well," Ernst said quietly. "We were very frightened for Nicolas," he explained to the others. "We did not know what was wrong with him until Maurice came, but now that we do know, we can treat him properly and he will soon be well."

"We were so puzzled," Helga said, rubbing her eyes wearily. "Nicolas was such a happy child and young man. We could not understand when he suddenly became irritable and had wild swings of mood. We consulted many experts but none could explain why he had changed so much until Maurice came. He knew right away, and helped us to find a good place to send Nicolas."

Veronica looked up at Helga. "It is my fault partly," she said. "I just couldn't be what Nicolas wanted me to be…" Her voice broke as she looked down at him again. "He is so beautiful."

Perhaps that was part of the problem, Laura reflected. Nicolas was so beautiful he hardly seemed real. It might be hard to fall in love with a man like that – and equally hard to discipline such a faun-like creature.

Helga kissed Veronica's cheek. "It is not your fault. It is Ann's fault if it is anyone's, and I am not sure she is responsible for her actions. But Nicolas must learn to be. We can blame Ann her for introducing him to drugs, but not for taking them. Nicolas did that. We have made life too easy for him, I think."

"Nicolas will be all right," Ernst repeated, and Laura wondered how many times he had reassured Helga with the words, and even more, himself. She hoped he was right.

"Now we must take Nicolas to the bed you have prepared for him," Ernst continued firmly. "He will sleep it off and then we will talk to him."

He and Max and two staff members carried Nicolas away, with Veronica supporting his head and Helga in close attendance.

Laura sighed with envy. Right now what she wanted most in the world was a nice soft bed to lie down on, but as far as she knew there were only two in the castle, and Nicolas and Ann would get them. The rest of them would have to spend the night on stiff-backed chairs or horsehair sofas, which was all the sitting room provided. It was marginally more comfortable, As Helga had said, but it was not a room in which one could put up tired feet.

Or could one? Makedu sank into a chair and promptly put her bare feet up on a low table. "You

337

should do the same," she advised Laura. "Feet swell at the end of the day, and this has been a long, long day."

Tossing off her shoes, Amina put her feet up beside her mother's and wriggled her toes. "Pointed shoes are fashionable, but at such a cost!"

Laura copied her, as did Catherine and Sigrid. When Thomas came back, looking invigorated but damp with snow, five pairs of bare or sock clad feet were grouped companionably around the table.

Laura patted the other side of the stiff loveseat she occupied. "You can sit here and put your feet up too," she invited Thomas, "but you have to take off your shoes first. Men's shoes are so hard, and they might scratch."

Thomas complied and put his arm around her shoulders. Oddly, he smelled of gasoline, Laura thought, sniffing. Where *had* he been?

Thomas forestalled her question. "If this gets too stiff, we could always try one of those boxes," he suggested, massaging the back of her neck. "Some of them are quite large. Maybe we could even lie down."

"With our legs dangling out the end," Laura said hopefully.

"And a major crick in your neck," Catherine supplied.

"On the other hand," she added, "Gustav and I might just try it if he ever comes back from guarding Ann. I bet there are extra tablecloths around for sheets. Has anyone caught sight of a pillow or two?"

"Victorians probably didn't have them," Laura said grumpily. "Decadent."

They sat in silence for a time, trying to find a comfortable position, or at leas a prop for their heads. There were none.

"Why do I have this creepy feeling that we're in a shadow play too," Laura said suddenly. "It's as if the mastermind we were talking about earlier has set this all up and we're all just playing our parts in a larger play. Maybe Felicia meant for Ann to hear her when she bragged that day in Zermatt about how she had always wanted to execute Henri. Maybe she knew Ann would get the idea of doing it herself and being so important, and then Felicia just kept us all going through our paces... She set up the shadow play to divert suspicion from Nicolas, who was known to hate Henri and could have killed him under the influence of drugs, but maybe she also hoped that Ann wouldn't be able to stand having someone else take the credit for her own brilliant plan, that she would confess just the way she did. Even if she hadn't done the murders Ann would probably confess just to get the credit. Felicia also knew full well that an elderly lady who is universally acclaimed for her generosity would be hard to charge..."

Violet came into the room. "What did you just say?" she asked sharply.

"That it would be hard to charge Felicia -" Laura began.

Violet cut her off. "No. About Ann."

"I said that Ann would probably confess just to get the credit -" Laura stopped in mid-sentence. "Oh, I see what you mean. Did Felicia know that, or hope it would be true?"

"That," said Maurice, "is a very interesting idea. I wonder too; I truly do. If I ever work up enough courage, I shall ask her."

"And she won't answer," Felicia said as Ernst and Helga brought her back into the room. "I still find resting uninteresting," she explained, "so I came back."

Laura wondered if she had gone out just so she could listen to them. She wouldn't put it past Felicia.

Felicia took the seat she had vacated earlier. "All is well now," she said firmly, "and I won't have my peace disturbed any more. It is bad for my health, which as Maurice keeps telling me, is not as robust as it once was. Ann will go into a hospital, which is where she belonged in the first place; the criminals have been caught or killed and their odious businesses closed down; Nicolas has been rescued in time for him to recover; the mysteries Violet and Laura came here to investigate are solved; the grant to build schools for girls will proceed as planned, and the children who were threatened are all safe."

"And you will go right along pulling us all around the stage, and we shall be unable to resist," Maurice joked as he helped her into a chair.

"I admit to no such thing," Felicia said testily. "But everything *is* all right now – what more could anyone want?"

"Art," Thomas shot back. "I want the solution to the mystery *I* came here to investigate. You can provide the answers I need. So let us begin."

Felicia brightened. "Ah yes!" she said. "The art. That is a subject I really would like to talk about. Maurice, will you start?"

Maurice nodded. "Thank you, Felicia. I believe all of you know my early story, how I vowed at my mother's grave to recover all my family's art and the records that proved our ownership. For many years that was difficult, however. I entered University to study art and psychology and then became absorbed in a demanding and draining career. Depressed at my failure to make progress, I came to the mountains to walk and to think what to do. The walking did help, but it was the woman I met while walking, the woman who walked with me, who gave me the courage to fulfill my pledge. She was and is the warmest, most compassionate woman I have ever known."

Maurice's eyes misted over. "She is also Veronica's mother. Ignoring the consequences - which for her were grave though I did not know that until recently - she took me into her arms and comforted me, encouraged me to fulfill my promise. She was a university student then, much younger than I, and she had her own goals for her future. We agreed to go our separate ways and perhaps to walk again next summer."

He smiled. "Elisabet and I stayed in the little cabin in Gimmelwald, where I found Veronica and Laura found me. It was an ecstatic interlude.

"But to continue: Shortly after that trip, I went abroad and began to search seriously for the art. I was out of the country for more than a year. It was then that I met Felicia. She was writing articles about art stolen by the Nazis, so I got in touch with her and we began to work together. She had contacts that I did not, more knowledge, and infinite energy for tracking down lost paintings. Together, we have found at least some of the stolen art. We also found some of the old records and returned what we could to the rightful owners. Other paintings and valuables were impossible to trace, and these are now available to be sold, with Ernst's help. Felicia will tell you about that, and what we plan to do with the money."

Maurice laughed, remembering. "Her energy now is high; her energy then was phenomenal, as was her courage. Felicia took risks that terrified me to put illegal art hunters out of business. I have seen her face down one of them by threatening to shoot off his ear. She could have, too."

"Indeed I could," Felicia agreed. "I've often wished I had."

Laura was gratified. One question at least was answered. But if Felicia really was a good shot, why had Lindsey said the opposite? Was it possible that she too didn't like the idea of Felicia as villain and wanted to protect her by implying she couldn't have done the murders?

Maurice's deep voice interrupted the thought. "When I finally returned to Switzerland I heard that Elisabet had married. I thought it best to stay away. I know now that she had become pregnant. With her usual resourcefulness, she found a good husband, a widower with a young son. Max and Veronica and Max were brought up as sister and brother. Elisabet believed it was best. Life is hard for an out of wedlock child in Swiss mountain towns.

"She and her husband were happily married until he was killed. Then, only a short time ago, I met Veronica. I think I knew immediately who she was. The resemblance is uncanny. And so I looked up my old walking companion and re-discovered the love of my life. The well-meaning story of Veronica's parentage unraveled, and the truth has been liberating for us all, but most for Veronica and Max. The terrible burden of being forbidden to love each other has gone.

"But that is enough of my story except for the fact that it has a very happy ending. Now, Felicia, I turn the stage over to you."

"There is not very much to add," Felicia said tartly. "We have a great deal of art, mostly paintings but also other valuables. It is well-protected in the safe but we still feared for it when Henri decided to use the shelter for his illicit drug enterprise, and his gang of unsavory people - many of them delegates who were recruited by Karl - swarmed into it. That was rather a nightmare. All we could do was to watch over the art as best we could, and wait."

Violet pounced. "Did you write the letters threatening the children?"

Felicia looked horrified. "We would not do that!"

Violet nodded, seeing satisfied. Ann, Laura thought, to ingratiate herself with Karl, or perhaps Joe or Nina on the instructions of Dr. Nezam.

"Though we are certainly glad to be rid of the criminal element, even if not in the way that we might have preferred," Felicia continued. "But that too is over, and we must get on with our plans. That is why we are now looking for art experts who can evaluate the paintings for us."

She glanced at Thomas. "You are – and were – on our list."

Thomas grinned. "That's good, because if I wasn't, I would put myself on it by hook or by crook, as they say."

"I gather you found the safe," Felicia said dryly. "I imagine you are eager to look inside."

"Catherine found it, actually," Thomas admitted. "Laura found the tunnel. And eager hardly describes my feelings."

Felicia nodded. "Then we will try to get in as soon as possible. The only other people who found it are Ann – she is a sneak who followed people, so she probably saw one of us go into the tunnel – and Lindsey. How she managed it I don't know -"

Felicia stopped abruptly, a stunned look on her face. "Lindsey! That was not Lindsey! Why, oh why, didn't I see that before?"

****

"How do you know?" Violet was on her feet.

"Lindsey is left- handed, and the woman who came here as Lindsey pulled out her gun and held it with her right hand. Lindsey uses only her left."

"Has anyone seen Lindsey since she helped take Ann away?" Violet asked.

"She said something about checking the dungeon again," Maurice said.

Thomas and Violet were already running for their jackets and boots. "I'll look there," Violet yelled back. "The rest of you search inside the castle or the outside if it's possible. Ask the staff too."

"Snowmobile," Thomas called to Laura. "I saw one. Hurry."

Laura sprinted into the cloakroom, stuffed her bare feet into her boots and her arms into her jacket. Before she had even gone two feet she was shivering. The snow was ferocious now, a full-blown blizzard.

The roar of a snowmobile racing away brought her to a halt. The storm made it impossible to see who was at the wheel, but there was little doubt in Laura's mind that it was Lindsey.

"She won't get very far," Thomas said with satisfaction.

"Because of the storm?" Laura asked.

"No. Because I drained the gas tank," Thomas replied.

Laura laughed. "So that's what you were doing! But how did you know?"

"I didn't know, absolutely," Thomas admitted, "but a snowmobile hidden behind the bushes indicates that someone might want to get away fast. So I took the precaution of making that difficult."

Violet joined them. "Thomas, you are a genius," she said.

"Thank you," he answered. "Now maybe we should go inside, get warm and see who we can rouse to rescue Lindsey when the machine stalls. She might be a villain, but I can't help but admire her."

"Yes," Laura said. "I agree with all those sentiments – especially to go inside and get warm."

"I took another precaution," Violet told them as they divested themselves of boots and coats. "I made marks with indelible ink on the boxes we saw in the dungeon, so they will be picked up if they go through security."

"Brilliant!" Thomas congratulated her.

Ernst and Felicia were waiting when they returned to the sitting room. "I asked Ernst to call my niece in Texas to make sure she was there," Felicia told them.

"She is exceedingly garrulous and I did not have the energy to listen, so Ernst did it for me. He will explain."

"Felicia's niece told me that her passport and driver's license were stolen and that a woman posing as a magazine editor doing a story on beautiful homes had interviewed her and prowled all over her house taking photographs," Ernst reported. "No doubt she took notes on niece Lindsey's appearance too."

He laughed. "A highly versatile lady!"

"And a highly gullible niece," Felicia retorted. "The Lindsey we met here would have no trouble getting niece Lindsey to talk and be flattered into the bargain. I'd rather like her for a niece instead. She is far more interesting.

"She is that," Violet agreed. "And polite. She even left a thank you note for you, Felicia, as well as a memento of her stay which she discovered at the bottom of one of the boxes. I found them in the dungeon. She took all the drugs – I imagine they are on the back of that snowmobile."

Grinning widely, Violet pulled a pizza box exactly like the one Laura had found out of her huge purse. Thomas opened it eagerly. "Not another Vermeer, but certainly valuable," he said. "Why on earth did she give it back?"

"Probably because she didn't know what to do with it," Laura pointed out. "To sell a painting like that you have to have connections."

"She may also have known we would be watching, and didn't want to take the chance," Thomas said wryly. "Maurice and I are aware that other paintings were missing, so we arranged for boxes from this area to be searched if they turned up at any of Henri's warehouses or in airport luggage."

"She's a clever crook," Violet decreed. "She only takes on jobs she knows how to deal with. No extras."

"Smarter than I appreciated," Felicia agreed, opening the letter. "It truly is a thank-you note! How delightful."

Thank you so much for having me, she read aloud. *I enjoyed my stay with you, and I hope one day we will meet again. I imagine we might have a lot in common and would enjoy comparing notes.*

P.S. *Please accept the contents of this box as a token of my appreciation.*

Felicia laughed uproariously. "What gall, giving me back one of my own paintings as a thank you gift! She's right, too. We probably do have a lot in common. Some of my methods for retrieving the paintings might match up quite well with Lindsey's methods for getting the drugs. If we must have an illicit drug market, she is certainly a more palatable villain than Henri."

"I hope she doesn't get caught," Catherine said wistfully. "I liked Lindsey."

"She might just get away," Thomas said. "The police report that they have found an abandoned, out of gas snowmobile, but no sign of the driver or of any boxes. Now how do you suppose Lindsey managed that?"

Laura grinned. "I bet she flagged down another policeman – there must be a lot of them prowling the roads for stuck cars - told him a sob story about all her mother's possessions in the boxes and asked if he could give her a lift to the train station."

"Where she has another completely different identity ready in a suitcase," Catherine added. "I bet she's on her way to Timbuktu or some other romantic place I've never heard of right this minute."

This time, it was Catherine's words that were prescient.

CHAPTER TWENTY FOUR

Felicia finally agreed to lie down in the staff room, and Helga and Ernst went with her to see that she stayed in place and to rest themselves. Veronica and Max were with Nicolas and simultaneously keeping an eye on Ann. She was easy to watch since she was sleeping so deeply that Veronica suspected Lindsey had slipped something extra into the brew Maurice had concocted for her.

Maurice was asleep too, snoring gently in a reasonably comfortable chair. Maurice knew how to take his pleasures when and where he found them.

"Just us again," Catherine remarked, casting an eye around their small group. "Expanded us," she amended, to include Makedu, Amina and Sigrid. Together, they had prowled the castle in search of a more comfortable spot, and after a hilarious interlude sitting inside the boxes and experimenting with the side-by-side toilet seats – Makedu had joked that she needed two, they had retreated to the stiff sitting room again. The cook had provided coffee and more tea to warm them up, enhanced by some re-heated rolls, which tasted delicious with butter and jam.

Thomas pulled Laura closer. "Not so bad," he said. "Makes me think of our over-extended stay in the shelter, but at least this is warm and no one is trying to knock us over the head or otherwise do us damage."

"Unless Ann gets loose again," Catherine warned, snuggling up against Gustav in their horsehair love seat. "I'm positive she's the one who slammed into Laura twice, pushed Sigrid off the cliff, slashed Amina's robe and wrote those nasty letters, and who knows what else?"

"But did she do the murders," Sigrid said. "That is what I would like to know. Is Ann really the killer?"

Violet suddenly began to laugh, a huge infectious guffaw that soon had all of them laughing even if they didn't know why. Helplessly, she tried to explain but only laughed more.

"Oh dear," she sputtered finally, wiping her eyes. "What made me laugh, aside from sleeplessness which perversely makes me slaphappy, is that when I walked into the castle I hadn't a single viable suspect for the murders of Henri, Ludwig and Dr. Nezam. Now I am swimming in suspects, but I still can't be certain who pulled the trigger. Felicia says she killed them, Ann says she did, Nicolas might have and so might Lindsey. For all I know, one suspect might be guilty of all three murders or three suspects are guilty of one each, and other suspects could turn up. Any guesses?"

Laura grinned. "Let's take a silent vote," she suggested. "I'll get a hat, we each write down a name for who killed Henri, Ludwig and Dr. Nezam. Then we'll pick the person who gets the most votes.

"Would a helmet suffice?" Thomas had found one in the armory and held it out for inspection.

"Perfect," Laura decreed. "Who has pen and paper?"

Violet produced that from her voluminous shoulder bag, and Laura printed out names.

"This one is for Henri," she said. "We'll do them one at a time and then put it all together.

"Keep in mind," she added, "that the killer has to be a good shot and in Henri's case, a good skier. In

Ludwig's and Dr. Nezam's case, the killer could have used a snowmobile. We know they are all skiers and that Ann and Felicia are good shots, but how about Nicolas and Lindsey? Does anyone know?"

"I may," Violet said. "I got the number of Felicia's niece in Texas and called her myself to ask various questions. She is indeed garrulous, and along the way I learned that Felicia had taught Nicolas to shoot. That suggests he is at least competent. I also made some calls about women who have recently become involved in the world of illicit drugs. If the fake Lindsey is who I think she is, she is an excellent shot. If that changes, the votes may change."

"That is good to know. It means any of them could have done it," Sigrid said. "Shall we give each suspect a number instead of writing their names? It might be best to keep this anonymous I think."

"Good idea," Laura agreed. "Alphabetically, Ann is number one, Felicia is number two, Lindsey is number three, Nicolas number four."

Each of them bent over their paper, thinking hard, and finally writing a number. When the task was completed, Thomas pulled the papers out of the helmet. He laughed. "Hardly conclusive," he said. "We have two of each."

"Well, let's try Ludwig," Laura suggested, unwilling to give up yet.

This time, the results were more satisfying. Nicolas got no votes, Lindsey got two, Felicia and Ann three each. They went on to Dr. Nezam.

Laura found her hand hesitating over the paper. The scene in the shelter when they had found Dr. Nezam flashed into her mind, and suddenly she knew what was different about his murder. Dr. Nezam's head was at the wrong end of the bed, and the bed was out of alignment with the others. Someone had moved it so that it was aligned toward Mecca, the direction Ben had knelt in thanks for Zaina's safe rescue. More telling, the soles of Dr. Nezam's feet, not his head as was customary, were facing the holy shrine.

Laura's heart seemed to drop into her stomach, and she had to clench her teeth to keep from crying out. Was that a deliberate sign of disrespect, a final message from the living to the dead? She didn't want this to be true, either. Her hand was shaking when she placed her paper in the helmet.

"This is even more interesting," Thomas said when he examined them. "Five of us left their papers blank, which seems to say that none of the above killed Dr. Nezam. Does that mean we have yet another suspect?"

There was a long silence. Abruptly, the levity that had accompanied the task was gone. This was no longer a game. These were murders they were talking about, and a person or persons who were real, who were known to them, had committed them. And some members of their group were deeply unhappy about it. Somber now, they waited.

It was Violet who finally spoke. Her face was bleak. "I am one of those people," she said. "I am also in charge of this investigation and can speak freely only to the people in this room. I trust that you will keep my remarks confidential.

"I cannot prove what I am about to say; I doubt that any one else could either. I would like your thoughts on the matter. This is a complex case, and I need all the help I can get before I present the evidence I have accumulated to the Swiss authorities. After that, it is up to them to make charges."

She took a deep breath. "To me, the most likely scenario is this: Nicolas shot Henri because he hated him so ferociously and was in the manic state some drugs can induce. Felicia shot Ludwig, a copy-cat murder designed to deflect suspicion from Nicolas. As for Dr. Nezam…"

"Better not to say the name." Maurice's voice came from his chair in the back of the room. "It is over now and the person to whom you refer has left the country. That, I think, is best for everyone, and safer for that person."

"He did not kill Dr. Nezam." Sigrid's voice was positive.

"How do you know?" Laura asked cautiously, hardly daring to hope.

"Because my husband kept Ben with him the day Dr. Nezam was released, the day he was killed," Sigrid answered. "Lars teaches Iranian culture, and he understood that Ben's first impulse would be to restore the family honor. I do not know what happened; I was not there, but I believe Lars talked him out of it. Lars can tell you if he feels free to share their conversation. Since this is a murder investigation, I will reveal, however, that Ben believed someone else would kill Dr. Nezam if he did not. He did not say who it was.

"I am eternally grateful to you and your husband," Maurice declared, the emotion raw in his voice. "I did not know, and I was afraid. Truly, I believe that young man has friends in very high places – and I do not mean political – who look after him."

"I wasn't going to say the name you feared, Maurice," Violet assured him. "I think Joe – his real name is Yussef Abadi - killed Dr. Nezam, and I hope to be able to prove it soon. He was released shortly after Dr. Nezam due to lack of evidence, so he could have done it. He also had motivation. He loathed Dr. Nezam, who muscled his way into Joe's thriving drug business and treated him like a lackey. Joe saw a good opportunity to get rid of a powerful rival and took it. As soon as more information comes in, I believe he will be arrested. In the meantime, he is not allowed to leave the country and we will be watching to see that he doesn't."

"Investigators from the art world will also be watching," Thomas inserted, "so he won't get very far if he tries, which I suspect he might.

"Well, *someone* hid those paintings at the bottom of the drug boxes," he explained to the others, seeing their puzzled faces. "I think it was Joe and Nina. They knew about the art and must have intercepted various paintings before they were deposited in the safe; at any rate quite a few paintings small enough to fit into boxes disappeared."

"Excellent," Violet said triumphantly. "Once I present all that information to the Swiss authorities, Ben should certainly be cleared."

Laura wanted to cheer. "What a relief!" she said thankfully. "When I saw that someone had moved the bed and put Dr. Nezam on it so that his feet instead of his head faced Mecca, I was terrified that it might be Ben."

"Is that what the man did?" Makedu was indignant. "That is an insult. I am glad Ben did not see it. Then he might have wanted to kill Joe instead."

354

Violet brought them back to reality. "I am pleased for Ben, but I still have Nicolas and Felicia and Ann to consider. I must report what we have observed to the Swiss authorities, including Ann's confession and the shadow play Felicia arranged. She would not have done that unless she was afraid that Nicolas had killed Henri, and the police will know that. They will also know that Nicolas was on drugs. Then, as I said, it is up to them to make charges, depending on who they believe to be telling the truth."

She ran her fingers through her hair in frustration. "If only I had proof that Nicolas could not have done it! But no one knows where he was from the time Laura and I saw him after the Braun's party until the middle of the next day. He doesn't remember either."

"His hands," Laura said suddenly. "Nicolas. His hands were shaking so hard when we saw him that he couldn't zip his jacket, so he couldn't have held a gun steady. Does anyone know how long the shakes last?"

"Until the next fix," Thomas said brutally. "But it seems to me that the drugs Nicolas took put him to sleep instead of inspiring him to grab a gun."

"I bet some of his friends found him and took him in," Catherine said. "If any of them were at the party, you can be sure they kept an eye on him. But they wouldn't rat on him, so no one would know."

"Another good idea," Violet said gratefully. "The police interviewed his friends in Zermatt, but they professed not to know."

"Of course they did," Catherine said impatiently. "Someone they trust has to ask them. They also need to be convinced that Nicolas might be indicted for murder if they don't talk. And them as accessories or whatever it is."

"I think I'll send you," Violet said with a grin.

"Send Max," Catherine said. "He would do a lot to help Nicolas."

"Even better," Violet agreed.

Her face sobered. "Then there is the final question: Ann. What are we to do about Ann? She might not have committed the murders. What am I to say to her, say to the police abut her?"

Amina answered this time. "The best thing we can do for Ann is to believe her. That is what she wants more than anything in the world."

"But is it the right thing to do?" Sigrid persisted.

"She is dangerous to other people," Gustav pointed out. "The best place for her is a psychiatric hospital, which is probably where she would be sent."

"That is true," Sigrid agreed.

"Don't forget Reginald," Catherine said passionately. "He counts too. Imagine what his life would be like with his mother loose."

"And Felicia," Laura said quietly. "She is not well."

An uneasy silence fell then, as everyone considered the dilemma.

Finally, Maurice uttered a long sigh. "We may never know the absolute truth of these murders," he said gently. "But I do know that Ann believes, truly believes, that she committed them. In a sense that knowledge, that triumph, is her most valuable possession now. She is a very vulnerable woman."

Laura looked at the sober faces around her and saw the understanding. "Yes," she agreed. "I think that is the best way for everyone."

"Amen," Makedu said softly. "Amen to that."

****

The next day dawned brilliant with sun. Laura put on her coat and boots and went out into the deep snow. The castle glowed in its white coating, giving it an even more fairy like appearance and enhancing the illusion that the whole setting was unreal, a kind of fantasy they were experiencing.

Thomas joined her. He didn't speak, just took her hand as they wandered across the bridge, breathing in the frigid air, listening to the stillness, aware of the trackless expanses all around them. No cars were moving, no other people stirring. Just them, in this perfection of snow and ice.

They went slowly back the way they had come, watching as the wind blew snow across their footprints, obliterating their passage.

Two hours later, they were on the train, on their way back to Murren. With commendable efficiency the Swiss had cleared the train tracks first in order to quickly move the largest numbers of people to their destinations. The high mountain roads would come last.

The trip was stupendous – just whiteness all around them, frosted limbs, snow-covered lakes, everything so buried in white that it was hard to make out the nature of lumps that could be barns or cars or piles of brush, the hollows that might be river beds or crevasses. Soon, when the sun strengthened, the branches would shed their burden and spring free, the rivers would resume their flow, the cars and barns would be cleared, and the landscape would revert to its normal state. But for now, it was spectacular.

The sensation of living in a fantasy stayed with Laura until she woke up the next morning feeling perfect normal. She was almost sorry to rejoin the real world. Her dream-like interlude had been mesmerizing.

After breakfast, she and the others who had been at the castle went to the conference room, where a final meeting with Maurice, Helga, Ernst and Felicia had been arranged.

Maurice came into the room first. "Good, you are all here. Before we view the art, there are details to be sorted out regarding the disposition of funds. I have asked Dashka if she is willing to be our accountant. She is very pleased to accept the post. Now I wish to ask Sigrid if she would be the administrator of the grant, the person who makes sure all is being done as it should be done. We hope that Makedu will oversee the African grants. We will find a place for Amina, too, though she and I need to speak together so I learn what might suit her best."

Makedu's eyes glittered with what looked to Laura like tears of joy and triumph, but Sigrid and Amina simply stared at Maurice. "I am not sure I understand," Sigrid ventured. "What grant is this?"

Maurice looked surprised. "Why the one that all of you discussed in the conference," he said. Seeing their stupefied faces, he laughed. "I see now that Felicia has not yet told you of our plans. I had better wait for her to come or she will never speak to me again, and that would not be a good idea!"

Felicia came in, with Helga and Ernst assisting her. She still looked frail but also curiously strengthened by the rigors of the last days. "Good morning, all of you," she said with surprising vigor. "I am glad to be here. I am very fond of Chateau Chillon but I have seen enough of it for a while.

"Now, we must get down to business. Maurice and I and Ernst and Helga have long had a plan to use the proceeds from selling the art for purposes that make sense to us. Like you, we believe that educating girls and women is the best way to achieve peace. I do not need to tell you about that, however. You are the experts, and that is why we wish to make use of your talents as we turn our plans into realities. We hope that at least some of you are in a position to accept our offers."

"Felicia, are you saying that you four are the anonymous donors?" Laura asked in astonishment.

Felicia laughed as she looked around at the stunned faces, delighted with the effect she had produced. "Indeed we are! I thought you would have figured that out by now," she said impishly. "I suspect Makedu did, Violet too."

"I had my suspicions," Violet agreed. "But I am delighted to hear them confirmed and rather overcome by such wonderful news."

"You will make a difference in the world, and that is not easily done," she added. "I will help in any way I can."

"I had guessed," Makedu said softly, "but still I dared not hope. So much has gone wrong with grants in Africa, and finally to be able to get one right... You must know how much that means to me, to Africa."

Robes swinging with each step, she went to Felicia and embraced her gently. "You are a woman after my own heart. In one of your past lives, you must have been an African queen."

"What a lovely thought!" Felicia exclaimed. "I have always wanted to stride across Africa, skirts swinging, dark skin glowing in the sunlight, and now I can believe that once I really did. Thank you, Makedu, for those words. I will treasure them."

"I did not guess," Sigrid admitted ruefully. "But this is the best news I have heard all week and I thank all of you from the bottom of my heart."

The four philanthropists seemed well pleased. "We wish to get organized as quickly as we can," Felicia told them, reverting to practicalities. "Maurice and I have created a good-sized fund which is available immediately, and the art sales will ensure that the work goes on for many years. We would like ask immediately if some of you will assist us. Helga can describe that."

Helga took over. "If you are willing to take it on, Sigrid, we believe you would be ideal as administrator of the grants, since you are experienced in work of that kind. That does not mean changing jobs, just administering this one as you do others, if it is not too much work."

"I will be honored," Sigrid said. "For me, it is a dream come true."

"Excellent. Now – Makedu and Amina will oversee the African grants, and we wish also to speak to Amina about the work she would prefer to do, since we know less about her background. We can sort that out.

"As for Laura, we thought she might undertake the research end of things. Tell us what works and what doesn't in a series of research articles."

"I too will be honored," Laura replied. "That is exactly what I would like to do, to have an actual on-going case that can be evaluated and measured."

"Excellent. We will use Hassan, too. We hope he will return to Pakistan from time to time to evaluate the grants and provide data. Dashka will be our accountant, Zaina will receive a grant to study nursing at the institution of her choice; Thomas will help us with the art, finding buyers and so forth.

"If you are interested, Catherine, we hoped you might act as liaison with the young people, and Gustav will be offered a medical residency near one of our study areas if that appeals to him. As for Violet, corruption is ever-present in these areas and I am certain we will need her investigative talents at some point. Who else?"

"Reginald," Maurice said. "I have spoken to his father. He is a good man and we are looking for a school in international relations for Reginald. He would like to specialize in that area. I have also told Ben what we plan to do and he will assist in whatever way we think is best."

After that, a general discussion and congratulations followed. Laura found herself blinking, as if this too was an illusion and she would wake up and find it wasn't really happening. All this time, through all the drama, the heartaches, even murders and illness, these four people had been thinking about how to ensure that their magnificent idea would come to fruition. She was stunned, and profoundly impressed. She had met villains on this trip whom she hoped never to see again, but she had also met an astonishing array of truly good people. Like her occasional glimpses of the Matterhorn, that was a gift.

Ernst stood up. "Now that we have settled the details, let us look at the beating, throbbing heart of our creation, the one that will keep the grants alive - the art!"

CHAPTER TWENTY FIVE

"I thought the Zermatt group was behind all this," Thomas said with satisfaction when they got back to the room after the viewing.

"They fooled me," Laura admitted. "Not in my wildest dreams did I think they were our benefactors."

Thomas laughed. "They might even be paying for that weekend we still haven't taken in Paris. Remember that?"

"Barely," Laura said. "So much has happened in the last week that all else fled my mind. Was it really only a week ago that all this started?"

She frowned, puzzled. "Why are they paying?"

"I never was entirely sure who hired me to take on this case," Thomas explained, "but I wouldn't be surprised if it was them. I think they wanted to vet me, so to speak. Probably they were vetting all of us."

"I'm glad Karl didn't pass muster," Laura said tartly.

She stopped suddenly in the middle of packing. "What are we going to do now?" she said apprehensively. "It's as if the world has stopped going around. All that chaos and drama and danger and then – poof – nothing."

Thomas laughed. "I can think of quite a few things," he assured her. "Like dinner by moonlight in Paris, a boat ride down the Seine, that wonderful chapel with the rainbow colors, and going up to our room on one of those funny little elevators that take only two people. Imagine the possibilities there!"

"Like getting stuck between floors," Laura suggested.

"Even that has its possibilities," Thomas teased.

Laura laughed. "Almost as uncomfortable as one of those boxes, or for that matter, the filthy men's room on the train."

"In that case, perhaps we should take advantage of our present situation," Thomas suggested. "That bed looks quite accommodating."

Laura looked at her gaping suitcases, with nary an object in them. "The train leaves in two hours and I've hardly begun to pack!"

But Thomas was already waltzing her around the room, humming a tune. *Que sera, sera, whatever will be, will be*... he sang, switching to words.

There was a knock on the door and Catherine came in, with Gustav behind her. Grabbing Gustav's arm, Catherine swung him into the dance.

"Perhaps after all, Paris," Thomas muttered into Laura's ear.

"Ah, yes, Paris," Laura said dreamily. "No mysteries, just croissants and coffee in the morning instead of the next disaster, no more dungeons or shelters, wine over dinner and our very own room without..."

"I just came to say we're off to Paris!" Catherine interrupted. "Gustav arranged it all. Isn't that fantastic! See you later," she finished, dancing Gustav out of the room. "We leave in about an hour."

She put her head around the door, frowning. "Seems to me Dad said that you two were going there. I'd forgotten. Anyway, if you are, don't feel you have to look us up. I suspect we'll be busy. We've only got two days."

"We won't," Thomas assured her. "In fact, we'll be pretty busy too." But Catherine was already running down the hall.

"Why do I suddenly feel very old?" Thomas complained.

"Because you're not in Paris yet," Laura told him. "Nobody feels old in Paris and you won't either. Even I won't feel old."

"Then let's switch to a speedy number to prove it," Thomas said, launching into a wild jitterbug. It didn't last long. Laura got dizzy from being twirled around, and Thomas got winded from twirling her. They fell onto the bed, laughing, but with evidence of youth unproved.

"We'd better get to Paris quick!" Laura said. And they were, a mere three hours later, where the city worked its charm. It was even a warm day; the sun shone, a few hardy flowers were blooming, and café life was going strong.

Leaving their suitcases in the small room whose charm survived its view of the fire escape, they closed themselves into the rickety elevator, emerged into the lobby without mishap, an outcome that seemed miraculous to Laura, and settled themselves into a busy sidewalk café to catch the last of daylight.

"This is glorious," Laura marveled, feeling the sun warm her face, pulling the ineffable scent she associated with Paris into her nostrils. Even mixed with car fumes and smoke and dust, it aroused all the senses.

Thomas leaned over to kiss her, ignoring the glances of passersby. Laura ignored them too, even when she saw, out of the corner of her eye, that two of them were Catherine and Gustav.

Better not to mention that to Thomas, she decided, lest it ruin the mood. Besides, there was no reason why a middle-aged couple couldn't indulge in romance in the city of love.

An apt quotation floated into her mind.

Love to faults is always blind, always is to joy inclined. Lawless, winged and unconfined, and breaks all chains from every mind, she recited.

"Charming, and exactly what I was thinking when I saw two familiar faces," Thomas answered. "Now, here's another.

A kiss is a lovely trick designed by nature to stop speech when words become superfluous. Ingrid Bergman said that, and she is exactly right."

Leaning over, he kissed her again.

SKIING INTO MURDER

A note from the author, Joan Dahr Lambert

I hope you enjoyed SKIING INTO MURDER. It is the third book in the Laura Morland Mystery series and follows WALKING INTO MURDER and WADING INTO MURDER. A fourth mystery is in progress.

When Laura discovers a two-hundred-year-old document written by the long-forgotten younger sister of Jane Austen, she is stunned. Did this sister actually exist and if she did, why is there no mention of her in the Austen family records?

With the help of her art detective and love interest Thomas, who is in England to determine if a two-hundred year-old painting of a prominent English barrister is a woman beneath his wig. Laura sets out to solve the mystery. Within hours, someone tries to rob her. her room is searched and her car disabled. She and Thomas flee, only to find themselves surrounded by enemies whose purpose is clearly to steal the documents and get her permanently out of the way. She is not alone in believing that Isabella Austen really did exist, Laura realizes, and vows to keep her precious manuscript safe. Adventures, narrow escapes and near fatal encounters are the result.

I am also the author of a prehistoric novel series: CIRCLES OF STONE, CIRCLES IN THE SKY and ICE BURIAL, the story of Otzi the Iceman.

15831976R00204

Printed in Great Britain
by Amazon